First Voices
Part Two: Abraham—Jacob

Other Books By Walter Schenck

The Birdcatcher, Part One:
The Formation

The Birdcatcher, Part Two:
The Reformation

Jesus of the Four Gospels

The Handbook of Jesus' Parables

The Final Comparative of the Synoptic Gospels,
Part One

The Final Comparative of The Synoptic Gospels,
Part Two

The no-nonsense, straight-to-the gut,
CCNA Study Guide

Yehohshua Mashiach, Unveiled

First Voices, Part One: Adam—Eber

First Voices, Part Two: Abraham—Jacob

First Voices, Part Three: Jacob—Judah

First Voices
Part Two: Abraham—Jacob

▼

A Novel Based On Biblical Genesis

Walter J. Schenck

Writers Club Press
San Jose New York Lincoln Shanghai

First Voices
Part Two: Abraham—Jacob
A Novel Based on Biblical Genesis

Writers Club Press
an imprint of iUniverse, Inc.

For information address:
iUniverse, Inc.
5220 S. 16th St., Suite 200
Lincoln, NE 68512
www.iuniverse.com

ISBN: 0-595-20734-0

Printed in the United States of America

Praise For Walter Schenck's "The Birdcatcher"

"Walter Schenck's work is outstanding. He truly succeeds in making one want to know why and what next. He has a power of psychological involvement which is exceptional."

Prof. Sir Angus Wilson

"Your work is often of astonishing brilliance…some of the most powerful writing I've ever seen…I would expect you to become a writer of serious note…I am deeply impressed by your book."

"Powerful writing…excellent action writing…amazing talent."

"Mr. Schenck is very talented and intelligent. The best of his written work (in my short story writing class) was a breathtakingly good story; a strong, violent, moving tale set in Vietnam…a visionary."

Prof David Carkeet

Praise For Walter Schenck's "First Voices"

I've often wondered what direction a writer such as Mr. Schenck would take after his warrior's tale on Vietnam. I never expected this spiritual road. I am dazzled by this enormous undertaking. This is an extraordinary book. His adventure into the spiritual field of writing humbles me. There is no other writer in the world who has as much in-depth knowledge of the history and characters of the time period of Genesis as Mr. Schenck which he has amply demonstrated in his marvelous and scholarly work. I always thought Mr. Schenck was a brilliant writer, but now he is more than that. He has transcended the extraordinary to a level that only giants can reach.

Walter, I read your book. The language is original, precise, and the clarity astounding. I do not believe there is any book anywhere that compares to this. Your writing reflects great scholarship investigation with the heart and soul of a saint. This is a rare look at the story of Genesis.

Dedication

To my Wife whom I dearly love.

Nothing achieved or accomplished
is worthwhile
unless someone is there to guide you
through the duress
of the task at hand.

My wife has been an anchor to me.

Without her, I am a shallow
man groping in the darkness of distress.

With her I am a giant
shouting on the pinnacle of success
for all the world to hear.

Preface

A man sat in a forest, not isolated nor alone, but enriched with a vast portrait of the beginning of life. A perspective endowed him with unending visions of what must be said, and in what form stated. Whispers lingered in his imagination. For moments he sighed and wondered how the reader would accept his latest forage into the words of God.

"I have held God's words tenderly in my heart," he said, "and sought a deep understanding of God's message so I could correctly and intelligently talk to others about His true meaning without conceit or arrogance.

"This question I ask to all: Why can you not hear that when the sun sets the cries of the birds recall that God once before exterminated an entire species of life? The birds' cries should serve as a reminder to us that our form of life may also be extinguished.

"What form of life will cry out, when the sun sets, that once we were?"

The man's breath rushed out. Tears covered his face, for he saw exactly what would occur as the veil of prophecy covered his eyes. He transmigrated from flesh to spirit in a wink of an eye then back again.

He set his pen to work.

Introduction

We all wonder why we are placed on the earth, why things are as they are, and what can we do to enhance our lives. The people who are driven by these thoughts incorporate in their personality a force that enhances whatever they do to a separate degree of achievement that may mean something to the world, or it may not mean anything at all.

To become someone, a person must first surrender to the ideas and wills of the cause they set themselves on. To be free, a person must first know every discipline that he is capable of learning. To excel, a person must become a slave to his desire.

A long time ago I determined to reveal the missing pieces between the lines of the Genesis account. I wanted to expand the abbreviation of the many books that originally incorporated the histories of mankind's first stages of spiritual discovery. In working this rendition, I wanted to make clear the inexplicable. To do so, I visited the lives of the cultures surrounding Abraham and his descendants. Like so many beliefs, culture seems more important than the religion that gives rise to the nations and their adherence to customs unsupported by God's words, whether it be Allah, Brahman, Zoroaster, Jehovah, Yahweh, or ?

Moreover, I felt this work would have been a pointless exercise unless I also provided textural clarity to the confusing verses found throughout the Book of Genesis. This is not to say that my conclusions are the same as the witnesses before me. I am only stating that in order for me to arrive at my interpretative destination I had to do a thorough rethinking of all the material that was provided to me. I had to ponder the words of the philosophies and debate with the ideas of the theologians. These things I did so the reader may understand the expansiveness of the Genesis account. This rethinking of man's origins may perhaps offend those who believe that the earth is billions of years old and mankind has existed for several hundred thousands of years—or more—and may cause an assertive reaction against what I have written. If that is the case, than that is the case. Evolution is a mere whisper of deceit echoed by a group unable to accept divinity in man, caused by divine grace. Creationism is not blind arrogance built on superstition by a group of men residing in a darkened cave, afraid of science. If so, than those persons limits their reason. Education should not be biased based on culture or accepted dogma. Religionists that give sway to tradition are more guilty than adulterers, for they fornicate God's word and intellect to selfish intolerance. They cannot challenge or discern for they are puppets of greed and inhumanity. If anyone is offended, what can I say? I am sure Jesus offended many. He must have. Wasn't he nailed on a stake? But if I am trespassing on your sacred beliefs, that is a matter between God and me—not the reader. Truth is always painful. Many bigots and close minded persons hate truth. They will kill to preserve a lie, and cringe away from God's word. Their faces twist in contorted visions reminiscent of Dante's characterizations. Milton would laugh at them. But I am not laughing. I am crying because what is obvious—escapes.

But why would God permit a man like myself to write such an interpretation of His divine word? Because I am egotistical and bent toward forming a new religious doctrine? On the contrary! That is not my intention. God permits this book, because He does. It's that simple. No elegant justification, for none exists. By the same token I can say that I do not like religious leaders who wear pretensive personalities singing "Hallelujah!" or who publicly bend to the east, or face the sky, declaring that a wondrous, personal plan has been entrusted to them to share with the world. I cannot accept it, given the condition of failure of their organizations.

Yet, I must confess: never has a single work compelled me to cry as often as I did while I was rewriting the Biblical book of Genesis. I underwent more catharsis than what my Vietnam book put me through. I came to realize in this endeavour that all the voices of all people who died throughout the ages will owe their resurrection to the men and women who formed the framework of my book, First Voices. Which brings me to this—the heroes in this book strived to perform a finite sense of balance with themselves and with God. All of them accepted God, as did the non-heroic. No one in this book denies His existence. They all wanted to raise themselves to a certain level of spiritual growth that could place them near His essence. Even a person who hates wants to be loved. Even a demon.

So, after all this, what is this book about? It is about God's love. It is a historic drama that builds on the performances of all of the characters in Genesis. Not one voice is omitted. This book allows every person to speak and move as real people do when faced with life's issues. The reader will closely follow the adventures of mankind's first multi-generations: each represented in a new focus, emphasizing character development and interaction with each succeeding generation.

The stories progress as real world events. The people lived. The history was. What happened we know. Why it happened, many of us don't know. So, to answer the questions of why, where, and when, and to stay away from preconceived philosophy and theology and "scientific-evidence," I created a fresh perspective unbiased in its rendering, based, however, on biblical words, events, and dates. Of course, I am flesh, limited by flesh.

And here I must state this: in rendering this account I followed the bible's path in deliberately omitting personality descriptions. I do not paint a man fat or thin. A woman tall or short. I do not talk of the landscape or sounds except here and there. In many places I could have expounded and beautified and rendered poetic appeal but I choose to limit the pictures of the characters in this book and to deemphasize the

environment in order to stress godly ideas and wills. That is biblical practice. We do not know what Yeshua looked like nor David nor Adam. One
thing though is for sure: they were not Aryans with blue eyes and blond
hair. God was not interested in their physical attributes but in their spiritual strengths. How they lost touch with grace and how they found it
again. This process may be one-dimensional, but then, I suppose, the
bible is very much one-dimensional. It clearly makes ten demands, without colorful compromise. No where does the bible say it is OK to have a
thousand different organizations proclaiming to worship and understand
Christ, yet each organization has a history of brutal intolerance against
any that thinks different from itself. These divisive organizations love to
hear themselves on TV and in the pew and the pastors make sure their
names are as large as Christ's over the signage. But enough of that. So, to
go on, in many ways this work is a body of literature, but it is not intended
to be read as pleasurable literature. Escapism was not my goal. Thinking
was. Literature invites speculation, and speculation can lead itself to fantasy. This is not Dune nor playful invention. Rather, the usage of literature
in this body is used to enhance the testament. Flesh and blood indeed
enhances and glorifies but it steals from the substance of ideas. A three-
dimensional work is wondrous if it is geared toward entertainment. But
this is not that kind of visit.

This new visit to the heart and soul of Genesis is an honest belief in an
unpretentious God that loves all humanity and wishes them to be close to
Him. Thus, this book is written from a man's view of dozens of books he
read, discerned, analyzed, researched, and came to a particular conclusion
that he wanted to share with others. In this sense I truly believe I present
the foremost conclusion ever written on Genesis. As evidence of this statement, I offer my other two books, *The Final Comparative of the Synoptic
Gospels.* They will demonstrate my profound and meticulous adventures
into the word of God.

And, that's why I wrote this book. To share my impressions with
humanity. I did the same thing with my book on Vietnam which explored

the depths of chaos foretelling the world we now live in. My four books about Jesus went into his soul and intellect and unveiled his emotions in an earthly context. The one about computers is perhaps my most impersonal, given the nature of the subject.

For all the complexities of science and philosophy and religion, it all comes down to a simple quest: to understand. To become enlightened a person must shed away his former prejudices. Paul experienced this on the road to Damascus. To become one with an entity, one must try to think as an entity, however difficult that goal is. Jesus thought not as Jesus, but as the Creator. Buddha did what he could as did Confucius. To understand a small piece of the puzzle, you do not need a complete puzzle in front of you. Small glimmers of light testify to the sun's existence. A closed door testify to darkness. When a person really wants to understand the whole, he takes whatever piece is available, and with that small piece, injects it into a stringent thought, as though it were a sonnet wanting to find harmony within a symphony. Focus, energize, then subtract yourself from the surrounding events. A single tone can be beautiful. A single beat can mesmerize. Clarity becomes yours. The puzzle is solved.

And if that is not the case, I have no case to make to you other than this promise: by the time you finish reading this book you will know more about the Biblical book of Genesis than you ever had before. Its history will reveal itself from a tiny layering of information to a colossus of possibilities. Religion is such a stratum. God reveals Himself in exact fortitudes of realities, and it is our responsibility as His children to gain His trust so he may share with us His intents. But what man is humble enough to accept this fact. It is not the roar of a lion, or the swift flight of an eagle, nor the strength of an ant that impresses. It is the gentleness of a dove and the softness of a lamb that symbolizes who God's power touches. After all, who was more powerful: David the King or Elijah the prophet? Who survived: Josiah or Daniel?

The persons who pray and devote themselves to Godly study needs only to listen to a brook and to watch the sway of a branch amidst a deep forest to find what God wants from us. It is harmony. It is peace. What a miserable shame it is to equate the roar of the river's fall and the volcanic eruption with power. A drop of water can rust iron. A small indention in the earth can cripple a horse.

That is the essence of this novel. Adam changed everything. In turn, Noah also changed everything. Then Abraham came along and changed everything again. Jacob is the representative of our millennium which will see the fulfillment of Abraham's quest. The adventure that Adam set mankind's course on will find God's redemptive decree fulfilled in a very short while.

So, who am I that I should commit so many years of study to write this book? It doesn't matter. The only reason I used my name on the cover page is so the reader will know that a very sinful man can come close to God in a balanced manner befitting redemption.

If I can, surely it should be an easier road for you.

Chapter Thirteen

▼

Avram

This is Avram's story.

Three years after Eber left the city of Haran, during the month of Shebat, in 1943 B.C.E., Terah died.

Terah was 205 years old when the breathing energy of his spirit expired. The breath that had sustained his life-force now failed to enrich his bloodstream. The spirit which preserved and motivated his body's cellular reproduction, quieted. His thoughts and impressions and reflections totally ceased. His heart perished as did his soul. The children lowered the stiffened, rigid body that was once composed of the living earth's elements and Yahweh's sustaining breath of life into the ground.

Terah's soul, the totality of his personality, and Terah's spirit, his life-force, the men, women and children walked away from. Whatever there had been concerning him no longer mattered. The only thing left was for his surrounding companions to remember him, and in their prayers, ask Yahweh to remember him, so He could restore his personality in a new physical body to live forever on the face of a perfect earth.

Seventy-seven years prior to Terah's expiration, Noah died in the mountains overlooking the vast valley leading to the Zion. Shem was 525 years old when Terah died. Arpachshad was 425 years old. Shelah was 390 years old. Eber was 360 years old. Pelug died 87 years earlier. Sixty-seven years prior to Terah's death Reu was buried on the mountain overlooking the village.

Serug, at the time of Terah's death, had been dead for 34 years. Nahor, Terah's father, died 86 years earlier, 9 years prior to Noah's own death.

The trading processions stopped and the family wailed their mourning cries throughout the night. The children ripped their tunics and bathed their hair with the dust of the earth. The moon was sheathed behind immense layers of clouds.

"Did Father ever convert to Yahweh's name?" Nahor, Terah's son, asked Avram.

"Never."

"Will Eber be coming for the funeral?" Lot asked Avram while Nahor, Terah's son, respectfully listened.

"No."

"Where is he?" Lot again asked.

"With our patriarch."

"Who could be older than him?" Milcah inquired.

"His own father: Shem."

"You really believe that, don't you?" Nahor insisted on knowing.

"Why not?"

"You've changed, Avram," Milcah chose her words carefully. "That intense logic and discerning mind of yours seems to have surrendered to Eber's influences."

He ignored Milcah and separated himself from the family. He went off by himself and wandered to one of the cool creeks that flowed through the lavishly rich lands that were forested with cedars and pines. The flowers' fragrance filled his nostrils with an overbearing scent.

Alone, in deepest thought, he paced the ground that indented with every step.

As he looked at the foot tracks, moisture seeped inside and formed minuscule puddles. He walked to the creek's edge. His face stared at his face. His beard was well groomed. His hair was perfectly shaped about his shoulders. His tunic was threaded with rich strands of gold cloth and his robe was bordered with purple silk against the green wool.

Overhead, the tree branches reached across the banks, touching the tree branches from the other side. Like a maniac who had lost control of his actions, he jumped into the water, running underneath the natural arch of leaves, splashing the water about his body.

"Father, Father, Father!" he shouted. "Everyone dies and there's no escaping its dark recess. Yahweh! Have you no solution for such pain?"

The wind's breeze swayed the trees. The treetops danced in circles, as if they were masts on a ship, the green land the sides of a boat. The stream moved swiftly beneath Avram's feet and small tadpoles darted around his sandals. Several paces away a rotten tree trunk lay in the water's path. The cascading water flowed over the break of a knot, making a sound that caught Avram's attention. The water spread out in a wide sheet. Through its clear depths he could see the river's bottom littered with old, rotting tree branches.

"Yahweh, are You as this water? Can I see You yet not see You? Look, I can touch this water. I can place it to my lips and refresh myself with it. Are You the same?

"YAHWEH!" he shouted as loud as he could, arching his back against the wind, "TOUCH ME!"

For a while he stood still, then he relaxed his arms. The water continued dripping from his fingertips, striking the stream. His left ankle created small ripples that formed into half-circles. On his right side the water flowed as if nothing had occurred to break its motion.

He lifted his head farther back and kept his eyes closed. Slightly parting his lips, he slowly raised his hands to the air until they were fully stretched over his head

Moments passed. The voices of the birds, calling to one another, seemed to fill the air. The clouds appeared to thicken. A moist wrapping composed of gleaming, twirling, dancing, cascading, electrical energy rose upward from the midst of the waters. Simultaneously miniature lights fell from the clouds above him surrounding his body.

"Avram," a voice spoke softly.

"Who is speaking to me?"

"I am Yahweh. I am He who purposed the existence of all life and the establishment of the heavens and the earth."

Avram shook with fear. He stuck his eyes, then opened them, expecting to see a materialized personage in front of him. Instead, he only saw the rustling of the trees and the rush of the water beneath his feet.

"Why is it," he finally spoke out, "that man's condition is what it is?"

"Man has determined to set about his own course, without regard to its consequences. Man falls prey to the evil tidings that Satan whispers to him."

"Why do you permit evil?"

"It is a question of true sovereignty."

"Is Your rulership over man more important than our welfare? Why must You permit our small disregards for Your laws to unfairly lead us into death? Surely, a power such as Yourself can permit us immortality. Surely you can forgive us our small misadventures"

"I had created mankind to live forever on a paradise earth. I had not intended for man to die. It was Satan's corruption and manipulations that caused man to fall. Havva was the first human to transgress against me, yet I permitted her and Adam to live for hundreds of years so they could see firsthand what their actions caused. I have, however, established a plan of eternal redemption for mankind, whereby they can once again live forever on an earth filled with delightful things where all man will find fulfillment and harmony."

"How?"

"I require an equal thing for an equal thing. Adam was a perfect man who sinned. Therefore, I require a perfect man to remain just and good toward all things until the very end of his life."

"What human can do such a thing?"

"I have selected from the earth your forefather to bring about this perfect human. Each generation will carry the seed until the right time approaches for his appearance."

"Why must we wait? Why can we not have this man with us now?"

"What do you propose?"

"A set of laws that will guide us toward perfection. A set of standards that will be written for all men to know and to follow."

Yahweh's voice silenced. The wind stirred the clouds overhead, making them more dense. Shafts of bright sun rays broke through them, radiating about Avram.

"I will cause a body of laws to be written. More, I will cause a legislative body to enforce My laws. Whatever evil acts man performs, I will permit other men to judge and hand out punishments against the offender. Man, for a while will be allowed to have the power to correct the evil things of the world. If they fail, then I will send My chosen representative to finalized the wrongs committed against Me. My chosen representative will be the eternal ruler of man's affairs. He will be the supreme law maker and enforcer."

"How long will man be permitted to correct the wrongs committed against you?"

"I will permit man two-thousand years. If he has failed, I will send my representative. After he has performed his perfection toward Me, I will permit mankind an additional two-thousand years to learn from his example toward Me. If they fail to establish righteousness toward Me, I will send out my army of angels to destroy disobedient mankind from the earth. Thereafter, My own representative will handle the affairs of man. I will permit him to rule supremely for one-thousand years, then I will test mankind again."

"May they not fail," Avram prayed.

"What must I do for You to make this happen?" Avram asked, as a friend would ask another friend.

Yahweh smiled. He touched Avram's heart and discerned the man's conscience decision to devote himself to all the good things that would please Yahweh.

"Leave the land which your relatives settled into. Leave your father's house. Venture to the land that I will show you.

"Out of you I will create a great nation.
"I will bless you;
"and I will make your name great,
"and a blessing you will be.
"Those who bless you I will bless —
"and curse him that curses you.
"And all the families of the earth
"will become blessed by means of you."

Avram lowered his hands down back to his sides. Around him he saw only the trees and the flowers and the stirring s of the small mammals. He saw the treeless banks and the yellow and green lilies. The breeze rested. Avram shivered and walked out of the water.

Two days later Avram met privately with his family.

"Nahor, Milcah, it's my task to leave Haran. I talked this over with Sarai before I spoke of it to you."

"Why?" Milcah asked. "Are you going to search for Eber?"

"Yes and no. My primary desire is to find for myself, myself. Yahweh's voice will lead me to myself."

"I want to come with you," Lot begged.

"Terah, my father, named this city after your father. You honor it with your presence. I ask that you remain in the city of Haran."

"I am too young to be it's mayor. Besides, Nahor, you are the eldest in the family. All things belong to you. What belongs to you, will pass to your sons, not to me, nor to Avram," Lot said.

"I will always be generous with both of you," Nahor replied.

"Nevertheless, I want to travel with Avram. Permit me."

Avram nodded. "I will think on it."

"Avram," Nahor asked, "is it because I am the eldest and because you fear you will not gain an inheritance that you want to leave this land, as Lot said?"

"Yahweh's generosity calls for me to go to Retenu: the land of the Canaanites."

"Soon?" Nahor asked.

"Yes."

"Eber has placed an unmovable vision in your mind about that land," Nahor said. "I say stay here where everything is a certainty. We all love you. Who will love you so far away?"

"Yahweh," Avram answered.

"I must learn about this Yahweh of yours," Nahor concluded.

After the conversation concluded, Avram returned to his tent. There he found Sarai waiting for his final decision.

"So, do we pack."

"Yes. And Lot will accompany us."

Sarai looked at his eyes. He was resolved to designate him as the heir. She was too tired to argue with him, so she finally resigned to Avram's wish to have her accept Lot into their camp.

Days later dozens of people and hundreds of sheep and masses of donkeys bearing tents and pegs and rugs and obsidian artifacts left the city of Haran. The entourage traveled from Haran to the cities of the region of Aleppo that was near the Great Sea. From Aleppo they wended their way to the famed city of Ebla. As they approached the greatest city of the region, they came across hundreds of other caravans similar to theirs. Many of the richest merchants brought their commerce from Ugarit.

ᛒᚷᛒᚷᛒᚷᛒᚷᚳᛒᚷᚳᛒᚷ

𝔉rom the city of Ebla the Babylonian caravan continued southward to the city of Damascus. It was Avram's uncle, Aram, who set the founding cornerstone of the city of Damascus.

Decades earlier, while traveling with Eber, Aram stopped at the natural crossroads of the land. As soon as he saw it, he understood the value of the site. It was there, in the flat plain, that he visualize the establishment of a commerce center. The mountain ranges naturally grew up at diverse points from the plains, and all paths led to the flat territory that Aram had discovered.

"Eber," Aram said, "I will stay here to establish my own family line. I will build an outpost here for other caravans. I, and my children, will always welcome you and those who represent you."

Several decades prior to Aram's death, he cultivated his firstborn son Uz toward leadership responsibilities. Under Uz the city's growth increased and flourished. The newest caravans, traveling through the paths of the Anti-Lebanon Range fostered the city's growth, adding to its wealth and prestige.

The encompassing mountains and the jutting ranges overlooking the great flatlands, however, the Canaanites and the Amorites demanded to possess for themselves. Years of futile bickering passed with no resolve! Finally, after numerous treaties and after numerous costly skirmishes failed to resolve the disputes, Uz rescinded his ambitious desires to control the paths leading to the very forefront of the mountain ranges. Uz, watching the struggle deplete his city's resources, diplomatically acceded to the Canaanites and to the Amorites the land's rising hills.

With the warfare's conclusion, Damascus was now able to prosper without interference or warfare from the wandering hill people.

"Avram," Sarai announced, "we must rest our family here. We need fresh fodder and we need to refill our food and spice supplies."

"Yes, Sarai. I agree with you. And please, also stock up on more lentils."

As Avram rested his staff on a well's wall, a man, who had been raised in the city, approached the lead donkey. Inspecting its harness, he placed his hands over the leathering. He shook his head, pulled on a strap, and loosened the load off its back. "Excuse me," he spoke to Avram in a condescending tone, "why do you feel free to rest from your burden, but fail to release this animal from its burden?"

Avram walked to the load that the man had placed beside the donkey and lifted it over his own shoulders. "Of course, you are correct."

Avram carried the bundle to a place where he wouldn't be in anyone's way. He settled down and began unraveling the contents. Carefully he spread open the utensils so his men could distribute the cups and pans for the cooking.

"Have you eaten?" Avram decided to ask the stranger.

"Before I am fed, or your men, would it not be best to reward those who brought you so far?" he replied, placing a handful of water to the donkey's mouth. It gingerly sipped it from his hand.

Avram, impressed by the man's kindness and receptive perception, confessed, "I traveled farther than I expected to without resting. I ran out of fodder. My wife and her friends are purchasing some now."

"From which stall?"

"The nearest."

"No. Go to the ones hidden behind the rising wall. The ones who are the nearest always charge the most because people are more anxious to be served by them, rather than walking the extra mile. The barley merchants, whether close or far, buy from the same farmers."

"Thank you, stranger."

"My name is Dammesek Eliezer."

"What do you do here?"

"I'm a scribe and a translator. I speak Akkadian, Egyptian, some local dialects, and of course, your own native Hebrew."

"So, you travel?"

"As the need rises."

"I am Avram. So, Eliezer, be kind, please. See, over there? That is my wife. She is talking to that merchant. Take her and her friends to the other wholesalers. Direct her efforts to an equitable deal for me."

"I shall do as you request, because all men, I believe, are entitled to the utmost courtesy."

"I concur. Afterwards, return and talk to me. I need a personal servant and guide, and, obviously, a translator. Besides, your thoughts seem to reflect many of my own sentiments."

Eliezer returned and agreed to work for Avram. During the course of many years the two bonded into an inseparable friendship. During these years, Lot became jealous of the friendship which Sarai always encouraged. One day it happened, while Eliezer and Avram were exploring their genealogies, they uncovered a hereditary link between themselves through the lines of Aram, Uz, and Terah.

Lot, when he learned of the hereditary link between his uncle and Eliezer, became more resentful. "Now I have a relative to contend against for an inheritance," he thought. Then when he learned of the direct hereditary connection, Lot started muttering under his breath whenever the two appeared together. Intentionally he made excuses to tend the flocks or to care for the donkeys rather than share his uncle's company with his newfound cousin.

"Actually," Lot once remarked, "he should never have been anything more than a servant."

Through the years Avram, Eliezer, Lot, Sarai and their hundred loyal friends and followers made their way farther south to the regions of Shechem and Moreh. To the northeast, Mount Moriah clearly rose above their base camp. From Mount Moriah's steep ascension, the travelers could see the immense stretches of rows upon rows of resinous trees that the laborers constantly harvested, collecting the oozy liquid from the tree trunks to sell to the Sea People. Large containers of the oil rested by the wayside, waiting to be refined for the merchants' acceptance.

And in every city Avram saw deities carved out of stone representing the citizens' worship to false Gods. In every city he traveled through, he witnessed male and female temple prostitutes and men and women having sex on the public streets, without regard as to who was watching them.

Avram frowned and wondered about his journey.

ഇൻരൽഇൻരൽഇൻരൽഇൻരൽ

While Avram's large caravan relaxed from its journeys and trials, Avram afforded himself the opportunity to drift off into a deep sleep. "No more watches tonight against lions," he smiled at Eliezer.

Nothing disturbed him that night, for all was calm.

Waking with the morning's brightening yellow rays, he felt a restless need, a compulsion, an irresistible impulse to get away from the bustling camp to climb the highest hill overlooking the giant trees of Moreh. He climbed so fast to the top, he didn't realized he was there by himself until he overlooked the vast plains below him. "Such a quick climb," he mused to himself, "and who is here to see it's accomplishment." He relished the solitude of the place.

For long moments he stared at the tree below. He shook his head in wonder. Then he saw a faint glimpses of spiraling smoke and its sight saddened him. Among the trees of the thick forest lay the Canaanites' villages. He was fed up with their sexual perversities which he had seen publicly performed on the streets of Damascus and the outlying villages. Avram stroked his beard meditatively. "So, someone tell me, who really owns this land? Me or them?"

It was Yahweh who answered him. "This land I've already assigned to your descendants."

Whirling around, Avram saw only the movement of a tree's branches. Glancing to his left, he saw the bushes swaying in the wind.

"Yahweh surely spoke to me," he joyously shouted to the treetops. "He confirms to me what He had earlier declared to me!"

He gathered the loose large and small stones and carefully placed them on top of each other, balancing them carefully so no one could topple them. This altar, thereafter, publicly signified the contract between Yahweh and himself. The altar became a firm testimony, a legitimate witness bonding the agreement between man and spirit.

From the heights of Shechem, Avram traveled twenty miles farther south to the region that would become known as Bet-El.

A few miles west of Bet-El, a group of people had established for themselves the foundation stones for the city of Ai.

While encamped in the region of Bet-El, Avram took another opportunity to build a second, stronger altar to Yahweh. After long moments of earnest prayer, Avram tired of the silence. He stood up and took a deep breath then invoked Yahweh's name.

"Listen to me!" Avram demanded. "I wait, so speak to me! Inspire me to continue continuing in a land that I am unfamiliar with! Justify to me my presence in a land that everywhere I turn I see another people already populating! Why am I here?"

Yahweh heard Avram's voice.

"What I had pronounced, I have performed. This land indeed belongs to your children. Those who have settled the land came deliberately on their own terms to defy My intentions. Avram, walk throughout the land."

"Wherever I walk I see hostile, sexual predators. How is it that you have determined to set aside this immoral and harsh environment for me?"

"I will protect you at all times. You shall never be harmed."

"That may be. Nevertheless, I do not want to live near such a carnage of people as the Canaanites."

"Journey farther south."

"I will travel farther south, as You command me to. This, however, I demand. If I am to be your servant, I must serve You openly using Your name publicly! Wherever I am, I want all to know I am directly appointed by You as Your earthly representative. I do not mean to say I want to subvert Your anointed and ultimate Mashiach, I just want Your name to be forever on my lips!"

"It shall be as you desire. You are my earthly Mashiach who represents My name. This privilege I bestow to you and to your descendants."

Yahweh, thereafter, bestowed His permission on Avram to dedicate the land to Him. Then, after divinely blessing the altar, Yahweh permitted Avram to testify the event to his followers.

From this period on, Avram spoke of himself alongside Yahweh's divine name. One name could not be mentioned without the other being mentioned. Both names became inseparable from one another.

And Yahweh came to love Avram and declared him to be his personal friend.

ཀ৪ঙ৪ঙ৪ঙ৪ঙঞঙঞ৪ঙঞ৪ঙ

In the years that followed Avram settled in the Negeb. During this time-line of man's existence, the climatic conditions and the land's productivity were dramatically different from the seasons of man's previous days. The Canaanites' fertile, plateau grasslands easily supported Avram's thousands of sheep and cattle and goats. Tamarisk trees grew isolated from the oaks and the plane trees. The curving branches of the oak trees spread far and wide over soft, rolling hills of grass. When the children discovered a tall, imposing sycamore tree, they played around its large girth, trying to touch each other's fingertips.

Hundreds of springs and pools rested beneath thousands of shading trees. Great quantities of fertile oases and luxuriant pools of water greeted the travelers and the pioneers and the settlers.

"Build for us as many cisterns as we need," Avram directed Lot and Eliezer. "The region is an endless stretch of grass and grains. We will thrive here!"

One afternoon during 'Stretch around the tree time,' Avram's loyal friends and followers gave an alarming shout. The harsh screaming warned of the possibility of hostile soldiers approaching the camp.

Eliezer rushed forward.

Mamre, the Amorite leader, stood in front of a vast crowd of unwashed and tired men. Behind the soldiers another assembly of women and children patiently stood.

Lot, in all his years, had never seen such a dark-skinned people. Their thick hair, their color, their very presence frightened him.

"Who are they, Eliezer?" Lot inquired.

"Amorites. They descend directly from Canaan."

"Hamitics?"

"Yes. Of course," Eliezer answered the whisper. "It appears to me as if they're just returning from their hunt. Farther south lies a vast haunt of lions and leopards. When an Amorite hunts, the family hunts with him. That way they can dress the animal skins and feed themselves without spoiling the remains. They're very effective and generous hunters. They fight well and know all the paths of the hills."

"Should we get Avram?"

"Of course. The leader of our people should confer with the leader of another."

"I too," Lot reared back his shoulders, "am authorized to lead. Many of the people who are present with us are Haran's friends. That is, before they became my uncle's friends."

"Haran, your father?"

"Yes, my father. It was he who began this journey. Avram just followed."

"It is as you said it is," Eliezer, desiring to keep peace between them, refused to refute him. "However, please, bring Avram and, bring wine."

"I shall, for it is not my place to usurp my uncle's presence," Lot, knowing Eliezer's mollifying tactics, mocked.

When Avram stood in front of the Amorites, Eliezer interpreted the formal greetings. As they tested each other's wits and intentions, the young girls of both leaders served wine and food to each party of guests.

While both groups feasted, their two leaders sat down on the wool blanket of peace. Satisfied with the arrangements, the two leaders kissed each other's cheek.

"The Damascenes, are they your relatives?" Mamre asked.

"Yes," Avram replied. "Through Uz, who is my cousin through the son of Shem."

"We are not familiar with the name. Who are his children?"

"Elam, Arpachshad, Aram, Asshur, and Lud."

"Aram we have heard of. His son Uz was the great designer and architect of Damascus. Elam's children we have heard of also. The king, Chedorlaomer, has forced contracts of trade with them. His soldiers and the soldiers of Ampraphel and Arioch and Tidal command impressive tributes. But we, being wanderers, are hard to tax," Mamre, happy with his joke, laughed. His family members immediately joined in the laughter.

"We also wander," Avram smiled. "We are here seeking our progenitor."

"Shem?"

"Our great-grandfather Eber resides with him this very moment."

"So, you are the Hebrews of whom I have heard. It makes sense now why you are here. But, of course, this land belongs not to you, neither for you to settle into nor build cities in. This, I know, you'll agree with."

"I have not been directed to build cities."

"Then what are those altars you have erected?"

"They are testimonies of communications between my God and myself."

"Are you a man who speaks with God?"

"I am authorized to speak in His name as well as use His name—for it is my personal shield against harm and terror."

"For such a benevolent gift against hostilities, travel as you desire. Travel in peace throughout these lands," his voice dropped to a low growl, "for who can prevent it." His voice quickly increased, testing the man, "Yet, for this favor, I must in return insist on a favor."

"Such as?" Avram humored him.

"Mutually agree with me, and with my friends, that should trouble arise you will come to our rescue as we will come to your rescue."

Avram quickly pondered on the idea and saw its benefits. At once he placed his hand underneath Mamre's thigh. "It is agreed."

Through the afternoon's passage Avram chanced to learn that Eber had earlier traveled through the land. "Rumor," his new friend stated, "has it that he is seeking a mysterious city called Salem."

"It is true. I am seeking the city. Do you know where it is?"

"I believe the city is hidden in the mountains. Somewhere, perhaps, between the Great Sea and the lesser lake." Mamre replied. "Each time we, the Amorites, try to find it, the trail become confused.

"Our team leaders become lost and return empty-handed. We have wasted countless days wandering about in the mountains in vast circles looking for Salem.

"Sometimes I think it is a myth."

Others, hearing, politely laughed.

ଅଓ୪ଅଓ୪ଅ୦୪ଅଓ୪ଅଓ୪

Alongside his chief servant Dammesek Eliezer, Avram journeyed farther into the Negeb region. This area rests south of Be'er Sheva and north of Egypt, acting as a natural land bridge between Africa and the Middle East.

Many years later, the first great dryness of the world stretched over Negeb's fertile fields, parching its land. The great land mass of Saudi Arabia lost its vibrant green fields and the once rich farmlands withered into a land of sand dunes and waterless regions.

The changing climate of the earth deeply affected this particular region.

The plants of the vast rolling plateau withered. Thousands of pistachio trees yellowed and the tips of their leaves curled and dropped off the dying branches. The fruit hardened and the heat consumed them without mercy. The insects sapped the remnants of their nourishment, destroying them. The crocuses also died. The tall stalks of grains fell upon themselves, dying. The southeastern sands blew into the Negeb, covering the bases of the tamarisk trees, burying the oases and cisterns. The plentiful ibex, foxes, and other animals, unable to sustain themselves, perished.

Avram's sheep and donkeys, pawing at the dried pools, bellowed through the night. In the morning the disheartened men found several animals lying on the ground, their stiffened limbs pointing to the parched spring.

Soon the goat skin tents dried, emitting a foul stench. The unrelenting heat baked the earth. Unable to walk about, many men let the animals roam freely toward the waiting lions and hyenas.

"Eliezer," Avram asked sit in a council meeting in his tent, "where are we to travel to? We cannot go north, for Chedorlaomer's soldiers steal everything. I cannot find Eber or Shem, nor do I hear rumors of their whereabouts."

The silent group waited for Eliezer to speak. He remained silent. Another man finally dared to speak. "We must travel to Egypt."

"Can we not venture southeast toward the Arabian interior?" another asked, then hesitated, for he secretly feared that crossing.

"I understand that the deepest dryness hangs there," Eliezer answered to the man's relief. "Even the mountains have become void of trees. Whatever pools of water there were have become marshes and whatever marshes there were have become baked and cracked earth. To voyage into that interior would devastate all our livestock and us as well."

"It must be Egypt then."

"Can we not return to Babylon?" another interjected. "I remember the black earth and the cool river and the height of the grass which the winds swayed through."

"What tribute can we place with Ampraphel?" Avram took his turn to speak.

"We have men here whom we can place in his service."

"What you mean is this: we have men we can sell to him as slaves instead of giving up our money. More clearly, you mean to enslave men for your own conceited safety."

"Is not economics one of the reasons we came with you? Honestly, did we not venture forth from Ur on the hopes of prosperity? Are we not traders and merchants who have traveled with Eber—and with Haran? Now, do we not travel with you and Lot so we may increase our portions of what there is for our purses?"

"I am here to serve Yahweh. I am here because I have been called to be here."

"Do not be a hypocrite with us, Avram," the second man took his turn to speak. "During our journey you refrained from using Yahweh's name until you reached this land. Your association with Yahweh is exclusively yours."

"What he says is true," another reinforced the man's words.

"And," another's voice proceeded to inject his thoughts, "what came to be in our possession did not come so by your gift as a merchantman nor as a skilled trader. The thousands of sheep that came with you, you easily negotiated for with the cities that stood between there and here. More, and this is the absolute reality of things, by using your aunt's and wife's skills, you easily bartered for gold and for silver and for everything else that rests on your asses' back." The man stood up, harshly pointing his finger directly at Avram. "On your own merits you've accomplished nothing."

"That is correct: 'On my own merits I've accomplished nothing.' It is on Yahweh's merits that I've gained everything that I've gained."

"Including more donkeys than anyone else?"

"What donkeys?" Avram finally raised his voice. "Have not mine suffered as much as yours? Are they not perishing as severely as yours?"

"Yes," another friend supported. "Avram's losses are as great as ours! The vultures eat his carcasses as much as they do ours! This journey serves two purposes: God and nation!"

"No, its purpose is for us to discover God. It is for us to discern His intelligence and His meaning for us."

"Yes, Avram, you are correct. But also, He speaks exclusively with you. Whenever you hear His voice, you erect altars that bear His name. But we all know that the altars' purposes are to document your claims to this land. Already you have grabbed the land from northern Damascus to Moreh to Bet-El. I'm sure you intend to build other altars for your land-claims."

"Yahweh has placed the lands in my care, and in the care of my children to come. The lands are placed with me because the first-father resided here. This land is set aside for the most holy of men."

"And what of the people who already reside here? Are not their labors and sacrifices just as valid?"

"Evil intents gilded their settlements."

"We will not argue with you, prophet. Bear this in mind though: for whatever reason that may be—we are here with you. We have placed our lives in your care. We have placed our trust in you. Right now we know you must do what you believe in to do, and we respect that. But we want to survive this famine. Egypt is the land that we will survive in. Therefore, Avram, this council unitedly asks you, please, to ask Eliezer to go into that land and present us with a report."

"Why Eliezer?"

"He is part Semitic, part Hamitic. The Egyptians will treat him fairly."

"He is my cousin through the line of Aram."

"That is an acknowledged fact, uncle," Lot broke his silence, joining on the side of the quarrelers.

Eliezer stood silent among the crowd. After a long time he raised his hands, quieting them.

"Allow me, please, if you will, to cross first into Egypt as it was rightly suggested. I will go as far as Zoan and what I see I will report it to you."

Avram rose from the wool blankets and cupped his hands into each other behind his back. Worried, his eyes tightened, revealing the radiating lines that stretched from the corners of his eyes halfway to his temples.

"Eliezer," Avram whispered, nearly inaudibly. His eyes moistened. Not wanting his companions to see the glistering tears, he walked to the tent's vigorously flapping cover. "Strange," he thought, "how the drier the wind is, the more intense is its strength."

He grabbed hold of the taut tent rope and aimlessly stared at the drifting sand. "Beyond the campgrounds the sweltering sand drifts resemble a rolling cloud that can swallow up a city, consuming to its innards all life." He shook off the thought and turned his attention toward several large, tumbling pieces of dehydrated plants. The rambling branches intertwined with each other, like all the other dried plants that covered the vast stretches of land.

"Travel in safety, dear cousin. Remain near the Great Sea in case you need to depart quickly. The Sea People will offer you refuge for a price." Avram then walked to another tent with Eliezer following closely behind.

A sailor, by chance, happened to observe from the distance the two walking together. For a moment the scene appeared as a phenomenon of his imagination. The brutal, drying heat and shimmering waves that rose from the desert sands danced about the two figures making them a single contortion of two heads having one body. Three legs with one back.

Through time's unstoppable passage, that same sailor observed the intense buildup of sand overtaking the oasis that once greeted his ship's arrival. It appeared as if the very same sand that once greeted him from his long journey was now the sand that viciously flew far inland. The fierce, hot wind seemed to displace the seashore's beige sands, carrying the pulverized rocks beyond the dunes. It was as if the earth were being redesigned! The only thing left was for the ocean to climb over the cliffs to take for itself whatever it wanted. "And why not?" the sailor shrugged.

"The ocean's borders already precede the land. And what land didn't rise from the bottom of the sea?"

The sailor picked up his clothing chest and dismally wandered into the city streets.

ॐ ॐ ॐ ॐ ॐ

As the billowing sands forced the merchants to hide in their tents, Avram's nephew Lot tended to the watering of his few remaining sheep and single donkey. He placed a protective veil over his nose and sought to ease the stinging pains from the blowing sand drifts. Tying the cloth tighter, he futilely fought to filter the decaying stench that lingered throughout the dying land. Dazed by the unrelenting fury of the suffocating heat, Lot haggardly walked from the well to the pen. On lifting the caricature of a water bucket he heard his donkey's cry. At first he believed it was crying for the water.

The donkey raised its head to the area behind the pen. Automatically Lot's eyes followed the pet's motion. From the billowing cloud of sand a dark image appeared. The deep brown image slowly worked its way toward him. Against the fierce background of billowing sand, Lot couldn't make out. A protecting arm hid the image's eyes. Another arm clutched his tunic about his body.

Minutes later the image settled into the largest tent. There Avram personally washed the accumulated and caked dust from Eliezer's face and mouth. For Eliezer it was. Avram shared the warm porridge with his best friend and closest confidant. After several hours of rest Eliezer called for an audience with the men.

"Egypt is rich with barley cakes and with grapes and with beer. They cannot even conceive of such conditions under which we are now suffering."

"Will they receive us?"

"They are a generous people. Be crafty, however, with them. They will allow us, but never speak of Chedorlaomer or of Ur. Rumors fill the air with invasion and deceit."

"Surely they will know we are from Babylon. Our accent, our manners, our very clothing."

"We can change our clothes. We can train our manners. And, you must always allow me to do your talking. That way they'll never hear your accents."

"Then we will be safe in Egypt?" Avram doubled the question.

Eliezer turned his face from Avram, the candlelight intensifying the crags of his beard.

"Are you hiding something from me?" Avram insisted on understanding Eliezer's glance away from his face and eyes.

"Sarai, your wife," he became silent, refusing to finish the answer.

Avram also became silent, duplicating Eliezer's stance. Finally, after each watched the flickering light of the candle dancing on the other's face, highlighting specific strengths, Eliezer broke the silent stand-off. "Permit me, please, these words: Sarai is an attractive woman."

"Of course she is. That's why Father pledged her to me—to make beautiful children."

The group of listeners laughed.

"Yes, you are a handsome man, my dear cousin. Perhaps too handsome."

"How so?"

"The Egyptian king, Amenemhet, is fond of attractive women. He believes they are all his providence. 'All beautiful women are born for my household' he brags to the world. And he means to have them all in his service."

"Sarai is married to me. Who wants a married woman?" Avram innocently demanded.

"The Egyptians are immoral," Eliezer sadly answered. "Are not the Canaanites and Amorites their neighbors? Are they not Hamitics and are they not accustomed to multiple marriages? Do not be surprised if they don't regard holy bonding as sacred."

"I can not believe a man as powerful as he would want another man's wife."

"I heard rumors of husbands' bodies floating to the Great Sea, minus their heads. Their wives now live with the sterile Egyptian king. Their children, by their former husbands, cultivate the lands in the upper regions."

Lot, raising his hand, called to speak. "Uncle, we cannot let this issue prevent us from going into Egypt. A solution will be discovered for Sarai's safety."

"Yes. Leave her here in Moreh," another shouted

"What!" Avram's facial muscles tensed. "The Perizzites dwell in those houses—and if it is true that the Egyptians are immoral—how much more so they? Sarai will not be left behind."

"Yahweh will protect her," Lot impulsively spoke.

"Are we to go into Egypt to test Yahweh? Be careful, nephew, of how you invoke His name! Never allow it to be in manipulative terms whereby you try to gain an unfair advantage over another for self-serving principles."

"We need to go to Egypt to keep from starving to death," Lot countered.

"Then Lot, tell me, if you were married and your wife was endangered, how would you act?"

"I would make it an individual concern. Whatever one acts on, it's the act of that single person."

"Then I will talk to Sarai."

While his followers lowered the best tents and while the women carefully, skillfully repackaged them inside their protective canvases, Avram studied his wife's movements. Hesitating to talk to her, he waited by the wayside. Moments later the noise of the youngest men running off to the distant countryside to gather their livestock forced him to act on his thoughts. Finally summing up enough courage, Avram approached Sarai.

"Truly you are an extraordinarily beautiful woman. My eyes feast on you daily. My heart races as the antelope whenever I come near you. I have never tired of your company nor of your embraces. Sarai, I love you even today the same as I did when I first beheld you in swaddling cloths.

"I was ten years old then. Father came racing out of the tent proclaiming to everyone: 'What a beautiful baby girl.' You still are. His words have never been truer!"

"Avram," her hand touched his chest, her lips nearing his, "what brings this conversation?"

"We will be traveling for Egypt this afternoon. There's a rumor that the king craves all beautiful women."

"I am married. I am not young."

"You have an eternal youth about you. You radiate with an intense glow that makes all men desire you. I am still in its spell."

"Husband, I also love you."

"Sarai, please, become even more loving and exceptionally kinder on our journey into Egypt. Maintain at all times a veil over your face and refrain from talking with anyone. Intermingle only with the shepherds' wives of our tents. Please, at all times, keep your head lowered to the ground."

"Why? Am I not Sarai, Avram's wife?"

"You indeed are. Please Sarai, do as I ask. I ask this not to denigrate your status, but rather, so I may preserve my own life. I am afraid of this journey. I am afraid of the consequences of the Egyptians' lustful behaviors and intents. I am afraid of their wanton disregard of other people's beliefs and cultural heritages.

"They act as they want to act, regardless of the people's pains. What they do, they do in direct defiance of everyone else. They rule without regrets or remorse or morality. They rule on their whims without restraint.

"Sarai, we both issued from the same father. Truly, are we not brother and sister? Say, therefore, if you will, that we are brother and sister. Do this so I may remain alive, thanks to you."

"I shall act as you want me to. You are always alive in me. I have spent my life beside you. Terah pronounced to the world our bonding and Eber performed the ritual that announced to the world our love for each other. I greatly resolve for no other man to be with me. May Yahweh allow me to die before you, my dearest love."

ಲಿಛಲಿಛಲಿಛಲಿಛಲಿಛ

Avram's group slowly advanced toward the Egyptian entrance guards. Standing beside the deeply bronzed, short-skirted soldiers, the fully clothed accountants inscribed on their papyruses accurate inventories of the refugees. After the scribes recorded the accounting, a division of the goods followed. To the right of the road, the scribes, with the guards' swords, set aside an equal portion of the traveler's goods for the king's use.

Eliezer, busying himself with the chief accountant, distracted the soldiers from lifting Sarai's veil and the veils of the other wives and daughters.

"Why shouldn't I see their faces? Are they so ugly?" the chief accountant laughed at him.

Eliezer shrugged his shoulders and also laughed. "Nomadic women are rough. Their feet are as leathery as their hands. Their faces reveal the stings of the sand. Why hurt your eyes?"

Eliezer presented another portion of silver into the accountant's hand. The accountant felt the weight of the purse and called for the soldiers to back away from the women and daughters. The official smiled at Eliezer and allowed the diminished caravan to pass into Egypt to the city of Zoan.

ಲಿಛಲಿಛಲಿಛಲಿಛಲಿಛ

The alluvial savannas stretched as far as the eye could see. It seemed as if the rich earth readily accept whatever the tillers placed into the ground. What the farmers planted, grew.

Tens of thousands of workers lined the King's Road.

Nearly effortlessly, methodically, meticulously the block-masters transported on the hard bed of trampled sand vast blocks of stone over rounded beams. Dozens of harnessed oxen pulled on the long, taut ropes, obeying the feverish cries of their masters.

Hundreds of other taskmasters lined the bed of the road, helping the religious cult successfully maneuver the blocks into place. They accomplished this by placing lifting staffs underneath the stones and wedging support blocks underneath the stones as they went up. Six men lifted the block and two women scooted in the support blocks. In less than a minute a huge three foot by three foot by five foot block could be lifted waist high. Other construction workers quickly erected dwelling inns for the continuous streams of refugees who willingly paid the entry fees. Those unfortunate enough to have no savings voluntarily enslaved themselves to the laborers' camp, preferring food, water, and shelter to the independence of the famine.

As the heights of the building increased, the proud civil engineers of Zoan mounted large blocks of precisely cut stones with the help of counterweights at the end of long poles to rest perfectly on top of another block of stone. The construction workers also built two and three story mud and brick apartments for their sleeping quarters. The primary foundation contained large storage rooms while the upper floor contained tiers of two and three bunk beds.

The narrow streets between the rows of housing held gutters and sewer systems that wound throughout their paths. The windows of the rising houses faced the inside streets while the solid, back outside walls stared emptily into the great expanse of humanity entering through the gates. Only the waiting blocks and hastily arranged lengths of boards saw the pitiful groups of incoming travelers.

Throughout the region sand ramparts and military guard towers blocked the horizon's view. Everywhere, the beginnings of temple foundations and great houses broke the tranquility of the smooth land.

Avram and his companions, awestruck by the immensity of the architectural wonders of the builders, stared at one another. Each great architectural accomplishment rose from hewed stones that fitted against each other without the slightest mistake. The merchant-refugees couldn't help but compare Zoan's eternal blocks of stone to Babylon's mud-baked structures and to Ur's brick and bitumen palaces.

Avram's group was given permission to settle on the remotest western parcels of land behind the northern town houses. There, the refugees quickly prepared pens for their livestock. Almost immediately they agreed to empower Eliezer to barter the wares that they had carried from Ur and from Nineveh and from Susa and from Damascus for foodstuffs and water.

Lot, having only his few sheep and one donkey, sold his sheep's milk to the other newly arriving refugees. On occasion he even rented his donkey for the carrying of their goods. With his profits Lot bought another sheep, then another, and then four more.

Then ten more.

Avram, concentrating on his merchandising abilities, also began to prosper. Gradually, Avram's reputation as an honest and fair negotiator became appreciated by the refugees and, by a few of the king's courtiers.

And so it was that Avram and his friends began rebuilding their finances.

ဢဢ

One evening, in an unguarded moment, Sarai, by chance, stood before the watering well at the same time that an important official of the king's court stood by it. This happened during the zenith of a spectacular sunset. Life, for a brief moment in time, seemed to harmoniously understand the brevity of existence and the importance of a moment's excitement. As she briefly relaxed in those moments of the clouds' breathtaking beauty, Sarai's veil fell from her face.

A flock of geese flew in front of the darkening clouds. The deep violet and orange rays, striking up from behind the mass of clouds, blackened the geese against the red sun. Sarai raised her face to gaze at the geese. It was then that her veil unfastened. When the king's ambassador saw her face and her voluptuous figure he gasped an audible admiration.

Three days later, in perfect silence, six highly trained teams of soldiers surrounded Avram's camp. Wielding their war axes, swinging their swords, and jabbing their bronze-tipped spears into the bales of clothing and straw, they roused the people from their town houses. Eighteen soldiers forced dozens of residents into a circle. For an eternity in frightened time, they sneered at the frightened collection of refugees. When the trumpet blew the soldiers snapped to attention. They stood by the wayside while the king's personal courtier inspected the figures of the intimidated families.

"What wrong have we committed against anyone?" Eliezer translated Avram's Hebraic speech into Egyptian.

"The Lord of the Great House wishes to be introduced to the woman who occupies the fifth dwelling."

"Avram," Eliezer pointed out. "That is Sarai's place."

"The woman who resides therein is my sister. I am her caretaker! I am responsible for her safety."

"King Amenemhet, in his generosity, has heard of her beauty. He has ordered me to escort her to his presence. Now it is up to me to protect her. I'll make sure she arrives safely."

"Why would Amenemhet call for someone he has never met?"

"It's in keeping with his generosity. The king desires to assure his guests of proper treatment and to lovingly provide whatever he may for their prosperity."

"Has he placed a seal on this request?"

"There is not an official document for this, no."

"Ask, please, for the king's guarantee of safety."

"There is no need for that."

"My pledge to my father and my pledge to my sister requires this."

Avram's first companion, nudging him in the side with his elbow, whispered, "Do not provoke them. We have no weapons. We are not prepared to defend ourselves."

The emissary, observing the frightened men, relaxed his manner, smiling. "I understand your trepidation. Allow my position to ease your worries. I will stay in your camp while your sister visits my lord: your carekeeper."

"I also understand the art of diplomacy," Avram responded. "I am not here to offer a challenge nor to denigrate your lord's kindness. I sensibly ask first for an audience: for a document impressed with the Seal of the Great House.

"Sarai is, as you well know, my sister whom I must protect."

"Your brotherly devotion is strong and admirable."

The emissary gestured toward the palace and a soldier immediately darted off. The other soldiers tightened their formation, trapping the refugees within their menacing circle.

Avram and the rest sat on the barren ground. Hours dragged by. The sun, heating their bodies, parched their throats.

The soldiers also became thirsty. Afraid of the consequences of breaking their ranks to go to the well that was dug beside them, the soldiers similarly suffered the pains of thirst.

A larger entourage finally came bustling from the palace walls. Over the shoulders of powerfully toned warriors a short man sat rigidly inside a large golden chair. In the middle of the formidable ranks a taller soldier commanded the troops.

The king, surprisingly, was a young, handsome, intently gazing man. His chest was finely tuned as was his stomach. He had a ceremonial beard underneath his chin. Winged scarabs rose above his head. A small amulet, exquisitely shaped from pure gold, hung around his neck, signifying his power and wealth.

When the formation stopped, a group of women ran from the rear to the very forefront of the troops. In harmonic rhythms, the female servants of Ra pounded into the ground thick, sharpened oak poles that had sitting cats carved on top of them. The cats' eyes, exquisitely chiseled from red rubies, glimmered, glowing from the sun's rays. The refractions of light nearly blinded the crowd forming around the Hebrew clan. The cats' cheeks brilliantly, uncannily shone from the thin inlaid of gold sheets.

The king refused to speak to the crowd. Instead, the king held out a parchment wrapped in purple silk bands to the emissary.

Bowing low, the potbellied, aged emissary kept his eyes focused on his own feet as he watched the lengthening growth of his shadow. He moved in another direction, assuring that his shadow did not infringe on the king's shadow. With quickening backward steps, he returned to Avram after he received the king's document.

Mystified, Avram slid the bands off.

Sarai, hiding in the midst of the refugees, repositioned herself so she could observe the events. She saw Avram's hesitating hands reaching for the parchment. She watched the king impatiently lean forward in his chair. Edging herself past the inner circle she made her way outside its geometric protection and isolation. She walked past Avram's bent shoulders directly to the soldiers and stood before the cats' images. She placed her hand over the left one and pushed it aside, forcing it to tumble to the ground.

The priestess quickly picked it up and returned it to its hole.

Defiantly Sarai walked past Amenemhet as well. She stared into his eyes and forced him to follow her movements with his head. Unaccustomed to such manners, he turned his head hypnotically, responding to her motion. Transfixed, awed by her incredible beauty, he and all the men and women watched as she walked unescorted to the palace doors. The Egyptian king turned with her movements and nearly lost his balance on his chair. Swiftly facing-about, the troops ran behind Sarai.

ෂෝෂෝෂෝෂෝෂ

Inside the great palace, thick, strong oak doors, lined with images of cats and geese, greeted the strange visitor. Never had an Egyptian witnessed such defiant behavior in a female guest. Sarai, walking the length of the corridor, failed to notice that the interior walls of the walkway depicted wonderful pictures of farmers tilling the ground. Large, prosperous verdant growths of barley fields adorned the walls of the otherwise empty hallway. In the deeper portion of the palace, blue and gold paintings elegantly depicted scantily clad women drawing water from the river. A few feet away, carved images of alligators freely roamed near the riverbanks.

A servant girl, dashing from the entryway, rapidly ran to stand in front of Sarai. She bowed and silently led her new mistress to her room.

Outside the sumptuously large room a set of black stone jackals guarded the private entrance.

Hagar waited patiently for her new guest to speak to her. She bowed again when they entered the room. Hagar expected the tall woman to receive her warmly, thankful to be inside such glamorous surroundings. Instead, the woman remained strangely silent, bitterly resentful. Puzzled, Hagar stared at the audacious foreigner. Amazed, she fixed her gaze on her figure. She had never seen such large, firm breasts on a woman before. Her acutely thin waist and curvaceous hips made her envious.

Sarai, finally noticing the small-framed dark woman, returned her bow. With heavy breaths she followed Hagar, her appointed handmaiden, to the baths.

ᔪᏏᏏᏏᏏᏏᏏᏏᏏᏏᏏ

During the last day of the following week, with the approach of the new morning, several female attendants and two male shepherds greeted Avram outside his town house door. The Egyptian king, in exchange for granting them leave to remain in Egypt, demanded their servitude. Behind them followed a dozen well-fed, luxuriant sheep.

"These are Amenemhet's gifts for you."

"They're the finest animals I've ever seen."

"We also are here for you."

"I have not authorized nor expected gifts. Say to the king that I cannot accept these gifts."

"It would please us if you agree to accept not only these gifts, but also to accept us in your camp. We pledge ourselves to your service. Eliezer informed us that you are a righteous man. If you deny us, it would be the same as condemning us to eternal, harsh servitude under a tyrant. We ask sanctuary."

"Is it mine to give?"

"We understand it to be so."

"Then, I must accept you. Not, however, as indentured persons. Rather, as a free people."

"Free?"

"Yes. But for the duration, act according to my desires so all may remain safe."

"We will obey you."

The following week another group of women and men also appeared at Avram's door. Behind them fattened calves and choice geese and strong white donkeys, whose eyes were alert and whose legs were stout, followed. The donkeys' manes flowed to their necks. Gold braids dangled from the tips of their manes to the edges of their knees.

Avram accepted those gifts as well.

Before the third week passed a new group of men and women greeted Avram at his doorstep. Behind them followed large camels. Over their humps bundles of camel hair hangings and floor coverings rested. Avram motioned to Eliezer and asked him to direct them to the station where the other men and women of the nations earlier gathered together. Eliezer, talking to them, organized them into separate divisions of labor and talent.

"Eliezer, inform Amenemhet that I am well pleased with his gifts, but there is no reason for such generosity. Inform him, please, that I miss my sister and that she must be prepared to return to her home."

Eliezer did as Avram requested and asked permission for an audience with the king. It was immediately granted. In the fabulous hall of mighty columns, Eliezer bowed before the king of Egypt.

"Avram is a kind friend," the king answered Eliezer. "His sister is a kinder friend. Indeed, she is among the most virtuous of my friends. I desire for her to remain longer in my household. She teaches my maidens honesty and she speaks forthrightly about everything. She has also become a counselor to my children. What they hear from her lips they share with my ears. Her talents impress me too much to share her again with her brother."

Eliezer became dismayed at the king's words. His rigid and commanding pose softened and weakened. The king clapped his hands to his servants when he saw how distressed Eliezer became. The loud sound vibrated throughout the chamber-room.

"Present Avram these additional gifts." The 'King of the Great House' pointed to a collection of barley and wheat sacks and several barrels of beer.

ᔆᘓᔆᘓᔆᘓᔆᘓᔆᘓ

In the privacy of the evening's setting, Avram tried to subtract from his thoughts all feelings. Isolated, the sun's rays filtered through the open bay, its redness striking his face. He rubbed his wrinkling forehead. He massaged his throbbing temples. Trembling, he placed his vigorously shaking hand over his mouth. He sighed deeply and wrapped his arms about his chest. Tears, for all his efforts against them, nevertheless watered his cheeks. He suddenly bent over and heaved to an empty vomit. He forced himself to stand erect. Just as quickly he redoubled to the floor. His body shook with anguish. Finally he lost emotional control and submitted to his anxiousness. An uncontrollable torrent of tears overwhelmed him. He clutched the blanket that he and Sarai so often shared and wrapped it about his body, trying to hide his anguish from himself. Opposite from his intentions, he openly submitted more deeply to his pains of loneliness and lost companionship.

"Sarai! Sarai! Sarai! Sarai! Sarai!" he kept moaning through the deepening anguish of tears, rocking back and forth in his trance of agony.

Inside the encampment the people moved slowly. Clearly they heard Avram's muffled tears. As they looked at each other, their eyes also watered. Their emotions identified with Avram's mental sufferings. Their nostrils became moist. Their sniffles, they swallowed.

Lot, not knowing how to respond, crossed and tightened his own arms around his chest. Eliezer, being next to him, suddenly embraced Lot and the two loudly cried without hesitation or embarrassment.

And Michael the Archangel, being in Avram's tent, sadly withdrew to the far depths of the universe. Pondering, Michael the Archangel returned to his Father's heavenly residence. There, he respectfully approached the golden throne where the two secretly conversed with each other.

The soft, descending twilight quietly met the morning's rise. The Egyptian cattlemen went to their pastures, leading their herds to the river's edge. The children played gleefully in the shallow water. Storks, swallows, bulbuls, and geese flew from one embankment to the other, their calls filling the land. A gathering of ibis settled to the far bank while a falcon, flying high overhead, observed the twitching mice in the field. A lone dog, seeing the falcon, sniffed the nearby bales. Dashing hard, the dog snapped one of the field mice in half, quickly consuming it moments before the falcon could swoop it up inside its talons.

Unaware of the outside world, a group of dedicated scribes busily prepared their parchments, drying out the leaves of the plant over heightened racks.

The farmers, with their spouses, emptied large baskets of recently cut stalks, piling them high in front of the teenagers who were winnowing the chaff from the seeds. The nearby observers became caked with the flying debris. They wiped off the powder and laughed at the wonder of the new day.

The butchers, hurrying to the meat warehouse, grabbed slabs of pork, frying it quickly over the fires while the bakers pounded and kneaded the yeast into their rolls.

Unexpectedly, an incredibly hot, humid afternoon swiftly wrestled control over the mild morning. The king's body sweltered in drenching sweat. His servants and his wives and concubines similarly suffered inside a vise of unrelenting heat. The weakened servants, struggling, lifted the bewildered king from his throne, gently carrying him to his bedchambers. Within moments the acrid, heavy air pushed away all the cool air.

Mysteriously, large swarms of mosquitoes buzzed into the palace. Simultaneously, ravaging hordes of maggots swelled in the pork. The lone dog, chasing another mouse, discovered an army of mice scrambling from behind the sacks of grain toward him. Biting into the unending largeness, he gave up, returning to his dwelling. There, he discovered another army of field mice scrambling inside his cove. The falcon, flying overhead, swooped into the crowd, carrying off one mouse.

The cooks, watching the falcon, ignored the fecal droppings of the mice on top of the harvested and winnowed grains.

ᛞᚳᛝᚳᛝᚳᛝᚳᛝᚳᛝᚳ

"Sarai, why is your voice silent today?" Hagar asked.

"I've been here too long. Each time I try to approach the door's exit, the guards prevent me from passing through."

"Why would you want to be out there? It's safe here. It's beautiful here."

"I am not one to be locked up."

"The confinement is in your imagination. There's more blessing to serve Amenemhet than there is in anything else."

"There's a deeper blessing."

"Yes, I've heard you speak of such things to the children. It's a wonder the king doesn't silence your voice for speaking about such things."

"The Egyptian king will never raise his hand to me! However, should he prevent me another time from leaving this stifling existence, Yahweh will intervene for me."

Several days later the guards again lowered their shields against Sarai's attempted departure. Amenemhet, at that exact moment, woke with an excruciating pain in his abdomen. The king rushed to the washbasin and immediately vomited his evening's meal. He heaved again and again. Murky, filthy liquids erupted from his stomach and intestines. Losing his bladder control, he soiled his richly adorned garment. Then he fell flat on his face and vomited again.

His wife clutched her tunic about her knees and folded herself again as her bowel movements refused to stop. The handmaidens panicked and ran for the priests and doctors. The frightened doctors and priests supplicated a loud offering to Ra and Osiris: the pagan gods of Egypt.

Red and orange and blue incense burned throughout the interior palace. Heavy red and blue clouds of smoke ascended to the ceiling, becoming a vapor of sickeningly sweat, stifling aroma that hung throughout the Great House. The overbearing sweetness mingled with the horrid smells of fecal and vomit matter.

Rapidly, the household became infected with the inexplicable illness. Among the household, only Sarai remained healthy. The doctors, mystified, took her into the king's bedchambers. There, his attendants raised his head to speak with her.

"How is it you are not ill? How is it your stomach is still flat and your brow is still dry? What magic do you possess?"

"Yahweh has protected me from what sickens you."

"Why would your God harm us? What have we done to insult Him? Have we interfered with His ways? Have we prevented you from worshipping Him. Have I silenced your voice against the stories which you have shared with my household? In fact, I, myself, found them pleasant to listen to!

"More importantly, I never violated your chastity. I never demanded for you to remove your garments nor even asked for you to lay beside me in my bed.

"I have been generous with you and with your brother and with his friends."

"Your generosity was nothing more than a bribery. Whatever you offered to my brother and to his friends, you did so to compel me to want to lie beside you. The gifts were nothing more than the payment by a man for a whore."

"You are then the most expensive of prostitutes!"

"A married woman who is firmly obligated to her husband cannot be called a prostitute."

"Married? To whom?" the Egyptian king incredulously demanded to know. Shivering, he forced his head to rise higher than his attendants' supporting hands allowed.

"My brother."

Amenemhet opened his mouth to speak another word. Instead, he silently collapsed back into his pillow.

He thought of his own spouse. "She also is my sister by my father and mother. Sometimes," he reasoned within himself, "a person may want something so much, even when they know it's false, they'll accept it anyway for its hoped rewards."

He brought his two fingers to his chapped lips. The doctor softly walked to him and placed a spoonful of beer and cubed geese and antelope meat into his mouth. Immediately the soup dribbled outside the corner of his mouth, soiling his silk pillow.

ᚱᚲᚱᚲᚱᚲᚱᚲᚱᚲ

The bronzed Egyptian guards escorted Avram to the remote bedchambers and placed him directly in front of the king. Afterwards they blocked the entry doors with their spears, preparing to slay the manipulating, deceitful, ungrateful Babylonian.

"So, you came here from Ur to gain our confidence. Subsequently, you devised to poison us for Chedorlaomer's arrival."

"That's not true. We came for refuge."

"From enslavement?"

"We are not runaways! We sanction freedom and the rights of men to be able to fulfill for themselves their maximum degrees of creativity."

"I believe otherwise. Only the fewest are born to be free. Someone needs to father and lead the majority. My forefathers have trained and subjected these peoples for specific purposes. Greatness cannot mature without the massive efforts of a single, controlling house."

"God's House is a House of free men."

"That's why you have infiltrated into Egypt! You intend to corrupt and destroy this house. Afterwards you'll cause my people to openly wage civil war and rebellion against Egypt, placing perhaps yourself as its new king! First you will poison me, then you will overturn the throne."

"I will not," Avram defended himself. "Others, however, will come who will. It is they whom you must protect yourself against. Not me, nor my sister."

"Is Sarai your wife?" the king softened his words when he realized the uselessness of his accusatorial tactics. Amenemhet sucked on a loosening tooth.

"As well as my sister," Avram also changed the tone of his voice.

"Yes. My culture also demanded for me to marry my sister. It is the way of Egyptian royalty. But I did not know it was also the way of the Babylonians."

"My father, Terah, permitted it to be so."

"Was your father a king?"

"He had desired it."

"He bequeathed his ambition to you. So, instead of fearing Chedorlaomer's armies and court intrigues, I should fear your presence even more. You are a landless king, seeking a country to possess."

"I am not here to own Egypt."

"Then why are you here?"

"The desert's unswerving refusal to provide grain and water to me victimized my livestock and the loyalty of my followers. I came here only at the urging of my companions. I asked my wife, that should it happen that someone discovers how beautiful she truly is, she should declare that she is my sister—for it is the truth.

"In Retenu, the land of the Canaanites, I was convinced you are a man who will not hesitate to take to your bedchamber whatever wife or woman you demand to have for yourself. I heard it said you will 'take whom you want' even at the 'point of murdering' whomever interferes with your desire to gain what 'whets your appetite'."

"You are bold to speak to me so hatefully. I am not such a horrid tyrant. I am not so merciless that I would murder all men so their wives will provide me with sexual pleasures.

"Take your wife—your sister—and disappear as quickly as possible from my country."

"I will leave. I will also leave behind what you have given us, for it shall not be said they were 'provided by manipulation and deceit'."

"I will not have you return to me those skinny beasts and tarnished metals. Soldiers, see to it that all these Babylonians are completely exiled from Egypt. See to it that word is sent to all my border guards that these wanderers: 'these just looking types,' may not be permitted reentry."

From Lower Egypt, from the city of Zoan, the king's special task force escorted Avram and his companions back to the Negeb. Ensuring Avram's departure, the captain of the guard erected a plaque forbidding reentry to Avram and to Lot and to his companions.

For long hours the escorting guards watched the multitude cross over with their hundreds of livestock and dozens of male and female servants.

A few guards, admiring Avram for his victory over the king, secretly wondered how it was possible for such an uncouth, inferior Babylonian to gain his wealth.

ಬಿ ಲ ಬಿ ಲ ಬಿ ಲ ಲ ಲ ಲ ಲ

The hill people of the Indus Valley, who happened to be migrating at this identical time through the borderlands of the Arabian Peninsula, also heard of the Babylonian's cunning deceit over the young, lecherous Egyptian king.

Recently these hills people lost a terrible, ferocious battle against the Elamites. In their victory celebrations, the conquering Elamites expelled the hills people from the vast, fertile valley.

Reaching the outskirts of the seemingly endless Egyptian savannas the Hyksos emigrants watched Avram's long procession. Decades later King Salatis of the Hyksos eventually ingrained himself into the Egyptian culture. As he knew their weaknesses, King Salatis subverted the Egyptian throne for himself.

ಬಿ ಲ ಬಿ ಲ ಬಿ ಲ ಲ ಲ ಲ ಲ

Avram returned northward to the region between Bet-El and Ai. Once there, Avram sacrificed another sheep on the same altar that he had previously erected, blessing Yahweh's name for His intervention in his dilemma.

ಬಿ ಲ ಬಿ ಲ ಬಿ ಲ ಲ ಲ ಲ ಲ

Several weeks after this Avram called Lot before the large assembly of men. In front of them Avram publicly congratulated Lot on his cunning skills at vastly increasing his livestock quantities. Throughout the harsh northern famine the once plentiful herds of gazelle and ruminants had depleted, becoming nearly extinct throughout the region. The gentle sheep, readily adapting to the land, became the new main meat staple of the people. Ironically, the pigs also increased in the hills of the land.

"You've done well in Egypt," Avram wrapped his arms about his nephew's arms. Lot beamed with pride.

"By paying strict attention to you, uncle."

"What you gained, you did so admirably. You've learned the success of bartering where there was nothing to trade and you've learned to develop for yourself what was necessary for you to develop."

"Eliezer watched over me. What he advised, I heeded."

"So, is there now peace between you two?"

"There is. Since the days of Damascus too many things have happened for me not to mature. I left my youth in Egypt."

"You are ready then, are you not, for marriage?"

Lot beam with joy and rapidly nodded his head.

"I will send for a wife for you from Nahor's home."

"Please, uncle," Lot countered Avram. "May I not choose for myself whom I desire to wed with?"

"That is not the custom," Avram frowned, his voice becoming unpleasant.

"We are in a new land," Lot again argued against Avram's desires, "far from my uncle's home. Allow me, I ask, to choose the Egyptian who has traveled alongside my caravan."

"An Egyptian?" Avram stood slightly away from his nephew. He had never conceived such a possibility between the two.

"If it is permitted," Lot bowed his head.

Avram turned to look at his companions and advisors. He noted their silence. He raised himself on his tiptoes, hoping for someone to object against the intermarriage. No one did.

"There are no objections from the camp. However, the Egyptian hand-maidens have grown accustomed to wealth and to pleasurable things and such desires may eventually cause you hardships."

"I am a wealthy man. Nearly equal to you."

Avram nodded his head, agreeing with Lot's statement. He dwelled on the matter for a few moments.

"Have you considered its consequences?" Avram finally asked Lot. "There are many nationalities in this camp," he carefully acknowledged the fact of it. "It may be wise to select her for your companion." He grew pensive again, waiting for someone to object to the marriage arrangements. "For three generations your children must only marry Babylonians," a thought unexpectedly invaded his senses. As he looked from face to face, he saw no one's lips moving. The thought came from deep within himself. A private, irremovable thought. He quickly dismissed it, forgetting such a thing had mysteriously occurred.

Again, no one objected to the intermarriage. Finally, he added, "I shall permit it."

Short months later, the marriage feast took place among the lush and pleasant trees. Hundreds of guests brought Lot and his bride gifts. After the candles of matrimony were extinguished, though, the example of Lot's unity to a foreigner failed to encourage the other Babylonians to intermingle with the other nationalities.

The ransomed Egyptian families, feeling the sting of prejudice, demanded to similarly stay together.

A bitter separatism developed in Avram's camp. He had to come to terms with it as the original Babylonian followers determined to issue a decree forbidding intermarriage in order to maintain their original bloodlines. The families of power refused to encourage their children to play with the children of the former Egyptian slaves.

A special session was called.

"It's not an issue of intermarriage," a member declared. "The real issue is of rights and power. We are Babylonians. They are a conglomeration of bloods, fathered by mongrels."

"Moreover," an important council member stated in the meeting tent, "because these former Egyptians and other nationalities are not witnesses of Yahweh, they cannot comprehend His laws. They are able to corrupt us. We may be assimilated by their words and ideas. We are few and they are many."

Avram understood this to mean: "The foreign strangers among us must never rise above their inferior status among the rest of the camp."

The small but highly influential group debated throughout the night why the other nationalities must never be seen as equals among the Babylonians. "The foreigners are jealous and unreasonably fail to understand why we deserve our wealth. We must be guaranteed territorial rights for our grazing flocks and the foreigners must tend to their own affairs as best as they can." Harshly, arrogantly, the Babylonian powerbase also refused to acknowledge and abide by the prearranged times for watering the livestock by the foreigners.

Avram hated the intensity of the situation. He looked at Lot and Eliezer and at his wife Sarai. "I admit, the nations which we brought out of Egypt divide themselves off not only from each other, but also from among us. To remedy this we must clearly inform them that they are not slaves to us nor to any other man. As to Yahweh, we must teach them who He is and what He means to us. Through this, we will all become equal. In this equality, intermarriage will be permissible as will the sharing of land and water."

"Freedom for the foreigners?" Eliezer whispered.

"Under Yahweh's directing hands."

"Remember Avram, we Babylonians are known for our prejudice toward all foreigners. Only Lot has been permitted to marry an outsider, and only after considerable debate and disharmony among our kind. The rest wisely, or unwisely, refused. If you wanted to show equality among nations, why didn't you, Avram, the leader of our people, take a concubine from a foreign nation. Through such an example peace would have been easier to maintain among our groups."

"Yahweh placed me alongside Sarai," Avram replied. "Not anyone else."

"If prejudice is to be completely vanquished, you need to set an example for us."

"Have I not done so by permitting Lot to marry an Egyptian?" Avram repeated.

"She is a slave. Her legs spread at her master's command."

"A slave?" Avram spoke the term. It seemed foul in his mouth. "Why do people become another person's slave?" Avram then asked Eliezer. He wanted to change the subject from women to slaves as Eliezer failed to discern the difference between the two states of service.

"War, debts, to lazy to take care of oneself—or the total selfishness of one human being toward another human being?" Eliezer answered.

"War certainly can conquer freedom. Laziness would make a man seek the cares of a stronger house. But, as you said, what if," Avram set this scenario for Eliezer, "a man becomes indebted and needs to barter his services to satisfy the burden?"

"As we said earlier, he, and possibly his family, becomes the slave of the master," Eliezer answered.

"A man can became a slave because he owes money?"

"Yes, we reasoned on that already."

"And could it be that debts arise either from laziness, or perhaps, misfortune?"

"Of course. Land loss due to famine, or floods, or other things."

"Then not everyone becomes a slave because he is lazy or is conquered by a stronger force."

"No," Eliezer answered. "But what has this to do with intermarriages and the inferior position of women?"

"Women are not inferior to men. They submit to their husband because Havva was the first human to transgress against Yahweh. Sarai is my equal in all respects. Man's desire to control has brought women to an inferior status. However, I wish to address the slaves who became slaves due to economic necessity. There are many such men in our camp, and I want to devise a way to free them from their bonds. I am using our conversation about women and their legal status among us as an excuse to broaden our conversation to involve the other classifications of slavery."

"The point that you desire to make is?" Eliezer pressed.

"I want to propose this: rather than a man and his family becoming perpetual slaves because they owe someone money, I say, let the debtor work off the debts to the lender for a maximum of seven years. No longer than that will his slavery be permitted. Further, I propose, while he is working off the debt, he may accumulate money and lands for himself and his family. Those will be his by the right of labor. These things may not be taken away from him."

"Who will enforce such dictates?"

"Courts of law will dictate the judgments of the community. The community will be under Yahweh's discretionary eyes."

"There is no nation like that, anywhere."

"Yes, there is. That nation exists now. In this land. We are the ones who will foster and care for it. Over time, it will be formulated into a living entity, and the influence of this nation will touch everyone's mind."

"Another prophecy?" Eliezer stated.

"A statement of how Yahweh intends things to be," Avram replied.

"How did this idea ferment in your mind?" Lot asked.

"I remember Eber's lessons. During the period of existence before the great deluge men lived in a dark, somber, ambitionless abyss. No government controlled them. No laws subjected them. Chaos created the day's desires.

"Abel rose to teach them the importance of sacrifice and prayer to Yahweh to bring us the Mashiach. Seth became the progenitor of that 'seed.' Noah carried the dream through the dread of Yahweh's vengeance against sin and immorality. Eber embraced the ideology and taught it to me. Yahweh's guiding principles reinforced that sonorous thought inside my being. In turn, I present it to you."

"I do not completely understand it," Lot confessed.

"I will note it in my chronicles for prosperity's sake."

After that Avram turned to Sarai and inquired, "What shall I write concerning your stay with the Egyptian king?"

"I shall not speak of what occurred nor shall it be recorded."

"You wish me to lessen your role?"

"I am Avram's wife. That fact is pleasurable enough to be recorded."

ཟ྄ཅ྄ཟ྄ཅ྄ཟ྄ཅ྄ཟ྄ཅ྄ཟ྄ཅ྄

In the ensuing years Avram's followers fathered many sons and daughters. Their growing tents encroached on their neighbors' tents and, during the night's private activity, all sounds clearly voyaged to the listener's imaginations.

Avram and Lot, concerned about the moral standards of their charge, established during the first, third, and fifth mornings of the week a learning period to teach the people Yahweh's principles. Gradually, through the passage of time, a few of the parents began appreciating the lessons. Through action and practice these families relished the concepts of freedom that the teachers taught them. Soon, they incorporated the new beliefs into their households and personalities.

There were others, however, who remained unconvinced of the lessons' truths and inspirations. The more they listened, the more baffled they became. The ideology of a single God who sought to present an eternal ruler over man confused them. In time, they rejected the ideology. Uncertain, they cautiously distanced themselves away from Avram's camp.

Occasionally a few of these young men wandered into the Perizzite camps where they met with the daughters of the village. Attracted to their easy lures, the young men attached themselves to these Perizzite households.

Finally, in the camp of tension and divided beliefs, the ultimate quarrel happened. It occurred during a mild afternoon. The pleasant breeze and the green, nourishing valley and the soft blue sky crowded with spectacular cloud formations. Underneath this beautiful calm day, brew great hostility. Several groups of men fought each other. Screams ripped through the valley as the cool air blew against their sweat drenched faces.

Contracting contradictions ensued. The trees and the clouds remained picturesque. A herd of animals gazed in the far off pasturage occasionally startled by a shout. The fighting ceased as the day darkened. The blood stained grass amidst an ocean of soft currents denied the onslaught. Only the vulture and the eagle that waited in the nearby branches, waiting to feast, admitted to its occurrence. The horrific hand-to-hand fighting happened during the course of a gentle afternoon.

It began like this. Teams of rival families demanded to water their cattle herds at the same time. Two rival families quarreled with each other and finally they forced an irreparable schism throughout the camp.

"Are we to permit the people of the nations to witness our behavior?" Avram appealed to Lot. "We are surrounded by thousands of Canaanites and Perizzites. Those same nationals may be aligned with Ampraphel and Arioch.

"King Amenemhet has now been replaced with King Tamios. From what I understand he is ready to be overwhelmed by the Hyksos. We must guard ourselves against internal confrontations."

"How am I to control my herdsmen?" Lot demanded to know. "They endlessly quarrel over the time of day they should be permitted to water the cattle and then they argue over eating mutton and then they argue over eating steaks then over eating geese. None can even agree if ale or beer or wine is best served with roast lamb! Then when it comes to beef, watch out!"

Avram smiled faintly. His eyes radiated with more wrinkles. Lot quietly added, "It's a tiresome display, uncle."

After a period of silence, Avram breathed out heavily, saying, "It's also a divisive display. Permit me, please, to make a suggestion."

Lot nodded.

"We must maintain peace between ourselves and among our herdsmen for we have brought them out of Egypt as slaves and granted them freedom. They had to learn its meaning and responsibilities, but they have not yet tempered their mentalities to its fullest implications. We cannot allow them to regress. What we have accomplished must one day become the guiding laws of a country's constitution.

"Moreover, you and I are directly related to each other first by blood, and to a truer degree, by the bonding of Yahweh's mission to the Mashiach. Most of the men who are here have stayed with us because of their emotional and economic needs. I prefer, however, that they continue remaining with us because of their beliefs and devotion to Yahweh.

"Realistically, though, that simply is not the truth. Can men remain together without a unified and devoted love for Yahweh? To love Yahweh, can the quarreling be permitted to continue?"

Lot answered, "We can do so if we build a city with walls and if we build a temple to Yahweh."

"We have not been directed to such a cause."

"There is still the City of Salem."

"I do not know where to find it."

"Won't Eber ever come back for us?"

"I cannot answer what I don't know."

"What are we to do?"

"Lot, we must divide our camp. There are hundreds of men here. Their wives and children are too numerous for this plot of land to continue to support them. Have we not learned in the Negeb that land is not inexhaustible?

"And, if we do stay here, what you suggested will become our reality. We may have to erect walls and houses and devote our energies into furnishing them.

"To do that would be a direct violation of my word to my friend, Mamre. Had we not concluded a contract with him that we would not build a city here? We must, therefore, divide."

"Where am I to go?" Lot, stupefied, begged to know.

"Wherever you choose. I will not permit further strife to occur. Look. See, the world lies before us.

"If the northern territory is for you,

"the southern lands will be mine.

"Should you prefer the southern horizons,

"the northern setting will be mine."

Lot pondered on the land's layout then answered, "Many of the young men have gone into the Jordan Valley. I have traveled there myself in futile attempts to persuade the young men to return home. The land is fertile and there are numerous lakes.

"Uncle, I have more cattle than I have sheep. You have more sheep than cattle. Allow me, if your heart is motivated towards me, to chose the Valley of Siddim."

"The cities of Sedom, Amorah, Zoar, and Zeboiim are situated therein."

"I know. My wife loves bartering her weights of silver for their silk dresses."

Avram burst out laughing. "See, did I not warn you! Go then, Lot, go. Go with my deepest love and affection. Go with my tears on your cheeks, my dearest nephew."

ഔൽഔൽഔൽഔൽഔൽ

The next few days passed with Lot's companions lowering their tents. After stacking their poles on the camels' backs, their caravan proceeded south around the smooth hills of the land, traveling until they reached Beersheba. From there Lot's camp turned due east, descending into the rich fertile green valley directly ahead of them.

As the people of the caravan journeyed deeper inland, they plucked the pomegranates from their hanging bushes and yanked out of the earth dozens of heads of cabbage and bunches of grapes. For the moment they feasted, joyously declaring to each other the opportune benefits of being in such a rich and fertile land.

As Lot's caravan neared the city of Sedom, the herdsmen became fascinated with the hundreds of radiating fires emitting from the wall's highest towers. The fragrant yellow, red, green, and violet plumes of smoke ascended into the blue sky. The collage of colors mingled into each other underneath the clouds' ceiling, painting it an eery, iridescent color.

The different colors rose toward the thick cumulus clouds and fascinated the children even more so than the parents. The city's engineers intentionally designed the smokestacks to emit the fumes to mingle with the clouds that continuously hovered over them. This was done to hide the city from the eyes of God. The builders' also ingeniously designed the city's causeways so the cool morning and evening breezes would flow into the homes, blowing upwards and away the pockets of smoke. Many of the citizens, enjoying the sky's collage, fashioned removable roofs to watch the multi-colored clouds.

The mishmashes of reflecting colors, however, painted a deceptive calm over the still waters of the numerous lakes surrounding the two cities. Occasionally an antelope or a cow or a buffalo, trusting the water's calm, ventured too far out into a lake. Then, while washing down, its feet edged into the bitumen bottom. The thick gel, wrapping around the animal's feet, pulled it deeper inside its trap. The bellowing and frightened animal, fighting against the cruel tug, sank deeper into the tar. Within short moments, the animal's corpus joined hundreds of other bones at the core's pit.

ഉ෫ങ്ഉ෫ങ്ഉ෫ങ്ഉ෫ങ്ഉ෫ങ്

The black underlayment of the clouds delighted the king. The stark white caps of the clouds forced him to frown. "Why can there not be a single veil of black above us?" he challenged the engineers.

This particular day, he gave up arguing with the imbeciles. Resigned, he sat on top of the highest tower watching the disjointed clouds and the infernal breaches of sunlight. While cursing the brightening day, the sounds of a newly arriving caravan sparked his interest.

"Bring me better wine," the stuporous king demanded.

A young boy immediately prepared the king's eighth cup of wine. Watching through dazed eyes, the king saw the distant small cattle gradually become larger and larger. It was as if he were looking through a reverse telescope.

Lot, failing to see the king, concentrated on the entry gate of the city. There were more people today than he ever remembered being in the city. He squinted his eyes and saw figures of men strolling alongside other men. Shamelessly they wrapped their arms about each other's waist. Purposely keeping their tunics wide open, immense gold necklaces flashed. Large emerald rings graced their fingers.

Finally Lot approached the main front gate. Lot looked ahead of his caravan. In front of several houses dozens of men waited in a single line, placing in the pimp's hand whatever he would accept for the favors of the prostitutes that were waiting inside.

He turned around and saw his followers eagerly smiling. "You accept this?" he asked the man immediately in front of him.

"It was the same in Egypt. Don't concern yourself with it."

"Lot, thank you for bringing us here," another companion merrily stated.

"I fear I made a misjudgment," Lot quickly apologized, more to himself than to his followers. "I did not know the extent of their wickedness."

"What wickedness? It's party time. Enjoy it!"

"Are you going inside the city?"

"Most certainly I am!"

Lot cleaned his upper teeth with a green plant stem, accepting the loss of his companions. "I'll pitch my tent over there, by those trees. The cattle need watering."

The men refused to walk toward the thirsty cattle.

"I suppose I can water them."

"Yes, please do so for us. And, if you don't mind, we're going to have some fun."

The men in the rear, excited by the bright, intense fires and by the frolicking of the music's inviting chords, began slapping the cattle's rears, forcing them to rush into the ponds.

"Boy," the king tapped the young child's shoulder, "watch what happens."

Several of the lead cattle, being pushed by the cattle behind them, suddenly skirted into the lake. Others, stammering behind, forced the lead
cows farther into the lake. A third group of thirsty, bellowing cattle rushed
unhindered into the pool's edge, forcing the first group deeper inside. The
herdsmen, unconcerned with the cattle's plight, wanted them to finish
drinking as quickly as they could. Encouraging the situation, they igno-
rantly slapped the hind ends of the third group, compelling the first bunch
to move more forward. Doing so, their feet caught fast in the bitumen.

Again the herdsmen callously slapped the cattle's hind ends. The rear
cattle, unused to the violent saplings and harsh quakes and sounds,
jumped over the ones in front of them. The unexpected weight of the
third and second group pushed the first group deeper into the trapping
muck.

"What are the men doing?" Lot asked the women who were erecting
the tents and preparing the meals.

"They're rushing the cattle to drink."

"Why are they crying so loudly?"

"See for yourself," the woman retorted, impatient with the questioning.

The king, amused, screamed for the citizens to stop, to watch, to delight.

The crowd, catching sight of the cattle jamming into the lake, jumping
over each other, and tumbling haphazardly into each other, mockingly
laughed.

"The stupid idiots!"

"Look! The bitumen trapped the cattle! They're drowning!"

Frantically, the cows' heads rose trying to gasp whatever gulps of air
they could. The weight of other cows on top of them forced the ones on

the bottom to buck. Uselessly, in extreme agony, the cattle cried to escape the drowning waters.

Lot, running to the herdsmen, took from the nearest man the rod, beating it against the last rows of cattle, forcing a few of the calves to retreat.

"You damnable fools! You imbeciles! The water's a deadly trap! Get the cattle away from the water."

Confused, the men became trapped with the burden of dual commands: one shouting forward, another shouting retreat. Finally comprehending the terror of the waters, the herdsmen broke into the lines, forcing whatever cattle they could to retreat.

While the herdsmen fought against the weight of the forward moving cattle, the Sodomites continued laughing. Inspired, they began pelting the drowning cattle with whatever stones they could find. The children, joining the robust torturing of the cattle, aimed their rocks into the cattle's eyes.

Lot, watching the unbelievable, horrifying event, stopped his efforts to free the cows from the sucking pond. Frozen in disbelief, he stood with bent shoulders, looking at the last drowning cow. Unable to run from the agonizing scene, the defeated man saw the last cow futilely twist its head upward from the encroaching waves. He saw it's anguished tongue hanging out as the waters flowed down its throat until all the animals disappeared underneath the waters.

"How many have we lost?" he finally brought himself to ask in the darkening of the day.

"Half, I believe."

"How could you not have paid attention to your job?"

"Are you placing the blame on me?"

"I am."

"You called me an imbecile today, didn't you?"

"I did so in anger. What you did was foolish and unreasonable."

"It wasn't unreasonable for you to rush into the city and for your best friends to lodge themselves with the whores, was it? I wanted some pleasures myself."

"At the expense of your work?"

"I am a freeman, am I not!"

"Yes, you are."

"Then it was my decision to do as I wanted."

"You failed to see your responsibility through."

"I have no responsibility, other than what I want to do."

"That is not the meaning of freedom."

"What is it then?"

"To be able to come and go as you desire. To be able to rationalize your role with another and to be…"

"Stop! All I care about is being able to come and go as I please."

"It's one facet."

"Then, good-bye! Tend to your cattle yourself!"

When other members of Lot's camp saw the chief-herdsman hastening out of their leader's tent and after overhearing the intense argument between the two men, they also decided to follow the chief herdsman into the deep valley that led to the four cities. Many people lowered their tents and quickly sold them to the nearest merchants for whatever they offered. They no longer wanted to be herdsmen or follow Lot. So many traded their goods and chose to live within the cities' hardened mud houses.

"Lot, let's return to Avram," Lot's wife begged.

"No," he quietly replied. "We still have quite a few cattle left. Today we learned a bitter lesson, but we're still safe. Besides, don't I know how to make a tragic course turn positive?"

"Have we enough money to survive?"

"More than enough. Go ahead of me. Feel safe to buy your necklaces and dresses. It's all right."

ഇരുഇരുഇരുരുഇരുഇരു

In the stretch of land between Bet-El and Ai, Avram quietly walked among the blossoming flowers of the meadow. Absorbed by the deep beauty of the yellow and purple and pink flowers and by the luxuriant softness of the petals, he ran his palms on top of the flower beds. For the moment it felt as if he had become a child again. It seemed as if he had discovered a thing of intense beauty and mystery. The soft petals of the lilies fascinated him. The beautiful white funnel that journeyed far into its stem. The long green stalk that gracefully supported the stem.

"Avram," Yahweh's sudden and unexpected voice alerted him. "Lift your eyes. Look around you. Everything you see is yours.

"All the land that stretches from you: east and west, north and south, I give to you and to your children: forever.

"I will make your children as numerous as the sands of the sea and as numerous as the stars. If one could count the sands of the ocean, they would also be able to count your children.

"Walk forward! Walk throughout this land. Walk throughout its breadth and length. I give it all to you."

Avram, energized, excited, dismantled his tent from its place at Bet-El. Within the afternoon he traveled south toward the land of the resinous trees. In the immediate vicinity of his friend and ally, Mamre, Avram grazed his herd of cattle on the outskirts of Hebron.

Avram perched his tent on the highest ground then proceeded to erect another altar. He stretched his hands out. The man silhouetted against the setting sun offered another sacrifice to Yahweh.

When he looked north, he oddly felt the presence of the city of Salem. He watched the cattle gently eating the grass and wondered: When would Salem belong to his children?

Chapter Fourteen

▼

Chedorlaomer

In the city of Elam the musicians of King Chedorlaomer's great army gathered on top of the ramparts of the wall. The blasting notes of their horns signaled the beginning of the procession of slaves entering through the gates. Thousands of people crowded the streets. Their cheering and screaming drowned out the beseeching words of the slaves. Tiny children, sitting on top of their fathers' shoulders, waved happily as the whips struck the naked backs of the haggard men and women. Unmercifully, the escorts forced the captured people to march up the steep slopes.

Behind them dozens of large oxen, dressed with gold ropes, pulled the strong wagons that carried tons of barley grains and figs and cedar planks. The oxen trampled the dry dirt, creating potholes in the streets into which the following, inattentive old women tripped over.

A procession of mighty soldiers closed the rear ranks of the last group of slaves. Over their shoulders they carried a fitting tribute: swords and spears and war axes. Long-handled slicing sickles rested at their sides.

Between the banners and horses, commissioned scribes noted the conquered inventory. Artists also joined the important guests of the day. They
were there to observe and commemorate the victory for the king's heirs.

"All we have! All we control!" a general boasted.

Chedorlaomer forced a slight smile, then firmly patted the supreme
military commander on his shoulder, patronizing him. He walked to the
zenith of the ziggurat and marveled at the lush, verdant forests that
impregnated the rolling landscape. He controlled a land rich in natural
resources. A land that had hundreds of natural and man-made waterways.
A land, however, that seemed forever thirsty. A land whose appetite for
water never ceased. Chedorlaomer nodded in self-approval and regret at
not having more of what he wanted to attain for himself.

His country had tall mountains that always provided him with enough
water. To be certain, however, that his land received its required quench,
Chedorlaomer placed tens of thousands of men to work on the irrigation
canals. On any given day he would contentedly watch them cut paths into
the earth. He enjoyed watching their bent shoulders struggling with the
weight of the stones. He observed every placement of the foundation stones
for the dams that he had personally designed to control the water's flow.

The time finally came when the building work satisfied him. "We have
no need for more canals," he pronounced.

"Where do we place these slaves?"

"Let them build walls. I want them a minimum of fifty, no, seventy feet
high!"

"Our armies are our walls," the general boasted again.

"We will need the walls. I may decide to war against Egypt."

The general, caught by surprise, lowered his eyes, his face blushing.

"What? No comments?"

"We've stretched ourselves too thin to invade such a powerful country.
Our supply lines haven't been fortified enough. We are too far from Ur to
call reserves and what reserves there are, are not enough."

"What do I care about such things? Don't the kings of the south owe us allegiance? We'll place their armies alongside mine and we'll walk wherever we please." Then, taking a batch of hardened, inscribed mud tablets from his private shelves, he added, "Read these reports. They speak of a secret city. A city of wealth. A city of mysterious strengths."

"I am familiar with this myth."

"I've been chasing that myth all my life," the king responded. "My father empowered one of the merchants to travel there. He crossed the Euphrates with his children and I have not heard of them since."

"My men continuously provide me with rumors of the Hebrews."

"Then where are they?"

"I don't know. They never stay still. They never remain anyplace where I can catch them. It may be that they reside in that secret city. If so, then what is the use of seeking them out? No one can find what is hidden."

Chedorlaomer laughed at the general's words. "Grave diggers find whatever they want! Look at those slaves. Don't they come from Damascus?"

"Yes."

"Doesn't Ampraphel collect tribute from King Shinab!"

"For twelve years."

"And during those twelve years has anyone found this mythical city?"

"Some people don't chase foolish rumors." Instantaneously the general regretted exposing his thoughts out loud.

"My words make you ill?"

"I apologize for that remark. It was not called for."

"But it's too late for your apology. Therefore, it is now your personal task to find that city for me. Find for me the merchant whom my father trusted and traded with. Find Eber. Find for me his children: the ones called Hebrews. Bring them all to me. Bring them here, or forsake your family's lives."

The general bowed and walked away backwards from the king. That very day the general hastened the formation of his troops and departed to the southeastern lands.

The trek was uneventful for the thousand soldiers. The advance scouts easily found the trade routes. Quickly taking control of the road, they forced the women who were washing their clothes and who were preparing the afternoon's meals to give up their tasks for the oncoming soldiers' pleasures.

The caravan-masters, hearing the commotion, studying the mysterious clouds of dust, trembled when they realized it was an invading army.

Halting, standing by the wayside, the merchants automatically opened their wares to the soldiers, seeking to spare their own lives through peaceful cooperation.

As the infantry and horsemen passed by, the unpaved road filled with the dust of the horses' hooves. The innkeepers swept their floors and the dirt that they swept out blew to the bushes, covering the leaves with dust, which the rear supply wagons trampled to the ground.

"Question these people about the Hebrews and about the city."

"We do not know anything about them," the men, having been isolated in their retreats, truthfully answered.

"What have you to say?" a brutal captain asked a merchant who, sporadically trembling, was unable to let go of his camel's belt.

"I saw a plaque carved at an entry post in Egypt. A skilled reader told me it spoke of a man named Avram who sought compassion in Egypt and in turn offered betrayal. I heard he was a Hebrew, but I don't really know."

"Why don't you know?"

"I couldn't understand the hieroglyphics."

"Who is Avram?"

"The people of Retenu say he is the leader of the Hebrew people. I heard he trades fair and honestly."

"The people of Retenu speak of the Hebrew? Are they allied with him? If so, have they become our enemy?"

The frightened man shrugged his shoulders.

"Tell me: Where does the Hebrew camp? What possessions does he have with him?"

"Sheep, he has sheep. That is all I know of him."

"Sheep! Those damnable, lazy, ineffectual pests! Thank the gods we loaded them on some foolish merchants decades ago from our lands!"

The merchant, forcing a smile, began relaxing, his hand only slightly twitching now.

"Why are you smiling?"

Startled again, the merchant replied, "I thought you were making a joke. I also hate sheep."

The captain grinned broadly. He once tried mutton when he was desperately hungry. It was bland. As he smiled the black decay between his teeth could be seen by the merchant. The soldier caught the man's eyes opening wider. He knew the merchant wanted to turn his face away from his decaying teeth. The soldier resented anyone who didn't accept him, regardless of the appearance of his teeth. He became angry and in a reactive instant, the captain plunged his sword through the man's stomach. The tip of sword's blade exited into the camel's chest.

The camel bolted from the pain and ran away with the screaming man still pinned to its chest. The captain burst out laughing. "Soldiers! Do whatever pleases you!"

Suddenly violent, inexplicable carnage reigned over the merchants. Broad swords split the skulls of the merchants in half. Harsh, swinging sickles savagely severed the arms of other men who automatically rose them to protect their faces from their castrating iron instruments. Horrific screams of anguish bathed the atmosphere with the gruesome testimony of men's cruelty to men. The blood-bath continued throughout the day and into the night. As the king's officers ravaged one area after another area their assistants looted the dead remains' for silk cloths, tin ingots, lead bars, and blocks of hardened salt.

Tears of excruciating anguish fell on deaf ears. In the quiet aftermath, the silenced soldiers thought of nothing more than the food that the daughters and young sons of the slain had prepared for them. The children's hushed tears dripped into the soup. Not far from the cooking fires their father's corpses laid dejectedly in putrid pools of blood. Rivets of red streams joined each other.

On the dawn of the third day the soldiers reassembled and continued their trek toward Egypt, leaving behind them smoldering ruins. The pigs which escaped from their pens feasted on the carnage. Stray dogs, hearing the cries of the men's last breaths, began nipping at their sides, ripping the flesh off into their mouths. Other packs trotted to their cubs and regurgitated the lacerated flesh for them to feast on.

Within weeks of this inexplicable butchery, the citizens unitedly rose in open revolt against Chedorlaomer.

$$\text{\textbf{80}Cℬ\textbf{80}Cℬ\textbf{80}Cℛℰ\textbf{80}Cℬ\textbf{80}Cℬ}$$

In the mid-western plains of Shinar, King Ampraphel's soldiers joined the soldiers of King Chedorlaomer of Elam. Beyond the Syrian mountains the two armies rode into the city of Ham that the Zuzim tribe occupied.

Embedded on the tips of the soldiers' spears hung the rotting heads of the merchants. Blood soaked banners draped the wagons' poles.

Immediately the soldiers roused the people from their huts. The Elamites and the Babylonians, seeing the Zuzim for the first time, gasped at their incredible height.

"How tall are they," Ampraphel's second captain asked the general.

"Eight, nine feet, it seems."

"They are too dangerous for us. Let's retreat."

"We cannot. Chedorlaomer is behind us and the Egyptian king is in front of us. We must do what we came here to do."

The Zuzim tribe, alerted by the war cries of the invaders, rushed out from their homes. The village instantly became filled with the screeching tears of the newborn babies and young children. Dogs fiercely growled at the Elamites.

The Zuzim, transfixed by the dripping blood from the heads on top of the invaders' spears, echoed their frightening sentences among each other. Terrorized, they fell on their knees, bowing before the soldiers.

"They're cowards," the second captain exclaimed. "As tall as they are, they are afraid!"

"Bring the interpreter here. Quick, question him!"

"The mayor knows nothing."

The general of the army slapped the mayor of the village viciously, knocking him to the ground. The general cruelly smiled. He stood on the man's face and pushed it deep into the muddied ground. "See, this man refuses to resist. Since that is the case, bond him to some stakes. Skin him."

A few cringed as a soldier proceeded.

The coward groaned deep within himself. Slowly his silent groans surfaced louder and louder. The other soldiers looked away.

"Castrate him," the general commanded. Then moments later he added, "Soldiers, whatever pleases you, do."

As he watched his soldier castrate the mayor, he demanded for the rest of his company to fan out among the survivors to torture and kill them. While the murdering and thieving overtook the sensibilities of the soldiers, the first captain plotted with the general on a scheme to find the secret hiding place of the people's treasures.

Coordinating their thoughts they decided to make it appear as if by chance several small children escaped from their tent undetected. In the midst of confusion, both permitted the sodden eyed children to escape from the city. Behind the whimpering boys and girls, the generals' scouts quietly followed.

ഇരുഇരുഇരുഇരുഇരു

While the first group of highly trained scouts followed the dazed children, a second group of tactical scouts traveled to King Arioch of Ellasar that rested near the southern trading route of the Arabian Desert. A third mercenary group rapidly advanced toward the United Confederacy of Tribes which King Tidal of Goiim controlled.

By treaty, all three kings joined Chedorlaomer's warring campaign.

With the increased number of soldiers King Chedorlaomer of Elam eventually fell upon a dark race of giant man and women. When the villagers heard of the armies' cruel tactics, they assembled in war formation at Ashetorth-karnaim. The men carried with them sling shots with small bags of rock projectiles, and forks. After a series of shouting and tauting, King Chedorlaomer of Elam forced his army to stand directly in front the giant men in an endless field of red grapes.

"How interesting," his general commented, laughing at the ironic battlefield. "As we slaughter these ugly black giants, we can quench our thirst."

The four kings brutally joined the general's laughter.

King Arioch then grabbed a handful of the fat grapes and tested them between his teeth. "Remarkably delicious."

"Good," Chedorlaomer replied. "Now, if you don't mind, I'll like to continue with my slaughtering of these people."

King Arioch threw the bunch of grapes over his shoulders and sarcastically spit the seeds at his two horses. Their tails tried to flick the seeds off their buttocks.

"Well, soldiers," Arioch stated in a high, feminine voice, "kill the black bastards."

"The general again laughed as he swooped his war banner down. The waiting soldiers, when they saw the signal, slapped their thighs against the horses, rushing them into combat.

"Oh," he spoke in his softest voice, as if the consequences weren't worthy of his talents, "try to save me one to kill."

The combined forces, unused to the softness of a commander's voice, were taken aback by the general's nonchalant methods. They did not like King Arioch.

Chedorlaomer, meanwhile, formed his spearsmen into a long front assault line. "Aim the points of your spears directly at the kneecaps of the giants," he commanded his captains. "Swordsman, strike your swords into their legs, then into their chests. Save the last stroke for their necks."

The other two armies, watching the easy killings, also charged into the carnage. They shouted praises to their pagan gods just before they struck their weapons into the enemies' flesh. In two hours the battle was over.

ಬಾಡಾ ಬಾಡಾ ಬಾ

In the following weeks the combined forces continued to wreak havoc throughout the southwestern territories. The 'Alliance of Four' defeated the Emim at Shaveh-kiriathaim, which is slightly west of the mid-point of the Dead Sea.

Immediately afterwards the 'Alliance of Four' encountered the entrenched forces of the Horites of Seir. Thereafter, the constant ambushes of the Horites hindered Chedorlaomer's advance. Night assassinations and guerrilla warfare decimated an important portion of his troops. Fed up with the lack of progress against the enemy, Chedorlaomer personally rallied his banner against the Horites. The 'Alliance of Four' finally overwhelmed the Horite resistance in the rugged western hills. Their decapitated bodies and spilled intestines covered the grounds of all the major southwestern cities.

After Chedorlaomer exterminated the Horites, he quickly advanced as far as El-paran on the Gulf of Aqaba.

After he destroyed the city, he spent the rest of that day studying the reddened waves that carried dozens of floating corpses. Chedorlaomer blocked his nose against the stench. "We were misled. This is not the fabled city."

The general threw a rock into the rising tide. Several bodies disappeared behind a wave. "Some of our western scouts tell me there is a very large body of water several days march from here."

"Larger than this?" he asked, surprised by the general's statement. "How large is this other body of water?"

"Ships larger than our war wagons ride over it."

"What is a *ship*?"

"A very big boat," the general innocently replied.

"Who makes such 'big boats'? The Egyptians?"

"I don't know who built them. There are rumors of a large island in the middle of this vast sea that controls all of its shores. I heard the leader of the island is called 'Minos'.

"What? Is he the leader of the fabled city which I am hunting for."

"It could very well be."

"Then call the men forward. We march again."

For the next several days the army advanced due west through the Wilderness of Paran and crossed into the Negeb.

There, Chedorlaomer's armies met another military force.

The Amalekites, after days of arguing and disagreeing and near inner-court hostilities, combined their tribes into a single army. The Amalekite farmers, arming themselves with whatever implements they could muster on the call of the moment, fortified themselves behind the thick walls of En-mishpat.

Laying siege over the city, Chedorlaomer uselessly bombarded the mud-hardened walls with fire arrows and flaming spears.

"What are we to do against such a defense?" King Tidal demanded to know.

"Look over your shoulder," Chedorlaomer replied. "What do you see?"

"Nothing."

"That is why I am the man in charge of this army," Chedorlaomer answered back. He stepped forward and spun Tidal around. "What do you see!" he insisted again on having his question correctly answered.

"All I see are fields of grain."

"Unharvested grain, you fool!" Chedorlaomer shouted. "Burn all of it. I want those who resist us to starve to death!"

"Oh," King Tidal meekly replied. "It was too obvious for me."

"Obviously," he sarcastically repeated before he threw a gazelle roast at him, smacking it into his chest.

Embarrassed, King Tidal faced King Ampraphel. "How's he going to act when he can't find the fabled city?"

"For our sakes and for the sake of the this war's campaign, he better find it."

"General," King Arioch begged the question, "how far away is Egypt?"

"Another four to five days march."

"Why don't we head there instead? The Egyptians are rich. Their necks beg to be cut off for the enormous amount of gold that they carry around them."

"Chedorlaomer told me to head north after En-mishpat falls. I am not about to counteract his orders. Are you?"

"Never," both kings rapidly shook their heads.

"Then the issue's settled."

ᏋᎧᏣᎾᏋᎧᏣᎾᏋᎧᏒᎾᎧᏣᎾᏋᎧᏣᎾ

Three weeks later the Amalekites opened their gates to Chedorlaomer's troops.

"Do we feed them?" King Tidal asked with some compassion for the frail and starving men and women.

"Nope," Chedorlaomer, now called *"The leader"* coldly answered. "Rape, mangle, and kill them. Our soldiers earned it."

"The women are skinny. The men are too weak. The children are consumed with hunger. Let's just take their gold and artifacts and leave."

"Leave?" he shouted. "I'll tell you what: Get for me the whereabouts of what I am seeking, and I'll peacefully leave."

King Tidal nodded. After a few moments of gazing from prisoner to prisoner, he approached an aged warrior. King Tidal brought his horse's head directly to rest in front of the old man. The horse's breath fell over the man's face.

"Don't raise your arm against my animal," Tidal commanded. "You're an old, old man. Tell me, do you want to become even older, or die today?"

"I want to become older."

"My king demands to know the location of the richest city on the earth," he gritted his teeth. "Tell me what he wants to hear and I shall withdraw my troops."

"The city lies directly north from here near the Great Salt Water's edge."

"North?" Tidal's eyes widen. "I misunderstood that babbling fool at Bab edh-Dhra. I thought he said *west*."

"And I thought he said south," Arioch butted in.

"What lies north of here?"

"The richest city I've ever seen. Thousands of merchants travel there. It's the crossroads of the world. Men sail from the Great Island in the Great Sea and the Egyptians beg for their wares as do the Orientals. Their land grows anything planted on it. If I was to dream of paradise, than that is my dream of it."

"If it is so famous, why are we having such a hard time finding it?" Chedorlaomer insisted on knowing.

The aged, wrinkled man shook his head.

The leader got off his horse and grabbed the old man's beard, viciously tugging it. After a few studious seconds, the leader replied, "I believe him. Mass our troops north."

He turned again to the old man and deliberately placed the sword against his stomach. With the slowest motion possible he eased the sword into the screaming, terrified ancient man. Writhing in agony the man grabbed the sharpened edges as the sword eternally went through him, slicing his hands as well. Unable to stop its entrance, the man's bloodied hands grabbed the handle of the sword, plunging it into himself.

"Dignity!" Chedorlaomer stated. "The old bastard had dignity." Amazed, he kept nodding his head.

"Now, does anyone object to me killing all the rest of the people?"

Tidal turned his horse around and headed toward the gate. "If it pleases you Great Leader, do it. As for me, it no longer pleases me."

"Then you personally shall be the one to slaughter the *'innocents'*. Do it now, or I will personally kill you. Slower and more painfully than you can ever imagine." The words drew our slower from his mouth than the sword penetrated the old man.

Tidal shivered as he galloped toward the first collection of starving people. He forced his horse to trampled into the crowd of screaming men and women. He lunged his spear into the nearest man then jumped off his horse and slashed his sword into the retreating horde. He struck one woman dead than another, after which he killed a crying child than another child, than one aged man after another aged man. As the helpless victims fell at his feet, Tidal began screaming a ferocious hate against humanity.

The ease of the slaughter infected the other soldiers and they joined in his screams, amputating arms, and decapitating as many victims as they could. This was the most extensive murderings yet that they engaged in.

ଔଔଔଔଔଔଔଔ

The Amorites leaders of Hazazon-tamar, Mamre, Aner, and Eshkol watched the rising flames of En-mishpat and wondered how they would face the encroaching enemy. After another night of debate, the three Amorite leaders amassed their warriors and formed their divisions directly in front of the Alliance of Four.

When the morning fog lifted, the cries of the dueling armies clashed. Hundreds of men rushed, massed, and collaged into each other. The fighting swept from land to land until the opposers viciously crushed the resisters.

Mamre, Aner, and Eshkol, along with their survivors, managed to escape in the darkness to the outlying resinous trees.

"Again, no one knows anything about the mysterious city," Chedorlaomer slammed his knife into an oak plank, splitting it in half. "That old fool at our last stop made a fool of me. Why is it that no one knows who Eber is?"

"Is it possible he took a boat to India?" Ampraphel answered for the general.

"Hebrews in India?" Chedorlaomer responded.

"Why not? The Sea Peoples have established cities there. And if Eber is the great merchant your father traded with, then surely he would know all the land—and, yes—even the sea routes to all points of trade."

"If that is so, we have wasted our time. Stranger yet, India is just over my own mountains in Ur."

"No, my king," the outspoken general stated. "Eber did not travel to India. Your father sent him west. But that was decades ago. Surely he's dead by now. Nevertheless, Egypt is days from here. Let's enjoy ourselves on their miseries as well."

"How many men do we have left?"

"Enough."

"Ah, so optimistic!"

"With the roads safe against the insurgents, Chedorlaomer, it may be best for us to enter Egypt. Two, three days from now we can rule the country." His trusted general finally agreed with the three kings, nodding his support for them.

Chedorlaomer paced the tent, studying the men. "I need your allegiance," he began orating. "I will lead you into Egypt and together we will conquer it!" The men, hearing his forceful words and watching their charismatic leader, shouted their approval. "But, I ask just this one last thing. Let us go farther north. Two days more. If we do not discover the fabled city, we will destroy Egypt! I promise you this!"

"Why not venture into Egypt now?"

"Have we not already conquered the world? We control everything from Ur to here! Show me a city and I will raze it for you. Show me a wall and I will destroy it. Show me a river and I will navigate through it. What, tell me, is in Egypt? A few trinkets! Mainly they chisel stones and play with crocodiles. If we go into Egypt, will we be able to venture north? Let's go where our plan tells us to go."

"It shall be as you command," the general acquiesced.

ೞೞೞೞೞೞೞ

The soldiers of the four kings continued traveling north, defeating whatever resistance rallied against them.

In the rising mountains that stood before the Valley of Siddim the armies of the five kings of Retenu met. From five separate roads the armies of the kings met. Five banners, symbolizing their nations, fluttered in the wind.

From the distance the shepherds saw them.

From the west came two kings majestically riding on top of their brilliantly arrayed camels. From the east came another king straddling an impressive white donkey. From the north came the fourth king, carried by his slaves. From the south the fifth king walked alongside his men, bearing identical arms and armor.

Five tents rose in the valley. Five hundred fires lit the valley floor. Five thousand voices cheered.

The king of Sedom, the king of Gomorrah, the king of Admah, the king of Zeboiim, the king of Zoar.

Five thousand soldiers performed five thousand sacrifices during the night. Five priests cried before their gods. Five kings drew blood from their arms, intermingling it into a single cup. When the five priests finished their chanting, the five kings drank a small swallow of the blood mixture from the lead cup.

The lush and verdant Valley of Siddim seemed impenetrable by the soldiers. Large oak and cedar trees rose far above the ground. Sharp, jagged grass, taller than the tallest men, waited for the trampling feet.

ജ൝ജ൝ജൌඥ൙ജ൝

Beautiful white lilies withered underneath the stomping feet of the soldiers.

The red sunrise colored the thick clouds red. The very hills became colored red.

During the slow drift and descent of the red evening, the five thousand men inclined into the valley, passing the red lakes and scarlet flowers to wait for Chedorlaomer's army.

The Elamite general, stealthily maneuvering among the luxuriantly green vines marked the encamped enemies' position. Impressed with the wealth of the merchants and with the fertile soil and with the vibrantly luscious fruits, he at last thought everything prior to today was worth the agony and the long marches and the tolerance of arrogant insolence.

"Chedorlaomer, everything is better than any of us imagined. Never again will any of us doubt your wisdom nor your leadership."

"Everything is as I told you! Now, once we find Eber and his Hebrews, we can enjoy gracious eternity."

"As long as we don't get sick, I'm for eternity: as long as I can have wealth, young women, and plenty to drink," King Arioch boasted.

In the meeting tent of somber flickering lights, the general and his captains studied the layout of the terrain. It was flat with a few rolling mounds. Countless, large trees bordered numerous lakes and ponds. Everything was either too easy to defend or impossible to conquer. "Silent swiftness will win our day."

Chedorlaomer divided his forces into three main groups. The first military segment he directed to the very forefront. The second segment he assigned to attack the left, while the remainder plummeted into the right.

Heavy breathing dominated all the men of all the encampments. Each looked at the other. Each looked at the dissipating clouds. Each looked at the ground. At their sandals. At their swords.

Sweat covered the faces of some men. The mouths of other men became dry, parched. No matter how often they licked their lips, they remained dry. Meanwhile the hands of other men became moist. It seemed as if the wet palms were too greasy to hold a sword, much less swing an ax. The fewest of the few remained calm—jovially waiting to greet their enemy. They spent their time memorizing their war cries, eager to shout terror into the enemy's face. The soldiers from the south consumed their time painting their faces red and black.

Overhead the vultures flew and eagles swooped. Lions came as did the jackals.

Morning also came.

After he wiped his brow, the Elamite general jerked his war flag down. The fire-tenders quickly threw blue dust into the fires, signaling the infantry to advance against the five kings.

The horsemen, yelling, waved their swords and plunged ahead of the infantry, forcing the timid horses to trample on top of the falling men.

The strongest ground soldiers, able to grab a few of the horses' reins, pulled the horsemen off. Whenever an opening occurred, the infantrymen struck their swords into the horses' necks. Throughout the battlefield, brave men pulled horsemen off their horses to the ground where the waiting men stabbed their spears into their eye sockets and throats and chests. The brave infantrymen took the horsemen's horses for themselves and they similarly rushed against Chedorlaomer's infantry, only to suffer the identical killings.

Flying spears filled the air. A few randomly struck a soldier. Most, however, fell harmlessly on top of the ground, randomly sliding underneath another warrior's running feet.

A few picked up the spears and flung them back toward the enemy, hoping to impact it through someone, anyone.

Soldiers grappled with soldiers, each crying his death cry. Hand to hand combat dominated. Where hands once held a sword, empty arms now sputtered blood. Deep gashes opened the thighs and stomachs of many men. Their flesh throbbed with jerks of pulsating blood. Veins dangled out of the skin. A few conscious men, trying to save themselves, futilely attempted to stop the jugular's expulsion of blood with their fingers.

Some, struck by the unexpected pain of the slicing metal, opened their eyes wide with the terror of the moment; their voices failing to emit the scream of death.

Some, frantic with the hundreds of bodies racing toward them, wildly swung their swords, striking anyone in front of them: friend or foe.

After intense, never-ending hours of warfare, Chedorlaomer's enveloping soldiers began overpowering their enemies, until in the afternoon's late hours, they broke through the ranks of the five kings.

Panic instantly infested the five kings. Their soldiers, unable to fight on, began running away. The victors chased them and threw spears into their backs, the points breaking through the enemies' chest.

"The lakes! Retreat to the lakes!" the Sodomite king screamed to his companion, the King of Amorah.

The two kings dove into the water, and with them followed many other men.

Arioch's soldiers pursued other soldiers into the waters and followed after them. Quickly the men engaged each other with their swords.

"You damn fools!" the Sodomite king yelled. "Take them to the middle. Take them to the underwater tar!"

The soldiers continued to press against the other side, until in the middle of the pond, their feet caught fast in the bitumen.

"Spear them!" the Elamite general shouted.

"Our men are also in there!" a Shinarian captain refused to obey the Elamite's orders. The general focused his eyes on the captain's eyes and stared until the other quelled his resistance. "Soldiers! Do it!" the Shinarian relinquished his hard stance.

At this time the Sodomite king convinced himself he had tricked Arioch's men. Content with his ploy, he started to swim away. Suddenly a man grabbed tightly to his tunic. Turning about he realized it was the king of Amorah.

"Let go of my coat!"

The King of Sedom punched him on top of his head, forcing the other dead king to sink deeper into the water. "What is this?" the king, panicking, shouted. "What is this?"

When he looked, he saw that the other king's symbol of power, a long golden chain, inextricably wrapped itself around his waist.

The force of the suction became stronger and pulled him deeper into the reddening waters. Blood, flowing from his friend's back, entered his mouth and nose. Soon the red pool covered his eyes. The top of his head drifted underneath the churning waters. Inevitably, his feet were sucked into the bitumen. Screaming, the waters rushed into his lungs.

₭₭₭₭₭₭₭

The weary survivors, too tired to go back into their camps, collapsed where they stood. Through the long night the survivors felt a strange sensation surrounding them. An unimaginable fluttering sound disturbed their sleep. The inexplicable gurgling frightened them. Submitting to the night's fear, the men rested where they laid, hoping to see the morning's sunrise.

With the dawn's revealing light, the surviving soldiers faced the night's terror. When they woke, they saw why through the night everything seemed to be jerking and shoving and pulling against and into them, disturbing their exhaustion. Insatiable birds of prey tore at the intestines and flesh of their companions and enemies.

Through the night's horror, the eagles and vultures and falcons of the surrounding lands feasted on the thousands and thousands of carcasses that lay throughout the valley's floor. In the interior of the forest and in the depths of the meadows, the lions and leopards and hyenas wiped their paws clean from the night's meal.

Discarded bones and rotting flesh littered the earth.

The putrid smell swelled in the survivors' nostrils. Some, rising, instantly vomited. The waking captains and generals clenched their noses shut. Many became hypnotized by the sight of the birds yanking out the corpse's innards. They were unable to remove themselves from the carnage. They watched the vultures' ripping the flesh of the former life-forces. They saw their eyeballs and lungs and flesh flinging from the beaks of the consuming birds. The fearless lions openly feasted on the carcasses as did the flies and maggots.

Stunned, shocked, all the soldiers of all the nations called to their friends and to their officers only to receive a silent reply.

"This has happened to us? To us, the might of the world? To us, by the hands of homosexuals and perverse immoralists?" Chedorlaomer, puzzled, screamed at his general.

"What is moral, great king?" he softly replied.

Chedorlaomer turned to look at the city's red and violet smoke rising from their towers. "Morality is the prize of conquest!" he replied. "Go into those cities. Strip away everything they have! Enslave anyone you find."

In the aftermath of the battle the victorious survivors stripped Sedom and Amorah of their gold, of their volcanic glass, of their bronze utensils—of everything of value.

ଓଓଓଓଓଓଓଓ

Lot, standing in the tallest tower, hidden within the veils of blue smoke, floundered to the side of the wall.

"We lost the battle," he choked. "My people. I must protect my people."

He rushed down the winding stairwell and went to his nearest friend's house. "Where is your husband?" he implored.

"With the alliance," his wife replied.

"Since when?" his eyes opened in disbelief. "I forbade him to fight with them."

"All the men who came with us joined in the fighting."

But why? We are not homosexuals or immoralists nor do we even have a vested interest in these regions. We can leave anytime. We can go any-place."

"We can never escape tyranny," she answered.

"If your husband is dead?"

"Then it is your responsibility to care for us," she whispered.

"I will care for you," he quietly returned her words and stares.

The second captain, first entering the city, immediately collected the survivors in a forced enclave.

The strongest guards surrounded them.

Chedorlaomer, unconcerned with the survivors, plundered the city, taking its gold and silver and jewels and rugs, and foodstuffs, and exotic cloths.

"Never have we seen such wealth! Such enormous provisions! This is now our city and our country!"

"One can leave one's country, but one can never truly possess another country. Oh, we may be able to live here for the rest of our lives, but is our mission to settle happily in one place, or is our mission in life to happily reside throughout the world?" the leader orated.

"We will strip this region of everything and return home," he answered for everyone.

"This must be the fabled city," another happily shouted.

Chedorlaomer stared at him. He tightened his lips. The man quieted.

"Are you so sure?"

The man shook his head.

"Then I suggest we discover what else lies about here."

"The men want to return home," another soldier whispered to the general.

"How can we return home," the general privately answered. "We lost three-quarters of our men. We lost nearly all our horses, and which one of us is an expert with the camel?"

"Yes," another man interjected. "Wherever we travel, our enemies will attempt to steal from us what we have stolen."

Chedorlaomer caught the echoes of the soldier's desire to return home and their fears of losing everything they had attained during their long, hard conquest. The leader glanced at the amassed prisoners and pointed to Lot.

"Take him for your shield. Take all of them for your shields."

෨Ᏻ෨Ᏻ෨ᏝᏉᏳ෨Ᏻ

Avram, lying beside Sarai, fondly touched her.

Outside the isolated tent Hagar tended to the hanging of the washed clothes. Bored, she thought she heard a faint shout. Uncertain, she stopped working. Straining her ears, she turned toward the western plains.

Eliezer, panting from the intense excursion, placed his hands on his knees, supporting himself. Painfully gasping, he spoke between the gulps of air. "Avram, Sedom has fallen to Chedorlaomer!"

"Lot?"

"Captured."

"Who brings this sad news to us?"

"The fugitive rests in my tent."

"How many others escaped with him?"

"Many more. They're hiding in the hills."

"Why is it Lot didn't run off into the hills?"

"He probably wanted to remain with his charges who traveled with him."

"Yes," Avram agreed. He reflected on his nephew, then suddenly asked, "Is Chedorlaomer's army pursuing us as well?"

"No. I looked and I sent out our best scouts."

"Isn't that strange? He doesn't know we're here."

"Or, he may believe we're only an insignificant people."

"Eliezer, rest a moment. After you've caught your breath, send word to Mamre the Amorite. Inform him what has happened. Inform him my nephew is in danger. Inform him I need his help.

"Remind him that I have kept my contract with him. I have not built a city nor established a permanent camp anywhere on his lands. Remind him also how the wells which his sheep quench their thirst with, I dug. Remind him that not once have I protested to him a missing animal or granary loss. Remind him, for I lost my nephew and intend to have him back," he smacked his fist into the tent's supporting pole.

ಬೞಬಬೞ

Mamre and his first cousins Eshkol and Aner immediately armed themselves along with Avram's male servants.

Avram, speaking to his companions, revealed the gravity of the situation to them.

"But Avram, we are not fighting men," a rich herdsman protested. "How are we to defend ourselves, much less, attack a professional army that has yet to be defeated?"

"Mamre the Amorite has fought Chedorlaomer. His cousins have fought the Alliance of Four. They stand now with us! They will teach us how to fight!" his energized voice shouted above all the other protesting voices.

"We have no weapons!" another angrily responded.

"There are ten thousand rusting in the Valley of Siddim," Avram softened his voice, forcing them to quiet in order to listen to him. "Pick as many as you want. Sharpen your swords while I prepare our retaliatory maneuvers."

"Avram, are you going to be travelling with us—even in your old age?" a final question rose from the back of the meeting tent.

"I will fight alongside you. I will train with the very same weaponry. It appears I must begin what shall never end: a warring against the peoples' who would seek to take this land. It is mine. It belongs to me!"

"The land is yours!" The men in unison shouted as they lifted their staffs into the air, for they believed in Avram's prophetic abilities and leadership.

Mamre silently watched Avram's resolved. He concurred to teach him, hoping that somehow, the weapons which he'd present to his friend and ally would never be turned against him.

₧₧₧₧₧₧₧₧₧

Avram's eyes hazed and glistened. He hugged Sarai farewell. Bravely he turned to be with his men.

And this was the world's first international war against tyranny and world conquest and against worldwide domination by evil, ruthless men.

Three afternoons later Avram and his 318 men ascended over the last hills. By chance, after they reached the apex, the seasonal rains began to fall.

Through this bitter, anxious journey the Amorite warriors taught the Hebrews how to wield the swords. They taught them the skills of the thrust, the dodge, the backward move and instant forward response. Skillfully they taught them how to grasp their hands on wrists and how to pull their enemy forward to the low-waiting sword. They taught them how to push their enemy backwards into a companion's waiting sword and how to sidestep an enemy's rushing play. By example they taught them how to extend their right foot to trip the left ankles of their enemy and how to plunge their spears deeply into the enemy's unmerciful heart.

₧₧₧₧₧₧₧₧₧

"Chedorlaomer," the captain interrupted his conversation with the other kings and with his favorite general.

"Yes, what is it?"

"We are being pursued."

Incredulously, slowly, Chedorlaomer lifted his eyes to stare directly at the man. He placed his hands directly into the recently executed clay moldings of the landscape and roads, and grinned. Then the grin became loud laughter.

"Pursued? By men wanting to give us their kidneys for our gods? Well captain, welcome them with your spears!"

"I've tried to meet them in the battlefield. They avoid us."

"I don't understand."

I advance—they retreat. I move—they follow. I expose my men to trick them into charging us. They rest and eat. I don't know how to fight these irresponsible tactics."

"General?"

"Let them be. They're stragglers looking for easy pickings. Or, it may be that our hostages prevent them from attacking us. Whatever the reason, Captain, I want you to regroup your soldiers with ours. If we stay together they'll be too afraid to attack us."

"Captain," Chedorlaomer questioned, "how many are there?"

Moving his head back and forth, he confessed, "I'm uncertain. It appears around three hundred."

"And we have?"

"Ten times more."

"So, do I have anything to worry about?" he asked the general while he scratched his arm and face.

"Only the quality of this wine," the general jested, passing to the king a fresh cup.

"Let everyone have their fill as well. Tomorrow we'll pursue the pursuers. I want their penises tied around my spear."

ಬಿಉಲೆಬಿಉಲೆಬಿಉಲೆಬಿಉಲೆಬಿಉಲೆ

During that night a heavy sleep overcame the enemy camp.

Avram, roused by the strange stillness and quiet of the camp, rose. He trembled. Profusive sweat covered him.

"Yahweh," he whispered. "I appeared strong and decisive to my men. Let me not fall apart and reveal my fears. Let me not shame myself. Let me not fall to the wayside begging for mercy from the enemy's sword."

Avram peered into the dense darkness. The constellations brilliantly shone.

"There are so many men against me. I am alone." Despairing, he walked toward a singularly strange tree. It was a night of misconceptions. Of hidden truths. He sat near the fingering outreaches of the tree and wiped away a forming tear. "Yahweh, I am afraid. I've never fought against another man. We are so few. Yet, allow me please, safe victory. Do this and I will take nothing for myself. Do this, and what is gained, I will forsake away from me."

Silence.

"Tell me then, Yahweh: Did I make an impulsive, unauthorized decision? Are you still with me—or am I truly by myself?"

Again silence.

Avram stopped speaking to the stars.

"Avram," a man shook him from his trance.

"What is it?" he inquired. His mouth dried.

"Mamre wants to see you."

He nodded.

He rushed to his friend's side and clasped his hand into his. His brother Eshkol embraced him as well.

"Chedorlaomer guards are asleep."

"Asleep?"

"Yes."

"The other men as well?"

Aner shrugged his shoulders. "Everyone, it appears."

"Eshkol, what do you think?"

"Avram, we should attack."

"Then let's do so silently. We'll slit their throats as quietly as possible. From soldier to soldier. From man to man."

"Slit their throats?" Mamre questioned. "I would rather plunge my sword into their hearts."

"And risk an outcry! Listen to me: What sheep or goat or dove cried out when the cut was mercifully given?"

Aner raised his eyebrows and sarcastically snickered, "We're to kill our enemies mercifully?"

ɮʊɾɮʊɾɮʊɾʊɭɮʊɾɮʊɾ

Night.

Avram led his 318 men against the enemy's camp. He cautiously approached the first guard. From behind, Avram raised his sword. With shaking and hesitating hands, he finally forced himself to place the blade beside the soldier's jugular vein. One swift jerk later Avram sliced the guard's neck open. Cupping his mouth, the startled man was unable to cry out. His panicked eyes rolled to peer deeply into Avram's similarly frightened eyes. Dying, the guard's teeth brushed Avram's inner palm, leaving small scratches on it. In this hectic, horrible moment the guard died. The blood poured over Avram's hands and wrists. It dripped to his black cloak, sticking fast.

Aner quickly brushed beside him. Without a second's thought he killed the second guard. Mamre, on Avram's signal, skillfully dodged by him and his cousin, killing the third guard. The 318 men correspondingly followed suit. The silent killings continued throughout the night. By dawn's beginning Avram's soldiers killed nearly a third of Chedorlaomer's army.

Retreating, Avram and his men reentered the seclusion of the thick, forested hills.

ɮʊɾɮʊɾɮʊɾʊɭɮʊɾɮʊɾ

The exposing rays of the sun fell directly on the general's eyes. He threw his arm over his eyes and he twisted to his other side. Again the sun disturbed his eyes.

"Someone close the damn flap!"

His rectum muscles tightened and his bladder pushed hard against his kidneys.

"Doesn't anyone listen to me? Close the flap!" His shouting woke the kings from their tranquil sleep.

When the other soldiers heard the general they woke up nearly the same time with each other. Startled, they stared at the slit throats and streaming, coating blood of the hundreds of corpses surrounding them.

"My soldiers! My soldiers!" Chedorlaomer screamed when he exited his tent. "How could such a thing have occurred to my mighty soldiers!"

The general rushed outside and gasped at the enormity of the slaughter. Simultaneously feeling his bowels pressing against him, he ran to the privy behind the woods, cursing as his bowels exploded the fecal matter from him.

While he was inside the privy a few of Avram's men happened to spy his banner. They moved behind the privy. Quietly working their way behind the honor guard, the men, on cue, wrestled behind them, carving open their throats. Carefully they dropped the bodies to the ground.

Hearing the muffled falls, however, the warrior general instinctively understood what was happening outside the privy.

He lifted his spear and callously grinned. Patiently waiting for an opportune time to release it, he skillfully positioned himself directly in the center of the tent. He bent his powerful knees and hefted back the spear. He took a deep breath, stilling his anxiety.

A man's whistle from behind him ripped the silence apart. Automatically, with sharpened reflexes, he twirled around. At that very moment a dagger struck him through the eye, penetrating deep into his skull. With the slightest whimper the Elamite general fell on his knees.

Collapsing to his face, his own swift motion fully drove the dagger inside his brain.

During that exact moment King Ampraphel rushed to his men, only to discover what Chedorlaomer had discovered. Hundreds of their soldiers had been quietly, cunningly slaughtered by an unknown enemy.

King Arioch placed his delicate foot on his favorite captain's chest and turned his body over. Doing so, he fully exposed the gaping carving in his stomach. A colony of larva swarmed in the thick, deep pool of blood that drained from his body. His face was ashen white. An infestation of bugs completely ate away his tongue.

Shocked by the terror of the sight, Arioch screamed. Running, he grabbed his fellow companions in strickened panic. Their hands and arms danced about each other's body. Grotesquely, as caricatures, their intense movements prevented each other from running away. The rest of his soldiers, disturbed by their actions, ran to the hills. As they advanced away from the camp of undisputed terror, the Amorites and Avram's men met them with their swords. Within moments they ripped and gouged asunder their faces and chests and stomachs.

King Arioch watched the unrelenting and unfathomable revenge. The slaughtering scared him as nothing else ever had. He retreated to his tent and emptied as much of the heavy gold trinkets that he could out of his trunk and layered them over his neck and arms and ankles. After he grabbed as much as he could possibly carry, he wrapped himself in a heavy cloak to hide his gold. The weight bore down on him and slowed his trek toward his horse. A young man, who happened by, saw the ungainly fat man. Without hesitation he flung his spear through the man's back. Without watching to see if he struck him or not, he continued chasing another enemy soldier, felling him as well.

Confused, perplexed, in chaos and in utter pandemonium, the remainder of Chedorlaomer's army hastily withdrew north to Hobah. When they neared Damascus, Chedorlaomer managed to beat his army back into a sensible formation.

"Where is my general?" he inquired of his second captain.

He shook his head.

"We stand here," Chedorlaomer insisted.

King Tidal, hiding among his surviving clansmen of the primary tribe, refused to obey. When night was in its zenith, King Tidal tried to sneak away from the camp. Unable to find a horse to mount, and unable to penetrate the heavily guarded pens, he selected the nearest ass. When he jumped on the donkey's back, it loudly brayed, alerting the second captain. He caught the deserting king.

The officer stripped him naked then knocked him flat to the ground. Taking four spears he slammed the points through the king's hands and ankles. The fourth spear broke against the bone. Chedorlaomer walked to him and shook his head. "What strong bones! Not to worry captain. I'll simply remove his foot for you."

With those words Chedorlaomer violently slammed his sword down, amputating the king's left ankle. The brief flash of the sword caught Tidal's eyes. He clenched his teeth and felt the brutal, severing pain. He opened his mouth, hideously screaming and squirming about the spears in withering agony.

"Everyone who is a member of his confederacy, if you wish to live, remove a portion of him from him. What you remove, you eat."

Each survivor, not wanting to suffer such brutality, pulled their swords out, cutting away from the fighting man strips of flesh which they consumed. Through the night each man cut away at him.

ꙮ

By mid-morning the battle cry rose.

Horses crashed against Avram's footmen. Having learned, however, the tricks of warfare, the footmen fell down, rolling in front of the horses' hoofs. The unbalanced animals viciously bucked. The riders, unable to hold on, ejected from the horses' back, impacting to the hard ground.

Arching their backs, the calvary became stunned by their unanticipated falling. The sudden, hard impact expulsed the air from the riders' lungs. Dazed, unable to take another swallow of reviving air, Avram's men easily annihilated them.

Chedorlaomer, remembering his general's combat phraseologies, tried to issue directives at the retreating soldiers. All ignored his directives. The men kept running farther from him.

Frustrated, he gave up and determined to stop running alongside his soldiers. He faced Avram's men.

"Ha! Come! Try to kill me," he challenged.

Chedorlaomer wildly extended and circled his sword's sharpened tip. He hunched defensively, waiting for the first man to rush upon him. "Come on! Come on," he teased.

Mamre, unafraid, pushed aside the hesitating men and stared at the king of Elam. Meanwhile, Eshkol, happening to see King Tidal's skinned body and gouged eyes, heard his faint breaths. He stepped on Tidal's wrist and jerked the pinning spear from his hand. Quickly he slammed it into his exposed, pumping heart.

Eshkol then went to Mamre and presented Tidal's spear and heart to him. Chedorlaomer looked at Tidal's butchered chest and knew where the heart came from. He quickly studied Mamre.

"You're their leader?" the king arrogantly demanded to know, furrowing his forehead.

"I am not. Avram, the Hebrew, is their leader."

"The Hebrew?" Echoing those words, a drove of spears flew at him, striking him fully in the chest, stomach, and right leg.

The king fought off the weight of the down-pulling spears, but unable to fight it, he slowly, gracefully lowered himself on his left knee. He clutched the spear that jammed in his chest and yanked it out. In that terrible agony he refused to shout a painful cry. When he pulled it fully out he stared at it, and wondered at the amount of blood that covered its length. He flung it to the wayside. Lifting his face, he coughed. Blood and saliva driveled from the corner of his mouth.

He placed his arm against his bent leg and tried to support himself. He believed he had to stand straight up to present a dignified appearance. He did not want his body to indignantly collapse to the hard ground.

Glancing up, he saw a strange white cloud forming behind Mamre. Rays of sunlight splashed against a large grayed man standing behind Mamre. His silver and black beard blew with the rising wind. His black tunic was thickly caked with blood. Chedorlaomer lifted his head higher. He intuitively whispered, "Avram?"

"He knows your name," Aner, perplexed, commented.

Avram lowered himself beside the dying man and stared into his eyes. "I am Avram," he confirmed his identity.

"Avram tell me, please? Does the mysterious city exist? The city of Eber?"

"It is the city of Shem, Eber's father, who is also the father of the Elamites and the father of the Assyrians. In remotest terms, I am your brother."

"What is the name of the city?"

"Salem."

"The dwelling place of peace and righteousness," Chedorlaomer translated with his expiring breath.

A terrible sense of remorse began to overwhelm Avram as he gently pulled the last two spears from the king's body. The guilt engulfed his essence. He gently picked him up and personally carried him to the outskirts of the war-zone. The bodies of the other kings' lay side by side. Not far from them a large heap of the remains of the combined forces waited for the torches' flame.

A flock of vultures patiently flew overhead.

Avram habitually placed his index fingertip between his front teeth and shook his head in perplexing agony.

He folded his arms about his chest he began moving back and forth. Indeterminable sounds emitted from his throat.

Avram, unable to remove himself away from the dead kings, remained through the night, refusing to sleep.

Lot, discovering his uncle standing determinedly still, edged his eyes to an acute focus. With the morning's sunrise Lot caught the sight of a strange glow filtering around his uncle's body. It was as if the power of the world had descended over him. The directing force of God's holy spirit controlled the event. A facet of God's judicial power bequeathed to Avram the knowledge that what had to be done was sanctified by God. Through the night Avram beseeched forgiveness for the blood he had spilled. In the morning God forgave him. The power of the holy spirit transformed that night of violence into a dawn of calm.

Lot wanted to shout a greeting, a grateful thank you. Instead, he hesitated, remaining still.

Mamre, Eshkol, and Aner also witnessed the phenomenon. The men went to him, each taking their turn kissing him on the neck. Lot was the last man to kiss his uncle. When he finally did approach his uncle, his face blanched white. Succumbing to the stresses of the ordeal, Lot's legs weakened. His hands reached out, wavering. Unable to find Avram's tunic, he panicked. Avram supported his nephew to sit beside him. Lot could barely distinguish his uncle. The blood-bath sickened him. It made him dizzy with remorse. He nearly fainted from the smell that emitted from the accumulation of lifelessness littering the ground around them.

Avram saw on Lot's face a mirror reflection of his own horrid experiences over the past few days. As he lowered his nephew to the ground, he stroked his nephew's hair tenderly. In that time Avram clearly remembered his father and brother.

He saw their smiles, their tears, the passing moments of joy and love.

He broke out in a heightened sob.

Avram succumbed to the tension of the memory and allowed himself to cry openly.

Through the hours his tears exhausted themselves dry. At last he stretched his legs out on the ground and placed Lot's head in his lap.

Through the morning's rise the army rested in front of the decomposing bodies of the king, watching as the birds swooped to feast on the mangled flesh.

Chapter Fifteen

▼

Sedom

The boy-servant of the former king of Sedom filled a new lead cup for his own lips, becoming the new king. The priests stood behind him, again standing watch over the multicolored fires that rose from their towers to the skies. Again the lakes reflected the red and violet clouds. Again the goats and gazelles and ruminants roamed the rich, fertile land. Again the land-tenders tilled the productive farms. Again the caravans came with their wares to trade.

The survivors, because they were the survivors, became the new landlords.

Taking over the vacated leadership roles, the new masters worked with the same credit vouchers that their former wealthy landlords controlled. The child-king, needing them, readily allowed them to wear the rings of power that their former masters wore. The child-king also permitted the survivors to display around their houses the council chamber's Cylinders of Trade. And, no one protested nor contested their wearing the Seals of

Authorization around their richly adorned necks. Within weeks the survivors forced their presence into the council's empty seats.

The returning survivors freely took the best and largest houses for themselves. Those who had lived in the tents outside the city walls, now moved into the vacated, nearly dilapidated houses of the former impoverished families. The gathering homeless gratefully occupied the weathered and torn tents.

The refugees of the war, seeing the dilapidated houses and the forlorn tents, became thrilled to have them for themselves.

And the attitude of the survivors changed.

Each took for himself whatever he desired. Whoever protested, the quarrel ended with the sword. The returning soldiers, vacating their positions, allowed the people to run amuck. Civil obedience broke down. The former gave way to the might of the new.

ঔৎ঩ঔৎ঩ঔ঩ৎ঩ঔৎ঩

Avram set the piles of men on fire. He clenched his lips tight and his jaw slightly trembled. Mamre scratched his beard then turned to pour more bitumen over the corpses. All the men held black handkerchiefs around their mouths and noses. Whenever they saw a bird eating a body, their eyes became impervious to the sight. The lions freely ate until their stomachs bulged, forcing them to sleep beside the torn flesh. During these moments Avram's men scouted the forest, unmolested by the dangerous creatures.

The victorious campaign finally returned home. Purposely they took the least traveled road that led them to the Valley of Kings. The men, burdened by the battle, shamed by the victory, depressed by what they had done, silently walked through the land in five long lines.

Many nationalities haphazardly made up the five long lines. The men were not divided by rank and file, nor did they march very well.

Nevertheless the different nationalities remained together on the trek home as a deferment to Avram's God.

In their march many men staggered. Many kept their heads lowered. A few, feeling proud of their warring efforts, nobly walked with straight backs and high-held heads. All, regardless how they marched or thought or felt, kept their heads covered with mourning cloths.

ಬಲಿ ಬಲಿ ಬಲಿ ಬಲಿ ಬಲಿ

Shem, pruning his favorite olive tree, lifted the discarded limbs to his shoulders. He carried them to the burning pits. After that he grabbed a clay bowl and walked to another olive tree. Underneath its mid-branches he carefully plucked the ripened olives.

"Melchizedek," Eber disturbed him. "Father."

"I know. Prepare for them our best wine and cook our richest breads. Bring me the flask of oil that I have been preserving in my quarters."

"You've at last found a use for it?"

"Yes," he patted Eber on the shoulder. "It shall be used for what it has been intended."

ಬಲಿ ಬಲಿ ಬಲಿ ಬಲಿ ಬಲಿ

Avram and his men struggled through the morning mist that mysteriously hugged the rising landscape. It seemed especially significant this morning as if it held a deep meaning inside an ethereal shroud. Its silked appearance intrigued Avram. When they reached the last bends of the Valley of Shaveh, Avram refused to lift his head. Instead, he maintained his humbled position. With his head lowered toward the ground, he failed to see before him the eagerly waiting crowd of men. Despondent, he failed to see the banquet spread and the numerous skins of wine and the steaming loaves. Severely depressed, he failed to notice the dizzying configurations of colorful tunics and wraps.

He sniffed the air and smelled the cooked bread. As he neared the turn of the high road, he first saw the strangely trampled trail. He finally lifted his eyes. First he saw in front of him his legs of the men and as he rose his head higher he saw the full bodies of the strangers blocking his path.

The dismayed group of followers, also keeping their heads lowered to the ground, misunderstood Avram's hesitation. Immediately each man behind Avram bumped into each other. The caricature of the event caused the ones watching to laugh.

Uncertain why these strangers laughed at him and at his men, Avram stiffened. Just then, Eber advanced from behind the files of priests. Avram instantly recognized him and broke out in a loud, heartfelt laughter.

The two quickly embraced each other, kissing one another's neck. The watching ones, knowing all was safe, rushed to the distraught army, embracing them with joy.

"Lot, you're getting fat!" Eber joked. "And Avram, look how gray your hair has become!"

"At least it's still with me," Avram replied, again hugging Eber.

"Quick, come with me. Father wants to meet you."

"Father?"

"Shem."

Startled, Avram whispered, "He truly lives then."

Avram impulsively ran ahead of Eber and Lot and using the trees' branches and vines, anxiously pulled himself forward in spite of his tired and exhausted body and mind. Finally, he reached the top of the hill. Before him stood the city of Salem. Behind him the Valley of Shaveh rolled away toward the Dead Sea.

No fortified walls, nor towers of war, nor guards hindered his progression into the city's streets. The main entry road, manicured with flowers edging the curbs, led directly to the center. The rock houses behind the blossoming flowers had large open windows looking into the streets. Stairways led to the cool roofs.

Each street had its own well. Unlike Ur, everyone freely helped themselves to the water. In the center a large circular fountain poured crystal clear water into stone-lined ditches. From there the water softly cascaded into the richly endowed gardens whose walls were covered with vines heavy with large clusters of grapes. Everywhere fig, olive, oak, and plane trees grew right next to the houses. The large crisscrossing branches kept the city streets in perpetual shade and overshadowed the roofs.

Amazed by the beautiful city, Avram took a few private moments to study its layout. When he saw the construction attributes of the city, he readily understood why no one had ever found the city. From the distance it appeared to be a continuous forest. No house rose over fifteen feet nor was wider than twenty feet. Vibrantly green plants covered every roof. Vines crept along the windows and doorways. As soon as he stood in the middle of the street an incredible, mind-awaking, sweet aroma filled his nostrils. Walking about, he noticed everyone freely sharing the fruits from the trees and the vegetables from the maturing gardens.

Eber and Lot finally caught up with Avram. "Follow," Eber touched Avram's shoulder. Eber then turned left at the apex of the city square. The three men strolled toward the rear corner of the city. They soon reached an isolated, plain white house. In front of it a single brown chair, primitively assembled from thick cedar branches, rested outside its door. The chair's bark still remained on its legs and on its back slats.

Coming closer to the door, Eber motioned for Avram and Lot to stop, whereupon a very old man stepped out from the humble house. He carried with him a red blanket sewn from ram skins.

"Avram," he motioned with his fingers to step closer. "I am your great-great-forefather. I am Shem, Noah's secondborn. Now the people call me Malki-Tzedek. Or, Melchizedek."

"King of Righteousness and Peace," Avram struggled to recall the meaning of his great-Father's name. Feeling safe at last in the presence of this frail, old man and exhausted by his battle against the horrid thoughts that continuously invaded his conscious existence, Avram folded unto himself. Despite the encroaching shaking and intense trembling, he reached out for the ancient man who immediately embraced him. Avram collapsed in Melchizedek's arms. The old man comforted Avram in his frenzy of terrible tears and remorse.

Through his sobs, Avram fought his words out. "I've been in agony. I need happiness. I need joy. I need to be happy again."

Stroking the thinning silver hair, Melchizedek nodded. "I know you do. But first there is knowledge you must learn. Avram, we've entered into a new age of existence."

"What kind of existence?"

"An age of invisibilities—where everything committed is because of hideous, misleading whispers and covert underlayments of hate. Satan has committed everything he is to the overturning of Yahweh's purpose."

"I don't understand."

"Prior to the deluge, the demons freely roamed the earth, mingling openly with mankind, breeding with the women, and controlling the day's events. No central government existed for none was needed. No single army rose to conquer, for everyone was already conquered. No dictator emerged from chaos, for everything was in anarchy and in chaos.

"The demons resided directly alongside mankind, clothed in flesh. They ate, they married, they conversed as we do. Then they changed. Yahweh removed from them their abilities to cloak themselves with fleshly coverings. Now the demons live invisibly alongside us, influencing us with their quiet words and subliminal messages. Always insidious, always persuasive.

"This new existence brings to mankind a spiritual warfare unprecedented in history. What occurred between you and Chedorlaomer was a preview of things to come during the final ages of mankind."

"What do you mean?'

"You symbolically represented Yahweh and *'the leader'* symbolically represented Satan and his demons. Never has such horrific and unprecedented violence in such great extremities visited mankind. Never has such wanton disregard been exercised against man. What Chedorlaomer perpetrated, however, is nil compared to what will come. Though this physical warfare is new and treacherous and unmerciful, a harsher spiritual warfare is simultaneously occurring in Yahweh's residence."

"This—this what I went through—was symbolic?"

"Of the greater spiritual and physical war to come during the last days of mankind and evil. Many other things will occur which will prophesy the events of the last days.

"I also am the symbolic representation of what is to come.

"Noah renamed me so I may serve as the symbolic representation of the Mashiach who is to appear to us as a ransom for our sins. My purpose is to be King and Priest—the cohen—answerable directly to Yahweh and commanded directly by He who is the Most High God."

"Oh, Melchizedek! Help me! Since my encounter I've been unable to lift my eyes from the ground. My thoughts are heavy with distress. I wonder now about myself! I doubt everything, except my relationship with Yahweh. I trust only Him, yet, I need more than just being able to trust Him. How do I walk with my fellow human beings? How have I affected my state of consciousness; to what degree have I harmed my view of mankind? Do we men have the ability to rise above the depths of our anger and immorality, or are we all caught in a vicious depth that is so deep we can only escape it by becoming a part of it? Can I, now that I've killed, return to innocence—if truly I ever had it?"

"What are you carrying by your side?'

"My sword."

"Then I will answer all your questions this way. The sword is unworthy of a man who truly loves Yahweh. Throw it away and place faith beside. Carry it always, for it is stronger than metal. Faith and love are the swords of spiritual protection. Faith and love are the shields against a demon's piercing whispers of corruption. Let Yahweh's angels wage war not only against the demons but also against all national governments and all national conventions and accepted practices. All men who rule, govern by the powers of the evil one. Satan is the spiritual host of all governments and conventions. The anointed must patiently wait by the wayside for the gifts of the coming Kingdom. Do this, regardless of the consequences to your fleshly life. Torment, rape, murder are things that can befall anyone. How a person reacts is the measure of their faith. React by not reacting.

"In order to enter Yahweh's perfect Kingdom, make truth your protective tunic. Make truth your protective head-covering. Truth cannot be manipulated. It cannot be hidden. It cannot be mocked nor scorned, though many attempt to do so to impress listeners to their cause and personality.

"Few are chosen for anointment. You can desire it. You can falsely boast of having received the spirit, but Yahweh alone presents this encompassing gift. Regardless who you are, if Yahweh presents the veil to you, no man may refute it as a delusional event.

"Few men will enter Yahweh's perfection.

"Now, Avram, bow down before me."

Avram, once lowered on his knees, felt a sticky flow of liquid pouring over his hair. Instinctively he raised his hands to feel it.

"Keep your hands to your sides. I am pouring oil over you. Yahweh commissioned me to anoint the man who would one day come to this city after a victorious campaign over evil. Yahweh, from among the hundreds of millions of men inhabiting the earth, chose you, Avram, son of Terah.

"Today, I anoint you as the Messiah of our times.

"Through your loins many anointed kings will descend. Each of these descendants will raise to the world a new Messiah. Symbolically, they will continue representing the Messianic hope to the world, until the ultimate and final Messiah comes to take his place in history. The refining characteristics of our line will be inherent in he who will lift us from the pains of death."

Rising both hands in front of Avram's face, Melchizedek's thumbs touched each other as he grouped his fingers to form the English letter V, signifying the Hebrew letter *Shin*, ?, the first letter of God's name.

"Blessed be Avram of the Most High God," he solemnly pronounced, "possessor of heaven and earth!

"Blessed be 'El El-yohn.' He has delivered your enemies into your hands."

Melchizedek lifted Avram from his knees then wiped the tears away from Avram's face. Afterwards he kissed him on the neck.

"What further must I do?" Avram asked the progenitor of the Semitic race.

"You are obligated to learn everything I can teach you concerning Yahweh. You are to impart that knowledge to your people. Continue your traveling and continue erecting altars for they are indisputable land stakes for the children who will come after you."

"Have I any role with Salem?"

"In future generations one of your children will establish this place as Yahweh's capital. This very city is where Yahweh's throne exists. From here a theocratic, constitutional government will rule."

Gently pushing him away at arm's length, the king-priest stared deeply into Avram's swollen and reddened eyes.

"Avram, close your eyes. Listen to what you feel. And understand!"

Avram obeyed. Slowly he breathed in the fragrant air. His senses became acutely aware of a deeper essence surrounding him. An inexplicable sense of calm and assurance. His hair tingled. His mind raced to its innermost core where all reality became focused on the exact realization of meaning and understanding.

Mystically, Avram became one with Melchizedek.

"Men," Avram spoke to his companions after the trance expired. "Place before this great King and Priest one-tenth of everything."

His friends stepped up to Melchizedek's humble chair and separated from themselves the tenth part of their goods, the allotment filling the blanket that was placed between them.

"Great King and Priest," Avram asked Melchizedek, "when am I allowed to return?"

"Return first these people to their cities. Dwell then with us."

ᏜᏣᏜᏣᏜᏣᏣᏜᏣᏜᏣᏜᏣ

Shortly afterwards Avram met with the child-king. Cunning ambassadors surrounded the youngster.

"Great king," an advisor whispered to the child-king. "The Hebrew has more slaves than we do. If he continues accumulating men, he'll be able to overthrow us and take possession of our lands and properties."

"We can do nothing about it," another advisor responded. "We can not conquer the conqueror. All he has to do is walk to Elam. It is his by right of victory. We also are his by that same right."

"He may not know this. I suggest we give up and place him among ourselves. With his presence in our government, he may share with us his slaves. We do need them to help us in our flourishing trade."

Knowing their dilemma, Avram nevertheless refused to accept membership in their council. "Lot is the one to for you."

Gratefully, the council members bowed.

"Since you do not desire to be a member of our government, may I please be permitted to ask this question without your taking offense at me?"

"Your question will not offend me."

"The men you took from Chedorlaomer, will they work your herds?"

"They are not my men. I freed them not to enslave them again, but to permit them free-choice and self-determination. They may walk wherever they desire."

"We need extra people to help us rebuild our city," the chief financial officer said. "Avram, allow us, please, if it is in your heart, the care and management of these former prisoners. In return, we will permit you to keep all the war treasures for yourself."

"I made an oath to Yahweh, the Most High God, Creator of heaven and earth, before I fought Chedorlaomer: 'I will not take anything for myself. Not so much as a ram's thread or a child's sandal'. What belongs to you, allow to remain with you.

"You will not broadcast to other men that I have been made wealthy by the theft of another man's treasure. It shall not be stated that I became rich from consorting and manipulating as it was said of me when I left Egypt.

"You people of Sedom and Amorah shall not advertise to anyone, anywhere: 'I made Avram rich!'

"For me, nothing shall be given. I do ask, though: please, share with the warriors who taught us. Place with Mamre, with Aner, and with Eshkol their deserving shares.

"As for these other men, as I have stated, I am not their ruler. Walk where you desire. Think as you desire. I warred against Chedorlaomer not to conquer the world or to take for myself the world's possessions. I warred because evil faced good and the darkness tried to overwhelm the light. Knowing this, having experienced this, I pray all of you will follow the light that I follow. To ignore it, is to jeopardize yourselves worse than before."

The child-king, along with many of his ambassadors, thought only of the recaptured treasure. What Avram spoke, fell by the wayside.

ᴆᴄᴈᴆᴄᴈᴆᴄᴘᴆᴄᴈᴆᴄᴈ

Afterwards Avram, accompanied by Sarai, returned to Salem. Daily studying with Eber and with the progenitor of the Semitic race, Avram learned everything that the king-priest had to teach him.

While Avram and Sarai lived in Salem, Lot became honored by the Sodomites. Then population encouraged him to remain with them. They built a special house for him and immediately increased his trade contracts. Among all the merchantmen, his merchandise became officially designated as 'First Importance' among the people.

His wife accumulated the softest cottons and richest transparent purple silks and the heaviest gold necklaces and jeweled bracelets.

The citizens honored him and his family so much they permitted his two daughters to remain unmolested on the pain of death by the king's orders. For everyone else, however, no laws of morality applied.

ᔒᎰᔒᏻᔒᎰᏻᔒᎰᏻ

In the darkness of the city of Sedom a man believed he was safe from the eyes of any witness who might happen by. He did not believe that the eyes of Michael the Archangel and his first-in-command Gabriel could be standing beside him. A third angel also stood near him. The man was incapable of discerning the eyes of good. His evil acts seared his consciousness long ago. Evil thoughts forbade him to see the eyes of good.

What the three angels saw, however, they noted. They ascended back to heaven and presented their testimony to Yahweh.

"Prepare yourselves for the coming night of obliteration," He said to them.

A long time later, Avram fell into a divine trance.

Yahweh spoke:

"Fear not, Avram.

"I am your shield!

"Great will be your reward!"

Avram, submersed by the power of the trance, unable to break away, spoke exactly what his heart felt; without deterrence, without hesitation, without subtle coloration of his meaning.

"Sovereign Lord Yahweh, what more is there that You can give to me? I have thousands of sheep! Thousands of goats and tens of thousands of cattle. I have the strongest, swiftest camels. I have the choicest donkeys. Wherever I settle, the grass grows the greenest and the water tastes the sweetest. I have never lain under the sun without a shadowing, overhanging tree being nearby and without a cool breeze happening along.

"And," his eyes became sad, "the wives of my servants are among the most fertile women in the land.

"All this You presented to me. But why? Do you not realize I shall die childless? To whom am I to leave such a vast accumulation? In my household, though, there is my remote cousin, Dammesek Eliezer. He is the guardian of my estate.

"Since it has occurred that You have not caused me to issue a child, I ask this: allow him to possess my things."

Yahweh, seeing that Avram had forgotten His declaration that the Mashiach's seed would issue through Avram's genes, answered, "Eliezer will not be the inheritor of your possessions. No one else, except your very own issue, will inherit your possessions. Your semen and its genetic contents will bring you offspring. They, themselves, will inherit what has been given to you to have."

To further encourage Avram, Yahweh stated: "Step outside your dark tent. Raise your eyes toward the heavens. Try to count the stars. Are you able?"

Avram shook his head.

"That is how many children you will have."

Avram, twisting his neck, peered into the dense, uncountable constellations. Awed, and sincerely believing what he heard, he placed full faith in Yahweh.

Avram, at this time, was still uncircumcised.

A long silence followed. The resonant voice began again: "I am Yahweh! I am He who brought you out of the City of Ur of the Chaldeans on the fourteenth day of the month of Nisan, two thousand eighty-three years after Adam first received my breath into his soul. I give to you this land to possess."

Again Avram was unable to refrain his thoughts. In self-betrayal he exclaimed, "Sovereign Lord Yahweh!" His voice became tense, angry. "How am I to certainly know that I am to possess this land?" His fist tightened.

Yahweh, reflecting on the hostile demand for proof, silenced.

Overhead the stars appeared to dim. The universe seemed to quietly withdraw from existence.

Finally Yahweh responded. "Bring Me a three-year-old heifer, a three-year-old she-goat, a three-year-old ram, one turtledove, and one young bird."

"Three-year-olds?" he questioned himself. "One and one," he again whispered. "These surely are imperfect numbers. How can this be? I made Yahweh angry," he clenched his lips together, cupping his hand over his mouth, squeezing it. "I dare not question His purpose again."

Avram obeyed the command and walked into the deep center of his camp where the choicest heifers slept. He tied a rope around the virgin cow's neck that he had proudly set aside to mate with his prize bull.

A short distance away he examined dozens of male goats. After he examined their markings and teeth and toes, he finally found a black one with the correct markings on its horns.

Tired, he went on to study another group of she-goats. By near-dawn he came to the last few, picking at last the right one.

Avram placed a large handful of grain on the ground. Within minutes, several of the gentle and shy turtledoves flew in from their morning flight to eat. At that time he released a birdcatcher's net which dropped over the unsuspecting birds. He sifted through it and found the best toward the rear of the flock.

An hour later, Avram trapped a quail in the barley field, snaring it inside his trap.

After all was accomplished Avram returned to the exact place where Yahweh communicated with him. There Avram raised his knife. Coldly, detached from honesty, he praised Yahweh. Quickly, with a firm, strong pull he slit one throat after the other until all four throats surrendered to death.

He placed the she-goat, the heifer, the ram, the quail, and the turtledove on their sides and stayed with them as he studied the rising sun. He forgot to sit underneath the tree's shade. Perspiring, he wiped the sweat with his tunic. It was hotter than usual. Acrid.

Continuing the sacrifice, he carved the heifer in half as well as the ram and the turtledove. The quail remained in one piece. The carved halves faced each other on the ground. The grass absorbed the flowing blood.

Hours passed. The morning dew dissipated. The heat increased.

The afternoon's sun peaked. The earth began its cycle toward the evening setting.

The shepherds and herdsmen passing by, wondered why Avram sat by the wayside, in the full sun, staring quietly at the carcasses.

While Avram waited, Yahweh met with Michael the Archangel to discuss Avram's bitter attitude and Yahweh's subsequent request to have an imperfect number of animal sacrifices presented to the altar. Michael the Archangel gazed at the human and persuaded Yahweh to continue with His plan of salvation for mankind. Yahweh stared at the aging man. "An equality for an equality must visit him," Yahweh determined. Michael, satisfied, withdrew from the council chambers.

By late afternoon, as Avram began dozing off, vultures began to rapidly thrust into the intended sacrifices. As soon as he heard the commotion, Avram fully woke and ran to the fierce vultures. Underneath the flock, he swung his staff against their wingtips. One vulture, nevertheless, managed to land in the middle of the holy ground. Upset, Avram kicked his feet at the lead vulture as it spread its tipped wings against him. The vulture hissed at Avram for a few brief seconds before it flew back into the air.

And in the invisible world of evil, Satan and his cohorts laughed.

Finally, all the vultures turned away from the putrefying meat.

As he kept vigilant watch, the hours passed even slower.

He watched the sun color the horizon a deep red and grow larger and larger. "Somehow this powerful fire knows the exact distance to remain away from the earth," he thought. "What would happen if the sun moved a little closer, or perhaps, a bit farther away?"

Avram fell asleep.

Tossing! Breathing heavy! Sweating! Images: unfocused, unclear, uncertain, descended inside his mind. Explosive colors dominated his thoughts:

thousands of chains rattled in his mind. Boulders and logs appeared. Mud dancers came and went. Taskmasters viciously cracked their sharp, stinging whips into the air, threatening to hurt again the men whose flesh was already broken open. The snaps of the whip scarred their backs. Many wounds bled without coagulating. Everywhere screams filled the air. The screams seemed impossible to stop. The unrelenting screams fell on the taskmasters' deaf ears.

Avram screamed the loudest scream of them all. The dreadful cry woke him up.

Yahweh's voice revisited Avram during this moment of incomprehensible fear. "For an absolute certainty you will know that your children shall become strangers in a land which they will not possess. They will be enslaved and oppressed for four hundred years.

"Be it also assured, though, I will execute My judgment against the nation that shall oppress your children. In the finality of My judgment, your offspring shall be released from their bondage with a tremendous wealth of goods and gold and jewels.

"Concerning yourself; you shall die peacefully. You shall live for a very long time.

"In the fourth generation your offspring will return here. During their absence I will deal with the evils of the Amorites."

When the sun had fully set, the moon failed to appear as did the stars. In that period of bleakest black, when Avram couldn't distinguish one tree from another nor his tent from his neighbors, a smoking oven appeared to float toward him from an indistinguishable distance. The oven continued growing in size. It traveled to the very forefront of Avram's presence. Standing aside, he watched the flames rising from the oven. A fiery red and yellow and blue torch ascended from the oven's center. Traveling from sacrifice to sacrifice, the flaming tongue instantly consumed the carcasses within itself.

"Avram, this contract I pledge between ourselves: This land I will assign to your offspring.

"From the Nile to the Euphrates!

"The places which are illegally settled:

"the residences of the Kenites,

"of the Kenizzites, of the Kadmonites,

"of the Hittites, of the Perizzites, of the Rephaim,

"of the Amorites, of the Canaanites, of the

"Girgashites, and of the Jebusites.

"All the land which they now dwell on shall be yours.

"Sanctified war shall be between your offspring and theirs,

"for they have corrupted the land where I had placed Adam and planted and nurtured his Garden of Eden.

"They erected false gods and do homage to evil creatures.

"You have learned the method of war.

"So long as your offspring do what is righteous,

"they shall never be defeated in battle by any country or king.

"Whosoever wars on them shall war on me.

"This I pledge between us and between your offspring."

℠∞℃℠∞℃℠∞ℂ℅℠℃℠∞℃

When Avram was eighty-six years old, he fathered Yishmael. Hagar, the Egyptian and the concubine that Sarai presented to him, was the mother.

Yishmael, exercising total independence and arrogance was banished from Avram's camp when he was fourteen years old, along with Hagar, his mother.

Having a strong sexual appetite, Yishmael became the father of twelve sons and one daughter: Mahalath. She in turn married Esau, Yitzhak's son.

Yishmael's children, through his Egyptian wife, were: Nebaioth, Kedar, Adbeel, Mibsam, Mishma, Dumah, Massa, Hadad, Tema, Jetur, Naphish, and Kedemah. All the sons shared three parts Hamitic genes and one part Semitic genes. They became the restless men of the desert plains and the

Arabian peninsula. These children became infamous men of the regions for their fierce warrior activities.

Over a great period of years the children of Yishmael intermarried with the children of Avram through the mother's line of Keturah. By this time Avram was renamed by Yahweh as Abraham.

ઐલ્ઉઐલ્ઉઐલ્ઉઐલ્ઉઐલ્ઉ

Keturah became Abraham's second wife several years after Sarah died. With her Abraham fathered six sons. They were: Zimran, Jokshan, Medan, Midian, Ishbak, and Shuah. Moses wife, Zipporah, came to be born through the line of Midian and through the Canaanite line of Kenite.

Through Abraham's wife Sarah, Yitzhak was born. Through Riveka he had two children: Esau and Jacob.

Esau became the father of the Edomites with whom Yahweh contracted to protect for them the land of Seir.

Through Jacob, whose name was changed to Yisrael after the long night's wrestling with the archangel, twelve children were born. Reuben, Simeon, Levi, Yehuda, Issachar, Zebulun descended from Leah's womb. Joseph and Binyamin were from Jacob's second wife, Rachel. From his concubine Bilhah, Dan and Naphtali were born. From his second concubine, Zilpah, Gad and Asher were born.

From Jacob came Yisrael's scepter which was taken from Binyamin after a period of intense civil war.

From Levi came the priestly classes who historically aligned themselves with Yehuda.

ઐલ્ઉઐલ્ઉઐલ્ઉઐલ્ઉઐલ્ઉ

This is Yishmael's background.

Sarai, decades ago, ceased menstruating. In the night's embrace Avram cuddled her in his arms wherein they would explore each other's bodies and laugh of the day's events and evening talks. The years kept passing.

Hundreds of children were born to Avram's companions, yet Sarai remained childless.

Avram's herds kept increasing. More men were hired. When there weren't enough men to be found for the work, Avram began buying slaves from the Sodomites and Amorites and Kenites. After seven years of bondage he freed them, fully empowering them with the rights of his fellow men.

In the twilight of evening, when Avram sought the far corner of the bed, Sarai got up to lie beside him.

"Are you now shunning me?" she asked.

"I did not mean any harm. I'm just tired."

"Of my dry vagina and infertile tube?"

Avram expelled a deep breath. He looked at how beautiful she was and felt in his heart his deep love for her. Avram hushed her when he placed his index finger to his mouth. She walked up to him and placed her hand on his cheek. His beard felt soft, its wisdom reassuring, the strength of his eyes comforting.

"It is an acceptable custom among our people that you may write a writ of divorce against me for failing to produce a son for you. It will be honored among all men, everywhere. No one will blame you for casting me out of your tent."

"How can such a thought occur to you?"

"Since Lot married the Egyptian and she has presented him with a daughter, you seemed to become more isolated."

"I haven't fully recovered from my war campaigns against Chedorlaomer. His face and the face of thousands haunt me every night."

"Yahweh sent you against him. Did not Melchizedek equate it with the future picturing of the things to come?"

"Yes."

"You need a child to take the anguish of your nightmares away from you. More, you need a child by a foreigner to quell the long lingering prejudices away from our camp. How can a camp filled with so many divisive nationalities stay together? Remember, prejudices forced Lot and his followers to live in the Valley of Siddim."

"I remember."

"Then choose another mate for yourself. Preferably a foreign mate."

"Have I not only desired you since the day you were born? Yahweh has promised us a child and it shall happen."

"It will happen," Sarai breathed the words under her breath. "And, I know how it will occur. I just won't share it with you, for I know full well the cultural rights of our society."

She raised her voice again.

"You were unable to choose Eliezer, even though he is remotely related to you and has served as your chief steward because I, as your wife, had not consented to it."

"That is not correct, Sarai. There was another reason."

"No, listen to me! As your wife I have the absolute right to participate in the choosing of your heir."

"I understand that. I agree that what you have said sounds true."

"Also, as your wife, I can freely place in your arms who I dictate to be a reasonable and proper mate. By approved and witnessed intercourse between you and her, the child that is produced—by legal rights—I can receive as my own."

"I know of the legality involved.

"It is an acceptable act."

"Many men have committed to it and many women have raised the foster child as their own. But what has that to do with us?"

"I have thought on this for a long time. Avram, I beg for your patience and empathy."

Avram sat upright.

"Listen to me before you start arguing again.

"I chose Hagar my handmaiden to receive your semen in her womb. I will have my child this way. Legally, indisputably, the child will be mine. All nations will acknowledge the correctness of the act."

"Sarai," Avram insisted. "I will not do such a thing."

"In the night's passion, keep your thoughts on me. She who lies beneath you will be no different than I."

"Hagar is an Egyptian."

"Lot's wife is an Egyptian."

"This is happening too fast. Let me think about it."

"No. There's no time. The longer you think on this the more time passes and the older we get. Husband, I ask you, do what I say. Do this so I may finally end the shame of my barren womb."

"Let me think on it," Avram repeated, again turning away from Sarai.

Sarai suddenly jerked up. She walked away from her husband and paced back and forth for a few moments then suddenly darted out of the tent, going directly inside Hagar's tent.

"Rise, Hagar. I desire to talk with you."

"Yes, Sarai."

"I have a request to make of you."

"What is it?"

"I desire for you to conceive my husband's son." Then adding rapidly, before Hagar could speak, "Avram is wealthy beyond wealth. He has no heir to give it to. Think of all the treasures his son will inherit. Think of the power that money will command. Think of the men who will wait on him hand to shoulder and who will abide his every command."

"Is Avram as rich as the Egyptian king?"

"His heir certainly will be. All the land we have sojourned through—do you not know why?"

"To graze the cattle and sheep."

"Avram intends to claim it all for himself. All the altars and wells that he dug are legal vouchers testifying in court that he has settled and worked the land. Who can dispute it? His men are well armed. He has hundreds of strong men who are capable of fighting in any battle at a moment's notice. Who is mightier than Avram in this land? Did he not destroy Chedorlaomer?"

"What does Avram say?"

"Bare your clothes. He will agree."

"What assurance have I that my child will be taken care of? The Egyptian king of the Great House has many children. Most of them end their lives in the jailhouses and in the trapped chambers of the pyramids and in the hollow belly of the Sphinx."

"What I promised shall happen because the child will be Avram's. There is no better father for your child than my husband."

"Those things may be true, but Avram is prejudiced. He tolerates segregation. He does not influence integration."

"You say that because Lot left us?"

"I do."

"Then all the more reason for you to permit us to have a son by you."

"Avram said three generations must pass before his son can marry a foreigner."

"I never heard such a statement."

"The whispers of it are everywhere."

"Another reason, than, for your bonding with my husband. Your son will do two things: alleviate prejudicial thinking and force integration by example; and second, present him with a male heir."

Hagar finally consented, and after much preparation entered Sarai's tent where she knelt beside the sleeping man. Sarai helped remove Hagar's tunic. She lifted the wool cover that she had placed over Hagar in the Tent of Preparation alongside Avram.

"Husband, wake," Sarai whispered.

Opening his eyes he saw Sarai's figure through the dim light filtering through the tent's mesh.

"Sarai? Why are you waking me?"

"I want you to fulfill my wish that I have a son."

"We'll discuss it when the sun's warmed the earth."

"Hagar lies beside you. She has agreed to be your concubine."

"What?" He drew the words out very slowly. Jerking around he felt her naked flesh beside his. Her skin was dark, radiant. Her breasts were smaller than Sarai's but her shoulders were wider. Her longer, black hair revealed her youth.

"The time is now. Do what I have asked. I will watch to see it done."

Sarai, going into the darkest corner, watched Avram remaining motionless.

He wiped the sleep from his eyes and stared at Hagar again. Her cool body and succulent, moist lips caught his attention. She was young. Incredibly young.

Hagar awkwardly placed her arm on Avram's back. Scooting under his leg, she compelled him to raise himself directly on top of her. She reached between his legs, gently fondling his penis until he became aroused, erect. Her hands guided his throbbing penis inside her. She then placed her arms to her sides, keeping them motionless. She barely lifted her legs. Avram looked at Sarai as he inserted his painful erection deeper inside Hagar. As he motioned his body up and down over Hagar he refused to echo a sound from his throat.

Mechanically he went back and forth. As soon as he climaxed, he got off Hagar's body. He covered himself so he wouldn't expose his flesh to her then exited from the tent to the calm waters where he bathed himself, tears sweltering in his eyes.

"Hagar, get dressed. You can now leave our tent."

"Am I not to remain here? The semen may not adhere to my womb."

"It will. Avram will not permit another sexual encounter with you."

"You know him that well?"

"I know him well enough that I caused this event to transpire."

Days after Hagar bonded with Avram, Sarai began resenting her. She disliked Hagar's coal black hair. She frowned at Hagar's smooth skin. She began hating her full lips. She detested her youth. Her body was thinner than Sarai's. Though her hips were smaller, her face was not nearly as beautiful as Sarai's.

Prior to her bonding with the master of the camp, most of the women ignored the dark Egyptian. Now, in the coolness of the morning, they fondly greeted her, often presenting her with welcoming assistance.

Whenever a special cake was blended or a fragrant meal prepared, Hagar received the first portions.

During a certain morning, Hagar woke, vomiting.

The midwife examining her, discovered a hardening lump within her uterus. Within moments the news traveled throughout the camp. "Avram impregnated Hagar."

The feast lasted two days. Man after man congratulated Avram and Hagar.

Sarai, during this time, remained isolated in her tent.

Unable to focus on a meaningful task, she handled one empty clay vessel after another. Then she looked at the rows. "What a futile task," she thought, "figuring out what to place where. What difference does any of this make. It is meaningless." Sarai shifted her focus toward stacking one wool blanket on top of another. This task was worse than the other. After some time she determined to fold all the tunics that had been plaguing her for months in their unkempt state.

Sarai emptied the many chests that Avram had brought with him from Mamre's feast three years ago and as she did so, she accidentally discovered a comb that Hagar had misplaced. It was exquisitely carved from hippopotamus horn. As soon as she saw the beautiful object her eyes widened. Her face flushed red. In bitter jealousy she slammed the teeth into the chest, breaking them off.

During the third night, Sarai woke Avram again.

"What's wrong?"

"I want to talk."

"Now?"

"I don't want anyone to hear what I have to say to you," she gritted her teeth.

"Sarai," he resigned to her wrath. "I am listening."

"Hagar has all the joy and attention of the other women. No one any longer invites me to their tent. I don't even share in the evening meals. I don't receive a thing from anyone."

"They are happy for Hagar."

"It is me they should be happy for!" she screamed, spitting the words at him. A few neighbors woke up.

When the children's mothers heard the arguing, they placed their hands over their children's ears. "Go back to sleep. It doesn't concern you."

"Why do our leaders always argue and fight?"

"People of similar personalities always fight between themselves. There is nothing to contrast to, so the only excitement left is for them to argue with one another. Now hush and go back to sleep."

Inside the tent, Avram lit another oil disk. "What has been done has been done by you. You effectually made it happen."

"I? No, Avram. It was your doing! It was you who begged and prayed and beseeched me for a child. 'This is the right moment, Sarai' you would say, knowing I wasn't in the mood. 'This is the time and place' you would demand, making me strip for your all-important orgasm!

"No, Avram, what has been done was done as the result of your all-bearing and never-ending pressures on me to produce for you a son. I placed my servant under your naked body and now that she is pregnant with your child, my esteem has become vacated!

"May Yahweh decide who is right and who is wrong!"

"The servant is yours to do as you decide. Do not invoke Yahweh's judgment on what has already occurred. He had no part in it! Deal with her as you think right!"

Sarai, with every morning's rise and with every evening's setting, commanded that Hagar perform extra chores about the camp. Demeaning her status, Sarai demanded that Hagar needlessly walk to the last tent in the encampment to bring her a specific wool blanket that wasn't even required in the first place. "Somehow," Sarai reasoned, "everything that Hagar attempts to perform is improper. Somehow she fails at everything. She lacks the necessary vision to match the color scheme I'm trying to develop. She fails to understand the importance of having the specific pot for my cooking and the right needle for my darning."

Avram, remotely listening, turned his eyes toward the distant herdsmen. He wished he were walking among them.

"Hagar can't even place the correct measurement of porridge into the pot, let alone place it at the right temperature!"

"What does 'right measurement' have to do with being pregnant?" he muttered, catching only half her words.

"You imbecile. It has everything to do with how well the food tastes!"

Avram turned away from her, then after a few minutes he returned to her side and affectionately hugged her.

ଔଓଔଓଔଔଓଔଓଔଓ

Hagar finally grew tired of the continued abuse. She approached Avram.

When Avram saw her walking toward him, he turned away toward the flocks that were on the other side of Mamre's terebinths.

But she knew his ruse, and sidestepped in front of him. "Who will help me in this anguish?" she hoarsely whispered. "Has everyone forgotten that I am Avram's joy to come? Has everyone forgotten I was bribed and promised and compelled to lie with Avram?"

He didn't answer her.

Heartbroken by his lack of interest in her, she ran to her tent, falling on a pile of blankets. Large tears ran down her swollen, reddened cheeks. Folding the softest blanket, she clenched it tightly under her breasts.

"I was never treated like this in Egypt!" she screamed to herself as she beat her fist continuously on top of the blankets.

In the late afternoon, while the shepherds rested on the ground and while the women stopped the day's cooking, Hagar rose from the pile of blankets.

She threw a pile of food into a carrying sack. Grabbing a flask of water, she left the tent and quietly walked to the wayside road. Increasing her pace, she began running.

₧₧₧₧₧₧₧₧

Hagar followed the road to Shur and easily traveled from one hill to the other and from the nearby forest to the widening savannas.

The clear, crisp sky made her happy. The comfortable day excited her. For a few brief moments, however, she stopped to think of Sarai. "Once, before the unreasonable jealousy consumed her, she was kind and generous to me."

Swiftly walking, she thought about Avram. "He defied a king and destroyed a conqueror! He talks with God and makes demands!"

She reflected on where she was going. She had no answer. Coming to a fast moving spring, she stopped to rest. Tall cattails and beautiful flowers bordered the spring's banks.

Sipping the clear, refreshing water, she caught sight of several small fish darting from plant to plant. They nibbled whatever drops of food came their way. She rubbed her thighs.

She was getting hungry. From the bush overhead she plucked a fig, then another.

₧₧₧₧₧₧₧₧

Sarai, wanting a hot bowl of porridge, shouted for Hagar to bring her one. When Hagar failed to answer, she shouted again, this time louder, rousing the attention of the women nearby. Curious, angry, Sarai whipped the tent's flap open.

The men stopped their work and organized a search party for her. Avram split the groups, sending them toward various locations throughout the countryside.

Hagar, tossing the center of the fig into the water, watched as its impact forced the water to form one expanding circle after another in rapid motion. Smiling at her freedom, she tossed a second fig into the water. Its rippling circles inexplicably met the image of a man who was standing beside her.

"Sir, I did not hear your approach," she stated, a bit frightened. Then, seeing the kind eyes, the gentle smile, the handsome face, she blushed.

"Hagar," he spoke, surprising her, "maid of Sarai, where did you travel from? Where are you heading?"

Hagar, studying the man, instantly felt comfortable with him. She instinctively knew he meant her no harm. She easily confessed, "I am running away from Sarai, my mistress."

Yahweh's angel soothingly replied in a near-hypnotic voice, "Return to Sarai. Subject yourself to her mean treatments. Many children will be brought forth from your issue. Too many to count.

"You will bear a male child. He shall be named Yishmael, for Yahweh has heard your pleas."

Then the angel pronounced Yahweh's prophecy:

"A wild ass of a man he shall be compared to.

"His hand will war against every man's hand.

"Yet, he shall dwell alongside his brothers in this land."

In the childbearing tent all the family heads gathered together to witness the passing of Hagar's newborn son to Sarai. Avram, standing in front of the men, opened his arms to Sarai when she approached him carrying in her arms the newborn son. Two days later Hagar called Avram into her tent.

"You now have your son. Keep Sarai's promise to me."

Avram nodded, affectionately touching her forehead.

"Did you name him what I told you to?"

Yes, Hagar, I did. Our son is Yishmael, exactly as the angel's words commanded us to name him."

Thereafter, Sarai and Avram ignored Hagar. Avram placed Yishmael in their tent where he and Sarai raised him while Hagar spent her years isolated from them.

Yishmael lived to be 137 years old, then he died.

Chapter Sixteen

▼

New Truths

This is Yitzhak's story.

In the year 1918 BCE, when Avram was ninety-nine years old, Yahweh again appeared.

"I am El Shaddai—God Almighty.

"Continuously walk within the boundaries of My law! Strive to become blameless in all things and in all actions. Do this so I may establish My contract between us. Do these things, and I will make you a father of nations!

"This shall constitute our bonds: As you will become the progenitor of many countries, you will no longer be called Avram. Rather, you shall now be called Abraham. I will make you exceedingly numerous: 'Av Hamon Goyyim.' I will enrich your semen and reproductive powers. Kings will be born from your loins. Today, I will renew my covenant between us. I will automatically keep this covenant in force between Myself and your offspring. It shall be an everlasting contract throughout the centuries!

"I will place Myself forever as your God and, as the God of your offspring to come!

"I will give to you the land which you have traveled through—to you, and to your offspring to come.

"All the land of Canaan will be yours till time indefinite.

"I will be the God of your offspring to come.

"Furthermore, as for you, and for your offspring to come; you shall maintain My covenant throughout the centuries.

"Such shall be the covenant between Me and you, and your offspring to come.

"This contract shall be kept.

"Every man among you will be circumcised.

"You will circumcise the flesh of your foreskin.

"This shall serve as the symbol of our eternal contract between Me and you.

"Throughout the coming centuries every man among you will be circumcised at the age of eight days.

"This covenant of circumcision must also apply to all the male slaves who are born into your household and even to all the males who are purchased outside your home.

"Thus shall My covenant be testified to on the flesh of your penis as an eternal bond.

"If any man is not circumcised and, if he fails to remove the flesh from the forefront of his penis, that man shall be expunged from the house of his brothers and the house of his father. He has broken My covenant.

"Concerning Sarai your wife: you shall no longer call her Sarai. Her name will become Sarah.

"I will also bless her.

"Most assuredly, she shall bear you a son!

"She will be blessed and she shall give issuance to many nations.

"Great rulers will come from the recesses of her bowels."

Avram, caught in the circumstances of the conversation, fell down to his face, laughing with great joy. On covering his face with his hands he saw the reality of his aged and dried flesh. Starring into the cups of his palms, he shook his head, disagreeing again with Yahweh.

"Allow, please, for Yishmael to become your favorite son! I am nearly a hundred years old. Sarai is ninety years old!"

Yahweh answered: "Regardless of those facts, Sarah shall indeed issue forth a son to you. He will be called Yitzhak. I will maintain My contract with him and with his offspring to come. Yitzhak shall become My favorite son."

That very same day Abraham did what Yahweh instructed him to do. Yishmael was thirteen years old during this time.

Abraham wrapped his index finger and his thumb over the foreskin that grew beyond the head of the penis and stretched it out as far as he could. With the sharpest obsidian he swiftly cut the flesh off.

The other men, watching, jerked back at the sudden sputtering of blood. Nevertheless, taking turn after turn, all the men obeyed.

☥☣☥☣☥☣☥☣☥☣

Weeks later, Yahweh again appeared to Abraham.

This happened while he was sitting near the entrance flap of his tent that was pitched near the resinous trees of Mamre. Mamre is the same Amorite whom Abraham bonded a close friendship with and he is the same one who allied himself and his warriors to defend Avram and his family during troublesome times.

This particularly hot, stifling, acrid and stilled afternoon the smell of the rams and goats and sheep lay heavy in the nostrils of the shepherds.

Beyond, on the dwindling carpet of grass, three men walked toward Abraham. The sun's rays prevented him from clearly seeing them. Their figures appeared as an unfocused blur. Gradually their forms became clearer.

Abraham knew who they were. He became excited. He ran to them waving his hands and calling for them to stop. When he reached their path, he immediately bowed to the ground and wrapped small strands of grass between his fingers.

"I know who you are," Abraham exclaimed.

"How do you know us?" the leader asked.

"I can discern it. A man bonded with the Most High God can instantly recognize all his brothers and sisters and all those who are aligned with Him. Together we serve Yahweh."

The three spiritual-beings stopped to study the human.

"You," he pointed to the middle angel, "lead the other two. You are the strongest and where you move, they follow. You are Michael the Archangel. You," he pointed to the angel on the left side, "intellectually questioned me. You are Gabriel. You," he pointed to the third, "keep yourself at a distance from me. Yet, you observe everything and absorb everything. What you see, you surmise and act accordingly. I do not know your name."

"It is a precious name. A name to be kept silent."

Abraham nodded. "I will refer to you three collectively as Yahweh."

The lead angel smiled.

"Then, Yahweh," he directed to the lead angel, "please, do not pass by my camp without respecting my formal greetings. Allow me, please, to serve you a refreshing cup of water. Allow me, please, to remove your sandals so I may wash the dirt from your feet. Please, relax under my tree's shade. The wind there is cool, invigorating."

The lead angel looked at the two angels behind him. Abraham, desiring their company, continued: "I have fresh baked cakes. Eat to your content. Afterwards, if it must be, continue with your journey—but first, allow us to be together, seeing that you are already on this road and that my tent is already pitched?"

"That seems reasonable enough."

After Abraham hastened back to his tent, he requested to Sarah, "Please, make us some cakes. You'll need about twenty quarts of our choicest flour."

Abraham hurried to the pastures, where a clearing had been cut from the forest. Nearby, he quickly spotted a prime calf. "Boy," he commanded to the herdsman's son, "prepare this calf for my meal."

After he made them comfortable under the shade of the oak tree, Abraham personally served them his choicest wine. Encouraging them to eat heartily, he cut the tenderloins into large sections. Over the tenderloins he placed the succulent beef tongue. He went from guest to guest to guest, personally handing them generous portions of veal. Whenever their cups began emptying he refreshed them again from his personal wine collection. Finally, the three began relaxing under the huge, cooling branches of the oak tree. The guests sat on the finest red blankets, patiently listening to Abraham. Several hours later the leader inquired, "Where is Sarah, your wife?"

"She's resting in the tent."

He nodded his head, appreciating her effort in the meal's preparation. "Next year I will return to you. At that time your wife Sarah will already have had her son."

Sarah, eavesdropping on the conversation from her nearby tent began laughing, saying in a soft whisper, "I have long ago ceased menstruating. I can no longer respond to my husband's sexual play for I am old. My inside portion is dry and his insertion too painful to tolerate."

Yahweh heard Sarah's quiet speech. He asked, "Why did Sarah laugh?"

Abraham shrugged his shoulders and remained silent. Nervously, he shifted his position, once, twice, then again. Finally, he stood up and walked to his wife. With their eyes on each other, they understood what the other was thinking. Both refrained from answering the angel.

"Sarah said," Yahweh's messenger reminded them, insisting on clarifying the intent of the speech, "'In truth, will I bear a son, even as old as I am?'

"Abraham, answer me: Is there anything on the earth that is too extraordinary for Yahweh to accomplish?"

Abraham again stayed silent, this time staring into the angel's eyes. He averted his stare to a tree's outstretching limbs, one actually overgrowing into another, forcing itself under a thicker branch. "Strange," he thought, "why doesn't the branch grow around the trunk rather than trying to punch a hole through it?"

The leader restructured his words, "Abraham, indeed I will return to you here at this exact time next year, and Sarah will indeed have had a son."

Sarah, shaking, darted from behind the tent's flap and ran in front of the angel. She held her hands to her chest, blurting out a lie, "I did not laugh!"

The angel smiled. He affectionately touched her cheeks, as an old friend would touch the cheeks of a young girl. The angel understood the duress of the moment. He understood her fear of losing something precious due to an unintended mistake.

"Sarah, you did lie," he spoke softly, yet firmly and decisively. He placed his fingers on her lips then shook his head, quieting her from adding another word.

The other two angels rose from their seats and walked toward the road leading to the Valley of Siddim. Abraham accompanied them.

"Abraham," Yahweh's personal messenger began halfway through the trip, "shall I keep from you what I am committed to do? Especially considering that you are to become a great and populous nation and that all the nations of the earth are to bless themselves by the very action of your being? They shall all admit, 'Yahweh has determined that it is going to be you from out of all the men of the earth who is to teach, and who is to convey, and who is to manifest to his children and to his household what I want to be conveyed'.

"You must, therefore, keep sacred in your heart what is righteous as determined by Yahweh. You must dispense justice as Yahweh determines it to be. You must do all this because Yahweh has chosen you to represent

Himself and His purpose for man's salvation from the death trappings of sin. Do these things so Yahweh may cause that which has been promised to actually occur."

"Reveal to me what You intend to do."

"The sins of Zeboiim, of Sedom, and of Amorah are terrible. Their immorality outrages Me! Every day my messengers reveal to Me their transgressions. I am going to observe their sins against Me. If they are innocent, I will go My way."

"Yahweh," Abraham inquired, thinking of the deluge, wondering if the outcries of the good angels against those cities could cause the destruction of the earth. Will You destroy the innocent along with the guilty?" He swept back his long black and silver hair from his face and ears. His braided temple hairs flicked to his eyes. Yahweh didn't answer.

"Yahweh, Melchizedek taught me about the deluge. He taught me that billions of human beings perished. Women and children and newborn babies drowned. Did any of them beg for their lives? Did any of them offer to repent at the last minute?

"Even if they had not, wasn't there more than just one good family?

"Tell me, what if there are fifty innocent persons in the city? Will You still destroy it and will You fail to forgive the sins of the multitude on account of the fifty? I cannot conceive You doing such a thing! How are you able to destroy the city even though there are fifty good persons in it?

"Equaling the good with the bad! Could such a thought really be within You? Could it be that the Judge of the earth will not deal with justice?"

Yahweh answered as a friend talking with a friend, "If I find in the City of Sedom, or in the city of Amorah, or in the city of Zeboiim, or in the entirety of the Valley of Siddim, fifty innocent people, I will forgive the region and the three cities for the sake of the fifty."

"Allow me, please, another appeal. I know I am nothing more than dust and ashes. I know that I cannot dare say I understand anything at all; yet, please, grant me this hearing: What if there are only forty-five good persons within Sedom's kingdom? Will you truly sweep away the region and cities because five of the fifty are not righteous?"

"I will not destroy them if I discover forty-five righteous people."

Carried away by the drama of the action, Abraham began pleading. His thoughts turned to his nephew Lot, to his wife and to their daughters. He thought of the babies of the people. "How is it possible for such new newborns and youngsters to be guilty of committing sins against Yahweh?" He thought of the old and sick and of those who easily became influenced by their peers. Again, Abraham insisted on speaking. "What if there are only forty people there who can meet your expectations?"

"I will step away on account of the forty."

"Please, do not become angry against me, Yahweh, if I ask this: What if there are only thirty people who are good?"

"I will not destroy the cities on account of the thirty."

"Again, and I apologize, but let me ask, for I must know this: What if there are only twenty people?"

"I will not destroy the cities nor the region for the sake of the twenty."

"I am compelled to ask, for I cannot stop thinking these thoughts, and this shall be my last time asking You: What if only ten are found there?"

"I will walk away if ten are found in the entirety of the Valley of Siddim."

ಬಿೞೞಬಿೞೞಬಿೞಙೞಬಿೞ

While Abraham spoke with Yahweh during the first light of the day, Lot greeted his herdsmen during their morning chores of tending to the cattle's needs and to the grazing of the sheep. By now all the herdsmen knew the routes through the forest and where the hidden bitumen rested under the lakes.

Hundreds of cattle pastured among the valleys' trees. Farther up the hills, at the places where the forest turned to savanna, the sheep ate the barley down to the very knobs of the sandy soil.

In the king's park, where the forest hid small enclaves of barley, a few curious shepherds from Amorah decided to relax from their work. While the sheep were idling, the men drank from skins of ale. Through the lazy afternoon their shirts became soaked from the dribbling streams of ale. Stinking, the shepherds stripped themselves free of their tunics.

The shepherds stared at each other's naked bodies and the sight of one another caused them to laugh. Then, a wicked thought came into their minds as they glanced about their area. When they saw the meek sheep, a few men ran to them and tied a few to the trees. Without a care in the world as to who was watching, the men had vagina intercourse with the sheep. When the young children saw what the older men were doing to the animals they went to the darkest woods where they stripped and performed the identical sin.

The boy-king poured a bowl of violet dust on the fires and laughed as the smoke rose high, mingling with the clouds. The priests behind him, clapping their hands, commanded the boy's mother to lie before him. On so doing the musicians entered the room. On the music's start, dozens of naked, heavily buxom women danced a frenzied, arousing, stimulating performance for their audience. Soon, the hall became enmeshed in an orgy.

Outside the palace, Lot's wife busily instructed her chief steward on the trade's price for their bitumen and animal skins to the Egyptian merchants. After the contracts were concluded and the agreements finalized, she gave them to the chief steward of the house. Next she went to the main street of the city, to the merchant's row that she controlled. The merchants, exhausted from their day long haggling with the customers, were not happy to see Lot's wife. Surrendering to her privileged position, the merchants paid her the weekly rent for the stalls. Going from stall to stall she inspected the tally of their wares, making sure they did not cheat her on her rent. Satisfied, she dismissed them.

In the City of Amorah, young naked men prostituted themselves to the arriving caravans. The aged homosexuals, walking among the young ones, failed to attract the middle-aged customers. This day presented too many handsome young men for them to compete against. Unable to secure any money, the aged homosexuals offered to the rich and influential caravan masters their own sons and daughters.

In Zeboiim the gardens of the streets were luxuriantly beautiful. Dozens of brilliantly carved fountains cascaded multiple streams of water into deep pools. A grand display of carved, erogenously naked women embracing other naked women dominated the center square. From their nipples and from their vaginas clear, cool water freely flowed. The rays of the afternoon sun played with the mists of water. The sprinkling fountains bathed the carved bodies of the naked pre-teenage girls and boys in a sub-dued beauty that heightened the sexual senses of the people viewing them. The children, tempting the tourists, whetted their appetites further by associating food with sex. Behind the statues sweet-smelling inns cooked delightful batches of food. The tourists, seeing the fountains of children holding baskets of fruits to the sun, entered the inns.

On the fountain steps that glorified its prostitutes, real flesh and blood young girls and teenage women and mothers reclined nakedly. The women leaned back on their elbows against piles of soft pillows and spread their legs wide open. When the approaching visitors saw them sitting below the fountains and when they smelled the food, they entered the dark inns. Once settled down and comfortable, the older women tried to compete with the younger women. The eldest among them hurriedly offered their mouths and rectums for half the price of the younger women. The younger women, wanting to impress the priests, offered the tourists their sisters and partners for the price of one. Many offered them-selves, or their sister, or their youngest brother for the same price. The old-est and ugliest, unable to compete, offered the visitor their homes, their parents, themselves, and anything else they wanted, plus a meal, for the same price.

Some merchants looked at the fountain, then at the real girls, and wondered why the real ones couldn't be as beautiful as the stone ones.

In all three cities and throughout the roads that led from the Valley to the cities, sculptured fertility statuettes with large marble bowls in front of them waited patiently for the visitor. Multicolored and varied fragrant incense burned in the middle of the bowl. After the victorious campaign against Chedorlaomer incense burned perpetually in throughout the cities.

Near the entry gates large phallic poles stood. The men of righteousness who passed by, hid their children's eyes from the horrid view. The wives of the righteous spat at them. Not one of them settled in the city. Not one returned to do commerce with the citizens. They raised their voices in protest to Yahweh, who hearing enough, sought to rid the earth of the sinners.

The sinners ignored the righteous and laughed at them. Then one day it happened that a grand festive celebration was to take place throughout the region. All the righteous left the area when they heard of its approach. The main citizens of the Valley painted their faces red and purple while the leaders tattoo their bodies with snakes, lions, pigs, or quail.

All the row houses had their front exterior walls plastered with gold and purple colorings. The wood roofs were painted green—the floors, a radiant blue. The interior walls had antelopes fantastically having sex with lions and cattle eating sheep and sheep eating pigs and pigs eating the men who were dangling upside down from phallic poles.

The times that they did wear clothes, they dressed themselves in the most elegant silks with the gaudiest necklaces and bracelets and forearm bands.

Then, with the approach of noon, as the sun was peaking at its zenith, the fifty thousand citizens of the Valley retreated to their homes to sleep, preparing for the night's festivities.

Lot's daughters, knowing the safety of their garden, waited impatiently for their betroths to come to them.

As it happened, Lot's house was the biggest and the richest in the City of Sedom. His manicured garden blossomed with dozens of crocuses. A beautiful circle of yellow and violet flowers hugged a grand fountain that greeted the visitor at the entry gate. It's delicate balance of leaping fish gave an impression of the house's hospitality. An even larger fountain in the center of the backyard announced to the viewer that Lot's house was a safe haven for the weary traveler and an escape from the city's wicked infestations.

Bountiful fruit trees and grape arbors lined his northern wall. The other three walls had thorny plants growing against them to discourage a would-be intruder. All four walls were over twelve-feet high. In front of the entry a massive iron gate stopped the intruders of the night from gaining an unwelcomed entry. The curious passerbyers, wanting to see what they couldn't, always stopped to peer through the gaps in the iron bars. By twisting their heads a few could see a small glimpse of his living room. Outside the second floor an intricately carved balcony precariously hung from the exterior wall. Its sole purpose was to hold the carefully arranged flowering vines.

Lot finally returned from the fields and uneasily entered a series of nearly deserted streets.

The air was crisp and the smells of the flowers were intoxicatingly fragrant. Coming to the first stall by the roadside, he checked to make sure it was empty of the wares which he had earlier assigned to the merchant to sell. From there he proceeded to the second and third stalls. From each stall he pocketed his day's profits from the merchants. Near the end of that day he stopped in front of his iron gate where he took a sheep skin of water from his donkey's pouch to quench his thirst.

Evening rapidly approached. The sun quickly lowered into the horizon.

Lot wiped his brow clean of the sweat and happened to glance in the direction of the three angels. Instantly recognizing the leader, he dropped the water skin to the ground.

"Michael," he whispered. At the same time he lowered his head to the ground in full respect and humility.

"Righteous Lot," Michael the Archangel replied, "peace be with you and on your house."

"Peace be also with you," Lot returned the salutation. "Lords, please, follow me and enjoy the hospitality of my house. Spend the night with my family. Allow us to bathe your feet and refresh your hunger and to quench your thirst. In the morning, continue your journey."

"No, thank you. We intend to spend the night in the middle of the town, near the trading square."

"Why? This night is the Night of Yesterdays' and Tomorrows' Festivities. Why would you want to be in the middle of such a degrading spectacle?"

"We came to witness the celebration."

"Why be involved with such evil? Please, travel with me to my home. It is a safe haven for you. I have high walls and an iron gate. I have fine wine and geese and antelope meats. If you prefer, I can get calf meat or whatever else you desire. I do beg you, with all earnestness, please, stay with me. I cannot bear the thought of you spending the night in the merchant square."

"We must be in the square."

"If you must be there, I too must be there with you. I will alert my men to be with you as well."

"There is no need for that," Michael the Archangel finally consented. "We will accompany you."

The youngsters of the city, being the first to wake from their afternoon's nap, saw the three strangers walking alongside Lot. Gasping at their flowing hair, at the smoothness of their skin, at their muscularity and broad height and extremely handsome features, the children ran to tell their sisters. They, in turn, ran to their pimps, who in turn ran to see whether or not they were lying.

"We can chain them and make a hefty profit," the chief pimp told his men.

"Yes, their asses seem ripe enough."

"Get a few more men. Not everyone, however. We want this joy to be kept just among us. For now, anyway."

The homosexuals went to their friends, whispering the news of the three beautiful men. They, in turn, spread the word to as many others as they could.

Those, not hearing, saw the growing crowd. Curious and wanting to know if a different kind of party was in the making, they eagerly followed the men in front of them.

The pimps gathered before the iron gate and kept twisting their heads to see into Lot's living room. They watched as Lot cleaned the men's feet.

His hands gently moved between the angels' toes and behind their ankles and up their calves. Aroused, the pimps crowded closer to the gate. Each wanted to look at the sight. Excited, their penises hardened. The pimps shouted, "Lot, bring those men out to us!"

Lot jumped up from his place and looked at the huge crowd of men and boys pushing against his iron gate. They struggled with the hinge until they finally broke it free from the wall. Swarming inside his courtyard the men rushed to the oak door, banging frantically on it.

"Get those men out to us! Can't you see our hard penises," one screamed as he dropped his tunic to show off his huge, stiff erection. The crowd, laughing, also imitated the man. The women, when they heard the commotion, they laughed at the sight as did the youngsters.

"My friends," Lot pleaded, "please, do not place me in such a position by wronging my guests. Many of you know me! Many of you work for me and rent my stalls. You know you have always met fairness with fairness. Leave these men alone!"

"Lot, we are sick of your stupid morality. You call us '*friend*,' yet you are never in the square with us. You never eat with us. You never say a simple 'congratulations' during our birthday celebrations nor even a kind 'Happy

Holidays' when we celebrate our holiest days! You have never sucked our penis nor had any of us insert our erections inside your buttocks!"

"I trade fairly with you," Lot stated, not knowing what else to say, as if his fair practices were all that was necessary to quell the vicious circle.

"Always to your own profit. Who among us has such a wonderful house? Who among us receives such handsome guests? Share them with us, and your friendship will be true with us."

Lot briefly stared at the used and miserable looking prostitutes who were crowding into his courtyard. He went to his two daughters. "I am beside myself today. I don't know what to do."

"We cherish the law of hospitality. Offer us, Father, to quell their appetites."

"Mother, do you agree?"

She concurred. "Our guests shall not be harmed without our trying to prevent it."

"Sodomites, I have an answer for you," Lot raised his voice. "I have two beautiful daughters. They are both virgins. I know many of you have always desired them. I willingly present them to you. Do whatever pleases you with them. They will not resist anything. However, swear an oath to me beforehand: no harm of any kind will befall these men who are in the sanctuary of my house."

"Enough! Who are you but a damnable foreigner! You manipulate us with your salesman's words and take advantage of us all the time. In reality, you think you are superior to us! You desire to make yourself our king! Well, shithead, not only are we going to rape their asses, and your daughters' and wife's, but more so, yours."

The pimp, pushing hard against the thick oak door, began overpowering Lot, forcing it steadily to open wider. The angels, gathering together the terrorized daughters and fear-stricken mother, walked directly behind Lot. Grabbing his shoulder, they pulled him quickly inside. With an effortless push they slammed the door of the house shut.

"I am sorry," Lot tearfully stated to Michael. Lot hugged his wife and children to him. They all cowered behind the table.

Michael the Archangel peered over the frail balcony to observe the manners of the hundreds of old men and young girls and teenage boys and aging women and young men and older women. Among that vast crowd he distinguished the boy-king and his naked mother and the rest of the youngsters who were pointing to him in stark mockery.

"What you see, see no more," he spoke. A sudden series of swift lightning bolts struck out from Michael's hands, flashing instantly in front of the crowds' eyes, brightening the courtyard for a brief second.

The crowd groped about, trying to distinguish what objects they could with their fingers. Bumping into one another and into the walls and into the iron gates' sharp points, they stopped moving about.

"Sit down, sit down," they whispered to each other: dazed, puzzled, confused.

"Who else is with you in this place?" Michael hurriedly asked Lot.

"Who else?" he repeated, uncertain of what was being asked. Releasing his wife, stepping away from his daughters, he looked at the crowd, trying to understand what just happened.

"You have two men who are betrothed to your daughters?"

"Yes, yes, the contracts are signed."

"Anyone else?"

"No, no one."

"That's eight people total," Gabriel pointed out to Michael.

"Under ten," the third angel confirmed.

"Lot, hurry to their house. Bring them here!"

"What is going to happen?"

"We're going to destroy this Valley. The outrages of Zeboiim, of Sedom, of Amorah are to great to continue. Yahweh has sent us here to cease the outcries of the righteous against the evil."

"Won't those men harm me?"

Michael replied, "Can the blind harm those seeing?"

Lot made his way around the groping fingers and flaying arms and left from his courtyard to the main street. Strangely, the people outside his gate weren't paying any attention to his house. When a few did see him, they ignored him and permitted him to pass freely through the streets to his friend's house.

The singing merrymakers busily poured ale over each other. The women, embracing several men simultaneously, laughed at the man hurriedly rushing in front of them.

Frantically banging on his friend's door, he roused them from the back room.

"It's the third hour of the evening, Lot. Why are you here? Especially at this time. You never venture outside your home during the Night of Yesterdays' and Tomorrows' Festivities."

Lot shouted back at him, moving as a man possessed: "Angels are in my home! They've blinded the whole city! We need to get out of here! NOW! NOW! NOW!"

"Lot," the father shouted. "Calm down! We're not leaving!"

"Where are your sons?"

"Boys! Come here!" the father called out. "Lot is here to see you!"

"Lot?"

"Be quick! He's acting too abnormally for me to tolerate him much longer. Find out what he's talking about."

"Sons, we must leave this city this very moment!" Lot begged the groggy men.

"What are you saying?"

"The angels are going to destroy this city!"

The eldest son began snickering. His father, hearing him, broke out laughing. "Lot, what a funny way to greet us into your family. I didn't think you had the jester's spirit!"

"Wonderful!" the mother clapped. She held her hands to her mouth and bent over in an unstoppable fit of laughter. "Wonderful! Wonderful performance."

"I'm not joking!" Lot shouted, spittle coming at the end of his sentence.

"All the more funnier. Look at his eyes! My, how they bulge! Who taught you such a trick."

"Yahweh," he whispered, ceasing his shouts. "He's going to destroy everything."

"You and Yahweh," the youngest son spoke between his laughter. "Father, go on home. We appreciate your joke on us. Well done!"

As the morning began forming, Lot slowly walked through his gate's entrance.

The pimps and women and children who had invaded his courtyard had fallen asleep on top of each other. His wife and daughters, seeing him, ran to hug and kiss him on the neck.

"Where are our husbands-to-be? Their mother and father?"

"Their heart conditions were not suited to receive the gift of life. Rather than merely accept, they refuted me as well as God."

The two daughters looked at each other for long moments. The eldest wanted to run back to her man.

"Lot," Michael said as soon as he saw her feet face the street from where her father just returned, "take your wife and daughters and leave this land. The immorality is too great for this city to remain a moment longer than is necessary."

"I, I just don't know. I, I, should get some things first."

"There is nothing for you to carry away except your lives," said Gabriel.

"Husband," his wife injected, "what about my clothes and gold chains? My cooking pots?"

Michael the Archangel, unable to wait, seized Lot's wrist and forced him outside the city walls. The second angel grabbed his wife's hand, while the third angel took the two girls. All were placed outside.

"Run! Run for the safety of your souls! Do not look behind you! Do not stop for anything, anywhere on the road. Run to the hills! Run! Or perish!"

"No, my lord!" Lot panicking, screamed. "You have been kind and generous to your servant. You have already demonstrated extreme kindness to me so that you may save my life, but I cannot run fast enough to the hills. They are far from us and I will become exhausted! I, in my state, will collapse! I will be caught in the forces of destruction! Look! Look to the southeast. There is a small city there! It's not that far away! Please, let us run there!"

"It too is noted for destruction."

"But it's such a tiny place."

"All right. I will permit you this favor. I will not annihilate that place. But hurry! I cannot proceed with what I have to do until you are safe."

Lot obeyed the angel and began pushing his daughters and wife to the southwest where the forest opened toward deep meadows of grass. The family passed the red grape vineyards and rushed passed the fields of cabbages and ran passed the flock of sheep and resting cattle. They hurried beyond the clear, cool streams that fed into the large blue lake that rose beyond the protecting limestone walls of the Valley of Siddim.

"Don't stop!" he commanded his eldest daughter, who for some inexplicable reason had slowed down to look at a large fig tree.

His wife felt strange in the frantic. Automatically she rubbed her forearm then realized she forgot her arm-bands as well as her bracelets.

"Wait! We need to go back! I forget my gold and bars of silver! How can I conduct the day's business without my silver bars?"

Just at that moment, in the northern region of the Valley of Siddim the ground trembled with quickening waves. Just as the sea moves, so it occurred over the land's surface.

The fleeing family knocked and fell against each other.

"Keep running!" Lot commanded.

The sounds of the animals silenced. The earth quieted. The air stilled.

A pungent odor emitted from the crevice of the earth. Imperceptibly, the earth began moving. Gradually, the rolls of the land quickened, till it rumbled with a fury. A horrific explosion instantly overtook the land. A mountain erupted from the interior of the blue lake. The pungent odor that had slowly risen into the atmosphere now punctually spewed a sickening, stomach-wrenching vomit. Instantly a deafening roar followed. The sky ignited with blue flames and sulfuric outpourings from the volcano. The sulfuric cloud caught the forest and the grass meadows on fire. The down-pouring flames landed on the cattle and on the sheep and pigs and gazelle.

The flames stuck fast on the livestock skins and on the flesh of the running people.

ཀ᩠᩠᩠᩠᩠᩠᩠᩠᩠

As dawn broke over the lush, fertile valley, the citizens of Zeboiim woke extremely agitated. The violent shaking tossed many out of their beds. Many struggled to stand upright. Bodies quickly slammed into the side walls of the houses. Others, sleeping on the roofs' courtyards, rudely woke up. Uncertain of their steps, they fell from the rooftops into the flaming streets.

Before they could scream the scream of terror, the walls of their houses fell on top of them. Under the rubble and dust of the streets, crushed bodies momentarily jerked. Ruptured flesh and intestines and exposed livers and ejected hearts littered the ground. Kidneys and stomachs and brains splattered against the rolling construction bricks. Thick globs of blood spattered over the upheaved blocks of stone. Small children's bodies and the stiffened remains of newborn babies, clutching their mothers' necks, littered the streets.

The frightened and confused men rushed to the gates of the city of Zeboiim. There they met a flowing river of lava that rushed over their flaying arms. Others, fleeing to hide inside the massive walls of the palace, encountered the raining fire that catastrophically fell over them.

The boy-king tugged at his mother's skirt. He trembled in her arms and incapable of holding it back any longer, a horrific scream sounded out of his throat. A swift shadow descended over the mother and child. She turned to see the city's largest phallic monument fall directly on top of them.

Outside the city walls Lot's wife stumbled again. She rose but hesitated before she went on. She thought of her friends and of her preparations for the wedding feast for her daughters. She thought of all the gifts she had stored in her remote room.

As she reflected on the past, and as she dreamed of the future, she turned around. At that instant she saw a sulfuric cloud ball covering the valley. In that briefest moment, she saw Lot's terrified face.

ಬಚಚ್ಚಚ್ಚಚ್ಚಚ್ಚಚ

Far beyond the Valley of Siddim, Melchizedek and Eber ran to the clearing.

They watched the volcanic explosion in terror. Oddly, the sulfuric fires fell only toward the eastern horizon.

Other men stepped beside them, also witnessing Yahweh's fury taking shape against the sinners. Amazed, they watched as the lava raced toward Sedom and Amorah and Zeboiim, completely covering them over. They watched the fire's swift consumption of the trees and meadows. Even from their distant place they could hear the crackling forest fires. The stench of the destruction invaded their nostrils with an irremovable witness of the carnage.

The raging fires consumed the forest. The treetops danced with hungry yellow fingers. The black-gray atmosphere choked the sunlight away from man's eyes. The green meadows swiftly became blackened ash.

Continuous thunderstorms joined the volcanic eruptions, combining to an inescapable destruction for the citizens of the three cities. By evening the lightning bolts covered the horizon with an intense lavender.

The boiling waters of the blue lakes steamed, fogging the valley's interior bowl.

Explosions swiftly vibrated throughout the land. The mountain ridge, containing the blue lake above the Valley of Siddim, split asunder. As the waters arched, then spilled, then jettisoned into the valley, completely drowning it inside its perpetual waves.

"Another flood?" Eber asked Melchizedek.

"Yahweh promised my father it would never flood again."

"Destruction by fire," Eber concluded, nodding affirmatively.

ಬೃಙಬೃಙಬೃಙಬೃಙಬೃಙ

Abraham, Sarah, and Eliezer also watched the massive destructive of the three cities. An angry column of smoke colored the morning's sunrise, darkening the land. Aftershocks kept the inhabitants surrounding the Valley of Siddim off balance. Abraham stayed awake through the night watching the three cities blazing.

"Among fifty-thousand, not even five righteous people! Among their babies, their teenagers, their young, their old. Among the women, among the men, no, not even five!"

In the morning light he heard a rumble and stared in amazement as a wall of water burst over the landscape, burying everything underneath a sea of water. The natural dam that kept the water far from the valley thundered in a groan of terror as the frothing waves rolled and pitched over the trees and green land. The most fertile land in the east choked.

ಬೃಙಬೃಙಬೃಙಬೃಙಬೃಙ

Lot, penniless, went from Zoar's main street to the back roads. Studying the streets, he wondered which inn could best protect him from the howling night wind. Seeking refuge, he carefully explored the byway.

At the entry gates a large group of frightened people watched the spreading smoke overtaking the valley. A thick blanket of ash buried their streets. Dozens and dozens of roofs caved in from the fallout waste of the three destroyed cities.

A group of beggars, watching Lot and his daughters approaching them from beyond the hills of the deep valley where the destruction occurred, backed away from them.

Behind Lot's filthy figure, the bowl of the valley burned with unrelenting rage.

When the people observed Lot's torn tunic and the vicious bruises on his daughters' arms and faces, they gasped. Many wondered: "How is it possible that only they survived the cataclysm?"

Silently afraid, they stared at him and at his two daughters. Their eyes saw the torn tunics and smudged faces of the three survivors. As the three survivors crossed over the last hurdle, the crowd spread apart, allowing them ample room to walk through their ranks. The people refused to talk to Lot and his daughters.

When the youngest daughter staggered in front of a bread stall, a fat women slammed her door shut against her face, refusing to provide her a piece of bread.

Lot couldn't even raise his head to look at the people who cursed the large scratches on his knees. His cut and bruised legs testified of his horrific climb. His bleeding arms told of how the three had struggled to race up the cragged rocks.

Lot felt the intense hatred of the people. Regardless of it, he bravely kept walking forward into the midst of the city. Halfway inside, he finally stopped to look at his two daughters. They were famished. Their once beautiful curly hair clumped into tight, dirty strands.

"We cannot stay here. We must move on."

"To where?"

Lot pointed to the western hills and replied, "There. That's where Salem is. We need to go there."

"It's so far away," his eldest daughter protested.

"Then where do you suggest we go?" the harsh words slowly seeped out of his mouth.

Unable to answer, she shrugged. The she cast her head about and whined, "OK! OK! I guess that's where we'll go!"

The greenery of Zoar gradually gave way to the dry land that began appearing. The sulfuric smell repulsed the three. When Lot tasted the water, he spit it out. It was bitter. After a long time the surviving family found a clump of berry bushes. There the famished family ate all the berries as quickly as they could. A distance more they happened on some pomegranates. Lot squeezed the skin, rupturing the juice into his mouths.

Near nightfall Lot's youngest daughter caught the dark opening of a cave. Inside it Lot established a corner for himself while the girls gleaned whatever barley and straw they managed to find. Strides of depression overtook the family. That night no one slept.

In the morning Lot and his daughters determined to explore the mountain. The more they searched its surroundings, the more confused they became. Lot became uncertain of the mountain's path. The three foraged one trail after another, until Lot discovered an area of ripening grapes.

Near the wild and uncultivated vineyard Lot fashioned a stone chisel. Patiently he made a deep basin in a large limestone rock. After long hours he faced the valley which he had just escaped from. He saw the expanding waters rising toward the heights of his refuge. Hearing strange sounds, he peered into the sky. Large groups of vultures dived into the murky waters, retrieving pieces of flesh for themselves.

Stupefied, he entered a deep trance. Within this voyaging escape Lot saw his wife's eyes staring at him in utter terror. Reliving the moment, he watched her body transform from flesh to salt. Her skin and tendons hardened to stone. Transfixed by the nightmare's hold, he watched the solid stone that had been his wife moments ago, crumbling, disintegrating. The pillar of salt broke apart and merged with the ashes of the once lush forest and the once green meadows.

Depressed, Lot folded his head in his arms and started crying. The tears that fell from his eyes fell to the dying earth of the Valley.

Throughout the afternoon he cried tears of remorse, regret, and repentance. Throughout the night he cried tears of confusion. Throughout the morning he cried tears of anger.

By afternoon, he cried self-pitying tears.

The eldest daughter, seeing the grapes and the stone, spoke to her sister, "Our betrothed died in the grips of the eruptions and fires. Our father is ancient. He intends to take us to a city that is far from here and where it is said: 'the men do nothing but write books.' Who is left alive now who with us and who will give us pleasure? All those years I watched the women bare their breasts to the men. I watched them mount the waiting men. These women always laughed with an extreme and peculiar laughter that I have never known. Well, I want to know what sex feels like! And, Father is the only one who can provide me with its experience."

"Mother is dead. That I can agree with. Father cries for her. That I can also agree with. But there must be something we can do for him and for ourselves besides mounting on him?"

"The answer may be in the wine."

That same night, Lot's eldest daughter kept filling his cup. Unconcerned with the numerous cups, he kept consuming flask after flask. Lot, moaning within the deepest dark of the night, beseeched for his wife. His eldest daughter, hearing his whimpering cries, walked to his side. Impulsively she lifted his tunic past his waist and fixed her eyes on his penis. She heard a whisper in her ear telling her to lift her own tunic over her waist. She obeyed the voice and straddled herself over Lot's penis. She moved about and fidgeted with his erection until she managed to place it inside her. Softly moaning, she climaxed.

"Did you see what took place?" she asked her sister the following mid-afternoon.

"Yes, I watched. I heard the same sounds of the night that the other women used to make on the streets. I saw your body moving in such strange ways. Why?"

"The sex felt great. I never knew anything could feel that way. Tonight's your turn."

"I don't want to."

"You must do it. I did it. Think of it this way: if you don't do it, how is Father to get a son. You know he wants a son. Mom's dead. Who else can provide him a son but us?"

With the coming night, the younger daughter also intoxicated him. She also lifted his tunic over his waist and hers over her legs and straddled him.

In the morning's rise Lot woke to discover a wet spot beside him. Curious, he touched it. He rubbed the red liquid between his fingers. He leaned closer to examine the spot. Then he turned to look at his daughters. He stared at them as they stared at him. For an eternal moment the three remained silent. His eyes glanced at the ceiling of the cave where he discovered several cracks through which the sunlight filtered.

He grunted and left the cave in anger. For long moments he just stood still. His eyes found a few scorched trees. He walked to them and broke off a bundle of branches. With them Lot built a wall in the cave's far wall. After he finished he commanded his daughters, "Do not cross into my room. This is my privileged area. I will not violate your privacy, nor are you to violate mine."

ᴥᴖᴥᴖᴥᴖᴥᴖᴥᴖᴥᴖ

In the year 1918 B.C.E the older daughter bore Lot his firstborn son. Lot hurriedly picked him up from between his daughter's legs and carefully examined his body for defects and abnormalities. When he found none, he twisted and stretched the umbilical cord until it tore in half. Pleased, he touched the boy's forehead with his right thumb, naming his son Moab. Moab became the eponymous ancestor of the Moabites.

Lot named his younger daughter's son Ben-ammi. He became the progenitor of the Ammonites. Both were cousins of Yitzhak, Abraham's chosen heir.

Both cousins, in later centuries, waged war against Yisrael. And Satan laughed at the power of his own interference.

ೞೞೞೞೞೞೞೞೞೞ

Directly after the column of smoke blanketed the valley with ash and sulfuric clouds, its pungent odor hovered about the land as if an inescapable linen cloth shrouded the entire world.

On a particular day, Melchizedek, overlooking the valley, happened to see Abraham advancing on the mountain trail toward his house.

Sighing a long breath, the priest-king called Abraham to speak with him. "I need your personal testimony of what happened."

Abraham looked over the new expanse of water and nodded. The acrid, pungent smell of the disaster still hung thickly in the air. The contemptuous atmosphere of the Sodomites, Gomorrahites, and the Zeboiimans, who seared their moral consciousness, hung over the thoughts of the survivors.

Abraham motioned his hand toward a shadowed enclave under the great branches of an oak tree where the two went to converse.

Together, the king-priest and the prophet reviewed the immoral practices of the inhabiters of the land. Their perversions had become a constant in their daily lives. Their habitual badness infected every viewer.

Traveling merchants, learning from them what they never would have conceptualized on their own, carried the vile thoughts with them back to their lands. There they, in turn, inflicted the practices on their partners. Thus, the practices became universal. God, hating the immoralities, personally intervened to clean the land.

After Abraham finished his accountings of the event, Melchizedek thoughtfully stated, "Thank you, Abraham for traveling to me for this accurate accounting. Unquestionably, we now know that homosexuality can never be tolerated by our laws and society. We must shun and excommunicate it from our camps. If the homosexuals fail to leave, we are permitted, by Yahweh's direction, to stone them to death. May all sinners similarly perish."

And even though the judges of the land were empowered to exercise the decree of death against sinners, many judges decreed merciful sentences of punishment.

"Tell me, Abraham," Melchizedek said, "the slaves which you purchased from the Sodomites, are they vile or innocent?"

"Many were once practicing homosexuals. They shunned women for men. However, after I have professed to them my beliefs and taught them Yahweh's exacting fortitudes, they accepted His laws. After they understood the reasoning behind God's laws, they allowed me to circumcise them. They repented of their homosexual ways and I accept them in the fold of righteousness. Not one man in my camp hates those who had sinned. In my camp prejudice does not exist. The slaves which I purchased, I freed."

"Abraham, many people, however, are dismayed by your presence. You sold a lot of meat and wool and skins and threading to the Sodomites and Gomorrahites and Zeboiimans."

"The meat fed them. The wool and skins and threads clothed them. What man does not need to eat or have clothes over his flesh?"

"Yes, even though you never lived among them, many priests may disbelieve you are totally free of their corruption. Hagar is a case in point. You have never married her and your son Ishmael displays feminine behavior. The Sodomites immorality is insidious and infectious."

"As I said, my camp is free of sin."

"No camp is free of sin. I advise this: keep a careful watch on your son. Cultivate him toward masculine activities."

Abraham nodded, respecting the advice.

"Abraham, I have written your account of the matter. I shall return to my house. And you, dearest son, must journey to the Torrent Valley of Gerar."

"Is there anything else I can do for you?"

"There is only that which must be done. May Yahweh bless your path and keep your spirit righteous."

"Blessed is Yahweh's name," Abraham returned.

From the terebinths of Mamre, Abraham sojourned through the lush hills to the vast, rich, and fertile fruit and olive groves and barley pastures of Gerar. Slightly distant from Gerar the hills of Judea began ascending. Eight miles west lay the Sea of the Philistines.

Chapter Seventeen

▼

The Minoans

Gaza, the fortified coastal city northwest of Salem, appeared to the Minoan sailors as a welcoming jewel from the distant curvature of the sea. The Minoans, settling in the region, established a colony directly in front of the Canaanites. Swiftly the small fortress grew with the oriental merchants' visits. Where once no boat sailed, large ships floated to the docks. Where once only empty coastlines welcomed the lonely soldiers, large warehouses brimming with wools and rugs and spices and aromatic perfumes and obsidian and copper greeted dozens of ships.

The Minos, making sure the coastal city remained under his control and jurisdiction, authorized an *'Abimelech'* to rule the new province. The title authorized the ruler to act independently of the Minos while maintaining sole authority over the region. Similarly, the Minos presented a title to the military general, calling him *'Phicol.'*

From the top of the stone the soldiers, appreciating the cooling breeze from the seashore, vigilantly patrolled the shores and docks and houses and citizens and merchants. Their red-and-yellow-feathered headdresses and paneled kilts with hanging tassels swayed steadily with the wind's force. The corsets that wrapped around their chests seemed to the young children a menacing fright. To the thin-waisted women, who collected the murex shells, the soldiers presented to them a strong assurance that they would be safe.

The older women, popping open the necks of the mollusks, squeezed the creamy fluid into a large receptacle. The youngest daughters, watching the substance drip from the destroyed life-form, giddied when the drops changed to a deep purple.

"What pretty flowers," a child remarked.

"How many shellfish do we need to fill the receptacle?" another child asked.

"Tens of thousands. We'll be needing many more hours today before we can rest."

While the mother taught her children how to rupture open the large mollusk's necks, other children crushed the smaller mollusks inside a mortar to retrieve their creamy fluid.

As the women worked the wool threading and the sheepskins into the boiling water they faced the sea to receive its cooling caresses. "How much will you pay us," their cried as merchants passed by, for only the richest of traders could afford their labor.

To the left, on the drying platforms, mounds of kermes waited to be placed in the boiling vats to release the kermestic acid used in their dyeing process. A large pile of almond leaves and ground pomegranate skins and turmeric and safflower and madder plant roots and indigo plants also waited to be used in the dye manufacturing. Inside the warehouses deep accumulations of arsenic and tin, used for mordants, waited to be shipped to the Egyptians.

ᏅᏣᏅᏣᏅᏣᏅᏣᏅᏣ

In the Island of Caphtor, that is, Crete, the Minoan ruler presented his best and most courageous explorers his gratitude for the extensive jugs of purple dye that lined his harbors. A new formula, vermilion, also appeared in his collection of dyes. Happy, proud, he went into his palace. A group of dignitaries followed closely behind.

"What lies beyond Cyprus?" the blue-eyed and fair skinned ruler asked his brave explorers.

"Malta," the chief naval officer answered.

"And beyond?"

"Our ships are investigating. We'll know within the year."

"How is our northern outpost? The one directly above Egypt?"

"We have taken control of the coast. The Avvim accept us."

"And the Canaanites?"

"They also accept us. I believe we may be able to form an alliance with them against the Egyptians—should it be necessary to fight, that is."

"Are there any other nations that can meet our requirements? Should it become necessary, who can protect us against the Avvim and the Canaanites and, at what cost?"

"Are you proposing we commit ourselves to secret treaties?"

"Yes. One with every tribe. Whatever tribe battles with whomever, we'll help them through a careful selection of mercenaries. That way all nations will leave us alone. Whenever they need help, we'll rise up, and take everything for ourselves. No one will ever need to know for whom the foreign soldiers fight nor where the money came from.

"Our trade routes with India and the Far East and with the South and with the North will be guaranteed. Send word to the Abimelech and to his Phicol to be generous with the locals. In time, we'll be where we want to be."

ಬಿಜ಼ಬಿಜ಼ಬಿಜ಼ಬಿಜ಼ಬಿಜ಼

The Great Sea's trade winds carried ten small ships to the banks of Gaza. Fires continuously burned on the seashore. To let a fire extinguish was to suffer death. Large piles of murex shells and large assortments of carved ivory filled the storage houses. Behind the huts, dozens of well-armed men protected thousands of cedar planks and beams.

With the tide's rise the ships slowly crept inland. The sailors, on the bow's docking, instantly secured it to the harbor's posts. The captain of the fleet, after disembarking, turned his nose away from the land. His nostrils flared and his eyes became watery.

"What is that stench?"

"It's sulfur. It travels everywhere. The sunsets are strangely colored."

"Where's it coming from?"

"A volcanic eruption southeast of here, it seems."

"Volcanic eruptions? We seem to be cursed by them. Some of the Aegean Islands which I explored two years ago had ash and lava spewing to the seas. What a sight! Somehow, if I knew how, there must be a way of fashioning weapons from that liquid metal."

"What kind of metal?"

"I don't know. It's silver when it hardens, but impossible to extract from the earth. It never lasts, though. The water eats it away."

"So what good is the metal?"

"It's the hardest I've ever felt. It'll make a good sword."

"Ah, not if it rusts away!"

Abraham, meanwhile, had loosened his cattle from their pens to roam freely in Gerar. His herdsmen, excavating more wells, chiseled Abraham's name deep into the stone's surface so no one could violate or counter his legality to the water and the surrounding land.

The Philistines, advancing their caravan deeper into the torrent valley, heard the cries of the cattle. As they neared, they saw Abraham's tents pitched throughout Gerar.

"Report this at once to the Abimelech," the camel master instructed his assistant.

The wives of the Abimelech, when they heard the shouting man, watched the camel racing through the sand dunes. Quickly they alerted their husband. He touched their expanding stomachs and gently smiled. All were pregnant.

The Abimelech was concerned by the news, but he mildly asked the messenger, "When did they pitch their tents?"

"During the week."

"Are they entitled to do that?" the Abimelech asked the Phicol.

"We haven't been here long enough to know who is entitled to what. They may be asking the same of us. How do we know we haven't illegally trespassed on their coastal fronts?"

"We've been here too long now to be driven away."

"We may have passed each other since the last time they were here. Or we may have settled in just after they departed for other grazing lands. We need to find out who they are and how strong they are. We may need to exterminate them."

"No. That's too hasty a decision. We need an alliance," the naval captain interrupted. "The Lord-Ruler demands it."

After sounding the assembly, hundreds of naval men marched to meet Abraham. Easily finding his camp, they gasped at the large collection of cattle and sheep and geese and at the thousands of men attending them—all armed with swords and oak staffs.

"Their leader is a nation unto himself," the Phicol commented. "Approach him cautiously."

Abraham, having learned the art of warfare and the establishment of camp defenses from Mamre, the Amorite, already knew about the advancing soldiers. Their physiques impressed him. Their broad shoulders and strong chests moved him to admiration. The calves of their legs appeared as the oak staffs of his men. Each soldier carried with him an ax and a spear. Their red-feathered helmets amazed Abraham as did their kilts. He had never seen so many exposed legs. He smiled at their clothes.

"Are you laughing at us?" the Phicol demanded to know, actually testing to see his reaction.

"It's your manner of dress. I suppose you wear such clothes because you need to run so often."

"The man jests with us. He calls us to battle," the Phicol stated to his men.

"Stop this ridiculous reasoning. He has ten men to our one."

"So, are we to surrender on account of the odds being against us? I will not shame myself in such a manner!"

"No, we'll bluff him with our wits." The Abimelech placed the war banner in a servant's hand then went directly to Abraham.

"Why are you on our land!" he firmly demanded to know.

"I came to get away from the sulfuric clouds of the northeast." The Philistines began to relax. The Abimelech also smiled. "The smell is terrible, is it not?"

"Indeed, it is. I am called Abraham. These are my men. These are my livestock."

"All is yours? Single-handedly yours?"

"Everything is mine."

"Unbelievable! Simply amazing!"

"It's from obedience to Yahweh."

"Who is Yahweh?"

"He is the universal Power of Creation. Yahweh is God almighty before whom stands no other god."

"I have never heard of Him. But from what I can see, it won't be the last time we'll hear of Him. Tell me, why did He make you so wealthy?"

"I also asked Yahweh why He made me so wealthy," Abraham answered easily, humorously, "I suppose He wanted his friend on earth to be happy."

""You are God's friend?" The Abimelech instantly liked Abraham who congenially returned the smile.

"Indeed I am."

"I suppose gods could use human friends. They shouldn't all demand blind worship. So, I suppose, go ahead and enjoy the virtues of your worship! It does a man good—and it makes life good!"

"I'll tell Him you said that."

Momentarily startled, he stood slightly back. "You also speak with God?"

"Yes, friends do that with each other, you know. We like each other."

"This is too much. You're an unusual person. Unique. I never met anyone like you. Man, would I love to talk with God; even if only in a dream."

"I am Yahweh's anointed," Abraham responded.

"I never heard of such a term. I am the chosen king of the coastal lands. He is the chosen general of the coastal lands."

"Who chose you?"

"Our great *Lord-Ruler of the Lilies* of Caphtor."

"He worships snakes?" Abraham asked, after noticing the serpent bands around the ruler's forearm and around his brow.

"They strengthen the male genitals," he replied, again a humorous voice, nonoffensive, nonthreatening.

Abraham ignored the remark, pretending not to hear it.

"Well, prophet, are you not going to invite my men and me to a meal? Be hospitable with me and, I shall be equally generous with you."

"Forgive my lack of manners," Abraham bowed his head slightly. "Allow, please, for your men to choose whatever cattle they desire to feast on. I ask, however, that the blood of the cow be completely drained before it is consumed. It is all I ask."

"We shall do as you ask. We thank you for sharing them with us. Let's party."

"Without intoxication, yes."

"We'll party mildly."

The soldiers, desiring to make friends with the Hebrew chief, selected the remotest place in the camp to place their arms. After removing their heavy weaponry, they carefully selected the average cows so as not to offend the herdsmen. Abraham's men, concluding they were not unreasonable soldiers nor gluttons, assisted them in the draining of the cows' blood. While the herdsmen busily quartered the hinds, the women kneaded the flour for the cakes. The children, meanwhile, prepared the vegetables.

The fragrance of the delicious and moist cakes filled the air. The hours quickly passed in mutual enjoyment.

During the middle of the celebration of friendship, however, the Abimelech happened to see Sarah. Her beauteous figure and face instantly dazzled him, captivating his heart.

"Who is she?" he asked.

"She is my sister," Abraham again replied as he had done with the Egyptian king.

"Prophet, I had never seen anyone so beautiful! I have five wives. All are expecting children," he slapped his naval officer on the back. "He forgot to bring his! How foolish in a land so far from home."

"One should always travel with his wife. It's the right thing to do."

The king merrily laughed out loud. "I really like you! But, I am tired! May I rest tonight in your camp?"

"Of course. I will protect your valuables."

"Of course, I trust, you won't slice our throats in the night, will you?" he laughed again.

"I've been known to." When the Abimelech heard this, he laughed even louder. As soon as he became comfortable, he habitually beat on his wool blanket with his hands. Soon, the darkness overpowered his eyes. Fast asleep, his snoring mingled with the sounds of the other soldiers. He felt safe. He felt comfortable. The black engulfed him. Through the night his lips maintained a smile.

In late morning he rose, not excitedly, nor alarmed.

The majority of his men rose before he did. They had eaten their breakfast and rekindled their friendships with Abraham's men. Some, bored, played with the children. Others talked with the shepherds. Others yet played games with the herdsmen. Everyone seemed content.

"Who would have known this to be as it really is?" the Abimelech thought to himself. "Could this be their land and we the trespassers? Yet, do they not raise their arms against us! Should things change between us, are we strong enough to withstand their assaults? Perhaps I should formulate a plan—a manifest—just in case."

Wondering about his newfound relationship, he sought to speak with Abraham, attempting to digest more about him and his people and his intentions in the land. Searching, he disappointedly discovered that Abraham had left for the other side of Gerar.

Sarah happened to be standing nearby. As he approached her, he thought, "Perhaps I can learn what I need to learn from her." He walked directly to her and jovially asked, "Are you truly his sister?"

"I am his sister."

"Yes, I can see the facial resemblance. He's an extraordinary man. I've never had such fun. How long have you been with him?"

"All my life."

He laughed again. "Of course. What a stupid question. Tell me, though: when will your brother return?"

"When he finishes what he's doing."

"What is he doing?"

"Whatever needs to be done."

He put his hand on his cheek and continued flirting with her, "You are quite a diplomat. Do me a favor. Come with me and see my city."

"I've seen many cities."

"I'm right on the sea among the most magnificent sand dunes you've ever seen in your life. The sea breeze yields to me. The sails of my ships come directly to me as if no other course could ever exist for them. My white horses freely roam the coastlines. Come with me and visit my stables. Ride my favorite if you wish.

"Come! I insist on it!" he kept insisting. He grabbed her hand in his and played with her fingers. She liked the effects of his touch.

"You're such a child," she teased back.

"A child cannot hurt an adult, so come with me. I also promise you'll be perfectly safe. Come on. You'll have a lot of fun."

ᕙ(ಠ益ಠ)ᕗ

The waves of the sea washed Sarah's feet free of the clinging sand. The king's wives busied themselves with the netting and with the opening of the shells and with the preparation of the fish.

"I see the king's wives also work."

Embarrassed, his face turned red. "They do so to pass the time. We really don't know anyone here. And it's fun."

"There are hundreds of you here!" She placed her right hand over her brow and peered into the distant horizon. "Your ships are the finest I've ever seen. Better than the Egyptians."

"You've seen their ships?" perplexed, he questioned her.

"Yes. The house of the Egyptian king overlooks the Lower Nile."

"You've been with the Egyptian king?"

"I've been with many kings."

"I am a king," he childishly reminded her.

"Yes, so your title informs me."

He laughed again.

ᕙ(ಠ益ಠ)ᕗ

Night came faster than Sarah anticipated. She had forgotten the hours.

In experimenting with the various mixtures of the purple dye, she forgot to step near the exterior door to view the sunset.

"I need an escort back to my camp," she told the king.

"Stay here. It's far too dark to return to your camp," he mildly beseeched her. Still more gently, he added, "Besides, there's no moon to help my horses see the trails. Sleep here tonight. My wives will surround you and will prevent anyone from molesting you."

"I shall stay the night," she smiled back as she peered into the man's blue eyes and stark blond hair.

"Good. Good for you."

She placed her head to rest on her bent forearm and thought of her husband. Simultaneously with his wife, Abraham approached his blanket. He stared at the dark sky. He began counting the bright stars. He stared into the depths of the constellations. "Where, in all this vastness, does the earth lie?"

Immediately, he fell asleep.

⁣⁣⁣ ⁣⁣⁣ ⁣⁣⁣ ⁣⁣⁣

In the new morning Eliezer was the first man in the camp to wake. He went to his workers and roused them from their sleep. The men met where Eliezer told them to, and in that meeting he instructed them on the construction techniques of the new watering well.

"You can talk all you want, but I need to see a picture of it," one worker said.

Eliezer sketched an outline in the dirt and proceeded to teach him the principals of the well's design.

That late morning the men followed Eliezer's drawing. A week later the four teams exhausted themselves.

Eliezer inspected the construction and dismally shook his head.

"No water has been found," his construction chief bitterly spoke his thoughts.

Eliezer moistened his lips. "We'll stay another week," he said. "After that we will have to dig elsewhere."

"Won't Abraham mind?"

"No, he won't mind. He loves his wells. The more we dig, the more we can carve his name on the foundation stones. The more stones that have his name carved into them, the more he's pleased. So tomorrow we'll dig again."

ᔥᑳᔥᑳᔥᔲᑳᔥᑳᔥᑳ

Another day passed.

In the course of that day the king became fonder of Sarah.

His flirting increased.

During the customary sunrise walk, he stayed a slight distance away from Sarah. As the hours passed they entertained each other with diverse and insightful conversation. Each hour, each new exploration of a new subject brought him closer to her side. By sunset his hand often brushed alongside hers.

The third day came and passed. Then a fourth. Then a fifth. In the middle of the night the head mistress of his house intruded on his sleep. "King Abimelech. Your favorite wife just suffered a miscarriage."

"Is she safe?"

"She is. But she's ashamed of her failure. She thinks you'll divorce her."

"How can I when there's no scribe here?" he tried to be humorous. He got out of his bed and went to her side. With a heart full of love he placed her in his arms and wiped her forehead clean with his nightgown's sleeve. "It's all right, dearest. You're safe here."

"Husband, I failed to provide you with a son."

"Oh well, there's four other wives here to help you bear a son for me. Be content, dearest. Let life be good for you. You're still here with me to share in their raising."

In the late afternoon of that same day, his second general's servant asked him to meet him in his second house. Therein, the second general, and many other men, anxiously waited for him. "King Abimelech, my slave woman dried up! She began her menstruation; then hours later, it stopped flowing! It's inexplicable."

"Why are you telling me this?"

"The same thing is happening to all the slave women. All who began their periods, suddenly dried up! Our fertility rites are not being answered."

"Something must be in the food."

"Are you jesting again?"

"Half-so. I do not know why the women dried."

The naval captain bowed before him and waited for permission to stand up to speak to the king. "It must be because of the foreigner you brought into our camp. She's the only one who doesn't sacrifice to our fertility gods."

"Why do you insist on calling her a 'foreigner.' We are the 'foreigners,' not her."

"All mankind is a foreigner," the naval captain replied. "Hasn't it ever occurred to you that none of us ever originated from where he said he did. Even the Egyptians are said to be from some mysterious progenitor. And remember, even Abraham is a Babylonian! And who remembers who first washed ashore on Crete? Or Cyprus! Or Malta?"

Touching his forehead with his fingertips, he thought for a few moments.

Everyone, respecting the moment, remained silent. "I will retreat to my first home. I will concentrate on finding an answer."

That night he asked the slave girl of his third wife to sleep with him. She nodded and followed him to his bedroom. She dropped her thin dress off her shoulders. He got on top of her and gently worked his penis toward her vagina. He tried to penetrate her, but her vaginal fluids refused to moisten. Finally, reaching a dismal, highly disappointing climax, he examined himself. Only a few drops of semen oozed out.

"I too am affected!" he whispered to himself. "What is the reason for this?"

In the recesses of sleep, his eyes quivered rapidly. Restlessly, his body moved about in his bed, keeping him awake. His lips began trembling. His arms shook.

Yahweh, invading his sleep, whispered: "The woman whom you have taken for yourself is married. Because you have chosen her to become one with you, you will surely die."

"Are you Yahweh—God of Abraham?"

"I am."

"Yahweh, will you vanquish an innocent nation? He said to me: 'She is my sister.' She said to me: 'He is my brother.' My invitation is blameless. My hands are clean! I have not sexually molested her."

Yahweh, in the king's dream, replied, "I know you are blameless. Because you are innocent, I came to warn you not to err against Me. I am speaking to you to prevent an invisible influence committing you to undress Sarah.

"Abraham is my prophet. Restore to him his wife. Ask him to intercede for you so your life-force may continue living. Should you try to resist Me, know for a certainty, you will surely die. You, and everyone with you!"

His loud groaning sounds alerted his guards. Concerned, they vigorously shook him awake. "I dreamt of Yahweh! The naval captain was right. Sarah holds us helpless before her God."

"Then escort her back to her camp," the general demanded.

"I must do more than that. I must have an intercessor for my sins."

"What is an *intercessor*?"

"Abraham!"

The Phicol led his soldiers past the southern end of Gerar and used the dug wells to find the prophet. Coming toward him, the general presented him with a summons, requesting his immediate return.

Before the assembly of naval men and soldiers and women and children, the Abimelech waited for Abraham. He wanted a public trial. The broad leaves of the oak trees shaded the king's sitting area.

"Abraham," he interrogated him. "What have you done to us? I favored you above all men. I never denigrated your God and I never placed mine over yours.

"Regardless how different our beliefs may be, I never sought an unreasonable excuse against you to create distress between us. Now, I want everyone to know that I am not a thief of another man's wife."

Abraham lowered his face and remained silent.

"Abraham, why did you do this to me?"

Ashamed, Abraham lowered his head. After a few moments of silence he finally confessed: "I regret what I performed against you. I thought you had no fear of the true God in your heart. I thought you would seek an excuse to murder me so you might gain for yourself my wife.

"Yet, Sarah is truly my sister. Though we had the same father, we had different mothers. When God bade me to sojourn throughout the lands, I reasoned it would be a wise precaution for Sarah, my wife, to declare to everyone: 'I am his sister'."

"Sarah is beautiful," he replied as he gazed on her voluptuous figure and beautiful face. "I have never seen such a beautiful woman. I hold nothing against you, prophet! I have no malice nor anger nor vindictiveness against either of you.

"To demonstrate my sincerity and to beseech you and your God for forgiveness I wish to publicly present to you and to Sarah the gift of my finest white stallion. Take also my prize ibex and my strongest oxen. I also entrust to you their caretakers. And more than these gifts, take into your camp these male and female slaves. They are a treasured lot.

"Even more, travel as you desire without hindrance in this land.

"This I present to Sarah." He clapped his hands. Four strong men quickly carried a large cedar chest in front of her and placed the opulent gift before her feet. The strong men opened it wide, revealing the rich contents.

"I entrust to your brother one thousand pieces of silver. This will vindicate you before all who are in your camp. You are publicly declared innocent!"

Abraham placed his oak staff to his side and lowered himself to the ground where he stretched himself fully. His hands reached toward the west and the east.

He quietly prayed so no one could hear. In his prayer he beseeched Yahweh to intercede for the king and for his household, testifying to their innocence. Immediately the women began menstruating again.

The king, amazed at the joy of the women, broke out laughing again: "Enjoy! Enjoy life!" he shouted. "Let life be good!

"Abraham, dear friend. What an extraordinary God you worship. He is with you in everything you do. Please, allow me to affiliate myself with you. Let's lovingly conclude a mutual contract of fair dealings with one another. Swear to me your most sacred oath that you shall never deal with me nor with my relatives falsely. Swear on your most loyal oath that you will always deal with me and with them and with the affairs of the land out of loyal love. Publicly swear to love me as I'll publicly swear to love you."

"I shall swear such an oath. Love will be among us."

"Then, enjoy! Enjoy life!"

Abraham eventually traveled away from the coastal city and returned to Gerar. Shortly afterwards, in the exact time frame prophesied by Michael the Archangel, Yitzhak was born.

Everyone shared the joy and laughed with Sarah. It was the laughter of pride and of a great deed accomplished!

Chapter Eighteen

▼

The Binding

This is the story of the Akeda.

Yitzhak was born in 1918 B.C.E. This year marked the beginning of the 400 years of suffering which Yahweh declared for Abraham's descendants. By this time Noah had been dead 102 years. Reu died 118 years ago, while Serug died 59 years beforehand. Terah, Yitzhak's grandfather, died 25 years before Yitzhak was born and Arpachshad died 13 years after Terah died. Shem buried Arpachshad, his firstborn, during the rising of the sun near the olive groves that faced his city of peace. Shem, now called Melchizedek, was 550 years old.

Four hundred fifty-two years had passed since the deluge covered all the lands of the earth.

Eber, in the year that Yitzhak was born, became 385 years old. Abraham was 100 years old. Sarah, Yitzhak's mother and Abraham's wife, was 90 years old.

Yishmael, standing by Abraham's side, gasped in wonder when he saw Yitzhak emerge from Sarah's womb. Abraham reached for the baby and tenderly hugged the newborn. Melchizedek approached the newborn and radiantly smiled at the beautiful baby. Melchizedek picked up the umbilical cord, severed it, and tied a small knot on Yitzhak's stomach.

Melchizedek gave one portion of the cord to Sarah and the other portion to Abraham. "As the parents of this child, you must never abandon him, even should he abandon you. Love is eternal."

Yishmael was fourteen years old when Yitzhak was born.

೫ஜ೫ஜ೫ஜ೫ಟ೫ஜ೫ஜ

Five years later, when Yishmael was nineteen years old, the nourishing milk from Sarah's breasts was taken away from Yitzhak's lips. The weaning time called for a great celebration.

Eber, Melchizedek, Michael the Archangel, the Philistine king, as well as the great general of Sidon, appeared at the feast. The first family members to arrive were Lot and his two daughters as well as the two sons that he fathered through his two daughters.

A rich, joyous atmosphere permeated the encampment. In front of the one thousand guests, one hundred quartered yearlings rested over five hundred skins. The surrounding villagers, hearing of the feast, shared freely in the distribution of the cooked rye cakes. Everyone drank all the wine they wanted.

Softly the lyre's song began. Skilled and talented hands brushed the drum's skin. The flute, in unison with the lyre, sent its music cascading to the listeners. The smells of the smoking meats filled the people with joyful fragrance as the rising smoke mingled with the afternoon's clouds.

Sarah, surrounded by her friends, listened to the festive singers. As she watched the women and men dancers from the center tent of honor, she was fascinated with the juggling swords that flew exquisitely and precisely between the acrobatic stuntmen.

Then, as the wine loosened the women's tongues, gossip went from whispers behind the ears to front-face exchanges. Yishmael, going from grown-up to grown-up, kept pushing his words into their conversations. One opinionated sentence followed another, offending the guests.

"Mother," Yishmael retreated to Hagar, "no one is listening to me. Doesn't anyone like me?"

"They're all paying attention to Yitzhak."

"Why him? I have my bow and I want to show how excellently I can fire the arrow into whatever target I aim at."

"Yes, you have a hunter's eye and the brave heart of a soldier."

"Why doesn't everyone else tell me such?"

"It's Yitzhak's party—not yours."

Jealous, Yishmael went to his father. At just this same time Melchizedek handed Yitzhak a gift. Yishmael saw the exchange and rushed to grab the gift from Yitzhak's hands. "Let me see! Let me open it first."

"Yishmael," Abraham held his hand out for the package, "that belongs to Yitzhak."

"I know. I just wanted to see what it was."

"It's first for Yitzhak's eyes," Melchizedek softly spoke, carefully placing his words in a formal structure. "If he wishes, I'm sure he'll allow you to see it."

Yitzhak, eager, giggling, with his tiny fingers, unfolded the linen wrappings. Inside the wrappings a tiny olive seeding rolled out onto his palm. A bowed sliver of a purple papyrus sheet with cuneiform characters balled the fragile roots.

"What does the writing mean?" Eber tested Yitzhak by asking.

"It's the Tetragrammaton. Yahweh set in motion my birth."

"What a wonderful answer," Melchizedek responded. Michael the Archangel approached Yitzhak and smiled.

"Are you my angel whom I have heard of?"

"I am the one who has been with you even before you came to be."

"Are you forever?"

"Only the Creator is forever."

"Will you always be with me?"

Michael stared affectionately at Abraham, then at Melchizedek, then at Eber. He replied, "I will always be with you. Then, in later years, I'll be with your children as well."

"Really," Yitzhak, wide-eyed, was caught in the mystical moment between men and spiritual beings. With that word, drawn out as only a child could, dazzled with the extraordinarily beautiful angel, he blinked his eye. Then before he could open them, the angel disappeared.

Yishmael took the small twig from Yitzhak's hand. "It's only a stick. What use is it?"

"I like it," Yitzhak remarked, fascinated with the purple color.

"It's an olive tree," Eber commented.

"It's what our patriarch of the deluge received back from the dove that he had released from the ark," Melchizedek added.

"If I had my arrow I bet I could have shot that dove out of the sky!" interrupted Yishmael.

Abraham looked sternly at Yishmael and cleared his throat. "For a man going on twenty, sometimes, I believe, you act younger."

"Isn't that how you want me to act?" Yishmael returned in kind. "Look how you always play with Yitzhak. You haven't taken my hand in a long time. I haven't been on a journey with you in five years—ever since Yitzhak was born."

Abraham nodded and leaned over to kiss Yishmael on the neck. "As much as I love Yitzhak, I also love you. Go, enjoy the evening. Take Yitzhak with you!"

"Wait," Melchizedek motioned, and his firm command held Yishmael still. He picked up Yitzhak and raising the child above his head and over the crowd, he shouted, "Yitzhak! Yitzhak! Son of Abraham! Flesh of my flesh! Grow to be strong for nations of kings will come from you!"

Sarah caught the prophetic words and smiled. Hagar turned away, bumped against Sarah, and nearly knocked her down.

The next day Yishmael took Yitzhak to the wading pond. Both stripped and swam near the tall reeds, hiding from the world. Yishmael, pretending he was trying to catch a fish, cupped his hands, and cautiously at first, then gradually bolder, he intentionally grabbed Yitzhak's testicles and squeezed them hard.

"Why do you keep hurting me like that!" Yitzhak cried.

"All the Canaanite fathers teach their children obedience like that. You need to learn that you must never embarrass me in front of our guests!"

"They were my guests, not yours!"

For an answer Yishmael grabbed Yitzhak's penis and yanked hard on it, becoming more obscene with his play.

"I said stop it!"

Yishmael broke a reed and pointed the sharp tip directly above Yitzhak's pupil. "Do you want to keep seeing the world?"

"Don't play near my eyes! I don't like it!"

"It bothers you, doesn't it?"

"I don't like it when you do these things to me!"

Yishmael clamped his hand around the back of Yitzhak's neck and tightened his grip. Yitzhak struggled and jerked vigorously until he managed to break free from the painful grasp.

With a quick jump out of the pond Yitzhak found Yishmael's bow. Thinking it would protect him from Yishmael's unwanted touch, Yitzhak drew the string back. Unexpectedly, the taut rope snapped forward, welting his cheek. Yitzhak ran to his mother in frantic tears, leaving behind Yishmael's sadistic laughter.

Sarah knew with one look what happened and who was responsible for Yitzhak's pain. "Abraham!" she shouted. "That wild boy has abused Yitzhak again. Look at the welt on his face!"

"Was that from the bowstring?"

"Yes, Father."

"I too had welts on my face from the bowstring. It's a lesson all men go through."

"It was more than that. Our son told me Yishmael is touching his penis! He does to our son the very same horrible things that the Canaanites do to their children!"

"That is a grave accusation."

"It is truth. I am not fabricating it. You, as the leader of our people must accurately write in our history what Yishmael has done. Do not soften his harsh action."

Even though Abraham heard her words, when he spoke of it to Melchizedek, the record was rendered to reflect mere jealousy.

Sarah continued, "To silence our son Yishmael purposely scares him! That Egyptian woman encourages her son to hurt mine!"

"My son issued from that Egyptian!" Abraham shouted back, becoming just as angry as she. But then, calming, he stopped to reflect on his words. "If what you say is true, I agree, it is obscene."

Sarah, softened by her husband's grave face, added, "I know I made a mistake asking you to lay with Hagar. I deeply regret having done so. But we are, nevertheless, pure Babylonians! Our line is pure from Shem's line to Terah's line. Yitzhak's blood is untainted! He is your manifest heir!

"Get that Egyptian woman away from me and away from this camp! Remove her and remove Yishmael away from us!"

"Remove Yishmael? Sarah, he is my son. Where has your compassion and understanding gone?"

"This is not going to go your way, Abraham. I've followed you from Ur to here, where I can't even settle into a stone house, much less a wooden hut. We pitch and dismantle our tent far too often! If I cannot have a home, then wherever I am, that place shall be as joyous and comforting to me as possible! Hagar distresses me and she is interfering with my joy."

She tightened her lips. "I will not say this again: when I wake up tomorrow, I expect to see her tent dismantled! When I am washing in the lake, I don't expect to see her beside me!"

Depressed, Abraham walked away from his wife. He hugged close to the terebinths and resided in silent anguish under their branches. Long hours later God's voice came to him.

"Abraham. Do not remain depressed over the boy of your servant-girl. Do as Sarah demanded, for it will be through Yitzhak that your offspring will generate the seed of ultimate righteousness.

"Yishmael will not bear the seed of righteousness—only the seeds of deceit.

"Still, in consideration for your love of Yishmael and, as he has issued forth from your semen, he too shall become a nation. But for what he has committed against Yitzhak, all other nations shall continuously wage war against him. His children will never have peace, and in the final days of mankind, his children, unless they repent and accept Yitzhak as the true carrier of the seed, and that seed as the grace of mankind, will perish from the face of the earth. The children of Yishmael will not enter paradise, no mater how much they may knock at My door for forgiveness, unless they acknowledge the eternal contract between you and Me. It will occur that Yitzhak's descendants will overpower Yishmael's descendants."

ഈരൿഈരൿഈരൿഈരൿ

Before dawn caused the cock to cry, Abraham raised Hagar from her sleep. "I thought this thing through. You and Yishmael must leave!"

"So, Sarah finally turned you against us. She's been plotting this for years. She always wanted us away from you. Why is it you can't protect us now as you always have before?"

"Yishmael's nineteen now. It has been prophesied that he must be the progenitor of his own nation."

"How stupid! It's because his mother is an Egyptian! You are prejudiced! You laid with me once and never again disrobed me! Is my skin too dark for you? Are my eyes too black? My hair too stiff?"

"Prejudices are not possible with me. Soon, other nations will become a part of the ancestry makeup of the Mashiach; possibly even the Canaanites. Through my intercession, perhaps even an Egyptian will marry into my direct heirs."

"You are just trying to appease me. You are Babylonian. Your parents are Babylonian! I wouldn't doubt it if even your God is Babylonian!"

"Hush, Hagar!"

"Don't ever tell me to shut up! Don't I hear enough of that from Sarah! I was a virgin when you used and abused my body! My vagina was nothing more than a semen deposit for your sperm! I never enjoyed that night when you callously thrust yourself into me, breathing with a bull's breath! Your two minutes of sweat became my twenty years of suffering!"

"Hagar, dear Hagar. All your callous words are fraught with vengeful and hurt feelings. I cannot change what I have declared to you. What has been decided has been decided with tears and heartbreak. Take this flask of water and these loaves of cake."

"This is all you offer me?"

"God, not I, have outcast you from the righteous. For the sake of my love for Yishmael, God has permitted him to live. In turn, I give you the best of all things: nourishing food and the water of life."

"Where am I to go?"

To Gaza. It's only eight miles from here. Go and settle there. I'll always be able to visit! The king will protect you there. You will live a comfortable life."

"If I leave here, it'll be for Egypt!"

"To what purpose?"

"Have you forgotten? I descended from Egypt's greatest house. Unlike your fantasies of becoming a king and establishing a kingdom, I have a 'Great House' to go to!"

"It is you who has forgotten. Not I, nor anyone of my household, nor anyone who is in my service may return to Egypt. Your great master posted it on the border's gate. Go to Gaza where I have influence and where you can live in comfort."

"I'll go where I please!"

"Be stubborn. It's always been your trait. Your hands always rise against my concerns. Such shall also be with Yishmael. Nevertheless, I will intercede for you and for my son. Yahweh will protect you because I ask it of You—not because you descend from the House of Egypt."

Abraham walked to the tent's door. He paused, his sagging shoulders bent more. He forced himself straight, revealing his broad, strong back.

"Come, Yishmael," Abraham, out of concern and forgiveness, invited his son back to his graces, "hug and kiss me good-bye."

"No, Father. I shall never kiss you again!" Yishmael rejected the invitation. "I am permanently displaced! A son of a wanderer is absolutely worthless. I will have everyone as my enemy, and it'll be your fault."

"Yahweh has promised you lands and the right to rule those lands."

"Mother is right! You are obsessed by a false fantasy! Father, you are only a king to small children. I am grown now, and the crown I see over your forehead is no more than a misty thing, quickly evaporating. Father, I feel sorry for you."

"As I said, I will intercede for you with Yahweh. Go, leave before the dawn lights this camp."

Holding hands, the mother and son turned away; their heads and shoulders bent toward one another.

Abraham stood by the tent's edge and watched them walking away. Tears started flowing down his cheeks. As they fell on his knees, as a haggard old man would, he folded his arms across his chest, crying loudly and in deepest anguish for the exile of his loved son until exhausted from remorse, he fainted with grief.

As their figures disappeared in front of the rising sun, Sarah felt her heart tightening. She ran to Yitzhak's bed. He slept quietly. The morning wind blew the flap door open. She saw that the men had lowered Hagar's tent before the breaking of the dawn's new rise.

Hugging Yitzhak, she began to cry.

Chapter Nineteen

▼

Hagar

Hagar journeyed a quarter of a mile to the southeast. When she reached a small mound she stood on its top to study the land that led to the distant road that wound through the sand dunes into Egypt. She began thinking: "Perhaps within two, maybe three days, Abraham will send Eliezer to Gaza to check on me. But no, I won't be there!" She smiled and teased herself into believing her thoughts. "Nor will I be in Egypt. Commerce has made that route too well known. South again? No. All the merchants know those routes! Due east? Yes, but only by the foothills."

As she wandered along the region's newest road, she soon passed Abraham's last established water well. Beyond this one, his men were working on another. So far, their effort was useless. "The hole's dry," Hagar though. "Unrewarding. A futile attempt to expand his claims! His stake! He won't try there again. So, I'll travel on the route where the well failed. Good!"

The mid-morning became mid-afternoon, then late evening. In the full darkness she shivered, sleeping fitfully alongside her son. He drew his bow tight to them and kept an arrow prepared against the predators of the night.

They both woke. Their mouths were dry; their lips parched. Hagar took a small swallow of water from the emptying skin flask. Yishmael paid no attention to the dwindling supply. He took a large gulp. Then he quickly took another drink of water. Hungrily, they both ate several dry cakes, increasing their thirst. They both swallowed several more drinks. In the afternoon they both ate again. Then in the evening they unwrapped the salted beef.

By the morning of the third day they had finished eating their supply of food.

"I can hunt an animal," Yishmael comforted his mother.

"And leave me here by myself? No, we'll hunt together."

"We'll stay on this course," Yishmael stated. "Father once told me that all courses eventually lead to water."

"Let's keep walking."

As the distance increased, Hagar again thought of Eliezer going to Gaza, inquiring as to their whereabouts. "How funny it'll be when they find out we're not there. 'Where did they go?' they'll ask. 'I don't know?' will be the answer. 'Hunt for them!' they'll shout. 'Where?' 'East?' 'West?'

"Then 'South! North!' Abraham will demand! 'Bring them back to me! No, no!' he'll beg me. 'Stay with me forever. Never leave me again!' Let Abraham beg me to stay all he wants to! I'll make him suffer. I'll make Sarah suffer the most. Let her beg me instead to stay. Let them both beg my son to stay."

She continued with her hostile thoughts and failed to pay attention to the growing heat of the day and to the decrease of the land's vegetation. The ground grew hotter. The meadows thinned. The leaves became tall grasses. With the passing distance, the land became drier, the bushes fewer and farther apart.

She traveled in a state absent from reality, focused on delusional desires, so that she completely forgot where her feet carried her. Then, in a moment of time, she found herself in a distant, unfamiliar place. Looking about, she wondered how she had wandered to the point where she came to.

The fourth day passed. Their hunger and thirst increased.

The fifth day also passed. Then the sixth.

Steam seemed to rise mystically from the ground. Vapors of heat surrounded the two. Shrouds of dense confusion began lingering over them. Hungry, depressed, thirsty, Yishmael lost his ability to distinguish the few bushes from each other. When an animal finally did run by, his arrow missed its mark, sticking deep into the ground.

"Mother, I cannot go any farther."

"What am I to do?"

"Leave me here for a moment to rest."

Hagar touched his clammy hand and felt with her fingertips his parched lips. She looked into his reddened eyes and stroked away the buildup of dust from his forehead. Worried, she pinched her lips tightly together. "Come! Just a few steps more."

"Leave me under this shading bush. It cools my body."

Hagar pushed the thin leaves together and tried to make a denser tent from its branches. They kept bouncing back to their original position. Bending the center branch hard, she snapped it to conform to the shape she wanted it to be in. "I need to retrieve your arrow. It's the last one left. We may need it."

"Yes, mother. Go! Bring the arrow back to me."

Desperate, she forced herself forward and focused her thoughts and energies on the arrow. She staggered and her arms tingled. Then, finally, she reached the arrow. When she yanked on it, she discovered that the arrow held fast into the ground. Unable to gather her strength to the task, she surrendered herself to her weary state. She sat directly beside the arrow and felt a surge of tears overwhelming her as she leaned on her right hand.

"Yahweh," Yishmael called out. "Do let allow us to die! I am helpless before You!

"The sins I have caused against my brother; I am sorry I have committed them. Allow me, somehow, if You can, to find a way to forgive me. If I must die, then let it be so. My mother, though, allow her to live."

Yahweh heard his prayer and looked into his heart. He saw that Yishmael was indeed regretful for what he had done against Yitzhak.

The winds of kindness stirred.

Far above Hagar a dense cloud rolled over her figure, shading her from the sun's rays. A cooling breeze came upon her, swaying her hair. A voice spoke to her from beyond the clouds.

"Hagar, why are you troubled?"

"I'm lost!" she screamed to the voice, frightened that no one was visible to her.

"Do not be afraid. God has heard your son's anguish. Help Yishmael stand upright, for I have promised Abraham I would concern Myself with Yishmael's progressions. Take your son's hand and lead him to the well that Abraham had thought to be dry. It does indeed contain water! Drink from it, you and your son."

⁂⁂⁂⁂⁂

Several days later it occurred by coincidence that Abraham's camels wandered to the dry watering well at the same time that the Abimelech's exploring caravan arrived. Hagar and Yishmael were asleep behind the far rim as they approached.

Abraham's men, running behind the camels, saw the well at the same time that the king's men saw it.

Both chased toward the well, each trying to outrun the other. "Back away from this well!" the caravan leader demanded.

"We were here first."

"No, this camel was here first. However, it has no brand on it. How am I to know who owns it?"

"Abraham owns the camel!"

"What you claim, you claim only by your word. But, go ahead, take the camel. I return it to you. This well, however, is ours."

"How can you say that?"

"There is no mark on it. And we all know Abraham carves his name deep into the stones of his wells."

"Abraham must not have finished digging it."

"How could that be, there's water inside!"

"Then are you staking it as your king's?"

"We do not know if our king dug it or not. But we are here by the might of his title and position. It is our well."

The two camps edged closer to each other. Each man tightened his hand around his weapons. The loud bickering woke Hagar and Yishmael. She rose, startling the men.

"People, wait!" Hagar intervened. "This well was indeed dug by Abraham's men, but its water came by God! It was a dry well. God loosened the impacted earth. I drank first from it. See! Look at my water skins! They were filled from this well."

At first the men leered at her angrily, then when they caught sight of Yishmael raising his bow and arrow and pointing it first at Abraham's herdsmen then at the merchants, the two camps hesitated from attacking each other outright.

"The well is a miracle well," one of the merchants whispered to another.

"Their skin is perfect. Their clothes seem much too white."

"Let me test this miracle," the man replied. He held his right hand away from his sword and slowly approached the woman. "Tell us, what was your condition when you discovered this well?"

"We were both near death. Our lips were torn from the heat of our bodies. Our clothes were filthy! Our hair, tangled and dry! An angel's voice was authorized to speak Yahweh's words to us: 'Drink the water from the well. It is a sweet water. Crystal clear and cool. You may drink all you want.'"

Both camps cautiously approached the well. The bravest men inched their heads over the stone wall. Trembling, the first man swallowed hard at what he saw. He had expected a dark recess, full of mysterious fright. Instead the water lapped against the stone wall less than an arm's length away. He tasted the water and smiled. When the men saw the satisfied man, they also inserted their fingers into the water then into their mouths, testing the taste.

"It's delicious," both camps acknowledged.

"Both of your peoples may fill their flasks," said Hagar.

"We will purchase this well from you, woman!" the Philistine offered.

"I cannot sell what I do not own."

"You said an angel provided this water to you, did you not?"

"I said so, yes."

"We offer you weights of silver and whatever clothes you desire from our caravan."

Hagar stared at the weights then turned to look at the other men. "Abraham's men, leave this well. By certain rights, I do own this property."

"You cannot be serious!" a herdsman shouted. "You, yourself, are from Abraham's household! Yishmael is his son! By what authority do you do this?"

"By the authority of these other men."

"You intend to rebel against your keeper's house?"

"The keeper has cast us away! Now leave, or regret your stay!"

Abraham's chief herdsman smacked his camel's neck. When the animal rose from its knees, he struck its hindquarters causing the camel to bolt back to Abraham's camp.

⁢ೞ೮ೞ೮ೞ೮ೞ೮ೞ೮ೞ೮

Within an hour of the camel's return Commander General and Chief Abraham mounted his horse, leading five hundred men to Gaza. The dust storm created by the camel's furious race to the Minoan headquarters frightened the citizens.

"I have no knowledge of what you are talking about!" the Abimelech replied when he permitted Abraham entrance to his court chamber. "Let the Phicol investigate this before you commit your men to doing something regretful and shameful."

"We will all travel to the well. What truth there is will be waiting for us there."

Two days later Abraham and the Abimelech encountered Hagar. Both leaders interrogated Hagar, and compared her words with each other. Abraham and the Abimelech retreated to the center of their camp to discuss how they should resolve the crises.

While both leaders sat on top of the freshly woven red blanket from the ram's wool, other's sat on their worn, dusty blankets.

Through the long, tedious afternoon the negotiations progressed. By the hour of the darkening sky the contract of peace and trade was close to being finalized. To celebrate, Abraham sent Eliezer back to the camp to return with gifts to seal the contract's last concluding paragraph.

"It is," the Abimelech returned to the council after Eliezer departed, "a certain fact you had dug this well, Abraham. It is a certain fact my men desire to own it for their passing to the eastern trade routes. Moreover, this water is the finest I have ever tasted. It is a miracle well."

"Since it is acknowledged that my men have indeed dug the well, I must ask you to withdraw your soldiers from the area. Also, you must allow me to carve my name in the stones. By this token gesture, it will be firmly acknowledged that my God Yahweh caused the hardened earth to loosen so that the water could rise to replenish our thirst."

The Phicol gasped.

Abraham marked his expression. He diplomatically continued, "Yet, as we are here to quench our dry throats and not to war on each other, let us both relax. Your men have guarded this well valiantly for me! I must hospitably present you and your men with these gifts. Take for yourselves seventy sheep and twelve oxen."

"That is a generous gesture," the Phicol bowed his head. "What do you intend for my king?

"First, for us to drink some more of that water!" Abraham eased the fermenting tensions between them. "Afterwards, let us wait awhile. Let's see if the time doesn't warm your heart toward my present for you."

Hours later Eliezer came by the back road to the well, catching the Abimelech and the Phicol by surprise. The general, whispering, said, "They know a back route! A larger army may be lurking there. Abraham is already strong enough to destroy us. He defeated Chedorlaomer's legions. What are we compared to his strength?"

The Phicol nodded. "How do we negotiate a contract where our Lord-Ruler will become satisfied and not hang our necks in the middle of Crete?" he asked the general.

The king stared at Eliezer. His eyes betrayed his amazement at the quality of the ewes that followed behind him. "What extraordinary beauties! Their fur is magnificent!"

"The seven female sheep are yours," Abraham motioned his arm toward them.

"They are truly a wonderful gift. Their fleece is nearly golden!"

"By accepting these seven ewes you will bind the contract that I have dug and own this well."

"I accept your gifts, Abraham. Our Lord-Ruler will be pleased with this golden fleece. The miracle well is yours!"

"Then I shall name this land Be'er-Sheva. Hagar, you and Yishmael take whatever number of sheep and gazelles that you desire. Keep the merchant's weights of silver. Then, strictly obey me this time," he commanded. Then just as quick he softened his tone and added, "I beg for you to travel northeast to Paran."

"I shall do as you request. I've learned my lesson."

"This time, Yishmael, will you hug and kiss me?"

Yishmael nodded and kissed his father. He was grateful to have gained a number of animals and depended on the silver to establish his enterprise.

The following week Abraham returned to the well at the head of several hundred cattle and sheep. His last camel carried a tamarisk tree whose trunk was beginning to gnarl. After planting the feathery evergreen, Abraham dedicated the site to Yahweh.

Many years later, when the Philistine caravans traveled through Be'er-Sheva, the white blossoming flowers from the plant's spikes reminded them of the pact. As travelers tasted the refreshing water, they noticed the carvings on the stones. The children, inquiring, learned of the pact between themselves and the children of Abraham.

Three thousand years later Abraham's children replanted hundreds of tamarisk trees in the very same land. The tamarisk trees restored the desolate wilderness to its former greenness.

Chapter Twenty

▼

Yitzhak

When Yitzhak was twenty-five years old, Yahweh held a council meeting between Michael the Archangel and Himself. "You know, among the entirety of mankind, I selected Abraham to become the chosen one from whom the 'Seed of Righteousness' will come forth as the ransom sacrifice for Adam's transgression against Me.

"Through his line the perfect genetic characteristics will be incorporated so the prince of peace may travel among people to teach them My laws and values and expectations.

"Because Abraham is my friend, what I have promised to him, I shall fulfill."

Michael, listening, asked, "Will all of humankind's sins be forgiven through the Mashiach's mission?"

"Without hesitation."

"How will You accomplish this?"

"First, I will establish a set of laws whereby humankind may free themselves from sin without an intercessor's self-sacrifice. There will be specific commandments that, whenever they are fully obeyed, will release them totally from sin. Should it occur that no one is able to abide by the Law's standards then a perfect spiritual-being—an angel turned human—must take it upon himself to incorporate all of the world's sins into himself. That perfect spiritual-being turned human must be willing to be tortured and must be willing to suffer at the hands of other human's whims and degenerating abuses. That perfect spiritual-being turned human must be totally willing to set aside his heavenly residence to dwell among mankind, subject to exact desires and temptations and limited reasoning.

"I propose that this perfect spiritual-being turned human be reduced to human weaknesses. He must forfeit all his heavenly strengths so he may become vulnerable to human temptations.

"I propose this so the rebellious angel cannot say 'A perfect spiritual-being has ransomed humanity!' This must become so because I have instituted the 'Law of Equality' to be in effect. What has been done must be rescued identically as it had occurred."

"I, Great Creator, desire to be the spiritual-being turned human who buys mankind back for you. Allow me to be the one sent to them to be sacrificed for their sins."

"You are my first-created. We calculated and enacted our genius to form everything that exists. You now desire to be the one to die for their transgressions?

"Before you answer, realize, your mission is not guaranteed to succeed. You will be subjected to every vice and corruption that humans contend with. You will not be a supernatural being until the last years of your mission. You will not be able to transfigure yourself at the moment of danger. You will bleed and you will hunger and you will thirst and you will feel the heat of the afternoon's sun and the bitter cold of the mountain's wind.

"The rebellious angel will be able to kill you while you're in human form."

Michael stared at his Father. "I accept. Whatever befalls me, I shall circumvent."

"Before I inform the universal hosts of your decision, I desire again to test humanity. If I am to send my firstborn to death's torture stake, I want to see if Abraham will do the exact same thing for Me."

ℰ☯ℭℬ☯ℭℬ☯ℭℛℰ☯ℭℬ☯ℭ

Sometime later, Yahweh again spoke to Abraham.

"I am here," Abraham answered Yahweh.

"Take your favorite son, your most beloved child, Yitzhak, and travel to Moriah. I want you to sacrifice your beloved son to Me on top of a burning altar. I will select the place from which you will burn him to Me."

"Sacrifice Yitzhak to You?" Abraham, reeling with an terror, crumbled to the ground. He placed his hands over his eyes and wept bitterly. His hands pulled at his hair. He tried to reason out the strange and cruel demand. "There must be a purpose for such a command, otherwise it would not have been made." But Yahweh's voice did not respond.

"Great God and Creator, I will take Yitzhak to Mount Moriah as You desire."

ℰ☯ℭℬ☯ℭℬ☯ℭℛℰ☯ℭℬ☯ℭ

Abraham kept looking at the drifting clouds. Among the dazzling, mountainous white caricatures he believed he saw the faces of men he once intimately knew. As he peered into the billowing forms, he tricked his eyes and mind to see whatever he wanted to see. Then, among the clouds, flocks of birds glided. "They're free from all this ambiguity and stress."

His eyes looked at the swaying grasses. His thoughts drifted to the numerous herds and flocks of sheep that grazed throughout the hundreds of acres before him. He turned to look at his tents.

Sarah busily directed the women with their darning and with the weaving of new clothes and the cleaning and dyeing of skins for trade. He stared at his armed men who would instantly die for him at his command.

They kept their axes and spears and bows by their sides, always within easy reach. Even the Philistines were afraid of them as were the Amorites and the Canaanites.

Abraham's military strength and cunning had greatly impressed the surrounding nations. He could take for himself whatever he wanted. Sometimes his temperament revealed these hidden thoughts to his guests. Other times, he silently brooded on what the possibilities of conquest were.

"But why," he quickly reanalyzed those temptations. "Am I Chedorlaomer? Am I to present Yahweh's concerns to the nations through the sword? Others will come after me who will demand adherence to their beliefs by whatever means they can. To balance this, I must temper my beliefs with kindness. I must stress the importance of clear individual willingness to become a part of this new organization."

The surrounding nations, not wanting to war against such a powerful, insightful man, signed dozens of treaties of peace and cooperation with him. The negotiated signatures and the emblems of the surrounding kings and governing bodies were collected inside a large cedar chest that rested by the Entry Tent of Private Meetings. The primary objectives of the contracts were for the kings to acknowledge his wells and property. Each parcel, each well, the kings publicly declared were Abraham's by the rights of purchase, earnings, and bartering.

ಬಇಚ3ಬಇಚ3ಬಇ಄3ಬಇಚ3ಬಇಚ3

Ishmael at this time was forty-five years old while Yitzhak was thirty-one.

"It is time for you to marry," Hagar spoke to her son.

"I am ready," he replied.

"Then I will travel back to Egypt and solicit an Egyptian wife for my son."

After weeks of interviewing prospective households, she choose a mate for her son. When the wedding day arrived Abraham, out of love, attended the wedding feast as did Sarah and Yitzhak.

In the midst of the celebration, Abraham kept thinking about Yahweh's command. Instead of being happy at his son's wedding, he despaired. Yitzhak approached his father.

"What is wrong with you? You aren't dancing. You aren't drinking."

"My thoughts dwell that within another year Yishmael may possibly father a son. His family line will increase, while I may have no one to call my own."

"Yishmael will indeed be a strong breeder of children. His house will always outnumber you house, but the seed of righteousness will always be within your house—not his."

"Father, I want to marry. Am I not ready, Father?"

"Yes, that would have been nice."

"Would have? What do you mean?"

"I may not have you any longer in my life," Abraham shook as he released the words out of his mouth.

He affectionately hugged him.

"What are you saying?"

Throughout the next hour Abraham explained to his son Yahweh's plans.

"Do you consent to this act?"

"Yahweh is determined to perform it. So, I must obey," Yitzhak replied.

"Not necessarily. You can run away. You can hide in the mountains or in the cities. You can abdicate your heritage and escape easily through deception."

"I can do none of those things," Yitzhak answered. "You, my father, asks if I will obey Yahweh's demand. I say to you, I shall willingly obey you, regardless what you ask me."

Later, in the private moments of the day, Yishmael learned of the conversation between Abraham and Yitzhak. He approached his father, "What sin is Yitzhak guilty of?"

"It is not sin," Abraham replied. "It is the love of obedience and the willingness to exercise that love that Yitzhak permits his sacrifice."

"To love is the same as to sacrifice?"

"Yes," Abraham said. "The sin of transgression is on everyone. All men born are inheritors of death! Some sooner than others. The sin of Adam needs a redeemer to correct it. Perhaps Yitzhak is such a man."

Yishmael looked at his bride and mother. He kicked at an imaginary figure. "So always he must be first before me, even in such a thing."

ഇരുഇരുഇരുരുഇരുഇരു

Through the night Abraham tormented himself with the thoughts of the sacrifice of his inheritor. He developed one excuse after another to justify the act he was about to commit. Hope after hope came and vanished. On the morning's rise, with no retraction from Yahweh, Abraham prepared his donkey's saddle. Before his wife woke he went to the far wayside of the camp where he gathered up some firewood. He took an ax and he viciously split it into smaller quarters. Before dawn rose to wake the camp, he and Yitzhak departed, heading toward Mount Moriah.

Eliezer and his friend followed closely behind the two despairing figures. Eliezer knew what Abraham was instructed to do as did his friend. Yitzhak, also fully aware that he would soon die on a sacrificial mound, looked at his father. "When will we reach Mount Moriah?" Yitzhak asked.

Abraham didn't answer. He kept his misty eyes on the ground.

"We'll be passing right by Eber and Melchizedek."

"Yes. But we won't be saying hello to them. This business must be finished as quickly as possible"

"Am I not allowed to say good-bye to my Great-forefathers before I die?"

"No man can say good-bye to those he loves when he faces death. I wonder if he can even say good-bye to himself?"

"Father, what will you do once I am gone?"

Abraham shook his head.

"I suppose you and mother can breed another son. I will pray for this to happen for you."

"Why are we hurrying so fast?" Eliezer's friend shouted, confused by the haste for a father to kill his son.

"It's a necessary thing that we must do," Abraham answered him. "I cannot delay for any reason whatsoever. To do so may become my shame."

"Father, I don't understand your meaning. What shame are you speaking of?"

"Yes, my son. You are correct in what you say. There is no shame in obeying Yahweh. Whatever His command is, it is an honor to obey it. The shame is in wanting the duty to pass from your hands to another or never wanting the duty in the first place." With these words, emotionally spent, Abraham collapsed on the donkey's side, crying hard. Embracing his father, Yitzhak stroked his hair. "Father," Yitzhak insisted, "no matter what He asks, perform it righteously."

"Whatever He, as Creator of everything demands, is in itself righteous," Abraham quietly stated. "Do you, Yitzhak, agree with this?"

"Yes, Father, I agree. You have always taught it to be so. Melchizedek and Eber have stated it to be so. I have never questioned otherwise. Blessed is the name of Yahweh!"

"Then run to that pile of dried oak. Split them into smaller pieces so we may have more for the fire to consume. I want the driest branches to make the hottest fire."

The broad-shouldered and powerfully biceped thirty-one-year old man, whose strength was legendary throughout the camp, obeyed his father.

Yitzhak long ago had grown taller than his father. All the men easily distinguished him when he rode his horse across the hillsides. His long, luxuriantly embroidered tunic flowed behind him as though it belonged on a king's shoulders. His long dense black hair blew in the wind mingling with the black mane of his horse. His intense, rich brown eyes reflected his keen intellect. His straight, chiseled chin and the strong nose descending from his proud forehead continued with the fullness of his sculptured lips. Abraham, constantly watching him, constantly boasted about him. Never had he seen a more handsome man. A true progenitor of kings and nations!

Within no time Yitzhak had splintered and quartered the additional wood.

They journeyed through Be'er-Sheva and turned toward the western slopes below the city of Salem. When they neared the city, the four men distinguished the heights of rugged Mount Moriah.

"Is not this hill a part of Salem's borders?" Yitzhak asked.

"It is."

"Shouldn't we ask Melchizedek for his permission to build an altar on this land?" Yitzhak was again trying to find an excuse to visit the king-priest and great-father of the family line.

"Since when have I ever asked anyone for their permission to build an altar or to dig a well!" Abraham snapped fiercely at Yitzhak, catching all three men by surprise.

"Never, Father," Yitzhak meekly responded, startled by the attack.

"Eliezer, stay here with your friend. Yitzhak and I will travel the rest of the way by ourselves. After we finish our worshipping, we will both return to you," Abraham stated, clinging to his belief that somehow, by the end of this day, all would be made safe.

"The donkey may not be able to navigate through that jagged path," Abraham said. "The boulders are packed tightly together at the foot of the hill."

"Put the wood on Yitzhak's back. He's stronger than the ass!" Eliezer's friend remarked. He tried to smile. His nearly perfect white teeth showed through his tortured humor.

"Yes, I can carry it. After all, I am a grown man."

"Just because you're thirty-one doesn't mean you're a grown man," Eliezer also tried to lighten the event, but to no avail. "Strange," he thought, "why is Yahweh demanding a human sacrifice. Why does He demand Abraham's favorite son? Better to sacrifice Yishmael rather than Yitzhak!"

Eliezer spit on the ground. Bewildered, he shook his head.

"Did you bring the rope?" Abraham asked the companion.

"It's here."

"Yitzhak, may I tie it around you?"

"Well, Father," Yitzhak also tried to jest as Eliezer had done before him, "how else am I to carry all these sticks!"

"I don't care how!" he snapped again, forcing the three men to stop their imperfect attempts at humor. They now silently bound the wood around Yitzhak's back. This prefigured Yeshua's carrying of the torture stake at Jerusalem two-thousand years later.

"Eliezer, bring me my firestone and knife! Yitzhak, come on. Let's be finished with what must be finished," he harshly spoke.

Halfway up, Yitzhak stopped to shift the load. Its weight was beginning to hurt and scratch his back. Not too far from them the new towers of Salem became visible. Most merchants still avoided the city. It was full of priests and scribes. It was too boring to enjoy. Too sincere! Much too peaceful!

ଛ୦ଓଛ୦ଓଛ୦ଓଓଛ୦ଓଛ୦ଓ

Melchizedek, meanwhile, sat on a red ram's skin. He felt a strange sensation overpowering him. A tingling, nerve-pulsating coolness lingered over his body. The mystical, energized sensations rose to the tips of his hair. He shook violently. His right foot accidentally kicked against the clay bowl, scattering its contents against the wall.

"What is it?" Eber, startled by the unexpected movement asked.

"Abraham and Yitzhak are nearby." The strange sensations continued traveling throughout his body. Briefly, the queerest electrical fixation remained near his right eye. His right forehead began hearing a soft, wavering hum. The sensation traveled down his spine, suddenly dissipating.

Tears overpowered his eyes' vision. He wiped away the blurring tears, but more of them quickly formed. His body shook from the fringe touches of a cold wind. He kept blinking his eyes. Everything in front of him became hazy, indistinguishable. Wiping the sweat from his brow, he reeled to the ground.

Eber rushed to his side. "Father, dearest Father! What is happening to you?"

"Abraham, Abraham," Melchizedek choked out. His nostrils were wet. His eyes rolled to the back of his head. In a fainting trance he saw his son's great grandson walking with his own great-great-great-grandson to the crest of Mount Moriah.

"Father." He heard Eber's voice at exactly the same time he heard Yitzhak's voice in the inner depths of his psychic viewing. Eber's face transformed to Yitzhak's face and the background of the stone walls became the background of Moriah's landscape.

"What is it, Yitzhak?" Melchizedek heard and saw Abraham answering his son.

"We have the firestone. We have the wood. Somehow, looking about, I hoped Yahweh would change His mind. Where, I pray, is the sheep for the burnt offering?"

"Son, Yahweh will provide a sheep for His burnt offering."

Yitzhak studied the landscape and disappointed, he shook his head. "I am prepared to rest on the altar."

"Are you in such a hurry to die?"

"Since you told me of Yahweh's intent for me at Yishmael's wedding I have been prepared to die. It's why I traveled with you here. So, let it happen to me now."

"Yahweh may yet provide a sheep for the burnt offering."

The king-priest's acute perceptions continued seeing the pair walking up the steep slope. He watched as they gathered the loose stones. He saw them carefully arranging the stones to form a strong, sturdy altar. He watched as Abraham intentionally took his time, placing branch after branch on top of one another so the flames would quickly catch on fire and consume whatever was placed over the wood. Abraham knew how to generate the hottest flames, thus lessening the time of the consumption.

"Yahweh," Abraham prayed. "Is there still no sheep? Am I still to murder my son?"

The air seemed foul and stagnant. There was no beauty in the overhead clouds.

"Father, where's the lamb?" Yitzhak nearly cried out.

"Yitzhak," Abraham sighed heavily. He glanced again at the clouds, hoping for an angel to appear with a lamb in its arms. The clouds only thickened and darkened. He peered into the depths of the pile of wood that they had formed into a perfectly logical structure. He gazed at Yitzhak's broad shoulders. He looked deeper into his son's eyes.

"You are the lamb."

After a few quiet moments, Yitzhak forced himself to ask, "Father, what offense have I committed against Yahweh?"

Abraham shrugged his shoulders.

Yitzhak stared at his father's watering eyes. He lowered his head to search the ground and after a few seconds Yitzhak looked over Abraham's shoulder at the path that led back to Salem. At that moment he realized how old is father looked. He was nearly a hundred-twenty-five-years old. His hair was completely silver. His eyes were fully wrinkled as was his brow. The flesh of his neck hung loose. His chin drooped. Yet, his proud father remained strong! A true leader.

"I am this man's child," he said to himself. "This man is Yahweh's friend for whom he left Ur."

He looked back at his father and tried to reason out his approaching death. "Father, if I am to be sacrificed—what is to be gained?"

"Obedience."

"Father, I have not only followed every word you gave me, but I have also completely entrusted myself to you. If it must occur that I am to be sacrificed by your hand, I willingly accept."

Yitzhak then climbed on top of the sticks. A few points of the wood stabbed him. He winced at the splinters that jabbed and pricked into his skin.

"Son, I must bind you."

Yitzhak nodded quietly. After binding the muscular, strong youth, he placed his hand over his son's eyes, closing them. Aiming his experienced hands at Yitzhak's jugular, he lifted his knife, preparing to swiftly, cleanly sever the vein, hastening the death as fast as he could.

Michael the Archangel, at the very instant, knowing for a fact that Abraham was determined to obey Yahweh's instructions to sacrifice his beloved Yitzhak, shouted out: "Abraham! Abraham!"

"I am here," Abraham responded, easing the grip on his knife.

"Don't harm your son," Yahweh spoke through Michael. "Don't commit any maliciousness against Yitzhak. I know for a certainty that you respect Me! You have kept your promise and have not withheld your very flesh, your most desired child, from Me!"

Simultaneously, with the lowering of his flint knife, the cries of a ram startled Abraham. The ram's horn caught fast in a thicket where it had been trying to eat the succulent grass that was beneath the green shade.

Abraham cut Yitzhak's bonds off then picked up the ram. Abraham gently carried it to the altar. To his son he said, "Yitzhak, this place shall be named Adonai-yireh, meaning: 'There are visions on Yahweh's mountain.'"

Again Yahweh's chief angel Michael pronounced to Abraham the Creator's words. "What I say to you, I swear. Yahweh Himself declared it will be fulfilled: 'Since you have carried out this act, not withholding the very son whom you love the most, I will bestow My blessing upon you. Your descendants will be as numerous as the stars of heaven and as numerous as the sands of the sea. Your children will seize the gates of their enemies!

"'Each nation of the earth will bless themselves because of your descendants and because you have obeyed My command.'"

Leaving behind the altar and the rising smoke of the ram's body, Abraham and Yitzhak returned to Eliezer who was standing beside his companion and several other persons who had joined them.

Melchizedek and Eber, afraid of the visions that plagued him, journeyed to Mount Moriah. When the two fathers saw Yitzhak they ran to him and kissed him on the neck.

Chapter Twenty-One

▼

Sarah

"How is it possible for my body to hurt so much," Sarah could barely speak as her eyes penetrated lovingly into Abraham's. He shook his head and held her hand tighter in his. Without embarrassment, without shame or pity or having to pretend he was emotionally stronger than his herdsmen, or his son Yitzhak, the great leader bent his shoulders toward his wife's face, and permitted his tears to fall on her lips. Her tongue tasted the salty drops. She allowed them to linger on her face.

Her trembling hands fought to touch his wrinkled face.

His step-sister and wife devoted her life to loving him. She served his grandfather Eber and his father Terah, her husband's brothers: Nahor and Haran, and their single child, whom she dearly loved, Yitzhak.

"Abraham," she struggled with the word, "I hurt. I hurt."

He bent toward her as far as he could.

The candle's light in the tent flickered, revealing the soft shadows of Sarah's handmaidens. The oldest cupped her hands to her mouth, stifling her moans.

She wanted to rush to Sarah to push Abraham out of her arms to grab her and hold onto her last moments of life. Where was her husband when she was suffering these past five days? He and Yitzhak were always selling and buying cattle and sheep and cloth. Always walking about here and there or riding their donkeys over the craggy hills and widening valleys, boasting that every square inch of land that they touched belonged exclusively to them. Everything they saw, as far as they could see, both boasted, God promised to them.

The other herders of the other tribes, to whom she often talked and traded with, secretly confessed to her their resentment of this Babylonian intrusion into their lands. But Abraham's guards were more powerful than the combined strength of all of their warriors. Abraham had proven himself in battle and signed many treaties with the surrounding kings, permitting him grazing and watering rights throughout their lands. After all, the kings said, as they held their eyes down to the earth, did not Abraham's soldiers destroy the Council of Four? Did not his army keep away the invaders?

The people who settled the land long before Abraham, whose father's fathers were buried throughout the land, could do no more than wander away from the pastures whenever Abraham's came to feed their animals.

Everyone feared him.

Sarah loved him.

She closed her eyes, reflecting for a moment on Yitzhak's love for his father. She clearly remembered how twelve years ago Abraham made a sacred pact with Yahweh, the Creator of the Universe. She smiled her small sardonic smile that she developed after the episode when her husband took their only son, by then a young, mature man, to offer as a sacrifice to their God. That circumstance became the beginning of her illnesses. She struggled for more breaths as she saw in her mind her husband raising his stone knife to plunge bitterly into their child's chest, exploding apart his heart. She shivered.

Yitzhak came through the tent door at that moment. He glanced from side to side, felt awkward, but nevertheless walked to his father's side. He was afraid to enter his mothers tent. He wanted to pretend she was just going through another phase, another bout that would disappear. But her coughs refused to stop. She vomited and heaved and her body's hacking disturbed the camp.

Everyone hushed in expectation of death.

Yitzhak's eyes were filled with tears. His own body shivered as he hugged his mother. His tears similarly covered her face, and both men were afraid to look at each other, trying to maintain a pretense of emotional control in that tent of exasperating demise. The same tent where they once laughed and listened to the flute players and examined the quality of wool that their followers weaved, and where hours of conversation ensued of Abraham's dreams. Both mother and son sat spellbound as they listened to the great leader's words.

Yitzhak nostrils became filled with moisture. The fluid flowed to his mustache and beard. Sarah looked at her son's unencumbered emotions.

At her bedside, Abraham rubbed her shoulder and leaned over again to dab her forehead dry of the beading sweat drops. He shared the same cloth with his son to wipe clear his beard. Facing them, without averting her eyes from either male, she fought to lift her arms to draw both men closer to her lips. She kissed first her husband, then her son.

Again, she struggled to speak, "Abraham, I want a permanent place for my burial site. Without a moment's hesitation I traveled with you from place to place. Even as a vagabond. Even as a lost wanderer. Even as a disenfranchised person I traveled beside you. I isolated myself from my family and from my brother Nahor. After I left with you I never saw my nieces and nephews. I never met Uz nor Buz nor Bethuel nor Laban nor the other children of my brother's two wives.

"Promise me that you will establish a home for my remains! Do this so we may be buried together in peace. Do this so my children will have a place to rest their bones in."

Abraham nodded. He placed his arm around his son, and looked at his profile. His chin was strong, handsome. His eyes returned to his frail wife. She who had been so powerful in her opinions, so dominant in her beliefs. So vocal in her decisions.

"Dearest love," his trembling and pained words found a way to speak out of his mouth, "I promise I will establish a permanent home for your bones. My own bones will be placed beside yours as shall be the case for our sons."

Yitzhak also nodded as he leaned closer to her. A person passing by that distressed filled tent, saw two men as one. He recognized the broad and bent man and the lean and straight shouldered man. The handmaiden shooed him away when she noticed his shadow creeping into the tent.

The shadow neared Sarah's feet.

"Mother," Yitzhak wept. Not knowing what to say, he blurted through a stream of tears, "Let me bring you some water from the well that Hagar drank from."

Sarah silently laughed, "No. There are no miraculous streams of water nor wells of magic. Hagar died years ago, so the water proved itself useless for her, as it will for me. And look at your half-brother Yishmael. Look how old he is. All his wonderful skills at hunting and all his romances and the number of his children refused to keep him young. This worsening condition of man is the fault of our first-father and mother: Adam and Eve. You, my son, will the father of he who will come to take away this pain of death away from us all."

Yitzhak looked at Abraham.

"Did God revealed this to you?"

She smiled again. Just then her body slightly shook as if a cold wind rushed over her. She looked at the tent's opening to stare briefly at the bright day. "How odd," she thought" to see such a beautiful day while my body is racked with this pain."

Her words returned to her son. "I am certain," she said softly, "that Nahor has also passed away by now."

Her hand touched her husband's neck. She drew his ears closer to her lips. "See to it that our son marries Nahor's granddaughter."

He nodded.

Sarah then raised her arms to her son. "Yitzhak, kiss me. Let our embrace say what our hearts know. Son of my old age, never have I had so much joy and satisfaction than when I was with you. You are a magnificent child. You, Yitzhak, have been deeply loved by me—and by your father."

Her eyes, glittering, still retained their intense beauty. Her face still reflected the reasons for the Egyptian king's passion to have her numbered among his wives. The depth of beauty still defied her age and still showed the reasons for the Abimelech's wanting her as much as they Egyptian king wanted her. Her beautiful face, even though somewhat wrinkled, again concentrated on the eyes of the man who truly possessed her.

"Abraham, my dearest husband. How great my love has been for you. You are my life, my passion. How I regret not being able to give you all the many sons you so wanted to have." Abraham grabbed her hand as she softly stroked his beard. "What a handsome man you still are. Your belly sticks out somewhat," she softly laughed, her eyes glittered even more so, "but you are still an example of what men should be like. No wonder our son is so magnificent!"

Her magnetic smile caused Abraham to smile, too.

"Abraham, I still remember when I first saw you. You were Avram then and I was Sarai. How long, long ago has that been? Yet the years have passed by far too quickly.

"Why am I now called Sarah? Yes, yes, I know the answer. Abraham, tell me truthfully, without embellishing it with our father's impossible dream of being a king: Am I truly a queen?"

"You are the greatest queen of all time," Abraham replied, his words at times choking. "From you great kings will issue forth. From you Great nations will be blessed by virtue of your having being alive and keeping Yahweh's love and trust in your heart. From you will rise the greatest king of all time—the Mashiach! Without your faith, how could it be possible for any other woman to come after you to fulfill the Messianic mission?"

He rubbed his shoulder again and again, somehow caught in the thought he had to keep rubbing it to keep Sarah breathing.

"I am the queen-mother of the Mashiach," she whispered, turning her eyes to Yitzhak's face. "From me great kings will come." Gripping Abraham's tunic, she forced herself to sit upright in her bed. Raising her arm and pointing her finger straight out, she said to Yitzhak, "Open all the flaps of my tent. Let me see the sunset."

Quickly obeying, her handmaidens unloosened all the leathering straps and dropped the heavy cloths to the ground. As if God's heart had heard her desire, the setting sun colored the sky's clouds a deep orange and violet. The tamarisk trees became black figures of intriguing shapes with wandering branches, bent sideways to the sky.

Sarah's eyes closed, her breath hissing out from her lungs.

"SARAH!" Abraham screamed, both hands flung out for her, trying to catch her escaping life-force and turn it back into her body. Grasping her limp figure tightly to his chest, he moaned, "Oh great Yahweh! Sarah's dead! Sarah's dead."

Yitzhak, crowding beside his father, ripped his tunic. With loud cries he bathed his hair with the ground's dust. The men, women, and children, hearing the sobs, remembered the times outside the great Egyptian king's house. Listening, they also burst into horrific, wailing tears. Intense heartbreak gripped the camp, enclosing it in a vacuum of universal grief.

The angels, watching all, also cried. And Michael the Archangel faced his Father and bent his shoulders, his tears causing the clouds to darken.

"When will it be my time to lift this burden of death away from them," his body collapsed into his Father's receiving arms. Yahweh stroked his only-begotten's sons hair. His body tightened with grief as did Abraham's and Yitzhak's. He sighed, and the breath that emitted from the Creator stirred all the branches and plants of the earth.

"Sarah will be resurrected During the Day of Judgment" to a fair judgment, Yahweh's words whispered to Abraham.

And the echoes of the tears filtered throughout the campsite. The echoes of anguish and despondent futility carried to the very shores of Gaza. The Abimelech, learning of the tears' origin, also cried unabashedly. The mourning carried even beyond Be'er-Sheva and beyond the rising slopes of the mountains. The infectious tears betrayed Melchizedek as they did his household. Ten thousand times ten thousand men and women and children cried, their tears deepening the sense of loss that their hearts felt.

One hundred twenty-seven years after her eyes' first saw Abraham, her eyes closed for the final time, again with Abraham's face etched inside them.

Yitzhak, at this time was thirty-seven years old.

ঙ০৫৩ঙ০৫৩ঙ০৫৩৫০৫৩ঙ০৫৩

Moaning, rocking back and forth, Abraham spent that night with Sarah inside his arms and onward through the day and the following night, refusing to part from her. She whom he loved with all his heart for one hundred twenty-seven years, died in 1881 B.C.E. He kept squeezing her tightly, somehow believing he had the power to put her breath back inside her body or perhaps to squeeze her somehow into his own body, thereby providing her life anew.

"The Mashiach, the Mashiach," he whispered several times during the last hours he held her in his arms. "Why could he not now be here with us to free us of death's inhospitable encroachments?"

The third day's sun rose. Still, the camp members refused to withdraw from their mourning places. Finally Eliezer approached Abraham.

"Her body's decaying. We need to bury her."

"How can we? I have no ground to put her in."

"What do you mean? Our dead are buried everywhere."

"I promised her a permanent burial place. A place where we can all be buried in."

"How is that possible? We own no land."

"But my wells testify that we do. My altars testify that we do."

"All that you dug and staked are claims for your children. All the treaties that you authorized with the rulers of the surrounding cities forbid you to own lands or to build cities."

"What am I to do?"

"You have two alternatives. You have the most powerful army and the highest trained warriors serving you. No city or army can destroy you. You alone defeated Chedorlaomer. You alone make the rulers tremble. Therefore you can attack now all these city-rulers and force whatever you want to be yours, to actually become yours. Yet, Abraham, if you pursue this course, you'll violate every treaty and every principle that you stand for. So, to maintain your dignity and integrity to the One God whom you represent, you must honor all the treaties, which means you will continue landless. However, in this crises, in order to bury your wife, you must sign another treaty. Offer more than another to own a small portion of this land. Let it become your cemetery, for what king can say no to a place of remembrance? Therefore, I advise you to do this thing and to quickly enact this second alternative: talk to the sons of Heth. They admire and respect you. They often seek your counsel and act in accordance with your word. They have never cheated you in trade or falsely marked one of the strays from your herds as one of their own. So Abraham, talk to Ephron. What is a small plot of land to the man who owns the region? I believe he is as reasonable as he is wealthy."

"Arrange a meeting," Abraham, concurred with Eliezer's careful, well-reasoned, advice. "Do it before this day passes."

ঙ৾৻৶ঙ৾৻৶ঙ৾৻৶ঙ৾৻৶ঙ৾৻৶

In the immediate vicinity of the meeting gate that rose high in front of the city of Kiriath-arba, Ephron, son of Zohar, of the Tribe of Heth, came out of his house to meet with Abraham. In front of the meeting gate other residents gathered, for it wasn't often that the renowned prophet and patriarch came to visit them.

"I am a foreigner in your land," Abraham began. "I carry documents authorizing my residency in your land," he placed them in front of the crowd, "I stand before all of you and without anger or demonstration of power, humbly beg for the citizens of this land to present my cause to one of the residents of your land, Ephron. Permit me to approach him to ask him to sell to me a small parcel of land that I can permanently keep to bury my dead in."

"Great lord, listen to our reply," the master of the chambers orated. "We know you are God's chosen representative. Though we have created and concluded many treaties between us forbidding you to own any land and restrained you from building any permanent structures, we sympathize and emphasize with your loss. We, therefore, will rescind a small portion of our treaties with you. We unanimously consent to permit you to have a plot of land where you may freely and unhindered bury your wife.

"Not one of us will object to it nor prevent it from happening. Not one of us will violate the sanctity of your burial site."

"I thank you for such consideration. But, generous people of Kiriath-arba, help me, please, to convince Ephron son of Zohar to sell me the cave of Machpelah, which he owns. Allow him, please, to sell it to me for full value so I may have a permanent and indisputable burial site for my wife and for myself and for my son."

"Great lord," Ephron spoke for himself, "listen to me: I wish to place the cave and the land in your hands. I desire it to be so in front of everyone so they may bear witness to this transcribed action. So, scribe and legal writer and performer of the laws, draw a contract between myself and this great leader and make it effective immediately! Go, Abraham. Bury your dead in peace!"

Abraham bowed and fully extended his body on the ground. Respectfully raising his head slightly off the earth, he spoke loudly so everyone could hear him. "Listen to what I have to say! Allow me, please, to pay the full value of the land. Accept this token from me so I may bury my dead there."

Ephron, consulting with his accountant, also raised his voice so everyone could witness the transaction. "Great lord! Listen to me! What is four hundred shekels of silver between us? Go! Bury your wife."

Eliezer, bowing to the accountant, placed four hundred silver shekels in his pouch. Everyone, witnessing the land's purchase, acknowledged the fairness of the transaction that Abraham and Ephron concluded.

In this manner Sarah received her permanent burial site. The cave passed from Abraham to Yitzhak to Yisrael and to Joseph.

ઝબ ⁊ ⁊ ⁊ ⁊ ⁊

Immediately, a dark depression settled into Yitzhak's heart. In his unresolved mourning, Yitzhak withdrew from his friends and tended to his chores halfheartedly. In the still of the night his tears woke him from his sleep; his thoughts focused on his mother. Dream after dream infected his nights as fantasy invaded reality, the two continuously confused till the afternoon's clarity revealed the truth of loneliness.

Despair weighed heavily against his heart, crumbling his resistance against the others images that always seem to invade his mind wherever he turned. Through this miserable experience he groaned and moped about, discarding all his friends' approaches.

It happened one day that Abraham wanted to lower Sarah's tent and to present her belongings to the other members of his group. Hearing about it, Yitzhak hurried to her tent and placed himself in front of his father and the workers.

"No, father, please do not do this thing. Wait a while longer."

"It's only proper that I distribute her things to those who need them."

"Please, father. For a while longer, let them remain here. They will not tarnish or disappear. I will personally guard everything."

Abraham sighed deeply and nodded. With a slight motion of his hand, the workers returned to other tasks.

The two men stared briefly at one another. Neither one knew what to say or how to dispel the strange, incumbering atmosphere surrounding them. Abraham walked away while Yitzhak kept looking at the tent. Slowly he walked toward it. He hesitated before he entered the stagnant tent. After his eyes adjusted to the dark he walked to his mother's dressing table. A pile of blankets lay beside it. He ran is fingers through the wool and closed his eyes for a moment. As he looked about the room, he noticed his mother's preparation items. He touched her ivory Egyptian comb and ran his fingers over her hairpins. The smooth touch pleased him. He remembered how Hagar used them to arrange his mother's bound-up plaits and to braid her long flowing hair. Unbearably her images rushed forward and transfixed inside his thoughts. He quickly left the tent, but soon began to experience an unremovable sadness whenever anyone said anything about his mother. Often, just a slight gesture or a word in reference was enough to create a flashback. When the pressures of the trade were too great to understand, he hid in the recesses of his tent. With swollen eyes, flaring nostrils, and running mucus, he cried, "Mama, mama."

Abraham, on the third years conclusion of his wife's death, when Yitzhak was forty years old, became grievously concerned about his son's mental condition. Night after night, Abraham walked to his son's tent. Quietly, secretly, he lay crouched behind the leather tent door. Listening, he heard his son's tormented tears beseeching his mother's embrace. Listening, Abraham folded his head between his arms. He walked to the tent's side, touched its tight weave, and silently cried.

"Eliezer," he finally determined to direct himself on a solution to his' torment. In the privacy of the hillside, during the time of watering the livestock, he approached his valued friend. "You are my most trusted friend," Abraham said. "You are my cousin and a direct descendant of Aram, who descended from Noah. Moreover, your family line descended from the line of Shem as did mine. So knowing that we indeed related and that we must not deceive another, tell me: the night's tears, that I believe you also hear, do they wake you?"

"Always, Abraham."

"I am caught inside a void, Abraham confessed. "A great blackness hovers over my life. Its despairing quagmire refuses me a venue to escape from. My heart tightens inside my chest. My liver explodes watery substance from my bowels. I do not want to go on with my life. Yitzhak is here. Yahweh has kept His promise. I have a son. A truly wonderful and strong son. His thoughts, however, reflect only on his mother.

"Eliezer, please place your hand under my right thigh."

"What contract are we to incorporate?"

"Swear to me with Yahweh's name, Creator of earth and heaven, that should I die or should I become deprived of logical thinking, or should someone, somehow, attempt to manipulate me in my state of depression, you will prevent me from signing a contract of marriage between Yitzhak and the people of the nations."

"I so swear by Yahweh's name."

"Further swear to me this: should you become the head of my house, under no circumstances will you allow Yitzhak to marry a Canaanite woman."

"Yahweh shall bear a witness to such an oath."

"I request a third favor. You are knowledgeable of the northern trade routes. Among all my people you remember best the land of Asshur and the land of Haran and the land of Paran."

"Yes, I remember those lands well."

"My fourth request is this: travel again on those same northern trade routes. Journey to my homeland. There, seek a wife for Yitzhak."

"A Babylonian woman?"

"Yes, for am I not a Babylonian?"

"Hagar had spoken of your prejudice. Yet, since you've performed so many inter-marriages, I doubted the reality of her words. Now you intend to manifest it openly! Why not a woman from Damascus? They are just as beautiful, just as willing, just as ripe."

"For the same reason I refuse a Philistine woman and an Egyptian woman: the blood of the Mashiach who is promised to descend from my family's line must not be contaminated with genetic impurities. I am the chosen one above all others. My father, and my father's father and his father and father's father all came from one lineage."

"Since you so strongly believe in what you say, and since you are my dearest friend and blood-relative, I will sojourn to the north for you. But what if the woman whom I find refuses to come here? Shall I return and take Yitzhak up north to be with her?"

"Not under any circumstances are you to do such a thing nor even to hint at such an arrangement. Yahweh will send Michael the Archangel to guide your camels. Yahweh will protect you from harm, as he does with my child and will do with his children and their children's children. Yahweh's angel will lead you to the person whom He will provide to my son; just as Yahweh betrothed me to Sarah.

"Should it occur, however, that the woman refuses to come back with you, never mind. You are cleared of your charge. Again, I must reemphasize, under no circumstances is Yitzhak to leave this land!"

Eliezer placed his hand under Abraham's right thigh, binding the solemn contract between them.

On the backs of ten of Abraham's finest camels Eliezer secured gold necklaces, rich bolts of cloth, ram skins, leathering, bronze axes, and iron plows. Brand new tents hid the contents of the treasures. The women of the camp spent months arraying the tents with colorful weavings on their borders. When the talented women finished the weavings, they covered the seams with another layering of leather to protect the thread from rotting. Along with the ten prized camels, thirty of Abraham's best and most loyal fighters accompanied Eliezer.

ᏜᏟᏴᏜᏟᏴᏜᏟᏝᏴᏜᏟᏴᏜᏟᏴᏜᏟ

From the rounded hills to the flat plains to the mountainous regions to the forest and to the farms and to the meadows Eliezer journeyed. For months his caravan navigated through dense forests and tall woodlands and high grasses. They voyaged through the heat of afternoon into the chill of night. They crossed from the mild temperate grass-plains into the cold mountaintops.

The well-recruited caravan and highly disciplined soldiers sojourned from Be'er-Sheva to Shechem; from Dan to Qatna; from Elba to Aleppo. Finally the weary caravan crossed into Carchemish. From there, they traveled to the land of Aram that rested between the Euphrates and Tigris Rivers.

One year after Eliezer began his trip, his caravan finally reached the outskirts of the city of Nahor. The city resembled all the other cities that he had passed through. They had the same look to their walls. The row houses had the same appearance, and the interior seemed to be lifted from the village he saw last month a hundred miles away. Even the marketplaces seemed remarkably the same. Each city's colors and flavors collaged. The world, in reality, is one grouping, separated by whimsical fantasies of differences. All looked the same to Eliezer. Even the smells and the foods appeared identical. The only difference was the style of the clothes that the people wore.

By the time his caravan arrived the sun was low in the sky. Ahead of him a gathering of women surrounded the main watering well. Merchants and politicians and soldiers also assembled around the fountain. Through the years the place had become the center for commercial contract conclusions and the planning of military campaigns.

The camels knelt to the ground. Eliezer, not knowing where to find Abraham's relatives, prayed to Yahweh saying, "Yahweh, God of my friend and companion, God of Abraham, grant to me please this favor: I am standing here by the watering well. For a certainty the daughters of these men will pass by my caravan to draw water for their families. Let one of them approach me. Let her say to me after I have introduced myself, 'Drink from my cup. Also, please let me water your camels till they are filled.'

"Let that female be the one for Yitzhak. Thus shall I know for a certainty that she has been wisely chosen."

He had barely finished speaking, when a beautiful, delicate woman approached him. She had luxuriantly soft, black hair with dark long lashes and eyebrows to match. Over her left shoulder she carried a painted jar.

Fascinated by her, observing her confident walk, observing her kind face, he followed her to the well, compelled by the mystical moment to test her.

"May I please share some of your water?"

With a sweet smile, she lowered her jar to his cup. Another woman thought it odd that she would pour water from her jar to his cup when the man could just as easily have helped himself to the community bucket that sat beside him.

"Drink, my lord."

When he sipped the cup dry, she immediately refilled it. In front of her his caravan was still kneeling. Beside the camels thirty men stood continuous guard.

"Are you in charge of this caravan?"

"I am. They and my men are thirsty. But they are afraid to vacate their positions for we are strangers here and we are uncertain of the city's hospitality toward us."

"There's no reason to be afraid. Some of us still remember Yahweh's name. I will be more than happy to tend to your caravan. Your men should rest themselves."

"We need to take care of the animals."

"I will personally see that the animals are taken care of."

The young woman eyed the situation and the weary men. She pursed her lips, nodded, smiled, and immediately determined to work from the last group to the first group. Without any further hesitation, she carried her jar of water to the last camel and its team of three guards. She ran back and forth to the watering trough, and went to the ninth group, then to the eighth group, and so on. Instantly, she worked her way toward the third group, who gratefully, and full of respect, received her help. The cool water satisfied their thirst. As a commoner she continued to labor over the thirty men and ten camels. With strong energy and without complaint she poured out the contents of her small container into the larger receiving barrels until she became satisfied that the camels and all the men were no longer thirsty. Only then did she release herself from her volunteered task. The strength of a woman geared to a task, appointed on her own terms, revealed her inner essence. She instantly pleased Eliezer.

It took nearly an hour to water the caravan. While she watered the camels, Eliezer studied her movements. He gazed at her figure and at her face and at her manners. He made a point of listening to her conversations with his men. She had an acute sense of humor, easily jesting with the soldiers as they jested, providing a calm relief from the wearisome journey. Then he asked himself: "Is this truly Yahweh's selection for Yitzhak?"

"Girl," Eliezer approached her as she was walking away. "What is your name?"

"Riveka."

"Here, please take this gold nose-ring for yourself. It weighs half a shekel. I also have two gold bands for you."

"They're heavy."

"Each is about ten shekels in weight."

"You are more than generous for such a small chore."

He smiled at her, An emotional swelling touched his heart. A tear formed.

"Please tell me, whose daughter are you?"

"Bethuel is my father. He is the son of Nahor, through Haran's daughter, Milcah, who is the sister of Lot. Nahor was the brother of Abraham who is somewhere south of us. He may now be a king, or he may be dead. I don't know which."

Eliezer's eyes moistened more when he heard her mention his friend's name. He turned his head away, diverting his attention to the children playing in the street. He scratched the back of his neck, and pulled down on his robe.

"May I further ask: Does your father Bethuel have any room in his house to receive me as a guest?"

"He has plenty of straw and he has room for you and for your men and camels."

"Then, Riveka, run and inform your father that he shall have many guests tonight."

She thought it strange for the stranger to show such emotion. After all, she only watered his camels and joked with his men. All in all, she had a good time with them.

As her lithe figure raced ahead, Eliezer motioned for his men to bring the camels forward to Bethuel's house. As the caravan worked its way past him, the camels' kicked up the loose dust. Eliezer, inside the dust cloud that filtered about him, privately whispered his prayer: "Blessed is Yahweh, God of Abraham, who has not withdrawn His steadfast faithfulness from my master. Yahweh has guided my task, even to the very doorstep of Abraham's nephew."

ᏋᏅᏇᏋᏅᏇᏋᏅᏒᏋᏅᏇᏋᏅᏇ

Riveka, fascinated by the sentimental man and his caravan from the remote southwest region of the land, ran to the courtyard of her father's large estate. The walls rose high over their heads, protecting the stalls and granaries of barley and flour. Scribes briskly counted the bread and fruit and root baskets and marked the weights of the jars. Laban, Riveka's brother, supervised the process.

"It's just like you to do such a thing," Laban remarked to his sister.

"But, Laban, look at this nose-ring and look at these two arm bands. Feel how much they weigh."

"They are indeed heavy." Placing the band in his teeth he bit into it. "It's solid gold!"

"Did I not tell you so!"

"Where is this man?"

"His caravan is behind me."

Laban hurried outside his courtyard and encouraged the team-masters to step inside the courtyard. "Where is your guide-master?"

"He remains near the well," one soldier replied.

"May Yahweh's name be blessed," he invoked when he found Eliezer. "And why are you still outside, especially after I have prepared my house for your stay and have prepared my stalls for your men and camels? Come, come, come," Laban urged. Not wasting another moment, Laban grabbed Eliezer's sleeve and pulled him forward.

"See, your men's feet are being washed and see, they eat to full satisfaction!" When Laban clapped his hands, the cooks rapidly brought a table and plates for Eliezer. He sat in front of the inviting, steaming lentils and the porridge soup. Yet, as Laban and Riveka and Bethuel motioned to eat, Eliezer remained still.

"Eliezer," Bethuel placed his wooden spoon back on the table, "we cannot eat until you eat."

Riveka placed her chin in the middle of her palm, elbow on the table, and smiled. Her warmth, the intensity of her eyes, the wonder of her attractiveness, unexpectedly caused Eliezer to cry.

"What's wrong?" Bethuel empathetically inquired.

"I cannot eat until I lift this burden from my chest. Please, listen to my story."

"Yes, speak of it. I am curious."

"I am sent to you by Abraham, son of Terah. I am his closest friend. Yahweh has blessed him enormously! He is the wealthiest man alive! He has thousands of cattle and hundreds of sheep. He has hundreds and hundreds of female and male attendants. He has herds of camels and donkeys. He trades in skins, wool, threading, meats, and dye. He has commercial stalls in all the cities about him.

"Sarah, Abraham's sister and wife, had remarkably, in her 90th year of life, presented him with a son from the bowels of her very own cavity. Everything which he owns he has given to his son.

"A year ago today I swore the most solemn oath to him as he ordered me: 'You must not bring to my son a wife from among the people of the nations in whose land I live. You must go to the land of my fathers, to my own brother's lineage, and procure for my son a wife from them.'

"I replied to Abraham: 'What if she refuses to come with me?'

"Abraham said: 'Yahweh, whose paths I traveled on, will provide a protecting angel for your journey. Your task will be a successful one. A wife shall come with you from the land of my fathers and from my very own brother's lineage.'

"'You shall not be released from your adjuration unless my brother refuses my request.'

"So, as you understand, I cannot be released from my adjuration unless you exclusively free me from it."

"Unbelievable," Laban exclaimed.

"There's more," Eliezer insisted on continuing with his story. "Today, when my caravan approached your city's well, I tested Yahweh's intents. I prayed a secret prayer to Him. I asked: 'Grant me success this day. As I stand by the water, let a daughter of these men come to me and let her volunteer to water my caravan without payment or asking for a favor in return.' No sooner had I finished my silent prayer than Riveka came to me, fulfilling my very test!

"Thus, it is time for me to inquire of you: Will you treat my master kindly? If not, inform me at this very instant. I need to know for I must ascertain whether or not to take the right road or the left road."

Laban, with a penetrating gaze into his father's eyes, answered, "The decree has already been set in motion by Yahweh Himself. We cannot speak bad or good to you about Riveka. Nevertheless, take her, for it is she whom you desire for Yitzhak. Do this, for Yahweh has made it to be so."

Instantly Eliezer placed his face to the ground. He stretched himself out and gave thanks to Yahweh. After his prayer of thanks he rose and motioned to his second-leader. The camel assistant also gave thanks, then motioned his hands to the other thirty men. On cue they rushed to the camels and unloaded all the packs. In perfect formation, they unrolled the wool blankets. The curious family members, desiring to see as much as they could of the gifts, gasped in wonder as the wrappings of the gifts fall away. Great riches were camouflaged inside the weathered cloths.

The next morning Eliezer knocked on Bethuel's door. Laban answered.

"I ask that I may have your father's permission to depart."

"So soon? But you just arrived last night!"

"I am urgently needed back home."

"Please, remain another ten days. We have to say our good-byes to our daughter and sister. She has to say her good-byes to her friends and parents and brothers and nieces and nephews as well. It is only reasonable that you stay a little while longer."

"I understand your request. But, still, do not delay me. My task has been completed only insofar as I have found her. I must return to fulfill my requirement."

"Father," Laban turned to Bethuel, "let's ask Riveka what she thinks."

Her servant, going to the back room, brought her before the three.

"Are you willing to leave with Eliezer at this very moment?"

"I am ready, yes."

"Eliezer, it seems even her thoughts have been set in motion for you. Travel with our deepest love and concern."

Bethuel touched her chin and lifted her face to his. He gently hugged his industrious and dependable daughter and said, "Take with you your private nurse and take with you your ensemble."

Laban bent down to kiss her affectionately on the cheek. "My sister," he prophesied: "May you grow into thousands of myriads!

"May your children conquer the gates of their enemies!"

One hundred fifteen years after this Laban saw his own prophecy fulfilled when Jacob, before he was renamed Yisrael, out maneuvered him in Haran.

ଵ୦ଓଵ୦ଓଵ୦ଓଵ୦ଓଵ୦ଓ

During the year long trip to Abraham's camp Riveka saw the new lands and rivers and forests and large savannas. She wondered about the drifting clouds and the green meadows. Everyday she reviewed the things concerning the journey and how everything seemed to occur at the divine hand of inspiration. When the rains came and the men's heart saddened, she laughed and cheered them up, reminding them how soon they would all be at home with their families. They to their old ones, she to her new. One year later Eliezer's caravan finally returned from Paddan-aram to the regions where Abraham settled. The day before his surprising appearance, Yitzhak's caravan returned from a trading mission in the vicinity of Beerlahai-roi, in the region of the Negeb. There, Yitzhak honed his bartering and diplomatic skills.

Three years had come and gone since his mother's death. He still reflected on images that mother and child shared together during his thirty-seven years, and wondered, now that he was forty years old, with whom he would share new images. Yitzhak separated himself from his men. Quietly he walked through an isle of flowers. "If only she could see me now," he thought to himself about his successes whenever he represented his father at the council meetings of trade. Then, hearing camels' feet and hearing the soldiers encouraging their camels' to trot faster, he raised his head. "Ha! What is this? A racing challenge!"

As he lifted his despondent eyes he saw Riveka, who simultaneously saw him. He moved silently toward her in the midst of the chaos and excitement. The closer he got to the caravan, the thicker the welcoming crowd. His sad countenance vanished as he stared at the thirty men who so long ago traveled to a far land to bring him back a bride. A soft smile greeted his lips. The smile enlarged as did his desire to meet his old friends. Instantly he determined to be the first man to greet the caravan. Laughing with an energy long denied him, his feet dashed forward and quickened. Others also began laughing with him and joined him in the chase to greet the caravan first. The impromptu race developed into a merry and harmonious challenge where the best and the fastest joined the great leader's son in a race where the prize and reward was being able to say hello first to Eliezer, the thirty men, and the woman who traveled beside him.

"Eliezer," Riveka exclaimed, "look how fast that tall man runs to us! No other can keep pace with him! Who is he?"

"He, Riveka," Eliezer laughed, "is Yitzhak."

Modestly covering her face with her veil, she alighted from the camel's back to the ground, into a soldier's helpful arms. She quickly gazed at the men rushing toward them and out of respect, permitted Eliezer and his thirty men to greet their families and friends. As all were hugging one another, and shouting for joy, she walked toward the left side of the room. She did not want to stem the enthusiasm of the men and women. She stood by the wayside as Eliezer hurriedly related to Yitzhak the events that had occurred during the past three years.

Abraham's white stallion soon rode up. Abraham, sitting straight up, gleamed at the small figure standing beside the camel.

As his horse reared, she marveled at the man and at his skills.

"You must be my great uncle Abraham," she nodded, smiling radiantly at him.

"And you are my grandniece," he returned her greetings. "Truly, you are as beautiful as Sarah was beautiful. I see Nahor's eyes in you. Are you his daughter?"

"Bethuel is my father who is the son of Nahor through Milcah."

"Lot's sister?"

"The very same."

"On your journey, did you have a chance to greet him?"

"No," she shook her head. "We sent a messenger to him, but he refused to accept him"

Abraham took the news sadly. "He cannot forgive himself for what happened to his wife and for having sons through his daughters."

"Abraham," her eyes smiled, "Today, dismiss such thoughts. Laugh with the rest of us."

Abraham looked deeply into her rich brown eyes and dark skin and long black hair. She was the most beautiful woman he'd seen since his wife. He laughed loudly, and his eyes twinkled again after three years of somber misery.

"Nahor had two wives!" he shouted! "Now I remember! Yahweh's messenger informed me of such a thing." Then, eager to see if his son and Riveka had approved of each other, he asked, "Well, children, don't keep me suspense! Tell me! Do you like each other?"

"Your son is quite handsome! I've never seen such broad shoulders on a man!" Her innocence amused both father and son. She turned to Yitzhak and asked, "How tall are you?"

"My son is the tallest in the land," Abraham answered in his place. "I don't know how he grew so high. I guess his mother planted some trees in his legs." Abraham laughed again.

"Yitzhak," she gently asked, "does your father always do all the talking?"

Yitzhak nodded, his face turning red from embarrassment.

"Why are you so quiet?"

"He's developed a reservation about himself," Eliezer said quietly, remembering the day when he and Abraham and Yitzhak traveled to Mount Moriah to place him on the sacrificial altar. Since that day Yitzhak had rarely talked to his father. After his mother died, he delved deeper into his seclusion. "But," Eliezer felt a need to defend and strengthen him, "Yitzhak is strong about certain matters! All become aware of his opinion when it differs from theirs!"

ᏋᏅᏣᏋᏅᏣᏪᏅᏣᏋᏅᏣ

That night Melchizedek traveled to the camp. In front of the encampment, Yitzhak and Riveka united in marriage.

During the three years that Eliezer and his thirty men journeyed to the city of Haran, Abraham and his chosen craftsmen assembled an opulent marriage tent. Eager to show Riveka the tent, Abraham proceeded the man and wife and gingerly opened the flap door for them. The newly married couple remained where they were, uncertain whether to enter or not. Keturah, Abraham's head handmaiden and her friends had arranged the marriage bed and waited on the couple to come inside. For a brief moment Abraham reflected on his own marriage blanket of many years, now long gone. He recalled Sarah's waiting arms. He saw her image in his mind. "How greatly she comforted and reassured me concerning all things," he whispered to himself. For a moment she was clear in his mind. Then the vision faded.

Hugging his son, then his new daughter, Abraham laughed again.

The Abimelech, watching his friend, commented to Eber, "He's been in Gaza too long. He laughs as often as I do."

Keturah and Eliezer and Abraham closed the loosely weaved cloth that separated the marriage bed from the witness room. The coupled looked at each other and shared a faint, embarrassed smile. Yitzhak looked at his father and at his two companions as they both removed their clothing.

The parents and the witnesses remained in the marriage chamber until the marital act was performed. Afterwards, Abraham and the rest instantly laughed in the shared joy of the experience then left the tent to hold the bloodied cloth over their heads, presenting evidence to the assembled camp that Riveka was a virgin and suitable for marriage to his son. The camp members, throughout the night, and up to part of the following day, celebrated.

With the passing months Yitzhak learned to love Riveka deeply. She, in turn, loved him as much. With the passing months Yitzhak's memories of his mother began fading, as did Abraham's.

છઉછઉલઉછઉછઉછ

Two years later another wedding ceremony took place. Again, the countryside attended the sumptuous reception. Again, the carcasses of hundreds of quartered young calves roasted over the roaring fires that lasted through the night's festivities.

Abraham, looking at Keturah, slapped his hands to his knees. "Come, sit here for a few moments."

Doing so, she ran her fingers through his thinning white-silver hair. "Do you love me as much as you did Sarah?"

"You should not ask for such a comparison. In these days of multi-marriages we need to approach each other with the understandings of the moment. We should never reflect on what has been. Think only of what could be—not what should be. Concentrate on the individual qualities that you possess and energize them with Yahweh's purposes. That is how you must deal with me."

"Sarah was a queen, wasn't she?"

Abraham's lips opened. He thought of her in the Egyptian's Great House. "She was more than a queen. She's the mother of a great nation!"

"What of our children to come. How will they fare. How will I fare?"

"I thought we had settled this before we married."

"Read to me our marriage contract. I want to hear it again."

"Our prenuptial agreement, as witnessed by Melchizedek, states that whatever children we have are to be financially provided for. They will live in the eastern lands beyond the Jordan. Yitzhak is indisputably established as my heir complete. All children born to us must sign a pledge to forfeit their claims to my wells and altars. Furthermore, they cannot renegotiate my treaties to act against Yitzhak."

"Yes, the agreement is sealed. As Yahweh provides for you, may He also provide for our children."

ⅇⅇⅇ

Ten years after Yitzhak's marriage to Riveka and eight years after Abraham married Keturah, in the year 1878 B.C.E., Eliezer received a message from the northern province of Canaan. Apprehensively examining the seal, he saw that it came from Eber.

Two week later Abraham and Yitzhak stood in front of Salem's new stone towers. Holding their mounts steady, the father and son breathed hard. The passing viewer, staring, saw two powerful men sitting on top of great horses whose flesh foamed white from their heavy, unrelenting race to the holy city.

When Abraham and Yitzhak gained entry, they walked into the grand hallway of the palace of the city. The red and yellow plastered walls glowed with the entering rays of the sun. Deeply etched floral patterns and geometric symbols covered the hallway. White marble covered the floor. The blue painted ceiling reminded the visitor of the sky. Gold borders met the etched carvings. The elegant pattern amazed both men.

In the middle of this elegance, the king-priest quietly lay on his bed. He called Yitzhak to approach him and weakly motioned for him to sit beside his knees. He placed his hand over his head and caused Yitzhak to bend his head forward. Yitzhak looked at the ancient man's trembling hands and began trembling himself.

Abraham, remaining beside them, watched the assistants carefully opening a special vial of oil. Placing the vial into Melchizedek's hand (who was once called Shem, the blessed son of Noah), the chief steward stepped away from the dying man. Melchizedek's (Shem's), hands suddenly became calm. Without another struggle he poured the sanctified oil over Yitzhak's head.

"You are the anointed to come after your father," Melchizedek spoke. "I, the blessed son of Noah, who was once called Shem, confirm that you are the father through whose loins that Mashiach will descend.

"I am the father of the Assyrians, the Chaldeans, the Lydians, the Aramaeans, and the Hebrews. I fathered Arpachshad two years after the waters lowered from the earth, and I fathered Elam, and Asshur, and Lud, and Aram and several daughters. My son Aram fathered Uz and Hul and Gether and Mash.

"Among my father's children: Japheth, my oldest brother; and Ham, my younger brother, the blessing of Noah reached my ears and my heart. And through me I presented these blessing to your great, great grandfather Eber. And Eber passed these blessing through Terah, your grandfather, to Abraham your father and Abraham will pass these blessing to you as we all have to our designated children."

Yitzhak stared at the oldest living man on earth. He was 600 years old. The ancient man existed for nearly 100 years before the flood and personally witnessed Nimrod's rise to power and his downfall and the birth and covenant between Yahweh and Abraham. He was a king and a priest. The only man who ever held both titles.

The ancient man spoke again to Yitzhak. "Is there anything, anything at all, that I can reveal to you concerning Yahweh?"

"I studied for years about Him. Yet, you can tell me, am I to have children, or am I to remain childless?"

"Riveka will conceive."

"But why not now!" Yitzhak lost his temper, hitting the bedside.

"Yitzhak," Eber placed his hands on his shoulders. "This is not the time for this kind of outburst. Our progenitor is dying."

Yitzhak looked at his father and uncontrollably whined again, "Death and dying! Death and dying! I'm damn sick of it. Live twenty, thirty, forty, one hundred, or one thousand years, yet we still perish—and for what? To feed the maggots!"

"How can you talk like this?" Eber questioned.

Yitzhak scratched his neck and shook his head, confused by his own outburst. "I don't know why. I'm just tired. I ask for everyone's forgiveness."

"I say this now to you," Melchizedek added, "through you and your through your chosen son, will a god-man descend. He will present mercy and divine compassion and eternal leadership and power even greater than I, not just to our children, but to all the children of every men for every generation."

Yitzhak stared at him in disbelief. He shook his head and wondered why he said such a thing.

"Son," Abraham whispered, "please, wait outside."

"I did not mean to shame you. I will wait outside."

Melchizedek, after Yitzhak left, called Abraham to his side and counseled him, "There's a duality struggling inside him. He has been this way since the day you placed him on the sacrificial altar. Such an event scarred his mental state. In my histories, I barely have anything to say about him." Melchizedek shook his head. "Those troubles shall enact themselves in a bitter and in a joyful drama between his children to come."

Abraham and Eber turned to look out the doorway through which the sunlight filtered, creating a column shaft of dancing dust particles.

"Nevertheless," Melchizedek (Shem) continued, "Yitzhak is quite correct in what he said: Death and dying are too burdensome to have to continuously witness time after time. I witnessed the death of billions who were born before I was born and I've lived long enough to witness the deaths of thousands who were born in this new age.

"I tremble at the loss of life that will precede the final age that will be ushered in through the power of God.

"Thus, Abraham, it is now time for you to subject yourself to Yitzhak. He is the anointed. As you were the Mashiach for this age, allow him to the Mashiach for his generation. Let this symbolize the ultimate Mashiach that will come from the Creator of the Universe. Your son will take care of you."

Abraham bowed then left the bedchamber. Eber stayed behind with Shem, who had been renamed Melchizedek by his father, Noah, prior to his own death.

"Son," Abraham solemnly, stiffly, spoke. "We're returning to our camp."

"What of the king-priest?"

"His death is a private affair," he choked back his tears. Lifting his head to the clouds, Abraham sighed heavily. "He did what he set out to do. You are the anointed. Ride before me. I will now do the following."

Yitzhak nodded. He led his father down through the green trail where overhanging branches brushed the horses' sides. The bushes of the trail gave way under their hooves.

Moments after they reached the new path leading to the valley, they heard the ram's horn blowing behind them. Its high, shrilling sound penetrated throughout the countryside. Both, knowing its death announcement, remained silent, faces set toward home.

Chapter Twenty-Two

▼

Yitzhak

This is Yitzhak's story.

Ten years after Shem died, twenty years after Yitzhak wed, Riveka still remained barren. Abraham, by this time had through his second wife, Keturah, six other sons. During Abraham's last few years Midian became the father of other sons as did Jokstan, making Abraham a grandfather.

ഇൻൽഇൻൽഇൻൽഇൻൽ

Abraham had other concubines as well. They also bore him sons.

ഇൻൽഇൻൽഇൻൽഇൻൽ

A day came when Yitzhak approached Abraham. "Father," Yitzhak asked Abraham, "will my wife give me children?"

"Yes, she will. As to the time, that I don't know. When I was a young man your mother's womb was sealed shut. We both agonized and prayed to Yahweh concerning her inability to provide heirs for me. We both misunderstood why she could not conceive and we both made grave mistakes as to how to interpret God's word. His meaning is best left unsolved, and accept its fulfillment when the times comes and declares it to you.

"We both knew that one day we would together produce a child. Often we doubted the veracity of it. Today, I know for an absolute, indisputable fact: one day many kings and nations will descend from you and Riveka."

"How are kings to come from us when we are not kings ourselves?"

"Yahweh has anointed us. We represent the ultimate Mashiach to come. Today we both serve as examples of the Mashiach."

"No one here recognizes our symbolic representation of this mysterious Mashiach."

Abraham smiled at his son. "Perhaps," Abraham became sarcastic, "these Canaanites don't recognize our crowns because they came from an invisible God."

Yitzhak also smiled at the warmth and gentleness that his father was displaying more and more openly as he advanced in age.

"It's just that our crowns are invisible. You, Yitzhak, and I, Abraham, are the kings of this world. Terah, my father and your grandfather, always taught that to me."

"Should I take another wife?"

"No. That was a source of conflict between Sarah and me and Hagar and Yishmael."

Yitzhak remembered the sexually abusive event in the pond during his weaning days and blushed red. "It's been over fifty years since I've seen Yishmael. Yet I know his children run everywhere. They are chased away by everyone."

Abraham nodded. "Such occurrences happen because he teaches his children his abusive play. Yet, I beseech you, learn to forget what he perpetrated against your flesh. Even though he sexually abused you, I still love Yishmael. I still think of him in kind terms."

"Then why don't you ever visit his tents?" His father's confession angered him and made him jealous.

"To do so would be the same as to admit that I am divided between you two. He was my firstborn, but he is not the inheritor of the genetic perfection required for the Mashiach's arrival."

"Must my child marry a Babylonian as well?"

"Your true inheritor must, yes."

"And his child as well?"

"That remains for the times to dictate. But your son must not marry any other clan. Is this understood?"

"I will obey your words. I know no other way than to follow them."

"You are now the anointed. Consider my words to be an experience shared; not the dictates of a commanding person."

Later that night and through the proceeding months Yitzhak continuously entreated Yahweh to intercede for him: to enrich his sperm and to enrich Riveka's reproductive fluids as well.

☙ଓ☙ଓଔଓଔଓ☙ଓ

Satan, traveling to Yahweh's domain, entreated Michael the Archangel for an audience with the Supreme Creator. It was granted to him.

"Yitzhak prays for a son, does he not?"

"I have heard his prayers."

"He wants kings."

"I had so promised it."

"It's a wasted effort. Why do you trouble Yourself with such an effort. Just pronounce it to be so, and it will be done. Yitzhak will rule the earth if You so desire. Abraham has a powerful army! He has enough wealth to sponsor any warmaking and machinery he desires. He is an experienced commander. So, tell me: Why do You wait? Why do You play this ridiculous game with him? Why do You taunt him?"

Yahweh, answered, saying, "I have purposed a specific plan arranged in precise details. I will do what I purpose."

"For a redeemer to ransom what I had caused to happen in Your perfect garden?" Satan mocked. "Look at humankind. I rule them! They want what I offer them. I have created thousands of gods for them and I answer all their prayers. I provide wealth, beautiful women, handsome men, lands, and yes; I make and destroy kings and governments at will. I can have a hundred different powers on earth ruling simultaneously for me, so why can't You have just one overtake them all—if Your plan is so brilliant?"

"What you accomplished, you created for chaos's sake—not for uniformity or good continuance. What I purpose shall be forever."

"When?"

Yahweh remained silent.

Satan also quieted. After a while he spoke again, "I challenge to You this: let Riveka's cavity open. Allow Yitzhak's sperm to swim inside her ovaries and let two cells embrace and from these twins, let me whisper into one's ears."

"Whisper into the ears of both," Yahweh replied, "for I understand your intent. You believe you can determine the lineage and responses of the ultimate Mashiach to come. I shall allow it to occur, and by your own standards you will see that the genetic goodness cannot be corrupted."

"We will see!"

"I have already seen the outcome," Yahweh answered. When He spoke, Satan stood still. For the briefest second he wanted somehow to find an avenue to return to God's fold. The idea quickly dissipated. Sneering, he left the chambers.

ઠ૦ન૩ઠ૦૩૨૩ઠ૦૩૨૩ઠ૦૩

Night after night Yitzhak and Riveka embraced. Morning after morning they reunited. When her period occurred, she withdrew to her private tent to keep count of the days and to observe the menstrual flow and coloration.

Counting the days she again entered Yitzhak's tent, embracing her husband. The days passed, the mornings flowed into the afternoon, and the sunsets colored the horizon crimson red with an aura of royal violets.

When the time of her normal flow returned, she left Yitzhak's tent for her own. Her handmaidens brought her private containers of water to bathe in. While she sat on an embroidered cloth, the maids set apart her special menstrual cloths to the wayside. These they burned during the morning's rise. As she bathed she brought her hands between her legs. She realized her period failed to flow. The next month her period again failed to appear. In her third month she woke to a heaving vomit and severe cramps.

"Yitzhak! Help me!"

Behind him the handmaidens followed, carrying ointment jars and salts and fresh garlic.

"What ails you?" Yitzhak, frightened of the moment, feeling helpless and concerned, inquired.

A handmaiden, reaching around Yitzhak, felt along Riveka's stomach.

"She's pregnant," she replied, tears swelling in her eyes.

"You're pregnant?" Yitzhak's eyes also watered. "Yahweh has seen our desperation and has come to our aid. Blessed be the name of Yahweh!"

Riveka, hearing the words, also joined in their tears and joy.

Days later, the cramps became more painful, more intense in their severity, lasting longer. Tightly gripping her knees, she screamed again. And the screams increased through the weeks. "Yahweh! Yahweh! Why must I bear such a terrible pain? What other woman suffers like me? Why was I brought into this life? To anguish so terribly? Would it not have been better for me if I had never been born?"

Yahweh answered her through Michael: "In your cavity two nations lie.

"Two separate peoples will exit from your womb,

    "and one people shall be stronger than the other.

"The younger shall rule over the eldest."

Riveka, transfixed by the words, remained motionless. Gaining her senses, she rushed out of her tent to find Yitzhak. Distinguishing him in the far fields she watched him as he bent over a newborn calf. She watched him as he picked it up. Her husband, fascinated by the new birth, personally washed away the placenta. Moved by the recent birth and her husband's loving tenderness with the calf, she ran to his arms, hugging him.

She shared Michael's divine news with her husband.

"I must inform Father," he answered. He gently touched her forehead and his hand flowed down her arm to her hand. Both hands lingered in one another's.

"Please, invite him to live with us till the child is born."

"He's with Eber. I'll send word to him. Perhaps, when you're closer to your time, he'll be able to come and stay a while with us."

She agreed. She long missed her father-in-law's generous smile. Since Melchizedek/Shem died, Abraham and Eber occupied their lives expanding the writings of the history and genealogical records that Melchizedek/Shem treasured so much.

ഇൽ ഇൽ ഇൽ

While living together in the city of Salem, both Abraham and Eber, determined to travel through the countryside. Both aged men traveled to the seashore. After a while, from there, they journeyed to the Negeb. On the border near Egypt the two historians studied the Hyksos infiltration into the Egyptian king's household. From escapees they learned how the Hyksos corrupted the *Great House* with intrigue and counter-intrigue and false manipulations and hopeful manipulations until the whole house rebelled within itself. Its effectual incompetence finally gave in to the foreign shepherd kings. Through patience, relying on time and gradual assimilation, the Hyksos advanced themselves into all stations of power.

Eber and Abraham analyzed the events. Tracing the course of the political and geographic possessions, they continued observing the Hyksos diplomats riding their camels to the Asiatic mountains where they signed treaties of peace and cooperation with the Hurrians. Years earlier these same people gathered their armies throughout Mitanni. There, the Hurrians eventually routed the city. Surrounding the countryside, they forced their sphere of influence to dominate political and cultural policies.

The Hurrians, like the Hyksos, were displaced from Armenia. With the newly negotiated treaties, both nationalities, for the moment, became content with their possessions.

Feeling secure, the Hurrians allowed the Asiatic clans to pass safely through their lands into Egypt.

ಐಲೕಐೞಐಲಐೞ

When Abraham was one hundred sixty years old and when Eber was four hundred forty-five years old, and when Yitzhak was sixty years old, Riveka went into labor. Sarah had expired twenty-three years beforehand. Historically, the recorded year was 1858 B.C.E.

Through the afternoon's unmerciful heat to the midnight's humidity, Riveka labored in waves of spasmodic pain. Her hands tightened. Her muscles tightened. Her breathing became harsh. The handmaidens and midwives tended to her needs while the men waited outside the tent, staying silent around the large, loudly crackling fire. Embers flew high overhead, disappearing into the stars.

Inside the tent of pain, the flickering light played on the women's faces darkening briefly one face, then another, then another. First the light revealed a nurse's forehead, then her nose, then her left side; then another's right temple and ear. Hushed, methodical fingers spread Riveka's legs, exploring the vagina walls, cleansing clear the rushing fluids. Two propped Riveka on her hips. Two others held her arms while another two supported her weight over the birthing stool.

At late watch the chief-midwife demanded that her daughter hold the oil lamps higher. Finally, a small red arm, similar to a hairy mantle, appeared from Riveka's cavity. Then, with a tiny hand grabbing hard around the emerging first child's heel, a second baby instantly followed.

The first they named Esau, after his red hair. The younger they named Jacob, for his hand seized his brother's heel.

Abraham, receiving the news, arrived hours after the twins' birth. Eber talked to the nurses and immediately wrote down what had occurred inside the tent, witnessing and testifying to its authenticity.

On the eighth day Abraham circumcised both children. In the second year he returned with Keturah to teach them everything he could about Yahweh's covenant. In his tenth year, Jacob, while tending watch over his favorite sheep asked Abraham: "How is it Esau is so much like me in appearance, but is totally different from me in his thoughts?"

"It was prophesied that you shall one day rule over him."

"Am I to be a king?"

"Someday one of your descendants will become a king."

"Why can't I be one?"

"Be content with your son's scepter."

"Will I have to wage war against my brother?"

"Never raise your hand against your brother. Always love him. Use your intellect. Analyze the moments. Logically conceive the true thought through deductive reasoning. Be slow to speak, and always speak with humility."

"Esau speaks what he wants to and says what he thinks. Father hardly speaks at all."

Abraham sadly smiled. "So, what happened when he was twenty-five years old still lingers inside his heart."

"What happened?"

"I nearly murdered him!"

Riveka, approaching the two, clapped her hands, signalling for Jacob to rush into her waiting arms.

"Grandfather tried to kill Daddy?"

"Eliezer and Eber explained why to you, didn't they?"

"Yes, I suppose I remember something about it. But Daddy doesn't always have to be so silent toward us."

"Your father's manners speak loud enough for us. We obey his eyes and hands, don't we?"

"Yes, Mother."

Touching Abraham's hand, she gripped it tightly. "Reinforcing the way of things—or trying to create a way of things?"

"Riveka, after I'm gone, the anointing must pass on to Jacob—not to Esau. Already I see too many instabilities in Esau that make it unsuitable for him to become the anointed one: his marriage to foreign wives, his overbearing manners, his sometimes overly anxiousness to fight others."

"Yitzhak loves Esau the most. Never has Yitzhak felt so comfortable around anyone."

"You know in your heart the course of things."

"What could be the harm in having Esau anointed?. Does it really matter?"

"You think because they are both Babylonians all is well with your family? That is not so. Through the decades I have come to realize my prejudices. I can now feel comfortable in the thoughts that one day a grandson of mine—yes, even he who is the genetic carrier of the Mashiach, may intermarry with a Canaanite. Perhaps, even with a Philistine. Perhaps, even as soon as Jacob's children?"

"Why do you say that?"

"The human race is born from two parents. We are all the same blood. A time will come again when the Hamitic and Japhetic races will intermingle with the Semitic people. The Mashiach to come will not tolerate prejudice nor bigotry. Freedom of hatred, with clear understanding of variant cultures permits all of us to be accepted into the plan of salvation."

"Keturah, is she influencing you?"

"No. Yishmael is half Egyptian. His children are three-quarters Egyptian. I find my other sons marrying his daughters. No one is disintegrating from the union. So, perhaps it can come about. I'm receptive to the thought."

"I am not!" Riveka surprised Abraham. "In your old age you accept too many things that you fought against in your youth. You sent Eliezer on a two-year journey to secure me for your son. My children shall also marry Babylonian women, directly from my father's lineage! Tell me, why is it some old mens' philosophies, which were conservative, soften—while the other old men, whose doctrines were liberal, harden?"

Abraham laughed. "Yahweh never changes. Depend entirely on Him. Your path can never stray."

ଅ୦୪ଅ୦ଫ୨ଚ୦୪ଅ୦୪

War again visited the world.

While the armies of the Hyksos overtook the armies of Egypt, the Hurrians waged war against the Hittites.

Treaties and counter-treaties and *Pacts of Accordances* overtook the clans and tribes of Mesopotamia.

While one army after another advanced and retreated and regrouped and attacked and withdrew again to countercharge, the Minoan navy established more seaports in Lower Egypt. Adventuring into western Africa, the Minoan navy explored its coastal lands, finally reaching Spain and its silver mines. The maritimers, renewing their territorial expansion, enlarged Gaza.

The Abimelech and the Phicol of Abraham's time died. The Minoan powers replaced him with another Abimelech, then another, then a fourth.

In the year 1843 B.C.E. Abraham called to his tent all his children. Eber, witnessing the event, wrote the contracts. That year Abraham fulfilled his promise to Keturah, his second wife. "To Zimran, travel east with your inheritance. Acknowledge Yitzhak as the true heir."

"I so acknowledge."

"To Jokstan, travel east with your inheritance. Acknowledge Yitzhak as the true heir."

"I so acknowledge."

"Jokstan, let it be also the same with my grandchildren from your clan: Sheba and Deban."

"Your grandchildren from my loins will acknowledge Yitzhak as the true heir."

"Medan?"

"I will also obey the contract."

"Midian, do you and your children: Ephah, Enoch, and whoever comes afterwards, agree?"

"We shall always protect Yitzhak and Jacob and his descendants. If we do otherwise, may our clan become as the desolate wasteland."

"Ishbak and Shuah?"

"We will travel to southern Arabia to the coasts of the Red Sea. We will never harm Yitzhak."

"These then are your gifts.

"Now, all of you, kiss me, then depart from me. Do so with affection. Do so with love. Do so remembering the promise of the ultimate Mashiach who is come to destroy the evil from our midst, engraved in your thoughts just as the amulet seals are engraved in your minds, which I had authorized for your usage in trade and safe traveling."

He held Keturah's hand and turned his voice to Yitzhak. Jacob and Esau were standing behind their father. "Yitzhak, have you forgiven Yishmael?"

"I have long ago forgotten what occurred in the pond."

"Who is your God?"

"There is only one God on earth and on heaven. There is only Yahweh. There is no other god before Him."

"It is so! It will always be so from time eternal to time eternal. Tell me, are you still repulsed by the drama of death and dying?"

"Yes. I will never be comfortable with it."

"Nor should you be. Through you and through your children the redeemer of death will come to the earth. The Mashiach will ease your images of what now takes place with humanity's deterioration."

Abraham rose to stand between Keturah and Eber and projected his voice, "Yitzhak, all that remains with me, is yours. All my wells, all my altars, the burial cave of Machpelah, all my cattle, my oxen, my sheep, my camels, and those servants who wish to remain with you are yours to care for. Now, rest. Permit your mother's memory to come to you tonight so we may remember her kind tenderness and love and disciple for all of us. When you speak to your children and grandchildren, tell them of my journey from the city of Ur through the city of Haran and how it is and why it was that we settled in this land among these various tribes that hate us. In the morning, place me alongside Sarah."

Nodding, Yitzhak entered his mother's old tent which Abraham kept protected behind his bedchambers. During the night's vigilance not one fire burned. Not one person kept watch. Everyone in the camp retreated to their tents, residing in total darkness.

Abraham, in the recesses of the silenced camp, stared through the open flap of his tent to look into the deepest portions of the stars' constellations. Perplexed, he asked, "Yahweh, where is your home? Are you in the eastern spirals, or in the western swirls of light? I have never seen your face. Yet I know you are my closest friend. Long after my body has rotted and has been consumed by the nature of things, recall my personality in your memory.

"When you see my children's eyes and hear their cries, recall that they issued from me. When they commit their wrongs and transgressions against You, remember, please, they are my children. I have not forgotten your decree of affliction that they must suffer through, but when the time expires and they become free of their chains, recall in their hearts who I was.

"Yahweh, remember me in the resurrection."

As the sun brightened the darkness away from the earth, Jacob was the first to wake up. Entering his grandfather's tent, he witnessed a strange glow hovering over Abraham's body. A sad, omniscient presence resided in the tent with him. The light brightened, then instantly vanished.

Eber came up behind him.

"Was Grandfather a real king?" Jacob asked.

"How could you be a king if he was not?" Eber replied.

ᏅᏏᏌᏏᏋᏒᏏᏗᏒᏌᏏᏌᏏ

The following week, a new caravan arrived in Mamre. Struggling through the torturous sandstorms and the furious heat of mid-afternoon, the caravan finally approached the soft sloping hills of the village. Reaching the place in the road where all caravans stopped for military inspection, a lone, aging and unarmed man approached the team leader of the caravan. A brown mourning tunic covered his body.

"It's Yishmael," Eber whispered to Yitzhak.

"May I travel beside you, Yitzhak?" he asked only once after approaching the mourning caravan.

Without speaking Yitzhak stepped in front of his half-brother. Opening his arms, they embraced each other, passionately kissing each other's necks. A strange, electrical radiance traveled through Yitzhak's body and it similarly transferred to Yishmael. "You indeed are the anointed," Yishmael finally admitted.

"For those words, I forgive you of everything you have ever done against me. Come with us. Help me bury our father."

After the private burial, Yitzhak felt a presence descending over him in the deepest recesses of a man's heart, where all true things become exposed through the peelings of anguish. The sensation enveloped him entirely inside a mystical, transparent bubble wherein he understood Yahweh's directing purpose. Eber, touching Yitzhak, felt the spiritual bond. He stepped back and Eber stared into Yitzhak's eyes. Yitzhak was acutely focusing on the burial cave.

"Yahweh is speaking to your father," Eber informed Esau and Jacob. "Let's leave them alone."

Afterwards, in the calm of afternoon, Yitzhak and Yishmael forever separated.

ᔕᏫᔕᏫᏣᔕᏫᏣᔕᏫᏣ

𝔍our years later, while Yitzhak was living in the land of Beer-lahai-roi, he happened to be waiting outside the city walls when an old, toothless, nearly blind man walked toward him. Behind that ragged man an aged, decrepit donkey followed. A very old, extensively worn and tattered gold-threaded cloth rested over the donkey's back. Yitzhak became curious, so he walked to meet the man and his animal.

"Who are you?" Yitzhak asked the white-and-purple-robed man.

"I am searching for Eber's great-grandson, Yitzhak."

"You have found him, old one," Yitzhak smiled.

"A caravan of papyrus rolls follows me from Salem. The historic documents are being transferred to your care. Eber sends this note ahead of the caravan. You are to read it in front of me."

Precariously walking to the donkey, the trembling old man snapped back the purple linen over the donkey's box. Underneath the cloth an aged and small cedar chest rested underneath Eber's trading cylinder.

Yitzhak gasped and wondered at the meaning of it.

As he opened the chest, Yitzhak ran his fingers over the etched characters on the dry mud tablet. He looked at the old man who could barely see him in return. But the old man, feeling Yitzhak's staring eyes on him, placed his shaking hand on Yitzhak's shoulder. The violent trembling suddenly hushed.

When he read the tablet, Yitzhak's eyes moistened. Memories rushed over him. Unable to bear the pain of those times long ago vanished to the recess of history, he dropped the clay tablet. In slow motion the tablet descended to the ground, shattering instantly on impact. With the shattering, Yitzhak bellowed an anguished, deep-throated scream. All the silences that he had ever retained, erupted forth from his throat, flooding the plains with his remorse and love.

He folded his arms over his shoulders and collapsed to his knees.

His face fell forward to the ground where his tears fell on the bits of the shattered clay tablet.

He grabbed handfuls of dirt and rubbed the harsh grains into his cheeks and forehead.

The particles of grit skinned his flesh.

This event happened four years after Abraham's death. Eber expired in 1839 B.C.E. after living four hundred sixty-four years.

Chapter Twenty-Three

▼

Nations

The morning breeze alerted the group to the night's end. The planet Venus shone brightly through the eastern dawn, greeting the sun's rays. The earth continued rotating on its tilted axis, manifesting that only for a brief span of time can things remain the same.

The thief placed the stolen scrolls down.

He stared into the Greek's hazel eyes. He took note of his gray hair. For the first time the thief realized the caravan leader's dangerous strength. In the morning, when the dawn light reveals everything in its softest contrasts, the truth of the man's scars and facial wrinkles and broad shoulders and powerful biceps gave testimony of whose tent the thief had just spent the night in.

He quickly shifted his eyes to the rest of the audience. The six dozen men seemed to sigh a strange, soft echo. They rubbed their hands dry on their tunics. Their faces were characteristically different from each other. Somehow, however, they were briefly unified by the same thought. The moment quickly disintegrated.

"The reading gave me some thoughts to digest," the Greek merchant finally said to the two thieves. Arching his shoulders back, his tunic opened slightly. The thief sat back down. Somehow, during the night's reading, he had failed to realize the enormity of the man. "But now that you've read us the scrolls, why would we want to buy them?"

"To resell to someone else?" the thief meekly replied. Almost comically he added, "Surely you pass by scholars and religious temples where the priests and intellects would be interested in acquiring these writings."

"I never associate with them. I sat patiently here during the night, listening to your stories, for we Greeks are accustomed to storytellers and wine. We have Hercules and Zeus and many other grand stories that help us pass the night away."

"These stories should make good rereading then."

"Aren't you being silly? One reading is enough. The storytellers' trade depends on new audiences, not the same ears over and over. Thank you for your readings. We will remember what we heard, and in the future, should someone else state something similar to us, we'll have a comparative foundation. That way we'll eventually discern truth from your perspective and truth from their perspective."

The thief leaned forward and gritted his teeth. "I want a sale."

The Greek tensed his jaw in return and snarled, "How many other tents have you sought a sale from?"

The thief looked at his partner. Both shook their heads.

Behind them, a burly camel-master pushed to the forefront of the listeners. Eyeing the rolls, he asked in a slow voice, "Are we through?"

"No," the thief sharply responded. "We have only touched on the fewest of these writings."

"I'm tired. Read again to us tonight."

"Your caravan is willing to stay another night here?"

"Of course not. But you may follow alongside us."

"To where?"

"China."

"How long a journey is that?"

"One year there. One year back."

"And during that time you expect us to read to you every night?"

"Not every night. Only when the storytellers' song is needed."

The second thief unexpectedly jumped up, his hands drawn into fists. "I'm tired of reading! And I certainly am not going to continue reading night after night all the way to China then again back to here! Just pay us a sum of silver and keep them for yourselves to read or to sell or to burn for fuel or for your excrement folding! Just give me some money!"

Incensed at his outrage, the burly man rushed alone at the thief. His huge arms wrapped around him. In the briefest second, he lifted the thief off his feet, crunching him.

"Wait!" his partner shouted. "Release him!"

Momentarily freed, the thief fell to his knees, his shoulders bent over like a defeated dog that whines to the superior. The other men, who had eagerly gathered during the night's story-telling-time, leaned over to one another, whispering. Agitated by the Greeks unexpected seriousness they started to leave.

"Wait!" the first thief shouted at the departing listeners. "At least contribute something, anything to us for our reading efforts."

"Contribute?" the Greek leader mocked. "For stolen words? How ludicrous!"

"You stupid buffoon!" he shouted back in a trembling voice, much too fast to think of the danger he was in. "You unwashed, ignorant Greeks still think you own the world and that it must answer to your every demand! Well, we demand some silver!"

In the quietest, most somber voice imaginable, the Greek stated, "Then it appears we'll have to save the Roman soldiers the trouble of arresting you two manipulators!" And in a calm voice that directly contradicted the enormity of the danger, he added, "Seize them." And the softness of the whisper terrified the two thieves.

In a quick scuffle, the Greeks caught and bound the two thieves.

Harshly, violently, the Greeks tossed the two thieves into the center of the tent. There, mystically, the dawn's light cast its shadows over the leader's face. This time, however, the first thief, daring to look at the larger Greek, couldn't distinguish his features. It was as if the leader's features suddenly became blanketed behind a darkened mask.

While he stared at this, he failed to notice a group of men sneaking behind him and his companion. In unison, the strong group tightly grabbed both thieves' arms. Trapped in an inescapable vice, the first thief panicked, crying.

The burly camel-master, standing over the crying thief, became angry at his weakness. Not tolerating the whimpering crying, the burly camel-master slapped him on the face. The sound vibrated through the tent.

"Farther! Extend his arms farther out," the same quiet voice directed the action. Practically picking the first thief up off his feet, the invincible group stabbed his arms straight out. Before the thief could gasp, the caravan master plunged the dull sword through the thief's arms, butchering them off.

Wide-eyed, horrified, unable to break loose from the entrapping grips, the thief watched the iron sword flashing a bright reflection of the rising sun, capturing the grinning faces of the men who were holding him. The sword struck through his flesh and bones. Both hands tightened for the last time.

The group, tiring of the thief's screams and crying, dropped his writhing body to the ground, where they kicked him aside.

The second thief saw the blood spewing from the extruding arm bones. His senses froze at the sight of his companion's amputated limbs. The stiffened arms repulsed him. The screaming, turning and turning body that was unable to grab anything tortured him. His companion's face became a contortion of everything ugly he had ever seen.

He kicked his feet at the men in front of him and tried to force his way outside. Thrusting wildly, shouting fiercely, he tried to attract a rescuer's attention. No one came. None interfered.

The Greeks clamped his body tightly in their grasp. Throwing him into the center of the tent, the Greeks laughed as they held the second thief directly above the screaming and circling body of the first thief.

The strongest men forced the victim's body straight out to the severing sword. Then the merciless Greeks tossed them outside and abandoned them to bleed to death. And through the inconceivable pain, they bled to death as the stars shone over their withering bodies. The mesmerizing blood poured from their arm sockets, forming a coagulating red and brown pool that trapped a few of the loosely flying scrolls. The baking sun caked the blood a deep, dank brown as it spread over the earth and to the edges of the loose rolls. Vultures occasionally perched on the men, tearing the flesh off. Ants came by the thousands, their long military line feasting on the remains. Maggots grew from microscopic size to full size, consuming the rotting cast-off.

Hundreds of scattered scrolls lay about the silent bodies. Some became caught in the thicket of woods and vines. Some unrolled over the bodies as a temporary shield against the heightening sun. Some flew completely away from the camp, entrapped under a bush. The wind pushed other scrolls into the grass. Some, resisting the wind's push and pull, remained exactly where the violent actions discarded them. As rolled flowers they appeared over the grass plain. As cylinder flowers they appeared under the bushes. As elongated flowers, rising around the trees' trunks, they appeared. They had a separate existence. A separate life. An indiscernible breath that no one could hear but could only cherish in its intellectual possession.

The evil spirits laughed as the scattered scrolls flew about the desolate campground.

The angels wept.

The dismantled caravan tents left no evidence of their placement. The people left.

The small animals scurried about.

The crimson sun set on the horizon.

Other caravans began meeting at the road's junction. Relieving their thirst, the first group of travelers ignored the two corpses. The camel hooves carelessly trod over the rolls. A little later a second group of men walked by, leading their donkeys to the water.

The missionary group traveled in long, loose white garments. Another thick layer of wool wrapped around their hips. Braided cords dangled from their shirts as they walked. Long black strands of hair hung from the temples of their heads, hiding their ears. Behind them other men followed. Their girth belts held other cords of braided wool cords. Their feet had no sandals.

When a few of the men spotted the corpses, they turned their eyes away. Covering their noses, they tried to avoid breathing in the nauseating stench.

"Don't touch them," the eldest member warned the youngest recruit.

"I'm curious about the scrolls."

"Yes, I am too," his friend admitted after a brief pause. "Let us investigate them."

"Don't waste your time. They're probably accounting records."

"No. They're not!"

"What are they then? History books? Science books?"

"Even more important!" he answered, beaming after examining a few of the scrolls. "They contain a religious element. Yes, they're holy writings!"

"What?" the leader exclaimed.

The Essenes, caught in the moment of discovery, stood silent, staring at each other. "Gather them together," the leader broke the trance.

They bunched them carefully inside a purple linen cloth. Afterwards, they separated themselves from the other caravans they traveled with to journey to the edge of the dwindling forest that had once reached to the ocean's sand dunes.

In their hastened flight from the torturous campground, the Essenes became frightened of the moment's tension. Nervously, a few imagined an armed expedition of Roman soldiers chasing after them, reclaiming the scrolls for themselves. "What potent message do these scrolls contain?" a junior member asked his friend. "What injurious revelations are inside them? What do they reveal?"

They allowed their imaginations to fly to degrees of various scenarios. A few whispered among themselves: "How did the writing come to be where they came to be? What wrong did the two individuals commit to suffer such terrible deaths?"

Cautiously, the Essenes established their night camp beneath the canopy of shining stars. Not daring to unroll another scroll, they waited for the hint of light to unveil. In that immediate moment, they departed, heading for their enclaves.

They traveled through the expanding desert until they finally reached the cragged peaks of the rolling mountains. The sun was fierce. The travel wearisome. The flesh of their soles were leathered from the long journeys. The sharp points of the rocks jutted into their skins.

They had trained themselves to endure the climate. To abide by the lack of material possessions. To subtract themselves from women. They relished the possession of knowledge. They desired to understand completely all religious thoughts of their sect. Daily they judiciously sought an analytical ownership of the Mashiach's mission. In their attempts at total understanding, the Essenes created a biblical enterprise and institute for discerning the writings of the prophets. Only the most religiously astute male could bond with them. Only those directed in purpose with the Mashiach's mission could adhere to their sect.

Once they reached their enclave, the leader of the Essenes appointed the most trusted and knowledgeable among his care to study the discovered scrolls. The passing days held great expectations. The selected few, consulting with the few who understood the Greek language, formed an impassioned effort to reassemble the scrolls into their original chronological order. The chosen scholars, finally accomplishing the task, handed their work to the leader of the Essenes. Appreciating the great work, he began reading the reassembled scrolls to the gathered missionaries.

As he read the words he thought of the times when his own father read the story of Moses to him and later, how his teachers read the stories of the prophets and of the law. After several nights he found the scroll where the thief stopped reading. He nodded his head. He knew from the torn edges that this was the last thing the thief read. As if he had to take over, he began reading aloud.

“”“”“”

Yitzhak's story continues.

During the passing years Esau's skills as a hunter fortified him as the foremost leader among Yitzhak's men. He trained himself to read the footprints in the earth and led others into the deep forest. He easily determined the type of prey and the speed of its run from the remaining evidence. From the hunted's excrement he deduced the hour it had rested and the distance it had traveled.

Esau preferred to sleep under the constellations rather than inside the stifling tents. Out in the night air, he and his friends laughed and traded stories about the great run and kill. Their songs echoed through the camp and their camp smoke signaled to the women another successful catch.

Jacob, mindful of the rising smoke from the depths of the forest, turned away and walked inside his tent. "Esau always has all the attention!" Jacob said to himself. "And why shouldn't he," he answered himself. "What man hunts better and what man provides more for us?"

He sat down and unraveled one of the scrolls from the collection that Melchizedek and Eber had worked on. The cuneiform characters were distinctly different from the Egyptian hieroglyphics that he had learned to read and interpret. The characters were not as intensely shaped as the wedge characters of the Hittites that he had also learned to read and write. The linear characters which his great-great-grandfather had conceived were more compact, easier to digest, translate, and write. The alphabet was created because of the hundreds of histories and hundreds of genealogies that he needed to testified to. Gradually the scribes that Melchizedek and Eber trained in their methodology transferred their skills to the growing population that was settling in the Lebanon territories near the Mediterranean Sea.

Jacob's intellect kept increasing. Then, when his father was feasting on Esau's greatest hunting victory, Jacob turned his thoughts westward.

₭℃₭℃₭℃℃₭℃₭℃

*F*rom the cliffs of the Island of Crete, the *Lord-Ruler and Prince of the Lilies* stood on the edge of his balcony, releasing his falcon to the oncoming prey. Swiftly gliding to the escaping partridge, the falcon's claws grasped it, thrusting his beak into its skull.

Satisfied by his accomplishments, the *Prince of the Lilies* stood with his hands grasping the stone edging of his balcony. The Minos, for such he was called, stared beyond his multi-tiered and hundred columned palace. Democratically elected by the Minoan population for life, he resided in the palace as the nation's representative to the world. The Prince of the Lilies, after listening to the most important members of his council, spoke the people's will and course to the other nations.

The enormously large white, red and blue palace sat at the foot of the ascending hills. The hired construction workers eagerly designed the palace to reflect a harmonious lifestyle of freedom and courage. Their beautiful palace rose softly to meet the lush and thick evergreen forest of cedars and oaks and mulberry trees that journeyed to Mount Juktas.

The vividly frescoed walls of the palace depicted gentle blue dolphins jumping from frothy waves, greeting the ships with a welcoming smile. Great-winged griffins guarded the entrance doors. The walls of the adjoining rooms contained frescoes of bull contests: the heroic conquering the onslaught of death. The narrow waists of the performers heightened their broad shoulders. The sleek, slender, muscular red men faced the sleek, large-breasted Caucasian women. Politically, economically, and militarily, each status equaled the other.

From the port city of Knossos, the Minos faced the Cyclades Island of Thera that rested seventy miles north of his palace. On clear days he could see the smoking cloud rising from its volcano. On rare occasions, he felt the earth trembling beneath his feet.

"We've established a new post in Corinth and in Pylos," the great naval commander informed the Minos, speaking in the Luvium language, a proto-Greek dialect.

The Minos stared into the deep blue eyes of his naval commander. His slightly tanned skin contrasted with the Minos's sunburned flesh. Legends had told of times past when his ancestors came from the interior of the great continent's heartland: the Caucasus Mountains. His ancestors had been the children of Yefet: the Javan, the Elishah, the Rodanim, and the Tiras.

The Aryan race found it easy to navigate the waters from the mainland to the larger island. The water was not as deep then. The islands were larger. With the passage of time the shallow sea rose, covering the once faraway mountain to its waist. The rising waters erased from men's eyes the flat welcoming plains. What had been great heights of mountains became extruding tips.

The Minos summoned his personal accountant. "What has been brought in today from our colonies?"

"Our pithois are filed with new grains and fresh wine and olive oil. Silver ingots have arrived from Spain and our ships are returning from the northernmost port of Anatolia. A small settlement is being considered there."

"The name of the settlement?"

"Troy."

"Keep it to a minimum. Our trade with the Mitannians isn't as great as it used to be. I prefer a greater outpost on Thera."

"It's a volcanic island. We should concentrate on the Grecian mainland."

"Where the Mycenaeans live? Corinth is there already for that express purpose."

The Aryan naval commander stared at the accountant. "I'm sorry. I did not mean to question your authority."

The Minos graciously smiled.

"I always need someone around me who isn't afraid to correct me." Then, more seriously, he talked to the naval commander. "The Sea Peoples still threaten our commerce. What is being done to handle them?"

"Our navy is expanding. We're creating newer, stronger, swifter ships to fight them. One of our craft-masters has developed a keeled ship that has a rudder. He's created a war galley that has a convex stern. It can carry a double row of marines. It has a sharpened ramming beam secured to its prow. Along with our mussel boats, we should be able to defeat these buccaneers. Thus far we have militarily confined their activities to the Delta of Egypt."

"How are the Palastu doing? Are they holding against the Sea Peoples?"

"The Philistines are doing fine. I heard they had made treaties with them and are, in fact, intermarrying with them."

"As they are with the Canaanites?"

"Why not? The pussy's the same."

"I wonder," the Minos sincerely laughed, "white skin on top of black skin. Have fun! Enjoy!"

"Must be pretty exciting," the accountant theorized.

"If you like short women," the naval commander added. "Personally, I like our long-legged women."

The Aryan Minos nodded complacently. His thoughts shifted back to the harbor. "Build for me a city on the southern slopes of Thera. Name it Akrotiri. We'll establish it as a trading and commerce center to serve the

Ionian coastline and the new colony of Troy. Our turquoise and copper operations can benefit there."

ᏏᎸᏏᏯᏒᏏᎸᏯᎸᏏ

While the naval commander manifested his plans for destroying the buccaneers' ships that lay anchored near Ithaca, the flatbottom barges of their Caphtorim cousins cautiously exited from the Nile River. Inside these barges the merchants gambled on safely reaching the opposite shores with their ingots of gold and bushels of wheat. They coordinated their efforts with the naval commander's attack and together they landed on the Tyrian shore. There they saw the impassioned flames setting the buccaneers' sails ablaze. The horizon brimmed red with death and destruction.

A second group, not understanding the significance of the horizon's frightening brightness, stood their sails down. Standing watch, the frightened sailors hunched forward as a troop of Egyptian soldiers approached their encampment. A few men raised their weapons in uncertain response to the trailing dust of the swift-galloping horses.

"Hold your axes!" an Egyptian called out. "We're here to see your captain."

"Our passes have been notarized," the nervous captain said.

"We are not here to inspect your travel pass. We are here to tell you that the great Minos has vanquished his enemies!"

Astounded, the Cherethite, who was related to the Philistines, opened his mouth, bellowing a roar of laughter. "Our barge is safe?"

"For today! And, for generations to come."

"Then get over here and help us celebrate our Minos's great victory!"

The two nationalities celebrated through the short night the Cretan conquest of their dreaded enemy. Immediately the Egyptians dispatched ambassadors to Caphtor, who numbered among the descendents of Ham, laden with ivory and jewels.

During the next growing season the farmers cultivated the land of the Nile Valley to its maximum potential. The trading ships safely carried the excess grains to the Ionian island of Rhodes. From there the growing merchant class transported the grain to the Hittites. The Hittite merchants, in turn, traded the barley with the Mitannis and with the Assyrians.

𝕮he Abrahamites, settling in the Arabian Peninsula, intensively farmed their vast grainfields. Unaccustomed and unlearned as they were, however, in the methodology of irrigation, the Abrahamites soon hastened the death of their topsoil. Arrogantly, they refused to hire the Egyptian laborers who settled in their land willing to teach them their cultivation practices.

During the twentieth year of working and cultivating their farms, the children of Abraham and Keturah completely ruined their land. The winds that followed crept across their fields, carrying away the topsoil to the Philistine lands and to the Valley of Sharon. Other windstorms further snatched up the topsoil, blowing its brown clouds into the Red Sea and into the Persian Gulf. The earth cracked and the cabbage wilted and the carrots withered and the wheat dried, catching fire.

The ensuing firestorms raged throughout the Arabian settlements. In an attempt to calm the ravage, the panicking laborers mistakenly brought to the fields salt water, worsening the situation.

𝕰itzhak, unable to water or to feed his cattle, watched them slowly perish. Through the months he lost nearly his herd. Financially devastated, insecure, he withdrew to the shadows of his tent. Full of self-blame, he isolated himself from everyone. "It's because I survived the sacrificial altar that I've lost everything. I lost my father's prize oxen, his best sheep, his finest cattle. It is better to die in full grace than to live in the dismal mists of agony. Satan taunts me for having lived. Perhaps I should allow his victory to absorb me and be done with this episode."

"What do you mean?" Riveka demanded. "Are you talking about taking your own life?"

"My life has already been taken from me. What am I now? I just served to provide semen to you to bring about the birth of two children who constantly quarrel about everything. They are worse than Yishmael and I!"

"They are not homosexuals or deviants! For their continuous strifes, both still love one another."

"As Cain loved Abel?"

She snapped a cloth at his face, striking him hard. "Exhaust this depression away from yourself. Yes, we lost everything your father gave us, but we are still alive. We still have two brave, strong and highly intelligent sons. We still have men and women who follow you loyally. Never allow them to see you hiding in deep, depressive shadows."

"I shall not. Nor shall I involve myself with them. Better for me to keep silent than to let them know how much less a man I am than my father."

Later that month Yitzhak summoned his family together for a private conference. In the brightly lit tent, he asked them for their advice.

"We can go to Haran," Riveka suggested after everyone else failed to suggest anything worthwhile.

"Yes," Jacob reinforced his mother's strategy. Holding her in his arms, he gleamed, "We have family there who will be happy to feed us and let us graze on their lands."

"I cannot," Yitzhak quietly spoke, pinching his upper lip between his thumb and index fingers his thumbnail playing between his two front teeth.

"Father," Esau inquired, "why not?"

"I pledged to my father that I would never leave this land," his words almost sounded cowardly. "Do you want me to lose this as well?"

"Surely, he never foresaw this famine!"

"How is it you had forgotten the duress of his times?" Jacob spoke up, embarrassed at his father's lack of leadership and assertion. "Grandfather also underwent the times of a famine and came through them. We can too."

"How do you know that!" Esau insisted.

"I read about it in the histories."

"You spend too much time reading. It would be better for you, and for us, if you would learn the art of hunting. Two of us in the forest could bring back twice as much food."

Their mother interrupted them. "Jacob, is experimenting with a field of lentils. They seem resistant to the dry conditions of the soil. The plant seeds can feed us as well as becoming fodder for the livestock."

"Where did you learn such a thing?" Yitzhak asked Jacob.

"I've observed it."

"Observation? That's quite a keen feat," he beamed.

Esau walked to the tent's door. His jaw was tight. "Growing peas takes too long. Food is needed now! I'll hunt while he observes!" he mocked.

"Jacob, continue with your lentils," Yitzhak asserted his patriarchal role, speaking to his second born with a distant tone, "Esau," his smile broadened, affectionately, he touched his firstborn on the elbow, "continue hunting. Bring back some delicious meat."

"I will, Father. As your firstborn I will bring back your favorite meat."

"Go then," Yitzhak rapidly raised his finger, then instantly jerked it down. This gesture was habitual with him, as was the parting, lifting, and rapid lowering of his hands. The two brothers left their parents to walk into the bright, intense afternoon sun. The brutal heat baked the ground hard.

Hot! Exasperatingly hot. Unrelentingly hot!

The few surviving cattle, trying to escape the horrendous heat, rested under the skimpy shade of the oak trees.

Soon, even the large round water pond receded into a shallow, muddy lake. Within weeks the waist-deep waters became ankle deep. The vegetation disappeared into the blowing wind. The ankle-deep water then completely evaporated, leaving hardened, cracked earth behind it.

ঙ০Ꭷঙ০ᏮᏒঙ০Ꮾঙ০Ꮫ

The two brothers looked at one another. In that singular moment, where all visions returned to the past, memories flooded, tender and wonderful. They released the minute's hostility and held their arms out to each other. Both brothers embraced and tightly hugged one another for an eternal second. Jacob's clothes wrapped around Esau's legs and Esau's coat sleeves draped over Jacob's shoulders. Both kissed each other's necks. Over the two brothers, a few clouds drifted by, casting a fleeting escape from the sun's heat.

"How is it there are always these ridiculous altercations between us?" Jacob asked.

"Sibling rivalry," Esau answered with a dangerous touch of sarcasm.

"Esau," Jacob's eyes became affectionate, wet, revealing his love and admiration for his brother, "take care of yourself. May Yahweh guide your hunt."

"Let Him concern Himself with making rain—not in guiding my arrows," Esau smarted off, reverting to an argumentative state.

Jacob just smiled at him and watched with silent eyes as Esau and his band of hunters walked into the receiving arms of the forest's branches. For a long time Jacob stood where he was, fascinated with the play of sunlight over their bodies as they filtered through the forest. The fading colors of their clothes shimmered then blurred until they finally merged inseparable from the dying forest. Once, not so long ago, he would have been unable to see them in such a distant location, but the leaves withered and fell. The thick bushes dried away. The green vines became brown, brittle strings. "The death that swoops on man," Jacob thought, "grasps the lives of men more swiftly than the passing of the day."

He swallowed hard. The dry air hurt. Jacob nodded to the passing wind and walked southward to his lentil field. The pale blue flowers richly decorated the land. Yitzhak's men and women cultivated the fields from sunrise to sunset. Urgently they placed their baskets of peas into the beehive granary they had erected. Other times, Jacob worked through the cool night to compare that time's planting to the planting of the seed in the hot sun. Examining plant after plant, the skilled men watched for signs of destructive insects. When they found swarms voraciously eating the stems and breeding underneath the leaves, the cultivators set the fields on fire. Disregarding the futile effort, the men immediately began cultivating another field across the way from the first field. Quickly that parcel became as worthless as the first. To the far east a third field struggled against the heat of the day.

"Take the strongest wheat grains and cast off the weak ones," Jacob told his companions. "We may yet be able to cultivate a heat-resistant grain."

"You should learn to create heat-resistant sheep," a friend remarked.

"I prefer to preserve my grandfather's cattle," he replied.

"You better hurry then, considering what few we have left."

Nodding, Jacob returned to the lentil field.

 ⁊⁃

Weeks later, Jacob's field produced a large crop of healthy lentils. As he walked through the growth, his hands glided over the tops of the crop. The small leaves gently tickled his wrists. Meanwhile, Esau, while hunting, found the faint prints of an antelope. His fingers gingerly explored the print and his eyes expertly followed the trail of broken branches. Satisfied that he had accurately surmised its location, Esau whistled to his men and alerted them to its whereabouts. "Let's give chase."

"Lead on."

Excited, the band of hunters ran through the thinning forest. The small trees easily parted as they ran past the limbs of the trees. The brown leaves cracked underneath their feet and the twigs snapped loudly as they pounced from point to point. Esau outran his strength. He stopped. He hunched over and struggled with his breathing, capturing inside his lungs the hot, dry air.

"Quick, give me something to drink."

He gulped down the water and dried his lips with the back of his hand, the hair on it misted with minuscule waterdrops. "Let's continue, but not as loudly!"

The afternoon dwindled to evening. The tracks became easier to find. The experienced hunters shifted directions so that the wind blew their odor away from the game.

Finally they heard the sounds of animals. The hunters readied their bows and arrows and spears and slings. They cautiously advanced, soundlessly approaching the thicket. What they found was the antelope's fallen carcass. Their nostrils filled with the smell of its rotten flesh. A swarm of flies danced inside its intestines while a clan of lion cubs feasted on their mother's kill. The hunters lowered their weapons. Soundlessly they walked backward leaving the lioness's kill to her cubs. After retreating several hundred yards away, they redirected their hunt for another hour. With the sun's full descent, they pitched camp.

The following week produced the same dismal signs. The lions, the jackals, the hyenas competed with the men for the same food. So Esau led his men beyond the borders of the forest. Hours after they emerged, a few complained

"We've never gone this far out," a tired hunter roughly spoke to Esau.

"I didn't believe the famine extended this far," Esau answered."

"We would be better off robbing caravans than honestly hunting for food," the hunter doggedly continued.

"Hunters are not robbers!" Esau sharply rebuked. Then he added "Men who hunt honestly never have to resort to meaningless violence or refuse to share another hunter's burden."

"My burden is great," a fellow joked as he examined the soles of his blistered feet.

"Tha's why we should become a band of robbers," The other insisted again.

Esau refused to pursue the matter any further. He argued enough with his brother Jacob. He didn't want anyone else to fight with. Especially since everyone was tired and subject to making unsuitable and hasty remarks. "Love, hate! Hate, love!" he shook his head. "As much as I don't want to be around Jacob, I can't think of anyone else I would rather be around," he thought to himself again. Finally, he said to the others, "We're returning home."

"Then let's take the short cut."

"That route will take us to my brother's field."

"So what? He may have some food for us."

"It'll certainly not be meat," another hunter playfully teased the first hunter.

"Shut up!" Esau snapped, bitterly thinking to himself, "I can never get away from him." Speaking out loud, he barked, "If we're going there, then let's go there."

The straight shoulders of the hunters, after a long flight through the sharp, scratching twigs and branches of the dried forest, sagged lower at the trail's end. As they got close to the clearing, they smelled the lentil stew cooking over the open flames.

When the cultivators saw the returning hunting party, they immediately looked for the kill. They kept watching as the hunters approached, and when they stepped near the perimeter of the growing field, the cultivators stepped to the side, hoping that perhaps the last group of men had the catch tied between them. Instead, those men also emerged from the nulled forest empty-handed.

The hunters proudly tightened their lips and forced their pained shoulders straight. Those who permitted the ends of their spears to drag on the return trip, now lifted them straight and punched the air with the points as they neared the cultivators. A few even shouted their war cries, acting out scenes of a pretended kill. Esau quickly grew tired of the pretension. He heard his stomach growl. His legs hurt him as much as his back. He walked directly to Jacob and ordered, "Feed my men. They're hungry."

"The hunt was unsuccessful?" Jacob carefully chose his words. He didn't want to create another hostile confrontation between them.

"No!" He became angry at his obvious failure with the hunt. Certain that Jacob was being sarcastic, his face reddened. "Can't you see the dozens of gazelle and ruminants we killed?"

"Esau, I'm sorry. I didn't mean to imply anything bad."

"Just shut up and feed me and my men!" Esau shouted.

Jacob stepped away from the cooks and fixed a steady gaze at Esau and firmly said, "I understand the futility of your pursuit, but don't come into my fields screaming your abuses at me!"

Esau lowered his tone and shook his head. The futile hunt tired him. The failure made him angry against anyone who showed their success against the cruel task of the land. He tired to find the words to apologize with. He couldn't. So, he simply stated: "We're hungry!"

"I will feed your men," Jacob smiled at him and touched his upper arm.

He went to the chief cultivator and told him to boil more lentils and add to it whatever the hunters wanted.

Again Jacob smiled at Esau. "Relax. Wash your feet."

The hunters instantly dropped their spears and bows and formed a circle around the campfire. Several others started another fire with the discarded stems of last months' failed crop that Jacob planned to grind and mix with the cattle dung to use as fertilizer.

The group of men relaxed and joked with one another about the long hunt and how the land seemed unable to heal itself. Carcasses and vultures ruled what was left of the forest.

"It's the end of our times," one hunter remarked to one of the cultivators.

Jacob, when he heard it, said to Esau, "This is not the end of our times. This dry spell will end, and the rains will return."

"You think so," Esau replied.

Jacob looked at the cloudless sky. The sun painted the world yellow. "Yeah, Esau, I do."

"And why should God make it rain again? Don't you think, Jacob, that God is angry with men again, and this time He means to burn them to death?" Esau half-laughed at his attempted humor.

"No, God will not flood mankind again, nor will He roast us to death," Jacob also half-laughed with his brother. Esau scooted closer to Jacob. "So, tell me, how will we end?"

"Long after the designated and true Mashiach appears and settles the confrontation between evil and good."

"It's always a strife between two forces. The jackal against the lioness. The vulture against the eagle. The horse against the mule. Why, we even struggle against each other."

"Esau," Jacob touched his arm again, "There does not have to be a struggle between us. Accept me as the firstborn, and we will celebrate the wisdom of your decision."

Esau shook his head again. "This damnable, stupid principle of birthrights and firstborn rights are notoriously useless. It's a pathetic burden."

Jacob leaned back. He analyzed Esau's form. Esau appeared disarrayed, distraught. Lost in the quagmire of failure. A thing impossible to comprehend. Jacob turned to examine Esau's famished hunters. For the first time in years they sat separated from their leader. Jacob reasoned on the opportunity.

For decades Jacob had listened to his mother's stories about his birthright. He carefully reviewed her words. Esau snatched his birthright from him while he was inside his mother's womb. Even while they were inside her they fought each other. Bearing down too hard during the birth's event, Esau pushed him aside, rushing past him to find the light that coursed its way through their mother's vagina. Jacob grabbed his brother's heel and refused to let him go.

He stared at Esau's foot, then he stared at his hands. He had never let loose!

"Esau, relieve yourself of the birthright burden," he burst out.

"How? By killing myself?"

"Sell it to me."

"Are we now becoming as the people of the world?"

"You don't value it. There's a famine in the land, so you don't have to worry about losing your double portion to me. So, sell it to me."

"What will you pay me for it?"

"All the lentil soup you can eat," Jacob smiled. He stretched out his hands. "Look at my field. Nowhere is there a richer or more productive field. I will sell it to you and with it, feed your band of hunters and their families. Take the cultivators with the field. They will obey you."

Esau stared at his brother. He gazed deeply into his serious eyes. Esau suddenly laughed and scooted so close to Jacob, they felt each other's hearts racing. He grabbed him in a tight shoulder squeeze. "Sometimes Jacob, I hate you more than any man alive. Other times, I love you so much, I make father jealous. Come, kiss your older brother." Esau's laughter increased as did the laughter of his men and the laughter of the cultivators. "Dearest brother—bring on the lentil soup! Relieve me of my burden!"

"The birthright is mine?"

"It is! But, add some wine to this stew!"

Motioning with his index finger, Jacob commanded that the cooks quickly fill the clay bowls with the stew and hand it to each man.

Hours later the tired hunters fell asleep.

Esau, resting beside Jacob, hugged him tightly to his chest. "What a nonsensical thing, this birthright quarreling. Be content now, dear brother."

The morning rise discovered Esau contentedly, harmoniously sleeping beside Jacob. The cultivators and hunters, seeing the pair placed against each other, as if in the womb, walked quietly around them.

A week later the lentil field withered away.

ෂ෨෪෨෮෪෨෮෪෨෮

"𝔚e can no longer stay here" Riveka, in a quiet, yet firm, matter-of-fact voice, tried to persuade Yitzhak to leave Beer-lahai-roi.

"I must stay. As much as I've thought about it, I just don't know how to violate my oath against Yahweh."

"Father," Jacob softly spoke up. "I know the answer. Grandfather established wells everywhere."

"I know that."

"He also dug them in Mamre, and even in Gaza. Our land rights have been permitted by Yahweh to extend to the very shores of the Great Sea."

Esau, snickering, added, "I wouldn't doubt it if he dug them in Egypt itself."

"Esau!" Yitzhak reprimanded. "Never again speak so callously of my father! He was Yahweh's personal and deepest friend. You offend not only your brother, but me as well. Worse, you offend Yahweh."

Ashamed of his words Esau retracted his sarcasm. "Father, I beg for your forgiveness. And Jacob's, as well as Yahweh's. I should not have been sarcastic against my grandfather nor you nor Yahweh."

Yitzhak immediately smiled. "Come, my precious son. Kiss me on the neck. I know your words weren't mean to harm us."

Esau hugged his father and looked directly at Jacob with a smirk on his face. Jacob retreated to the farthest corner of the tent and resigned to the drama.

"We can, as a compromise, leave for Gerar," Riveka continued.

"That we can do," the head of the family finally agreed. "Children, pack our things in the morning."

ෂ෨෪෨෮෪෨෮෪෨෮

When Yitzhak turned ninety years old, his rumbling twins turned thirty years old. In 1828 B.C.E. the Hebrew clan departed for Gerar.

The adequate, barely subsisting pasture lands stretched out before the small, wandering group. Reaching the semi-arid torrent valley, the family immediately set to digging as deep a well as they could in their first day in the land to free the trapped water for their animals.

Not far from their camp, the increasing population arrivals from Capthor lived in the newly restructured city of Gaza. Prior to their disembarkation, discovery, and taming of the region, the original colonists, the Pelethites and the Cherethites had to be dealt with in an expedient manner. The sailors through the years had married the tribal women of the region. To equalize the marriages, the Lord-Ruler stipulated that all new marriages had to be performed with an opposite tribe and never within the same tribe. Forced integration took effect, alleviating segregation, prejudice, and racial bigotry. Within one generation the children became identified as the Palastu.

Further intermarrying with the native Canaanites, the Minoans managed to assimilate themselves into the region. Quickly the Canaanites accepted their presence, calling them Philistines.

⊘⊙⊘⊙⊘⊙⊘⊙

The Abimelech, the fourth appointed king of the Philistines by the direction of the Minos of Caphtor, patiently waited by the apex of the King's Road. By treaty the Egyptians and the Pelethites constructed the road so the merchants of the world could travel safely from Egypt, to Syria, to Babylon, and eventually to India.

White donkeys pulled the Abimelech's war chariot. A stiff red-and-yellow horsehair mane adorned the top of his helmet.

The Phicol stood beside him as did Ahuzzath, the Minos's ambassador. They chose this day to greet Yitzhak and his small, nearly insignificant entourage.

"We welcome you as we did your progenitor a hundred years ago."

"How is it you remember such a visit?" Yitzhak asked.

"It is in our histories. We still use the wells that he dug. His name is so deeply carved into the foundation stones, even the sand-blasting of a hundred years has failed to erase it." Stepping out of the chariot, the king went to Yitzhak.

Yitzhak's head, on the Embracing Ceremony, barely touched the ruler's upper shoulder. The king and the military general and even the lower ranking soldiers were taller and stronger than Esau. The blue- and hazel- and gray- and green-eyed people with their blond and light brown hair intrigued the wanderers. Jacob recalled reading about their strange light skin and strange-colored eyes. "Never will I again doubt what I read," he said to himself.

Esau smiled at the one red-haired sailor who happened to accompany the soldiers.

The king was surprised by the small number of men. The Hebrew clan struck his fancy. He had never seen such intense and thick black hair before. "Are these men the children of the people of India?" he thought. He studied them further. He saw their extraordinarily focused brown eyes. Whatever the men looked at, they looked at it till they knew every detail of what they were staring at. This acute stare unnerved the Phicol and the Abimelech.

Both men simultaneously stared at Jacob. They gazed at his manners and at how the other men looked at him. He was definitely the smartest among them. Jacob, in turn, studied the Phicol and the Abimelech. For long moments they just stood there and smiled and exchanged small courteous remarks.

Jacob responded with mystical answers to their questions on life and journeys and the body's need for nourishment. Every statement that Jacob made toward the ambassadors ended with a quizzical look. Finally Jacob shrugged his shoulder and walked away.

The high ambassador and the king looked at each other as Jacob turned his back on them. "You asked him how the journey went and he answered 'With God.' You ask him about the famine and he answers 'God replenishes the earth with thought of inner essence purposing toward divine, universal grace for all mankind.' Dare we ask him what he thinks about kings and their subjects?"

"No," the Phicol said, "Who knows if his answer will insult us or enlighten us."

Later, during the stillness of the night, as the stars invaded the earth with their brilliant light, the Phicol rehearsed the conversation that took place between himself and Jacob, wondering of deeper and greater intellectual questions and answers to challenge Jacob with. In the course of the dark night, images of fallen kings and destroyed lands, smoldered in ruins frightened him. A city, bigger than anything that ever existed anywhere on the face of the earth came to his thoughts. Then, as the sun came to encroach over the fringe edge of the horizon, the Phicol felt peculiarly silly for thinking the night away with such thoughts and scenarios. The link between greatness and folly was measurable by what true scope? The king, during the new dawn, felt obligated to wake to its beauty with questions that would say something, anything, to break the hold that Jacob's intellect held over him. Yet, he faintly remembered the strange images of tens-of-thousands of people walking through the streets of a grand city lined everywhere with gold and jewels and people dressed in white robes that glimmered as much as the sun. "The Hebrew clan possesses magic" he thought. "So, whatever extreme contrasts exists between our two peoples are unimportant," he temporized. "For our records," he later spoke with an air of efficient, cultivated arrogance, after he greeted Jacob and his father, "how many generations are you removed from Abraham?"

"I am his legitimate firstborn."

"Is this true?" his amazed words asked the twins.

"Grandfather had other children through Keturah, his second wife" Jacob confirmed the truth of his father's statement. "He also had other sons through his other concubines. Our father, Yitzhak, however, is the inheritor of Abraham's blessings. He is the firstborn of Abraham and Sarah."

"And how old was he when you were born?"

"He was a hundred years old," Yitzhak answered.

"Then you must be. . ."

"I am ninety years old."

"Simply unbelievable!" Then of Esau he asked, "How old was your grandfather when he died?"

"I and my twin brother were fifteen years old when he died. That was fifteen years ago. Grandfather was one hundred seventy-five years old when he died."

"This is simply astonishing! Our fertility gods need to meet your fertility gods!"

"We have no fertility gods," Yitzhak injected.

"Oh, yes. I forget. But it's not our nature to offend anyone. We are the greatest merchants of the world. We trade throughout the Aegean Islands and throughout Egypt and as far as the neck of Africa and Europe. We named both continents from our explorations! Even now our ships hug the northern coastlines of the Ionian Islands and, yes, even this very coastline. We will soon be building new cities in the deep harbors of the Lebanon coast."

"I know that land," Jacob again intruded in the conversation, insisting on an audience for himself. "The Canaanites reside there. Sidon, Canaan's firstborn, for which he named the city, was their progenitor."

"You lived in Sidon," the ruler, fascinated, asked Jacob. "How long did you stay there?"

"Why, never."

"Then how is it you know so much about its founders?"

"My greatest forefather, who was both king and priest, wrote their genealogies and histories. We have the intact histories of every family."

"How is that possible?"

"Research and revelation."

"Research, I understand. Revelation is too mystical for me to grasp."

"Yahweh has manifested all mysteries to us."

"To us," puzzled, he repeated the phrase. Esau squirmed in his seat.

"Of course," Jacob deflected the question, "I am speaking of my father's ability."

The Ahuzzath, the confidential friend and authorized spokesman of the Abimelech who accompanied him wherever he went, placed his hand on Yitzhak's shoulder and insisted on asking Yitzhak, "Are you a prophet?"

"I am more," he immediately answered, surprising Riveka with the swiftness of his response. She expected him to slide away, hiding under the table. The strength of his youth returned to him during the night's dinner. "I am Yahweh's anointed. I am the symbolic representation of the Mashiach to come. I am today's Mashiach."

"What is a Mashiach?" the Phicol asked.

"Today, it represents the true leadership to come. He will rule over the world in a reign of peace."

"Over the *entire* world?"

"Yes."

When the Ahuzzath heard Yitzhak, he stepped far away from him and walked to the Phicol and whispered, "We have a madman on our hands. Deny all of them entry to Gerar."

The Phicol looked at his trusted companion and counselor. He closed his eyes and remembered portions of his dream. He determined to ignore his friend's comment. The Phicol remarked, "So, the northerners are called Sidonians. See, Ahuzzath, instead of embarking expensive galleys northward, all we had to do was to ask this man's son who lives wherever he wants and reads whatever he wants, and informs to everyone every-thing, accurately."

The Abimelech, impressed by the entirety of these events, walked right up to the Ahuzzath. Refusing his whispers, the king further asked, "Yitzhak, do you intend to stay here?"

"No, you shouldn't!" the councilor now made his views known to everyone. "I recommend Egypt. The Delta is rich. The Egyptian kings' are constantly building. There is plentiful employment there. Great opportunities for the right family to become enormously wealthy and powerful. The Hyksos certainly proved that!

"And, it's so conservative down there! Nothing seems to ever change: either for the good or for the bad. Egypt just plods along in the framework of time. A person who has lived as long as you have will understand such an institution. You'll be a welcome blessing to the Egyptian kings. And, of course, by living there, you can become a tremendous help to us. Our Minos can appoint you to an exalted position. I just ask you to occasionally write to us the important things that you see happening there."

"Yes," the jealous ambassador saw an opportunity to tease Yitzhak. "You can keep the grave robbers away!" Caught in his own joke, he snickered loudly as did the soldiers behind him.

"Hush," the king mildly rebuked his men. "As I recall, we have a treaty between us. You may stay here! Or, if you prefer, we will escort you safely to Egypt. No one will harm you in Avaris. The Hyksos dynasty loves our Minos far too much to aggravate your family."

"I will sleep on it—figuratively," Yitzhak replied, directing his last word exclusively to the councilor's ears. A sudden chill penetrated the jealous man. He shook the sensation off and quickly stepped away from Yitzhak. An immediate trembling overcame him again. He stared at the Hebrew, and became afraid of him. An inexplicable essence surrounded and permeated through that man. Puzzled by his enigmatic fear, he hid his thoughts inside his mind.

"What?" the king, noticing the silence of the ambassador, teased him. "I thought the cats only clamped the Egyptians' tongues! I see they have yours as well."

Then to Yitzhak. "Indeed, sleep on your response. Either way, I'll honor your request. But, truthfully, Egypt is the place to be in. And, as I recall, your father visited there also. I believe, and correct me if I'm wrong, he became a very wealthy man down there. Something to do with his wife, I suppose."

Yitzhak, turning to face his children, refused to reply.

"Oh well. Rumors and history and speculation. Who can divide what into what? Enjoy! Enjoy life!"

ଓଓଓଓଓଓଓଓ

Yitzhak felt an intense fatigue overpowering him. He rubbed his neck and shoulders. He tossed and turned on his bed, forcing Riveka to leave the bed. She instantly fell sound asleep in the other bed. Long past midnight, he finally fell into a deep slumber.

In that deep privacy of the night's calm, Yahweh's voice spoke to him. "Do not depart for Egypt. Remain in the land that I had apportioned to you. Live fully in this land. I will bless you and I will be with you."

Enraptured inside a mystical vision, Yitzhak viewed the country that his children would come to possess. Yitzhak saw the mountains, the rivers, the valleys, the vineyards, the forests, the vast stretches of grain fields, the meadows, and the coastal sand dunes. From the southern tributary river of Egypt to the Euphrates River bordering Mesopotamia.

"All these lands I assign to you and to your descendants. This same oath I contracted with your father. Now, I contract it with you.

"I will increase the totality of your heirs to become as numerous as the stars of heaven. All your children will receive these lands so that all the nations of the earth will become blessed by the actions of your heirs. I do this because your father obeyed Me and kept My contract intact.

"You must obey My commandments.

"You must maintain My laws.

"You must remember Me and keep My teachings."

The new morning found Yitzhak the first one to rise among the household.

In the quiet period before dawn, when the wind stirs, when the branches move, when the stars become faint and the ascending light begins illuminating the paths of another land, Yitzhak sought an answer to the deep underlayment of his existence. But he already knew the answer. He clearly understood his place in the universe. He clearly knew where he stood in his relationship to everything and to everyone. His self-confidence soared! His timid humility, indecisiveness, and depressive/happy mood-shifts dissipated. He roused the sleepers and directed the people to gather around him.

"We will stay in Gerar."

When the Abimelech heard the announcement, he invited them to visit the seashore city.

🔪“🔪‚🔪“🔪

Eager to explore the new settlement, his family and household vacated their camp. The entourage, with their collection of animals, hastily walked toward the new area. During that journey the men and women wondered about their destination. The land's layout, the quality of the water, and how arable the soil was. Each step brought them closer to the designated area, and each step heightened their expectations of something wonderful to see and cherish. Their hearts swelled with joy as they neared the final hill. When they approached the last hill, they momentarily glanced back at the land that they had just traveled over. The tallest among them stared beyond the hill's crest, and the camp, together, ascended the soft-rising hill.

The first man to reach the top froze. Not shouting, not waving, not moving, the man just stopped there, as if he had turned into the long-gone tree that once grew where he stood. When Yitzhak caught up to him, he peered with the man beyond the crossing of the last hill.

Yitzhak tried to comprehend the architectural wonders of the city that lay before them. High towers and multi-floored risers dominated the skyline of the seacoast city. Yitzhak stood as frozen as the man beside him. When the others caught up, they also stared at the city in disbelief. They watched hundreds of men, women, and children going in and out of the condominiums that the people lived in.

As the Hebrews gathered, the city's welcoming committee walked in front of a large procession. Colored cloths waved and horns sounded and great cheers broke the amazed stares of the Hebrews.

"How high are those houses?" Yitzhak asked the lead citizen.

"Five stories,' he replied. "Some six. Some seven. Everyone wants a condo by the sea. This was the only way I knew how to satisfy them. But watch the wind. It's fierce on the top levels."

"How do you keep them from falling down?"

"Beams crisscrossed to beams and cedars riveted to cedars. As our ships are mighty, so are our high-risers. We have over ten thousand people living on this small coastline. Beyond those sand dunes, a sufficient amount of fertile land supports us. Once, that plot was able to support our homeland. But this famine has affected us as much as it has you."

"At least you can still grow crops on your land. We can grow nothing on ours."

"So, not only do we compete with what is best between us, we also compete with what is worst between us." He smiled, enjoying Yitzhak's company. "But what does it matter? Enjoy! Enjoy life!"

"Father," Esau asked, "where will we be living? Up there?"

"No, no," the king stated. "The upper floors are for my most royal staff members and richest merchants and greatest sea captains. Take the lower floors for your family."

"Can I be a sea captain?" Esau asked.

"So you can live on the top floor?" the king gently asked.

"For the trade's sake."

"Good answer, young man! 'For the trade's sake!' Be a merchant! Get rich!"

"Yes," Esau quietly commented, more to himself than to anyone else. "I shall indeed become a wealthy and powerful man!"

ᏋᏬᏣᏋᏬᏣᎡᏬᏣᏋᏬᏣ

Riveka, setting up her house, allowed her veil to drop, revealing her soft cheeks, and the lips that smiled radiantly. Her ear lobes held precious jewels and her eyes spoke a thousand love songs. When the sun rose, if a man turned to a specific degree, he easily could distinguish her body's curvaceous outline. But only for a brief moment. Inside the house she became comfortable. She had forgotten that from the seashore sailors could see through her open windows. It happened one day, that a mariner, espying her, determined to knock boldly on her door.

"Who are you?" he asked her. His eyes were bewildered by her figure and her queenly stance.

Yitzhak, noticing the sailor's earring on his nose and the hammered, solid gold symbol hanging from his neck, representing a pagan goddess, answered tersely, "She is my sister."

The sailor nodded and returned to his friends to inform them what Yitzhak had just spoken. Riveka turned to her husband and said, "Why did you tell them I'm your sister?"

"My father did that when he felt threatened in Egypt. That statement probably saved his life."

"What have we to fear here?"

"Pagans and sexual predators."

The Abimelech, curious as to why the sailors kept purposely walking in front of Yitzhak's condo, eventually forced himself to knock at his door.

"What goes on in here?" But before Yitzhak could reply, he saw Riveka's face. The morning sun revealed her interior form inside her silk covering. "Never mind the answer. I know it already. Is this your wife?"

"She's my sister," Yitzhak replied.

"Well, that's fortunate for you. But let's get your household moved near my high-rise. There's a single-story dwelling there. It's larger than this one. It'll provide you with greater privacy. It has a nice courtyard in the middle of it and a double entryway. I like the style a lot."

"Why don't you live there then?"

"Because I'm the Abimelech. My title requires me to live in the highest condo. Go, and enjoy it. It's a big house."

Yitzhak agreed with the king.

During the next few days he and his two sons transferred his belongings on the donkeys and happened by chance to pass a break in the sand dunes, revealing beyond them the struggling greenery of the farmland.

"Jacob," he called out. "Those seeds that you were experimenting with, did you happen to bring some with you?"

"I remembered to, yes."

"How will they perform in this salt air?"

"This soil used to be the richest around. With a few fresh wells the grain should perform. I trust it to grow."

"Esau, why don't you and Jacob find some land for us to buy? Let's experiment with those seeds.'

"Father, I'm a hunter."

"Esau, what's to hunt here? Fish?"

"Yes. I can be a sea captain."

"Well, that's not going to happen. You're bonded to this land as I am bonded to it. Besides, you should learn how to till the land. An experiment is an experiment. And, as the king commands us every day: 'Enjoy! Enjoy life!'"

Esau, hugged his father and laughed merrily. "For you Father, I will farm the land. Temporarily!" he slowly drew the last word out.

After he acquired permission to till several adjoining plots of land, Yitzhak and his twin sons and his household servants began breaking the ground with their copper implements. While they were tilling the ground and digging the irrigation trenches for the freshwater, the women occupied themselves with weaving the flax into long, broad cloths. They used two patterns: the closed twining and the open twining. The women punched holes in the ivory hooks of the tandem rods that stretched between six chairs and performed the quilting work using the long fish bones to thread pattern throughout the cloth.

While the women were working, the young men also began cultivating their newly purchased land. The Philistines, who happened to walk by, stopped to observe the hard farming work. As the days passed, those who walked by, wondered in amazement as the cracked earth began healing, returning to a rich black soil. The tender wheat shoots broke through the earth and expanded throughout the fields, generating new growths that quickly thickened. After Yitzhak threshed the grain, he sold it to the sailors and to the passing merchants. The leftover stalks he sold to the camel caravans.

Esau dictated the final price for the fodder and grain heads. Within two years Yitzhak became one of the wealthiest men in the city.

Riveka, meanwhile, increased the productivity of the women's efforts at the same time. Her weavings became the best in the land. The sea captains were impressed by the strong cloths and requested her sails for their galleys.

Everyone who passed by her house stopped. Seeing her for the first time, they were unable to take their eyes away from her face.

Eventually, the family began mingling with the citizens of the city. One day, while Esau was shopping in the marketplace, he happened to see a troop of men wrestling each other. He sat by the water well and spent the afternoon observing their arm movements, the placement of their feet, the grappling of each others necks and how they leverage their bodies to unbalance their opponents. He listened to the cheering audience and became intrigued with the wrestler's conquering ability. As soon as the wrestlers concluded their match, the people ran to them and bought them food and fruits and presented them with weaved baskets and new sandals.

"I will learn this," Esau said to himself. From that new morning on, Esau and his trusted friends congregated by the rear barn and practiced what he saw, and gradually improved their skills in the new sport. And even though the Philistines were physically larger, stronger, taller, broader, than the Hebrews, and could still outwrestle Esau, the Hebrews insisted in participating in the games events. Holding their pride and integrity, and never resorting to breaking the foreigners' fingers or squeezing the testicles, the Hebrews established an honored place among the citizens for their fairness and good sportsmanship. Simultaneously, their farming and trading skills drastically improved. Soon, the Hebrews became better at buying and selling than the Philistines.

A traveler to the city of the Philistines would often stare at the strange sight of a tall, blond-haired and blue-eyed mariner bending his head downwards to talk with a smaller Hebrew. The Hebrews, in turn, had to stand on special benches to see eye to eye with the Aryan seamen when the final negotiation called for it.

The traveler looked at the tall Aryans and wondered at the strength of the Hebrews who had no fear of such giants.

꙰Ⴆ჎ჇᏒᏒᏒჇᏒჇႦ჎

At a later period, by coincidence, the Abimelech happened to walk by his window at the same time that Yitzhak and Riveka walked about freely in their courtyard. Amazed by her large, firm breasts and excitingly thin waist, he stared out his window to watch her. He saw her walking to Yitzhak. Intrigued by her form he watched her walk toward her brother. Sipping his wine, he continued gazing at her. Somehow, he hoped he would catch her eyes. Instead she caught the loving stares of her brother.

When she disrobed, the Abimelech gulped. At the same time Yitzhak disrobed. Not believing what he was seeing, the Abimelech leaned farther out on his window sill. He saw her lie on the ground. He watched as

Yitzhak placed himself directly on top of his sister! He watched as Yitzhak had sex with her!

Infuriated, he kicked over a plant. The pot rolled to the wall's edge, breaking. "That damnable liar," he clenched his teeth. "That manipulating cheat!" he tightened his fists. "The curses of the gods be placed over his household!" As he stormed out, dark clouds ascended directly over the coastline. The king summoned a team of soldiers to follow him. The king burst through the courtyard doors, rushing up to the two lovers.

Yitzhak and Riveka, still naked, turned to face the king. Embarrassed, they robed themselves. Everyone, staring at each other, quieted. A deep stillness fell over the group. Baffled, shocked, the soldiers and the king kept on staring at the lover's trembling figures.

Finally Riveka spoke. "Husband, ask them what they want."

"Oh god! You two are married!" the king, mortified, blurted out. "Yitzhak, why did you deceive us by telling us *'She is my sister'*?"

"I was afraid to tell you otherwise. All of your men, including yourself, are giants compared to us. All of you are taller and stronger than we are. All of you are trained fighters. We are not. Your features are strange to us. With your blond hair and with your blue eyes, I wasn't quite sure how to act in your presence."

"What kind of excuse is that? What if one of my sailors had raped your wife? We, by our custom as seamen, could not have been prevented from such a possibility. She is extremely desirable, and it would only have been a matter of time before one of us finally did take her to our own bedchamber. Then, how could we have lived with such a guilt? We are sailors. We go for months without the companionship of a woman, and yes, at times we are compelled by our desires to take for ourselves whomever we want. Our captains never punish anyone for rape, but our ethics demand for us to honor the integrity of a marriage bond. We are not forcible takers of other men's wives! But, who here knew she was your wife?"

Yitzhak remained silent. He had made a mistake. These men were not Egyptians. More, he was not his father. Worse, history did not replay itself.

The king turned to his soldiers and commanded, "Spread this news to everyone: Anyone who molests this man or his wife will be executed on the spot!"

"Thank you, great Abimelech."

"Oh, now I'm great," the king remarked. "Before I was just me. That's what I liked about you so much. You never cared that I was a king legally appointed by our Minos. You always seemed absorbed by your own making, as if somewhere in you lies a secret kingdom waiting to burst upon us. It truly puzzles me. Well…"

"…I know," Yitzhak interrupted, "'Enjoy life!'"

�����������

Over time, word spread to the other citizens that Riveka was in truth Yitzhak's wife. Seeing his growing herds of cattle and the buildup of his flocks and the hiring of his many shepherds and herdsmen, the Philistines became jealous. Adding fuel to the fire, Yitzhak had the most beautiful woman in the land for his wife!

In the distant horizons, where shadows merge with shadows, the Philistines secretly maneuvered their way to the wells which Abraham had dug years ago. In haste the jealous men dumped hundreds of large and small rocks into the wells. Then, to completely block the water's flow, they maliciously threw into the deep well dozens of buckets of dirt. Through the night they stopped up the other wells, preventing any water from rising.

The Abimelech heard the news of this and investigated the foremost wells personally. He lowered a soldier into the deep well and shouted, "Can you loosen any of the rocks?"

"They are compressed into each other. It's like a single stone formed down here."

"An unbreakable impact," he spoke formally to himself. "Not only have they harmed Yitzhak, they harmed us just as badly."

His closest friend and most favored advisor, the Ahuzzath peered into the dark well. "What are we to do? Yitzhak is to blame for this."

"Did he plug up his own wells? No, I think not. He did, however, did he not, expand his business better than we did? And, did he not use our own methods against us? What herds he gained, he gained by our rules and standards of conduct. Now, in our own jealousy, we will die of thirst.

"Tell the naval commander to ship us water for the meantime. Then set up a task force to dig new wells for us. As for Yitzhak, send him to me."

Yitzhak was also working to free the impacted stones. He stopped when the messenger stood before him. Heavy sweat covered both the messenger and Yitzhak. Jacob's fingers were swollen, as was Esau's.

Yitzhak obeyed the directive and appeared before the king on the eighth floor of his high-rise. The wind blew fiercely from the sea, toppling whatever stood above the windowsill. The darkening skies continued passing by. From the window Yitzhak could see the floating barges and the mass of grain and cloths and implements that the laborers secured on their decks.

"For all these things I'm responsible," the king pointed to the docks, the ships, the wares and goods. My counterparts in the other cities bear the same responsibilities. We are all subjects of the Minos and serve him to the best of our abilities. You, I know, carry your own concerns regarding your own personal agenda. You don't care about our Minos, nor about our city or its inhabitants. If we were suffering in poverty, would you have settled here? I think not."

"I act according to the desires of my God," Yitzhak replied.

"Who is this God that has granted you such authority, I do not know Him."

"I have told you. My authority comes from Yahweh."

"I do remember that specific conversation. Evidently it must be true. You have hundreds of cattle, hundreds of sheep, granaries full of wheat, and a warehouse of the tightest sail weaves I have ever seen in my life.

"Yet when you arrived here, you came here with a few straggly cattle and a famished family along with a few miserable servants." He shook his head in absolute wonder. "Still, we welcomed you with open arms and with fanfare. We blew our trumpets and unfurled our flags for you. Things, however have changed. It's now difficult for me to say 'Enjoy life' when there are so many people around you who do not 'Enjoy life.' So, Yitzhak, I must say this thing: If your family continues to stay, I'm afraid one of two things will happen. You'll become richer and more powerful than I. With that extreme wealth you'll be able to demand my city for yourself. And with Gaza in your control you'd be able to establish your own kingship!

"The second scenario: your very success will cause a civil uprising in my city! You and your wife and your children and your household will be massacred by my jealous subjects. In turn, your revengeful God will perpetually forget to cease this famine.

"You, Yitzhak, my dear friend, must leave because you have become so successful."

Acknowledging the truth of the matter, Yitzhak departed from the city.

ఎంఈఎంౖఎ౿ఈఎంఈ

Yitzhak traveled on the same route that his father once traveled. After a while Yitzhak came upon the same well that he had helped his father dig out long decades ago. He removed his cloak and returned to the task. For days he labored to remove the embedded rocks and hardened clay. The passing caravans, when they saw the stones' removal, reported it to the Philistines, who in turn waited behind the mountains' rise for Yitzhak to complete the clearing task. Moments after his companions broke through the last obstacle, the water gushed, flowing free again. Immediately, a large group of armed herdsmen approached the well.

"Yitzhak!" They were hostile. Esau saw their gleaming daggers and reached for his own sword. "This water belongs to us."

"How can that be? My father and I dug this well decades ago. I have just finished freeing it from your idiotic abuses."

"Keep the water, perish with the water."

"Let's go," Riveka interceded. "We'll find water elsewhere."

"Yes," Yitzhak said. "Let us. Keep this, which I named Esek, for yourselves."

The same drama occurred at Sitnah.

ଧୁଔଧୁଔଔ

In the midst of evening, as the sunset colored the horizon a mute lavender, a young child hurried to the water well to raise up a bucket for his mother's washing. Dropping the line, the child heard a strange thud sound. Another woman, hearing the same sound, immediately rushed to the well. Leaning over the waist high wall, she was startled to discover that the well had gone dry.

ଧୁଔଧୁଔଔ

Days later, at Rehoboth, the Philistines left Yitzhak alone. After his men finished watering the cattle and flocks, the men and women pitched the tents. That night the camp rested peacefully. That night appeared free from hostilities and stress. For a while he remained in the land. After a few months, he became agitated, inexplicably nervous. he became obsessed with moving and he finally convinced everyone to dismantle the tents. With that afternoon's rise, he returned to Be'er-Sheva.

On that very night Yahweh again spoke to Yitzhak. "Do not be afraid of anything. I am the God of your father, Abraham. I am 'El Shaddai', God Almighty. I am the 'Elohim' God of creation: the sum and substance of infinite powers. I am 'El-roi', the all-seeing God. I am 'El Elyon', the Most High God. I am Yahweh Ser-Yihweh: He brings into being whatever comes into being. I am the Supreme Sovereign. Future generations shall know Me also as 'Eh-yeh' 'Asher' 'Eh-yeh': I shall prove to be what I shall prove to be. This will impart My purpose to your generations. Yitzhak, I am with you. I am with your children.

"I will bless you and I will increase your descendants for the sake of my friend Abraham."

෫෮෯෮෫෮෯

In that very same spot Yitzhak's servants began digging a well. While they were removing the rocks and the earth a caravan sounded its ram horn from the nearby clearing in the forest.

Through the path of renewing growth the traveler could easily visualize the stems and branches alight with buds and embryonic small green leaves that had colonies of insects dancing nearby. Throughout the sky, flights of migrating birds approached the thickening forest. From this regenerating greenery the Abimelech, the Phicol, and Ahuzzath rode in the midst of a powerful, colorful procession.

Esau hurriedly prepared his men. Taking their defensive positions behind the trees and rocks, they aimed their bows and spears into the procession's ranks. Yitzhak nervously approached the Philistines.

"Why have you come here? Do you seek to drive me away from these waters, even knowing the legalities of my father's ownership of them—and mine as well?"

"Yitzhak, we have erred against you," the king placed the tips of his fingers on each other. "We sealed your wells and violated the treaty between your father and the representatives of Minos. For such great harm, we apologize."

"Why?"

"We have cleared the damage that my people caused, yet the wells are still dry. Wherever you dig, fresh, invigorating water springs up. The wells that which you recently dug up, and which my people, out of envy, stole from you, have also gone dry. We know you are God's servant, and we have trespassed against His Mashiach.

"So, Yitzhak, I had to admit this to myself: How are we to enjoy life if we are dying of thirst? Even our vineyards are spoiled. What water we import from the Nile Delta becomes rank.

"We were wrong to offend you. We acknowledge before the world, and, yes, we testify even in writing, you are a true prophet. You serve Yahweh."

Yitzhak had matured from his experiences. He quietly nodded. He remained silent, discerning, observant. He had learned now to pay attention and to conceal his private thoughts.

"Thus, we desire to pledge a new treaty between us," the king continued. "Pledge to us you will cause us no further harm. We, in turn, pledge to you no further harm. After all, did we not send you away in peace?

"Therefore, please, do this act between our peoples, for we know for a certainty you are Yahweh's most blessed."

Esau faced Yitzhak. He then signaled for his men to lower their weapons. To Jacob he directed the selection of the choicest cattle, preparing for the camp and visitors the Celebration of Understanding.

The next day the two parties formally signed new peace treaties with each other. Hours later it happened that Yitzhak's newest dig ruptured with a fresh supply of water. Yitzhak, tasting it, joyfully smacked his lips. "Name this well *Shibah*."

Afterwards, in the land of Be'er-Sheva, Yitzhak's prosperity continued.

During this same time Esau established new military checkpoints on the King's Road. Each passing caravan, in order to travel peacefully on the road, had to place in Esau's hands a protection fee. His best warriors escorted the camels, honorably maintaining their protection against raiding Horites, vanquishing time after time the thieves and life-destroyers.

"Six times I faced the enemy," Esau boasted. "Six times I destroyed him." And his reputation as a powerful and valiant warrior spread throughout the land.

In the afternoon of extreme clarity and bright skies, admiring men approached Yitzhak's tent, praising Esau's name. And whenever Jacob heard the people cheering for his brother, he retreated deeper into the tent's recesses to read more scrolls.

ಬುಲ್ಲುಬುಲ್ಲುಬುಲ್ಲುಬುಲ್ಲು

Some time later, while a certain entourage set camp near Ebal (a city near the Great Sea, north of Lebanon), four separate merchant-masters from northern Mitanni and Subartu and Anatolia combined their units with the Hittites. The unified allies formed the mightiest train of camels ever seen. From the beginning of their enterprise they employed hundreds of guards. However, contrary to their plans and intents, the combined forces failed to withstand the attacking marauding bandits. Each succeeding week saw more and more mercenaries killed. Quickly the caravan's defensive capabilities weakened.

Opportunistic thieves continuously attacked the forefront of their caravan train. The attacks began this way: In the dawn's harsh rise, the bandits, after they flung a series of deadly, long, sharp spears, rushed against the middle encampment. With a great shout and a terrible pounding of the drums, the bandits created a massive confusion among the merchants. Disorganized, confused, in massive panic, the hearts of the bravest mercenaries fainted. The bandits increased their onslaught.

"When will they leave us alone?" a young wife asked her husband.

"Only after they've completely subjugated the caravan will their war cries cease."

Meanwhile at the rear of the caravan, slingshots fiercely jettisoned mid-sized rocks into the helmets and chests of the paid warriors, felling them by the dozens. High overhead, vultures followed the caravan.

"Who is strong enough to protect us against the Canaanites?" Beeri cried.

Judith stared at her father at the same time that the route-master stared at him. Depressed, the Hittite merchant-leader responded to the stares, "We are near your Esau's tents." He turned and face the caravan leader. "He is the best and most honorable of escorts. I will personally persuade him to offer us protection for the remainder of our journey."

"How many men does he have?" the caravan-master asked.

"He only needs himself," Judith's father said. He grinned, exposing his diseased gums.

"Surely no man is that strong?" his partner, Elon, ridiculed the remarked.

"Children gleam when he passes by them. Old man run to look into his eyes. Young men die for him. His father is the beloved man of Yahweh as well as His prophet. Esau's brother is an intellect. An observant genius. There is no finer man to protect us anywhere than Esau."

"It's imperative we reach Egypt with this caravan intact. Summon this giant of a warrior—otherwise Salatis will have our heads on his poles."

"Beeri, how can you say, 'Summon him' when we have already expended our allocated funds on these other mercenaries?"

"We will find a way to pay him. What other choice do we have? The Egyptian priests of Sutekh require these implements and myrrh."

While the caravan speedily encircled itself three rows deep, the route-master departed, searching for Esau. The mercenaries, uncertain of the territory, defensively pitched themselves at distinct intervals, maintaining an alert status. Intense hours later the route-master made his way back to them.

Behind him a hundred warriors followed. They quietly marched with long spears held rigidly to their sides. Long swords dangled from their waists.

"They ride as the Amorites!" Judith, the daughter of Beeri stated to Basemath, the daughter of Elon. Adah, the youthful sister of Basemath, wide-eyed, curious, stared at the approaching men. The horses of the silent, strange force betrayed their presence with a cloud of dust rising behind their horses' hooves. Somehow it seemed appropriate: great warriors exiting from a mysterious cloud.

Elon and Beeri, sitting beside each other on a red ram skin, waited for them.

After the two Hittites dismounted, Elon and Beeri reeled back with surprise. The men were much shorter than they had expected. Smaller than the raiding thieves of Lebanon. Smaller than the rushing advance of the screaming demons from the hills and valleys beyond Damascus. Yet, they were stout! They were strong! Broad shoulders! From their walk their agility testified to their warring experience.

Elon was satisfied.

From their ranks Beeri tried to distinguish the leader. He stared at the hundred men. His eyes traveled from bearded faces to smooth faces to craggy faces. Not one seemed more powerful than the other. Exasperated, he finally gave up. Embarrassed at his inability to distinguish Esau, he spoke to the route-master using the Akkadian language, "Who's the leader?"

A man quickly grabbed the arm of a red-haired man whose sunburned skin and freckled face surprised the speaker. The route-master introduced Esau to them.

Elon rose up and intently studied him. He watched his eyes, his gestures. He looked at his sword and caught hints of nicks on its edges. He looked at the other men. They casually encircled the horses, remaining separate from the caravan, respecting its circle of neutrality. "How odd for such short men to act so fearlessly," he thought.

"You seem to be a true warrior," Judith forced her way to the council place, talking to Esau.

She looked at the route-master and eagerly waited for him to translate her words to Esau. In exchange, Esau replied good-naturedly in Hebrew, "I defend the roads."

The softness of his voice surprised her. Basemath, Judith's sister, also came forward.

"But you're not at all a tall man," she said, in a nice teasing voice.

The two girls enchanted Esau. Especially their youngest sister, Adah, who remained by her father's side.

The other men also stared at the three beautiful women, and admitted to each other how desirable they were.

"Esau always gets their eyes," his best friend Nebaioth, Yishmael's first-born son whispered to another friend. The rest, hearing, laughed. The Hittites became annoyed, for they didn't understand their speech and turned their daughters away from the meeting and from the stragglers' staring eyes.

"We need your services," the route-master translated the Hittite's Akkadian speech to Hebrew. "We can only, however, pay you on the safe completion of our journey into Egypt. The Hyksos king Salatis will reward you and your men."

Esau lifted his head to look at the swiftly passing clouds. He carefully contemplated the man's words. He stared into both girls' eyes.

Suddenly shy, he faced the ground for a few moments.

He kicked aside a small pebble.

"I cannot go into Egypt. I had so sworn it to my father. I will, though, protect you to the very borders of the land. If you send a messenger to the Great House, an escort can replace us at the border."

"The messenger will have weights of silver waiting for you there," Elon stated.

"I agree."

ಐﬡ೫ﬡೞﬡ೫ﬡ೫

That very afternoon Esau sent the Ishmaelite trackers forward. The experienced scouts rapidly picked up the telltale signs of the enemy. Pursuing them through the morning and through the afternoon, the

Ishmaelites finally saw in the distant horizon a large congregation of thieves. Acting swiftly, the warriors surrounded the enemies. Within moments of raising the war-cry, Esau's soldiers killed sixty raiders.

Two weeks later another small skirmish followed. Esau, leading his hundred men, confronted the caravan robbers in a front row attack. Hand-to-hand combat ensued. Both lines wavered, till the darkening clouds burst in a furious rainstorm. Refusing to retreat, Esau pursued the fight, giving chase through the thunderous storm. With every lightning burst, another enemy fell. Not giving up to rest, Esau's warriors fought, exterminating every raider.

Wet, bloodied, the remaining warriors dragged themselves into the circled campsite. The fierce storm equaled the fierce fight. Entering the caravan master's tent, Esau tossed his sword aside, collapsing into a thick pile of wool blankets. In the mid-afternoon he woke discovering Judith and Basemath lying naked beside him.

A shimmering, translucent curtain surrounded the three lovers. Outside the curtain the two fathers sat, watching them. Adah was outside the tent, playing.

"What's going on here?" Esau asked the route-master.

"Their daughters are your brides. They will wait here till your marriage is consummated. The rags with your semen will be spread before the camp, witnessing the marriage ceremony."

"I never heard of such a thing."

"It is their custom. No one can then deny the consummation. Go ahead. Perform the intercourse. There is nothing more satisfying than a morning's embrace."

"While they watch?"

"It is the law. Refuse, and you dishonor them. You dishonor me. You dishonor your family. If you wish, rush through it."

Esau, not believing what he was hearing, reflected for a moment. Then he broke out laughing. When the others heard him, they also began laughing. The laughter traveled throughout the camp. Satisfied with the arrangement, the parents of the girls insisted on a marriage feast, inviting the camp to celebrate the union.

ঝ৹৪ঝ৹৪ৰ৹ৎ৹ৎঝ৹৪

Days later Yitzhak received the news from one of Esau's runners. Riveka tore the papyrus and crumbled it, throwing it into the fire, temporarily smothering it till the edges enflamed the paper. Yitzhak stared at the intense blue flame.

"He violated our ways, marrying those Hittite women."

"But he's still your favorite son," Jacob bitterly commented.

Riveka, wrapping her arms around Jacob's forearm's, hushed him. "Don't increase your father's temper. It'll only draw him nearer to Esau. He always feels compelled to defend him. And the more he defends him, the more he loves him."

"The more he loves him, the less likely I am to be remembered during his bequeathing time."

"I will not allow him to provide you with any less than what has been set aside for you. Son, let me do the talking. I know how to do it better than anyone else. He'll never lose his temper at me." Riveka's eyes shone into her son's eyes. He patted her hand.

Riveka turned to her other three sons and ushered them out before her. The four walked to Yitzhak. With their three youngest children acting as shields, Riveka determined to add a little extra pain to his mental anguish, testing his intents. "So, one hundred years old, and your forty-year-old son dares to marry outside our race."

"It may be that Yahweh is softening His direction for our line to intermarry. After all, Yishmael intermarried as did the Philistines. Why even Lot married an Egyptian."

"And what happened to each of them?"

"They all had problems. But, before you add another conflicting word, their problems came about not because they married with another race, but because they married into a false religious belief. One belief system does not equal another belief system just because both systems say they call on the same god."

"For the present age," his wife deliberated stood in front of him, "the true carrier of the Messianic hope can not be burdened with tainted blood. We are pure Babylonians. Your five sons are pure-blooded. We can not be anything else."

"Yishmael, my stepbrother, I repeat, is half Egyptian. His children are related to us and they are three-quarters Egyptian. Do we love them any less because their skin and hair are different from ours? I desire for this prejudice to cease. I will talk to Yahweh about it."

"Remind Him also that we still have a second son—an obedient, dutiful second son."

"Why are you badgering me? I know I have a second son. A brilliant, learned son. One who is always reading everything under the sun. That reminds me, I'm extremely hungry. Go and cook. I have personal matters to attend to."

She smiled and placed her hand on his cheek. "You are a handsome man. We have two handsome grown sons and three wonderful siblings. Tell me, as I want to know, do you love Jacob as much as I love him?"

Surprised by her question, he looked at her. "Am I still as shy today as I was when I was a child?"

She vigorously nodded her head. A youthful twinkle still glowed in her aged eyes.

"I will answer you. I love Esau because he has become what I've always wanted to become. Esau's strong. Energetic. Popular. Everyone always beckons to be near him.

"I also always wanted to be exactly as Jacob is. I wanted to learn all the genealogies and the histories as Jacob has done. I want to speak Akkadian and Egyptian and Aramaic: just as Jacob has mastered."

He touched his wife's shoulder gently.

"Yes, I love Jacob as much as you love him. But, Riveka, wouldn't it be nice if just once he could catch a gazelle for me? Just prepare one delicious meal for me! What a blessing that would be!" He placed both his hands to his face, emphasizing the joy of the moment. Gazing into her eyes, they seemed for a moment to be receding from him. He rubbed his own eyes. Strange, no pain. Yet she seemed slightly unfocused—her features hazy. But the colors were vivid, bright. He looked at the far distance where a group of men were approaching the camp.

"What is that befuddled mess?"

Riveka, looking at the horizon, instantly recognized the men. "They're Esau's soldiers: the Ishmaelites. Wave to Esau. He waves to you."

Embarrassed, Yitzhak waved, uncertain to whom he was waving. He rubbed his hundred year old eyes. The men appeared strangely out of focus. As a shimmering heat wave rising from the hot desert floor.

Riveka caught her husband's strange stare toward the men coming toward them. She observed him step forward after a moment's hesitation. He uncertain movements surprised her. "Yitzhak," she asked, "can't you recognize your favorite? Or do the two women beside him blind you?"

Yitzhak smiled. "Only a beautiful woman such as yourself can blind me."

"A hundred years old and you still think of sex!"

He smiled at her, then patted the heads of his three youngest sons. "Hush. Have our sons select a few cows for the meal. I believe Esau is quite hungry."

The group of friends, when they returned from the borders of Egypt, they greeted Yitzhak, his wife, and Esau's four other brothers. As tradition demanded, the company of men remained overnight to enjoy the Feast of Welcoming. When Yitzhak placed the ram on the altar for sacrifice, Adah, the youngest child of Elon, screeched! "What are you doing?"

Startled, Esau answered, "Father's honoring our return. We sacrifice to Yahweh the best of our allotments, praising Him for caring over us."

"How awful! We never kill living animals to our gods—do we Basemath!"

"No."

"What do you do for your gods?" Yitzhak asked.

"On the day of maturity, when we're fourteen years old, we go to the city and select a man to lay with. Whatever he gives to us we give to the priesthood. We do this every year."

"Every year!" Riveka screamed in her loudest voice. "You were not virgins when Esau married you?"

"Only Adah's a virgin. What an unhealthy state to be in! It's a waste of spiritual energy not to have one's body given over to pleasure!"

"I can't believe what I'm hearing!" she groaned.

Yitzhak put the blade down and asked, "Esau, how is it you didn't know this?"

"How was I to know? No one ever explained anything to me."

"You didn't know they were prostitutes?"

"How? I never had a woman before!"

"We are not prostitutes!" Judith jumped up and shouted at the distraught parents. "I resent you accusing us of being sluts!"

"Well what do you call your activities?"

"I call our *activities* a demonstration of good will toward the practice and respect for our beliefs."

"Get these idol worshippers and prostitutes out of my camp!" Riveka screamed again, slamming her fist into the table.

The group of men remained quiet and refused to eat. "If they leave," Esau finally broke the gripping silence, "I must also leave. I cannot dishonor them by such a disenfranchisement."

Riveka lowered her eyes. No one in the camp dared to speak during the family dispute. Esau's mother again loosened her tongue. "Did you climax inside them?"

"Yes, I think I did."

"Then I curse them so they'll not have children by you. No grandchild of mine shall issue from these two demonic whores! Let it be as I have spoken it!"

"Mother?"

She picked up a cabbage and flung it at Esau, striking him in the chest. "Yitzhak, there will be no sacrifice tonight."

The bitterness, the unexpected disappointment, weighed heavily against her. Retreating away from them, a furious storm of tears overcame her. Jacob rushed to his mother and escorted her to her private tent—the one erected for the *isolation from husband* time.

"She's on her menstruation!" Esau tried to joke, futilely.

ᏸᎤᏣᏸᎤᏣᏝᏏᎤᏣᏸᎤᏣ

Decades later, Jacob, holding council with the twelve heirs, vividly testified to the following genealogical histories: "The land of Seir, by Yahweh's direction, passed legally to the Edomites.

"From age forty to age sixty-three, Esau stayed married to Basemath and Judith. Unable to conceive children with them, the Treaties of Peace between the Hittites and the Hebrews grew fragile and nearly disintegrated. Esau selected Adah to marry. She immediately became impregnated with Eliphaz. This news helped to maintain the peace treaty between the Hittites and the Hebrews. From Eliphaz the clans of Teman, of Omar, of Zepho, of Kenaz, of Korah, of Gatam, and of Amalek rose to rule in the land of Edom (which is the same as the land of Seir).

"Eliphaz, through his concubine Timna, fathered Amalek.

"I had not yet married.

"Esau during these twenty-three years became fonder of Yishmael and his firstborn son, Nebaioth. Basemath (no, Simon, this is not the same one as the daughter of Elon) and Mahalath were his sisters. (Yes, Levi, Esau had two wives with the same name.) (Reuben, as I said twice before, Basemath, daughter of Elon, sister of Adah, was the first of that name. Basemath, daughter of Yishmael, sister of Nebaioth and Mahalath, was the second by that name.—May I continue? Thank you!)

"This second Basemath bore Reuel. Reuel fathered Nahath, Zerah, Shammah, and Mizzah. Zerah fathered Jobab who eventually became the king of the city of Dinhabah, which was established by Bela the son of Beor.

"Decades later Husham, a direct descendant from the line of Teman, a son of Eliphaz, became king of the city of Dinhabah.

"Oholibamah, Esau's sixth wife, was the daughter of Anah, who was the daughter of Zibeon who had descended from the Hivites. With her Esau fathered Jeush, Jalam, and Korah.

"Each of the sons of Esau through Adah, Basemath, and Oholibamah became the leaders of their specific family clan.

"With Riveka's curse hanging over them, Judith and Basemath bore no children of their own.

"Mahalath refused to have children.

"I testified to these facts in my writings. I spoke without shame of the events and circumstances that surrounded my children and myself. I spoke of their beliefs and of their human frailties. The ancestral record of my parents and my children are indisputable. I spoke of where we came from and said to all that we have forged many legal contracts with many kings that we have a right to settle in the lands that Abraham raised his herds and on which my father dug his wells. No nation, no people, will conquer us. We are the true children of God, selected among all the families of the world, to present to the earth the ultimate Mashiach.

"Thus, I, Jacob, after witnessing all these things, and testifying of it, seal this record."

☙⳾☙⳾⳾☙⳾⳾☙⳾

In the year 1795 B.C.E. Yishmael died. He was one hundred thirty-seven years old. He died as he had lived: quarrelsome, fighting against all the tribes surrounding him. Only Esau and Nebaioth attended the funeral.

Yitzhak, in the privacy of his retreat, held Riveka tenderly in his arms. "Yishmael sexually molested me as a child. My love for him was great, but

I was too young to understand the obscenities of his touches. Now Esau attends his funeral. Esau feasts with his children. Esau trains them as his allies. What is to become of Esau?"

"Should you not ask: 'What is to become of Jacob?'"

"Jacob is always here. Jacob is dependable. Solid. I never worry about Jacob. There is never any grievance against him."

"A man who reads so much should be encouraged by his father to visit us once in a while. Why look at how light his skin has become and how he burns in the afternoon sun."

"He chose to study the scrolls. The life that he lives, he choose for himself."

"Yitzhak, you're a hundred twenty-three years old. I know your eyesight is failing you. Daily I watch you as you place the needles closer and closer to your eyes. Daily I watch you as you need to approach the cows' udders closer and closer whenever you milk them. I've seen your feet stumble against rocks too large to ignore and I've seen you walk straight into the overhanging branches."

"Yes, all those things are true. I am old. I am terribly nearsighted."

"You are completely blind, dear. Not near-sighted."

His empty eyes stared at her. He saw only black.

"I am blind."

"Know this, dear husband, perform the anointing now on your son. Pass to him the blessing."

"I have time enough for that."

"No one knows how much time he has have left. All of us, even you darling, are subject to circumstances and happenstance."

"Riveka, should I have attended Yishmael's funeral?"

"For what purpose? Even his children refused."

"To inform him that I had forgiven him."

"You already told him decades ago that you forgave him."

"Yes," he recalled, "that is true. However, I never invited him to dwell in our camp. I never wrote to him, nor he to me."

"What did it matter. Esau always kept up with him, so you both always knew what the other was doing. Let the matter be lost forever from your mind."

"Even though Yishmael was born half-Egyptian and half-Babylonian, he was nevertheless a child of Abraham, who was from the loins of Eber and Shem. So, for all his follies, Yishmael is still a Hebrew." His face contorted and he let loose a long scream of regret and grief.

His wife tenderly hugged her sobbing husband. She simply said, "Yishmael is dead. May his children know that when he died, Yitzhak cried for him."

൚ഗ൞ഗൕഗ൞ഗ൚ഗ

Days later, after Esau returned from the northern hills with his entourage following closely behind, Yitzhak's personal attendant called him to the side.

"Your father requires your presence!"

"To complain again about my wives?"

"Something more pleasing," he replied.

Curious, he dropped the horse's reins in the attendant's hand.

Yitzhak, sitting in the middle of the tent, listened closely as Esau walked in. Recognizing his footsteps and gruff sounds, Yitzhak welcomed him.

Riveka sat on the far side, purposely distancing herself from the two. Watching her son coming into the tent, she remembered the past three days wherein husband and wife had argued incessantly about Esau and Jacob.

"Esau is a warrior," she recollected the words. "The world respects him. The world trembles before him. He is the man who can lead us to victory against all opponents! He can preserve us from being assimilated by the surrounding tribes."

"Listen to your foolish logic. Who is more assimilated among us than Esau? His children run loose with the Canaanites and with the Hittites. Esau freely travels to Gaza and even up toward the Egyptian borders."

"My father said this land belongs to me. Esau is the only one among us strong enough to make it so. With my possessions in his control he can raise a larger army than the one he has and he can take for himself the land that rightfully belongs to us."

"Where are you coming from?" his wife countered. "Abraham's army was larger and more powerful than Esau's! Yet, did Abraham march against the surrounding tribes? He conquered the conqueror of the world, yet he kept peace with all his neighbors. We are not to gain by fighting. We are to gain by obeying."

Yitzhak shook his head. "What woman understands?" he excused.

"This woman understands," she answered his sigh.

"I will not listen," he commented.

"So, are your ears becoming as useless as your eyes? I hope, when you pray tonight, that your mouth does not become as blind as the rest of you!"

Angrily, she exited.

In the dark confines of his tent and eyes, his mind similarly darkened. He clasped his hands and bowed to pray.

"Esau," a voice whispered. "Esau," another voice whispered. "Esau," a third voice whispered.

Michael the Archangel, appearing beside these manipulating demonic angels, hushed them.

"Yahweh permits me to influence him," Satan rebuked Michael for his interference.

"Then continue whispering to him. I, in turn, will whisper in another's ears."

Satan waved him off, laughing at him.

When Riveka entered the tent, Michael sat beside her bed. "Remember Abraham's words," he spoke only once.

Riveka woke from her recollection and clairvoyantly watched the drama unfold in Yitzhak's tent.

"Esau," Yitzhak's voice rose louder than usual, "kiss me on the neck."

Esau hugged his father and warmly kissed him.

"Esau, I am grievously aged. I am uncertain about how much time I have left to live. Because of my physical condition and mental duress, I am now willing to ask this from you: Take your weapons and go to the savannas where the partridge hide. I want you to prepare for me the best meal you have ever undertaken to prepare. I want it succulent and memorable. Do this for me so I may pass the blessing to you before I die."

Riveka rose silently from her place and left her tent. As she walked away, she clearly remembered Michael's words to her. Then she remembered how often she spoke to Abraham, and how he always looked at Jacob with fond and tender eyes. Her memories gave her no choice. She determined to take the matter into her own hands.

Satan, engrossed with Yitzhak, failed to notice Riveka's countermeasures against him.

She found Jacob tending the sheep and quietly approached him. She studied the terrain to make absolutely sure no one saw her talking to him.

"Jacob, meet me quickly in my tent. It's urgent for you to do so, now!"

He obeyed her and followed her from a distance. No one paid any attention to the drama taking place.

"Your father is mentally preparing himself to pass on the blessing. He's in a trance at this very moment. When he wakes from it, his facilities will be slightly impaired. At that time present yourself to him for the blessing."

Without a second thought Jacob replied, "What must I do?"

"Bring me the two best goats you have. I will cook them tenderly over the slowest fire with cabbage and carrots. I'll flavor the stew with salt and other spices. Take the meal to him. Walk so the smell will fill his nostrils. Let the blessing take place over you."

"How am I to fool father when he touches me? Have you forgotten that my skin is smooth? Esau has coarse hair throughout his body. Father will come to realize I have attempted to deceive and manipulate him. Instead of a blessing, it's a curse I'll be receiving."

"May such a curse fall upon me, my son. Meanwhile, do exactly as I have instructed you, for I do this to fulfill my oath to your grandfather, Abraham."

During the heat of afternoon the herdsmen took the cattle to the furthermost springs of the land. By this time the lakes had regained their water levels. When the rays of the sun shimmered in the distance, Riveka and Jacob conspired together against Yitzhak.

"I taught Esau to be a great cook, and then, as it should have been, he began surpassing even my skills. But today, I have salt and I have spices."

"But even that wonderful aroma won't disguise my body odors and smooth skin."

"I have thought about that. For such a bright man, I'm surprised you didn't think of it yourself. Here. Dress in Esau's clothes. Then cover your hands and arms and neck with these kid's skins. I've already plucked them so they'll feel like Esau's own skin and hair. Jacob, go on. Put them on."

"Are you certain?"

"What I compel you to do I am certain of. Now go, before Esau returns."

Jacob did as he was told, then left his mother's tent. He refused to turn his head to the right or to the left or behind himself. He walked straight ahead, forcing himself to carry out the conceived plot. His breathing pains increased. His heart raced. His face flushed. His mouth dried. The palms of his hands became wet. Unable to stop sweating, the dinner plate began slipping from his hands. The path that he so often walked, now seemed to go on forever. Then, as it had to happen, he reached the tent's entrance.

"Father?"

Yitzhak, hearing the trembling voice, groggily came out of his trance. Reeling from the power of it, he swooned. He rubbed his eyes and tried to focus on the figure that stood before him. Unable to recognize the harshly blurred figure and uncertain of the voice, he asked, "Which of my two sons are you?"

"I am Esau," Jacob, manipulating, deceived his father. Then clarifying his statement, so it would become a prophetic answer, Jacob added, "I am your firstborn."

And the tension in the sentence, mystified Yitzhak.

Jacob tried to ease the tension and to avert the questions in the face of his father and to avoid being caught in the deceit by continuing to speak, "I did as you requested. Sit up now, Father, and eat the meal. I am ready for your blessing."

"Tell me," Yitzhak insisted on understanding what was occurring in his tent, "how was it possible for you to so quickly prepare my meal?"

"Your God, Yahweh, permitted it to be so."

Yitzhak sniffed the air and tilted his head slightly. He listened to the heavy breathing, to the pounding of the man's heart. Yitzhak sensed an inner struggle in the man. Perplexed, he briefly pondered. He desired more time to wake from his trance. Yet, strangely, his son insisted otherwise. "Perhaps my son had already waited too long?" Yitzhak reasoned within himself.

Disregarding his hesitations and doubts, he spoke: "There is something wrong here. Please, son, come closer to me. You are in the direct sunlight. I cannot distinguish you at all. I want to touch you."

"You've touched me a thousand times."

"But your lips are not on my neck as they always are when you greet me. Your voice trembles. It has never been uncertain before. Is it unreasonable for me to verify the presence of my firstborn son?"

"Of course not, Father. Touch me."

As soon as Jacob drew nearby, Yitzhak grabbed his hands and pulled him closer. The ancient man stroked his son's arms and tested his son's hair. The eyes that failed to clearly recognize any image, tested his son's neck by placing a long, lingering kiss near the earlobe. Still uncertain, the son's Father tested the smell of the clothes which he wore.

And all the while, Jacob's heart pumped fiercely in is ears. His face flushed. His knees weakened.

"I don't understand this," Yitzhak said. "Your body is as Esau's, but your voice is as Jacob's."

"Is it not because we are twins? It's the anxiety of the moment. I've waited all my life for your anointing and proclamation of who I am. Your blessing is mine to receive."

Yitzhak hesitated again. He was troubled. He said, "Are you really Esau, my son?"

"I am truly your firstborn."

"Then feed me the food that smells so delicious. Could it be that the smell has dazzled me so much that I have become doubtful of your identity? Truly, I have never smelled a finer meal."

"Taste it," Jacob dipped a copper cup into the copper bowl that his fondest great-great-grandfather had brought them from Assyria. Yitzhak played with the taste of the food and rubbed his tongue between his lips. Satisfied, he smacked them apart. Yitzhak smiled broadly. "Salt and spices. How wonderful! And what kind of wine did you bring me?"

"Taste it. Take as much as you desire."

He breathed the bouquet into his nostrils. Yitzhak smiled again. "It's Babylonian! How appropriate! I didn't know we had any of it left." Impulsively, he took a deep breath, expanded his chest, and released a loud burp! "Stupendous cooking! But why haven't you yet kissed me? Surely, as important as this is, is not one kiss on my neck more important?"

Jacob rose up and kissed his father's neck as Esau had always done.

"Yes, it is true. The smell of my son is just exactly as the smell of the fields that Yahweh has blessed."

Yitzhak reached behind him and brought out the same jar that Shem had given to him on the day of his own anointment. He bent his son's head down and freely poured the oil over his hair, allowing it to drip from his temples to his cheeks. Large droplets fell to his knees. In the sudden twilight of emotions, Yitzhak's eyes blurred with tears as did Jacob's.

With a firm voice, a voice resonating with the holy embrace of prophecy, Yitzhak declared:

"May the true God give you

"the dews of heaven and the fertile soils of the earth.

"May the true God grant you an abundance of wine and grain.

"Let the people serve you.

"Let nations bow low to you.

"A master over all of your brothers you will become!

"Thus, let it become that all of your mother's sons will bow low to you.

"Cursed are they who curse you.

"Blessed are they who bless you."

As Yitzhak pronounced the prophecy, a tingling sensation embraced both men. Yitzhak at that very instant affirmatively knew he had anointed the correct son.

Jacob stared at the small jar that Melchizedek had given Yitzhak, and in that moment, felt another presence in the tent. Afraid, he quickly left the tent and went into hiding.

ༀༀༀༀༀༀ

Within the hour it happened to occur that Esau also appeared in his father's tent.

Yitzhak, by this time, had fallen asleep when Esau brought inside the tent a freshly prepared meal.

"Father, rise up! Up! Up! Up," he teased him, reaching to grab him by the toes.

"What?" Yitzhak questioned. His mind and emotions were groggier than the last time. His stomach and mind and senses swam from eating his latest meal and fully drinking the wine that Jacob provided to him. "Who are you?"

Esau, hurt by his father's tone and lack of enthusiasm and response, replied, "I am Esau! I am your firstborn son!"

"Whhhaaaattttttt! Bbbuuuttttt, but, you were just here!" Then, like an epileptic, he went into a convulsion. His head and upper body began shivering! Violently shaking, his eyes bulged. His tongue hung outside his mouth! His face flushed deep red.

Esau wrapped his father inside his arms. Affectionately he wiped the heavy sweat from Yitzhak's forehead. "What is it, father? What is happening to you?" He was frightened but he nevertheless tried to control his voice. Yet his tone betrayed the helplessness in his heart.

Yitzhak came back to himself with Esau's nursing. "Who have I anointed with the sacred pouring of the oil? Who brought me the food that I consumed before you came here?"

"How am I to know? What exactly are you saying to me?" Esau was fighting for control of his voice.

"Esau," Yitzhak, now knowing for an absolute fact what had occurred, and knowing that Yahweh was the source of the drama, flatly stated, "I have anointed your brother. Now he must remain the anointed. The true Mashiach of our family. Through him will the ultimate Mashiach of man descend!

"There is no water pure enough on the face of the earth to wipe clean the sacred oil that I have just poured over Jacob's head. No amount of wine, no amount of ale, will take away from him what has entered into him. The spirit of God will never leave his soul."

Esau drew in a long, deep breath. He raised his fists to his mouth. His face tightened. His eyes watered. He threw back his head. His chest filled with anger. He reached out blindly and pulled his father against him, holding on to him as tightly as he could.

It was no use. Esau cried! He sobbed like an infant. But it was the full passion of his grown man's inner depths that burst out of him. It was like a hidden quagmire had suddenly erupted in front of his face. A thing so detestable he had repeatedly hidden it from sight and thought and action. A hatred that demanded to be seen now filled his thoughts and passions.

Beside him the demons also cried at their failed attempt to thwart God's plan. And in the farthest parts of heaven, Michael the Archangel walked to his Father and placed his head in his lap.

Not wanting to come face to face with the monsters within him and the monsters outside him, Esau wept and screamed out the long hidden epitaphs. No forged sword existed that was powerful enough to defeat his desired revenge! No word existed that was gentle enough to vanquish his thoughts of retaliation! No thought existed that was intense enough to alleviate his hatred. No song. No poem. No music harmonic enough existed! Nothing existed that was strong enough to squelch the passions of the reality of what had occurred.

Burying his face in his father's shoulder, the agonizing tears penetrated even through his father's clothing, wetting him. Unable to concentrate on words, Esau kept pouring out the intensity of his sufferings in his father's arms.

And never had any person seen such turmoil and anguish from another, and never has any father from his own son.

"Father," Esau managed to speak between the sobs, "bless me also.

"Jacob, with cunning conspiracy, stole your blessing."

Esau again managed to talk: "Such is the truth of his name: Jacob, the supplanter!

"Twice he took from me what should have been mine. As a youngster, returning from the hunt, when I was tired and hungry, he manipulated me to sell him my birthright for a bowl of lentil soup. Now, when I am seventy-seven years old, he steals my anointing. Never has a man abused me so much as my own brother!"

As Esau gained control of his emotions, he was able to ponder the events: "Father, were these separate dramas focused purposefully against me?" He rubbed the back of his shoulder then tried to ease the tension from the back of his neck. He became calmer. His crying lessened. In a moment of calm, he asked, "Father, have you reserved a blessing for me? Surely, somehow, you had to be aware of Jacob's prophetic purpose against me. Surely, somehow, you placed something away for me to ease my burden."

"Esau, my most beloved child," Yitzhak answered, attempting to soothe away the hostilities, "I have made Jacob your master. He is now in charge of all the household tasks. He has complete accounting rights for all of Yahweh's promises. Not only you, but your other three brothers must also serve under him. You and they must ready for him the wine and the grains. Still, though, there must be something else I can do for you, my beloved child."

"I want no wealth from you. No possessions of any sort. No promises of land. I want to be the acknowledged forefather of the Mashiach! Let the true one descend from my loins!"

"Such a powerful declaration! Such a bold desire! Evidently it was not mine to give to whomever I chose. Yahweh directed the Messianic choice."

"Then give me any sort of blessing! Don't allow me to perish without some sort of historic acknowledgment. I cannot reside in the recesses of forgottenness, nor in the river of unfathomable abysses! Is my life to be so futile I cannot even become a memory to anyone?"

Yitzhak closed his eyes. His arms rose even with his cheeks. He spread his fingers apart and formed a V sign with both hands. With his thumb pointing to his temples, he became mesmerized. Again an electrical bonding occurred in the tent. The spirit of unification, of purpose, came to where Yitzhak was. Esau felt the currents penetrate into his body. He relaxed and allowed the calm breeze of the transaction to migrate into his subconscious.

"Absorb this prophecy:

"Your land of residence shall be placed away from here,

"even away from the quench of the heavens.

"You will live by the power of your sword.

"You will serve your brother;

"but when you become calm and discover the inner tranquillity of your life, you will at that moment break his yoke from your neck."

Esau pushed away from his father and searched deeply into his eyes. They could not return his gaze. He rubbed the hairs on his chest and became confused. He repeated his father's words over and over to himself. With widening eyes, he suddenly shouted, "I'm to serve Jacob! Even you cannot reverse such a travesty? By the sword? Am I to be as Yishmael? Must I continuously be at war with someone? What kind of blessing is this?"

"It's one that has a promise of peace for you."

"Peace? I asked for remembrance, but not this way."

"Touch the tranquillity that I have given to you. I, because of my deepest love for you, have passed it on to you. Do not forsake it, for it is nearly impossible for a man to grasp the inner harmony of his consciousness. It is a far greater blessing to be at peace than to be a master who must one day vanquish the world."

"Father, I love you, but I can no longer love Jacob. Let the peace stay within yourself. I only want to own hate. Hate and vengeance!" Esau then whispered to himself: "Please, hasten the death of my father so I may murder my brother Jacob!"

ೞೞೞೞ

That same night, when Esau went into his tent, he sat brooding alone, intensifying his hatred for Jacob. Adah, Elon's third daughter, brought Eliphaz, Esau's firstborn into the tent to sit beside him. "Father, why are you so troubled?"

Sighing, Esau placed his arm about his son's neck. "You are thirty years old. A man. And, I haven't an inheritance to pass on to you. Jacob, as always, robs me of everything."

"Jacob is the anointed Mashiach?"

"Yes. He won."

"But my wife is pregnant! What are we to receive?"

"Nothing, for I have been given nothing."

"Will Jacob allow us to stay?"

"I am going to kill Jacob. So, yes, we will be able to stay."

"Murder Jacob?" Eliphaz's angry thoughts instantly dispelled. He reflected on his father's words. Years ago he felt his uncle's tenderness and concern and compassion and his interest in everything he ever tried to accomplish. His uncle taught him to read as much as his own father taught him to hunt.

"Father, I like Jacob," he said to his father. "Never, not under any circumstances, will I permit you to do such a terrible thing to your own brother. Jacob, for all his cunning and manipulations, has a compassionate heart. He knows how to gently smile and how to laugh. He never frowns. Of the men in this camp, I like him the best."

Vainly trying to reason with his father's emotional trauma, he added, "Jacob's an intellect—not a warrior."

"His intellect is more dangerous than a sword. His deceitful, arrogant, manipulative cunning has ruined me!"

"Jacob will take care of us."

"A dead man can not care for the living! How can a childless, unmarried man become the anointed one? I have wives! I have children! I have responsibilities! He sits! He reads! He ponders! And to what good?"

"Eliphaz, go to your uncle. Bring him to my tent." Saying that, he drew his dagger out. "I will not wait a moment more. Let my blind father stay blind to what I am about to commit myself to doing."

Eliphaz rushed out of the tent. In haste he reported his father's exact words to his grandmother, Riveka.

In a panic, she mounted her donkey and rode to Jacob's hiding place. "Esau is making peace with himself by scheming your death. You must do as I command."

"I will, Mother."

"Run away from here! Run to Haran. Seek out my brother Laban. Stay with him until your brother's anger subsides. Stay there until Esau completely forgives you for what has been done to him. I promise I will send word to you when that happens."

"How do you know such a forgiveness is possible with my brother?"

"His father is a man of inner harmony. Surely, in the Tent of Pronunciation, such a harmony has been bequeathed to Esau. Never has a man needed such a state than Esau does at this very moment. If Esau kills you, surely he will also lose his own life. I cannot lose two sons in a single day."

"Mother, I cannot leave unless Father permits it to be so. He has bonded me to the land as he has bonded Esau. How can I break such a pledge?"

"I will think of a way. Meanwhile, go deeper into the forest. Esau would never conceive of you hiding in such a place."

"I've never been afraid of the forest. The crowded trees just never appealed to me."

"Son, I've always known you were never afraid of anything. Some display their courage in different manifestations. For now, let me leave. I must convince Yitzhak to allow you to break your pledge to him so you may leave this land."

ℬ◯ℰℬ◯ℛℰ◯ℰℬ◯ℰ

During the first morning of his anger, Esau invaded everyone's privacy! His eyes filled with rage as he tossed and threw out the belongings of the people residing in the encampment. Failing to find Jacob hidden behind a bundle of clothing or inside a package of goods or within the depths of the chests, he called his finest scouts to continue the hunt for revenge! Several teams converged toward the surrounding forest where they devised many unsuccessful plans for capturing Jacob.

A few days later Esau's teams tired of the hunt. The scouts also failed to find Jacob.

During the late evening of the sixth day Esau's best friend determined to hunt through the cattle and sheep herds for Jacob. That plan also failed.

Disgusted, his friend returned to his wives. Esau's spouses, unable to gain his attention toward their beds, regretted fermenting his hatred against Jacob. On the seventh day, Esau's wives, isolated and mocked by Riveka, silenced their pleas for revenge against Jacob. That night his wives surrounded him and embraced him in tender caresses. An hour later, Esau finally relaxed his hunt against Jacob.

ಐﬗಐﬗﬗಐﬗಐﬗ

In the new morning of the eighth day, with his energies exhausted, Esau determined to wait patiently for Jacob. In that new morning, his anger quieted. The hour of human trembling ceased.

Comfortable among his wives, Esau reasoned: "Sooner or later, he will make his announcement to me. I will expose his flank. I will wait for that exposure. At that moment, when the night removes the day and when the branch wilts and when the drought dries the grass, at that very moment I will kill Jacob! Even in front of Father, if need be, I will kill him!"

He raised his hands to pledge on it. Hesitatingly, he looked at the drifting clouds. "Strange," he thought, "I've never pledged on anything during my lifetime—except to remain in this land."

He walked away.

ಐﬗಐﬗﬗಐﬗಐﬗ

Riveka brought her husband another warm meal and placed the bowl in her lap. She fondly fed the meal to his lips.

"This meat tastes exactly the same as the one that Jacob served me."

"That's because I was the one who prepared it."

Yitzhak's breath caught. Uncertain, he began to rise out of his seat. Uncertain, he refrained. His hand began to reach out to her. She saw his movement and reached out to touch his hand. Before their hands could meet, Yitzhak withdrew his, enveloping it inside his cloak.

"You?" he whispered, astounded.

"I was compelled to intercede," she pleaded. "You had forgotten your father's words."

"What has my father to do with what you conspired today against me?"

"Your father told me Jacob would be the chosen son to carry the Mashiach's seed."

"My father said that to you?"

"And more."

She placed her hand softly on his long, gray beard and gently tugged on it. "Tell me," she asked, "was I mistaken to do what I did?"

"In the manner that you did it—yes! Yet," he again reached out for her. This time both hands met, embracing tenderly in their love for each other, "when I placed the oil over Jacob's head, I knew that the man whom I anointed was indeed the correct man. Yet, you erred against me. You failed to trust my judgment."

"Husband, your judgment was biased with favoritism. You are as figuratively blind as you are physically. You never considered that our two sons symbolize the social balances of the world. Esau represents the nations who will be saved through the Mashiach, whereas Jacob represents the class of man who will present to mankind an eternal blessing of prosperity and goodwill under a united and single law that equally applies to all people of all nationalities. The true law is good. It will never bend nor be influenced by a corrupt law. A good action will always conquer an evil action. If evil triumphs on earth, it will only be for a short while. Heavenly intervention will occur and all injustices will be balanced toward the good and eternal things."

"Dear," Yitzhak replied. "Though evil actions can assimilate, the good acts must never be compromised. It may appear to unknowing eyes that a good person bows to evil on occasions, but truthfully, when it rises, truth has no ceiling. All things lay underneath the shadow of the law."

His wife added, "This thing that occurred on earth is but a small enactment that foreshadows heaven's actions against all the evil forces."

Yitzhak smiled. He nodded. For a second he felt an inner satisfaction that what happened between him and Jacob had to happen to permit the descent of the ultimate Mashiach to be born into the world with the correct genetic makeup in his veins, as inherited by Jacob from the line of Abraham and Eber and Shem.

He spoke: "I should have remembered that not one of Esau's wives is from the line of Shem. The lineage cried against Esau's anointment. His firstborn, Eliphaz, would now be standing in front of his father, asking for the oil to be placed over his locks. Could Eliphaz truly receive the blessing?"

Yitzhak became silent. He pondered his own question. He slowly added, as though he was answering himself, "Yahweh is not prejudiced. I am not prejudiced. Perhaps," reflecting on a distant time, "I did not want to face the issues of segregation during my lifetime as my father faced it."

"I," she raised her voice, "know of those issues. Nevertheless, I am prejudiced! Not against their racial traits, but, distinctly, against their religion. After these long years they have failed to subject themselves to Yahweh's laws and principles. They bow before stone images and say strange words to rocks and trees, and burn the cow's dung. Those things makes me very prejudiced. Whoever says we must preserve these false stone images because they represent culture and man's talent, forget God's words: 'There is no other God before me.' So, regardless how beautiful a stone may be carved and how elegant it may be rendered, it must be totally destroyed. And, because Esau's wives and children can not tolerate Yahweh's presence in their hearts, I can no longer tolerate their presence in my heart. Hittite women they are, and such they remain!"

"Yes," Yitzhak thought, "it is true. Esau never taught his wives Yahweh's principles. Though his children know the Great Name, they do not understand the meaning and purpose behind the name. Only His anointed can flourish in Yahweh's task of cleansing man from false worship and pretended entities."

"Yitzhak," Riveka said, then paused and went on, "what if Jacob marries a Hittite woman? How much more would life be unbearable for us if that occurred?"

"Yes, the Hittite women refuse to adapt their hearts' toward Yahweh's mercies," Yitzhak confirmed it to himself by echoing his wife's concern. "They refuse to learn His history. They want to play with legends and with hearsays. They read superficially and, what they see, they place aside to another's creation—or formation from it's own power through time and motion. They do not make within themselves the necessary heart-conditions for a person to draw close to God. By willful direction, they align themselves against Yahweh's entrusted mission. Doing so, they become allied with demons and with Satan."

He let his wife's hand loose. He placed the meal aside and wiped his chin.

"I need to speak with Jacob. Do you," her husband teased with a glimmer in his smile, "know where Jacob is?"

She moved her head ever so slightly to her left side. She returned his smile. "I may be able to find him."

"Bring him to me tomorrow. Do so when the sun is at its full zenith. No one expects for Jacob to walk inside this camp during the afternoon's light."

ৡﺭৡয়ৡﺭৡ

With the sun's full rise, when the encampment lay underneath pitched tents to escape the glaring heat, Jacob's shadow touched the base of his father's tent.

Yitzhak, recognizing his son's footsteps, welcomed him.

"Are your arms smooth again?"

"They are."

"And are you sure you are whom you say you are?" Yitzhak tried to be humorous.

"I am Jacob."

"You are more than Jacob," Yitzhak whispered back to his son's voice. "You are the Mashiach who represents the ultimate Mashiach to come through your loins. You are the embodiment of a greater symbolic idea, rather than just the mere trappings of flesh and name. Yet it is odd that you are still childless and still unmarried. Have you ever thought on the subject?"

"There are no Babylonian women here for me to marry with."

"Does she need to be a Babylonian?"

"From the context of my understanding, yes."

"Mine also," his father's eyes, for a moment, seemed to brighten, as if he could really see his son again.

"Unlike grandfather, though, you never sent a servant to Haran to fetch a wife for me. And worse, I am thirty-seven years older than you when you got married. I'm seventeen years older than you were when Esau and I were born."

"I know how old you are," Yitzhak tartly replied. Apologizing, for there was no need to get angry in the first place, he lowered the tone of his voice. "I meant to send for a wife for you. After Yishmael died, I intended to do so again, but things kept interfering with me. Yet, we both know this for an absolute certainty: under no conditions are you allowed to marry a Canaanite!"

"Oh?" Jacob played with his father's emotions. "Should I instead marry an Egyptian?"

"Never!" Yitzhak protested.

"Perhaps, then, a Horite? Maybe, even, a Philistine? They do have, after all, such exquisite blond hair and such deep, green eyes. Their breasts are magnificent. And they're so tall! Wouldn't it be nice to have tall grandchildren?"

"Stop this Jacob. Your mother was right. You need to be married. First, however, I must release you from your pledge—but only temporarily."

Yitzhak gingerly walked about the tent. He knew exactly where every pillow was in the dimly lit space.

"Jacob," his voice turned merciful, tender, "I, in fact," his eyes began swelling with tears, "must send you away from our home. Esau is bitterly angry against you. The evil one's cunning entices his mind with thoughts of murder. When Esau's temper calms, return home. Return to your mother and father. Return to where you belong."

Yitzhak motioned with his hand. Jacob, understanding, knelt before his father. "Jacob, you have my permission, and my blessing, to travel north to Paddan-aram. Go to the house of Bethuel."

"My northern grandfather?"

"Yes. Go see your mother's father. Ask Laban, your mother's brother, and of course, your uncle, if he may have a spare daughter for you to marry. Here," his father handed him a parcel, "I have already prepared the necessary documents of introduction."

"Now, my firstborn son, quickly bend your head before me."

Scooting on his knees before his father, Jacob bowed his head. Yitzhak placed his hand over his head, saying: "May El Shaddai bless you.

"May He make you fertile,

so you may cause numerous children to be born to you.

"May He transfer to you and to your children the Abrahamic covenant.

"May it become so for you that you will possess the lands which you sojourn through.

"It is right to do this,

"for God has assigned all these lands to Abraham;

"from him to me to you and to your children."

Jacob took nothing for his long journey, not even a donkey. Jacob departed for the northern lands after saying his farewells to his mother and to Deborah the nurse.

ಬುಋಬುಋಬುಋಬುಋ

𝔄 week later Esau went into his father's tent. Pacing back and forth in front of his father, he struggled to contain his anger within himself. "I cannot find Jacob anywhere. I, nor my Amorite warriors. How cunning is my brother that he can so successfully hide from me and my Ishmaelite trackers?"

"I sent Jacob to his uncle Laban," Yitzhak quietly confessed. His blind eyes rose to stare into Esau's. Esau's body suddenly shook. He stepped away from his father. Puzzled, he fought for his composure and fought his tears back inside. A terrible, unexpected loneliness invaded his body. He silenced the words that cried to erupt from his mouth. He realized that what he suspected all along was correct. Yet he didn't want to face the ultimate realization that it had actually occurred.

Riveka, hearing the sudden quiet, cringed.

She rushed into the tent, taking with her her three other sons. Esau stared at his three brothers. He wanted to say something wicked to them, but found no words to say against them. "Strange," he whispered, "I never considered their existence, nor the meaning of their names, nor their circumstances. Will they ever be remembered by anyone?"

He swallowed his bitterness away from his mind. He scratched his forehead and tugged on his earlobe. He softened. His anger dissipated.

"To Haran?" Esau shook his head, knowingly repeating his father's thoughts and unspoken words.

"Yes," Yitzhak answered.

"That's so far away," Esau whispered. "So far north." Amazed at his own compassionate words, Esau silenced himself again. In those few reflective moments, Esau recalled their childhood. He remembered how often they held each other's hands as they explored the heights of the nearby meadows. He recalled how they caught the long tails of the cattle, snapping them as whips against the cow's backside. He recalled how they quietly studied the fish movements in the clear creeks. He remembered again how Jacob patiently tried to invent the draught resistent lentil and his many failures in perfecting the pea that cost him to sell his birthright.

The great famine not only cost Jacob his confidence in his ability to create, it cost Esau his anointing. Then Esau remembered that the things that he read, he read only because Jacob taught him the characters' meaning and deciphering.

As he reminiscenced, he felt his hands tingling. He bent his head to look at his fingers and saw again a distant time past when he carefully held the ropes that held Jacob suspended in midair in the middle of a deep, dangerous well. He had lowered his brother so carefully into the depths of the dry wells. Once in the deep pits, Jacob had studied the packed clay and devised a way to free the blockage. Ever so gently, Esau remembered raising the ropes so his brother wouldn't hit his head against the jutting rocks. He remembered his hands' strength and the dryness of his mouth, afraid to lose his grip.

He moistened his lips. Esau recalled sitting beside his brother while his father taught them the great histories of their lineage. He again saw the fire's kindling and heard the crackling embers. Affectionately listening, both together repeated their father's readings.

His eyes fully moistened.

"Is Jacob finally going to get married?"

"Yes." How did you know?"

"I deduced it. See, I can be as logical as Jacob. I believe he has gone there because, as he has become the anointed one, it is required for him to marry a Babylonian."

"Such is true," Riveka answered her son. Yitzhak, surprised at his son's honest evaluation, nodded.

"Mother," Esau looked directly at her. "you never loved my wives, did you?"

"Their ways and manners and beliefs are not suitable for us, no."

The gentle memories of his brother dissipated. Angry, he whipped his green and blue striped robe up to his shoulder. His renewed anger swelled. He snarled at his mother: "But they know how to make me feel as a man!

And, they don't mind performing whatever I ask them to do! They'll swallow buckets of my fluid if I demand it!"

Yitzhak, shocked, stood up. His leg bumped into the jar beside it. As it rolled away, it hit the tent pole and shattered.

His mother screamed, "ESAU!" while his father bellowed, "Arrogant and rude!"

Before either of them could find another word, Esau fled from the tent to his waiting horse. He jumped to its back and squeezed its side as he leaned hard forward, prompting it to rush away. After a distance, he went to his tent and pushed past his wives to the chest that rested in the farthest corner.

"Husband," Basemath said, "why are you taking our silver pieces?"

"To whom are you talking? And since when did either of you own anything?"

He climbed back on his horse and continued on the road until he reach its fork. He nodded and cruelly whipped the horse's side, galloping furiously toward Nebaioth's house.

ℰℭℬℭℬℭℛℰℭℬℭ

After he plunged down the last steep embankment, Esau slid off his horse, and threw the reins to a servant who ran to the visitor.

"Your master?"

The servant meekly pointed to the far tent.

"Bring me that sack of weights."

The servant swiftly followed the great hunter.

"Esau!" Nebaioth greeted his best friend

"These weights of silver are yours."

"Why such a generous gift?"

"I'm offering a contract of marriage for your sister."

"For Mahalath? Why? You already have three wives."

"I've been married to them too many years. Their skin has become wrinkled. Your sister's skin is smooth. Her breasts don't sag. I want her!"

"Since my father died, she has been in need of a husband," he examined the large weights of silver as he was speaking. "Who better for her than my best friend?" he jubilantly shouted as he wrapped his arm about Esau's shoulders. "Marry her Esau! She is yours!"

Chapter Twenty-Four

▼

The World Expands

Jacob brushed his long hair out of his eyes. Large perspiration beads covered his forehead. His wet clothes felt gummy and sticky. He rubbed his eyes clear of the dripping, humid sweat. His nose felt oily. He wiped his face clean, soiling his cloak. He rubbed his mustache away from his mouth and as he observed the long road's journey, he thought on its path. Northward lay the great cities of the King's Road.

Throughout the day and into the setting sun, Egyptian and Minoan soldiers passed by him. The tramping of their feet against the road crushed the grass, withering it. "How much like they trample the grass do men tramp over each other," he contemplated as he walked. "The western civilizations are expanding. India and Mesopotamia now seem closer to each other. How much closer are they in fact to each other than when my great forefather blazed the trading trails for the merchants and kings? The miles may be the same distance, but the mental realization of their existence and the trade goods exchanged between them lessen the distance's meaning.

"The Sea? What mysteries fog it today? The Minoans have no fear of the Sea. I must develop within my consciousness this bravery. To do this I must strengthen my body. In my body's strength, I must incorporate a forward boldness. I must back up this appeal with proper actions. I must reinforce and fortify myself so people will not remove themselves away from me, but will approach me with understanding, care, and loyalty.

"The Egyptians, in their treaties with the Minos, colonized the lower and upper sections of their vast river. I must, in my journey, ferment and bring to perfection the realization of personal colonization. I must form and develop methods whereby I can be the first in my family to actually own land throughout the land that God has promised me and my descendants. I will not be a third-generation wanderer. Before the Minoan sailors round the Cape of Africa, I will become a great landowner!"

ဆ၊ဆ၊ဆ၊ဆ

At the time of Jacob's traveling, an age of intense exploration and mythology developed among the nations. The Egyptian priests studied the skies and invited the Babylonian mathematicians to their land to formulate precise calculations for their newest building projects. The Egyptian sailors, learning from the Minoan sailors, determined to travel down their southern river to map its breadth and length. These explorers forged the new cities with patriotism, settling them not only to trade from but also to directly oppose the Hyksos regime. Eventually in their brave conquest, they discovered the deep, southern mother well. Egypt, becoming jealous, guarded its trade secret. Only the most trusted captains consulted the river's maps.

When they had conquered the river's mysteries, the priests felt empty and deprived.

The Minoan navy, blocked by recent treaties from entering the depths of the Nile, set out to discover the rest of the world.

The Egyptians were unable to find another river outlet from the other side of the gigantic lake. They felt themselves betrayed by their own haste to secure a treaty with the Minos. "Where can we sail?" a priest challenged. "What is there left for us accomplish if the Minos contains us locked inside a narrow bed of land, split between a long river going nowhere?"

"Is everything discovered?" another priest pompously retorted. "Is everything invented?"

The priests spent days huddled together in a secret conference as they tried to answer these challenging questions.

"Many of us are too old to maintain our systems. Many of the young men who are in our ranks, refuse to accept what we present to them. We are entering a chaotic upheaval. It is best for us to die today, rather than face the uncertainty of tomorrow."

"Yes, but who will replace us? We will all soon die. Vanish. Become forgotten. How do we endure? What can we do to be remembered?"

"Cities! Yes! We will build cities!"

"Cities preserve civilizations!"

Surmounting their different ideologies, the priests united into a secret clan. The Egyptian king seized on their ambitions by codifying himself as the embodiment of everything actual and possible in Egyptian culture. He proclaimed himself as the true representative of the people to the gods. The priests followed the king and thereafter, testified to the truth of their religion and ideologies to the people. Civilization bent itself to the king's will

The people of Egypt accepted the words. They traded their finite mortality for the bricks' immortality. The bricks' long-term existence outweighed all other considerations.

The commoners, viewing the heavenly bodies, reflected: "Within the stars' outstretch of light, our own physical energies pulsate. The heavenly bodies symbolize our gods! The stars accurately measure the distance and placement of all things. By following the brightest stars, we can survey and plot our land and designate the exact locations where our new buildings will stand and be eternally placed."

All the priests nodded approval.

☙ဪ☙ဪ☙ဪ

Jacob grew tired of his long journey. After many lonely weeks, Jacob decided to stop outside the borders of the city of Luz.

Night descended.

He lay down on the firm earth. He had no blanket, no other possessions. At first he tried to use his arm as a pillow. But, his arm became uncomfortable and woke him.

As he walked around, shaking his arm out to eliminate the sharp tingling, he found a suitable rock to lay his head on. That worked, and his body instantly adjusted.

He yawned a second time and fell asleep.

☙ဪ☙ဪ☙ဪ

Mystic images, swirling colors, jettisoning patterns. Geometric, circular, green and brown and yellow and red and violet flowers. Western mountains, eastern ridges: jagged, rocky, sharply dropping into steep, deep valleys filled with grape arbors and ribboning streams. Unending lush, thick forests greeted his dreams.

Then all vanished.

A clearness unlike any he had ever experienced descended over him. A vast emptiness where no colors existed covered him! No light could escape the void that entrapped Jacob in its midst. No light existed and the terrible void that descended, veiled his body in dreaded darkness. Fear invaded his thoughts!

No thoughts! No words! No images!

A state of total surrendering to the moment, wherein absolute consciousness is completely handed over to another's willful control, possessed him. Total clarity, as if in a vacuum of invisibility, possessed him. Absolute nothingness possessed him. In that state where his mind could see to the farthest point of essentialities, the essence of existence became real.

Colors formed.

Green, brown, blue, yellow appeared collating on top of each other till the brightness of their inner core extinguished itself, leaving impenetrable black in its wake.

From the inner mists of advancing and retreating images, all quieted.

Silence.

His eyes searched forward, racing swiftly. Acutely, he focused on seemingly distant objects. The soft, blurred forms appeared to be dancing, convoluting in a secret ritual known only to the highest essence of life. Gradually the hazy images became clearer. Gradually the unfocused images became sharply distinguishable.

He realized, seeing the images clearly, that he stood in the middle of their three-dimensional landscape. A grassless landscape littered with gigantic boulders and small rocks.

In the midst of this realm a single ramp ascended from the small tides of land to the vast collection of clouds above the planet. On the steep ramp a multitude of angels passed each other, hurriedly going back and forth.

Some rising, others lowering.

Jacob saw himself standing on the bottom ramp stair, waiting to join within their ranks. He desired to travel alongside them. He felt an intense, inner compulsion calling for him to lift himself from where he was sitting to journey among the visiting angels.

He knew that if only he had the courage he could ascend with whomever he wanted to. He felt the magnetic pull of his deepest desires beckoning him forward. It was as if he belonged to the class of men who one day would be allowed to climb the flight to the clouds. Yet in the deepest recess of his heart and mind he clearly understood that he was forbidden to step on the ramp.

He became afraid and his body trembled. Unable to stand still, he quivered. As he watched and viewed, seeing everything, he became aware of the slightest sound. His heart pained with the longings for a comfortable excuse to cease living beyond this incredulous moment. "What, after this, can be compared to it?"

Jacob lifted his head up and instinctively understood that the ramp's rise was a prophetic revelation of the stairway to come for the anointed children who survived the aftermath of the Mashiach's mission.

A soft breeze blew his hair upward, separating the strands. He tied his long hair back and felt another's presence standing directly beside him.

He shivered and turned around.

"I am Yahweh," the image declared God's words to the human with a majestic voice. Jacob listened, more with his mind than with his ears. He realized he was hearing a gentle serenade. A musical delight that tingled his senses.

The voice that spoke directly to Jacob was not Yahweh's, but the voice of Michael the Archangel who spoke his Father's words in complete harmonic balance. It was as though the representative knew exactly every thought that was about to be pronounced by the Creator of the Universe. "I am," the voice continued pronouncing his master's words to the awestruck man, "the God of your father Abraham and the God of Yitzhak. The earth on which your feet are standing I have assigned to you and to your children. Your descendants shall be as the dust of the earth. You will spread out to the Sea and beyond. To the east. To the west. To the south. To the north. To the Negev.

"All the families of the earth will benefit and receive blessings because of you, and because of your descendants.

"Remember, I am always with you!

"I will always protect you wherever you go.

"I assure you, you will return to this land, for it is yours.

"I will not abandon you," Yahweh's speaker continued translating the godly words to the human, "until I have completed what I have determined to become what has been promised to you."

A small crackling sound exploded between his ears. A small flash of blue light sparkled between Jacob's eyes.

Jacob woke.

Nervous, afraid, overwhelmed by the enormity of the extraordinary experience, he nevertheless jubilantly shouted, "Yahweh truly exists! This place testifies to His presence!" He grabbed a handful of dirt and flung it high into the air. As the dust filtered about him and into his hair, mingling with his clothes, he added, somewhat ashamed of himself, "I had not known this before. All the books I read, all the languages I learned, all my studies into the matters and essence of things, but of He who created everything, I knew little."

He fell silent, then joyously shouted again, "How fantastic this place is! This land is no less than the very House of God! That rise, no less than the very stairway to heaven!"

With the hint of the earth rotating toward the sun's rays, Jacob took the exact same stone that he had slept and built an altar underneath it. After capping the rigid monument with the pillow-stone, he looked about the area. On his left side stood a mid-sized olive tree. Pulling off large quantities of its fruit, he pulverized them until they emitted from their substance a sufficient amount of oil for his task. Praying over the pool of fragrant oil, he asked Yahweh to bless it. Cupping the middle portion, he poured the sum of the anointing oil over the altar. Taking his hands, he vigorously rubbed the soothing oil into the peak pillow-stone.

"This land that was once called 'Luz' shall now be known as 'Bet-El'."

He lifted both his hands to the heavens and the oil dripped from his wrists to the ground. As loud as he could, Jacob declared: "This, I vow," creating a verbal contract with Yahweh, "that first, if God truly continuously stays with me; and if, second, He truly continuously protects me during this journey that I am undertaking; and if, third, I am truly given bread and water to nourish me and clothing to place over my naked flesh; and if, last but most importantly,—I am truly safely returned to my father's house—then Yahweh will forever be my God!"

Confidently stroking the pillow-rock, Jacob stared into the face of the passing cloud. "This same stone that I have erected on top of this pillar shall testify to my declaration: This place is indeed God's house!"

Jacob placed both palms over his forearms. "This I further pledge: everything that You shall provide to me, of that, I will in turn set aside ten percent for You."

The cloud's face dissipated.

(Remarkably, hundreds of years before Moses understood the significance of the meaning of Yahweh's name, Jacob immediately understood the deepest essence of Yahweh's character.)

Chapter Twenty-Five

▼

Travels North

Jacob traveled north behind the Minoan caravan from Bet-El to Shechem. He carefully studied the terrain that he traveled on. Its hard exterior defied any type of grasses to grow on the road. "Only Yahweh can fertilize this route with the grasses' growth," Jacob mused. "Centuries from now, after the greenery covers the routes with dense forests, who will accidentally rediscover this pathway?"

The hooves of the camels stomped the ground harder with each passing and arriving trip.

Throughout the length of the road entrepreneurs established resting and dining inns where the Egyptian and Philistine soldiers quietly and peacefully shared their meals. Occasionally a foreign banner waved. None cared during these journeys who belonged to what country. The trade was more important. The commerce too precious. The journey was too difficult to insult another merchant because he happened by circumstance to be born near a river distant from the mountain range.

Peacefully the various merchants entered the inns, bedding down for the night.

Jacob, penniless, separated himself from the merchants, staying outside.

Unaccustomed to an impoverished lifestyle, he refused to play the beggar's role. Jacob leaned against an oak tree whose branches divided at the junction of the stars' brightness. He nodded. "Penniless? So what! For now, the constellations make me wealthy." While he observed the stars' movements, he clearly saw their paths and understood their rotations. Long ago he had separated the facts from the myths.

A merchant's servant, happening to be passing by him, momentarily stared at Jacob. "Such a man with such regal clothing," he thought to himself, "What does he see above?"

Curious, the man sat beside Jacob. "Hello."

"And good-greetings to you," Jacob bowed his head.

The two men remained silent beside each other. Both studied the stars' filtering light that wove among the branches of the great oak tree. After a long trail of clouds caught up to them, hiding their view of the stars, the servant inquired, "You must be quite satisfied."

"Why do you say that?"

"Let me guess: you're a rich man hiding from the world so no one can identify you?"

Jacob smiled. He turned his head away, refusing to answer. Undaunted, the servant continued his inquiry. "Or, you're a prince in search for truth." He picked up a handful of dirt, letting it filter between his fingers. "There are so many princes doing just exactly that. Inherited power seems to leave one destitute. Better to achieve on your own your greatness rather than being born to it."

Jacob looked amiably at the servant. A small scar ran from his ear to the corner of his eye. "Or," the man insisted on knowing, "you're on a religious quest for inner exposure." The man bolted up, "And I've met many of those types as well. It seems that many men want to become mystics. It's all about control—exactly as a prince would want to do."

Jacob stretched, indicating he wanted to be left alone.

The man studied Jacob for a few moments more. He looked at the man's sandals. They were filthy. He had walked far. The bottom of his cloak was unraveling. The threads had become caked with the road's magnetic clinging. "Or, you really are a beggar who hasn't yet prepared himself to beg from me! Or, could it be that you've just eaten; perhaps even received a weight of silver in your hand?"

"Actually," Jacob finally answered the man, "none of your guesses are correct." The man's face saddened. Jacob had hurt his feelings. Seeing this, Jacob sought to compensate. "Then again, it may be that everything which you surmised about me is indeed correct."

The man generously smiled. Jacob returned the smile.

The servant seemed good-natured. Jacob decided to confess, testing the man's genuineness. "Then there is the possibility that I am famished and that I am broke."

The servant's eyes widened. What an opportunity to speak boldly! "Then you must be too lazy to beg and intend to die of hunger!"

"How can a man die of hunger when fruit trees grow around us and the grains flourish nearby? As for laziness, I do not understand its concept. Doesn't a person need to wake and to go to the edges of the camp to relieve himself? Yes, and more. No, I am not lazy. I am content."

The servant kept smiling. He liked the stranger in regal clothing. "Broke, hungry, yet content? Unbelievable!" Softening even more, the compassion of the man shone. He continued speaking. "I am the route-master's assistant of that caravan. You do not appear to be a beggar. You certainly do not speak as an unlearned man. Your manners are imposing, even though you appear to be short."

"I'm about five foot three inches. My twin brother is about one inch taller than I. No one can tell except for us. Our eyes never truly stare into each other whenever we face off. It's humorous at times." Jacob let his breath out in a long, slow exit.

"Ahh, so you have a family! Are you lost from them? Are you, maybe, an advance scout for them?"

"So quickly you ask me so many questions. Write them down for me so I may take my time reading them. I'll answer at my leisure."

"Write? I cannot write. That's why I am only an assistant. Oh, I've managed to memorize the symbols of numbers and I can distinguish the signs of the cities, but I cannot create a sentence."

"It's not that difficult. I can write in every language that I've encountered."

"Yes," the servant acknowledged its possibility, "it's obvious you speak Akkadian well, yet I've not heard your accent before."

"I journeyed from the south."

"Where are you heading?'

"North."

"Elba?'

"Beyond."

The assistant continued to observe Jacob while they were talking and thoughtfully nodded. "I don't know why I stopped to sit beside you, but I am glad that I did. We can always use a scribe. Tell me, do you know this route?"

"I know all the routes."

"You must be a great traveler."

"I've never traveled beyond my home ground. What I mean is: I've studied all the maps and learned the locations of every known city," Jacob immodestly stated. Yet his demeanor showed he wasn't being arrogant. Jacob spoke in a matter-of-fact tone. The man liked the stranger's style. His genuine self-confidence. His careful, exacting tone of voice.

"What do you think about joining us?"

"If your master permits it, I will do so."

An hour later the route-master, himself, met Jacob. "Do you know accounting?"

"I know mathematics. I know how to work the symbols of the numbers."

"I speak several languages myself. But then, of course, all route-masters speak several languages. We need not only to speak the languages of the countries we trade with, we also need to understand the laws of each principality and the methods of accounting that they use."

"As well as the roads' turns and the location of the stars," the route-master's assistant interrupted.

At that point the route-master tested Jacob with the languages. Jacob proved that he clearly understood them all. The route-master was impressed. "Write my name," he commanded in a further test.

Jacob produced the writing on the loose dirt on the road. He wrote the man's name first in his native cuneiform wedge language then in Hebrew.

"Your style is simpler than ours," the route-master commented. "It's linear and more concise."

"It can be used for any word or sentence. It can present into writing any idea that exists. My great-great-great grandfather Shem taught the style to my father and he to my brother and me."

"Join my caravan and teach your writing to me. It's simplicity is amazing!"

Jacob agreed to stay with the caravan. It journeyed north. They eagerly traveled through Damascus where they bargained and negotiated additional commerce. The trading went better than expected.

With the enriched cargo, the larger caravan traveled hundreds of miles farther, heading toward Elba. Nearby rested its sister city, Ugarit.

Jacob overlooked the twin cities and studied the massive ramparts and fortifications that surrounded Elba and Ugarit. Elba's glacis were twenty feet thick. Adjoining ditches, called fosses, tactically resisted the battering rams of the city's enemies. Furthermore, the fosses hampered the war-charges of the horse-drawn chariots of its enemies.

Elba's intense commerce fascinated Jacob. Thirty thousand permanent residents lived in the city. Jacob observed their clothing and saw the cloths of other Minoan merchants as well as Egyptian and Assyrian and Mitannian. The Hurrians, unlike the rest, carried broad axes and swords with them. They refused to negotiate, demanding massive discounts from the merchants.

The route master grew tired of the Hurrians' demands and his quick losses. That same day he abandoned Elba. The caravan proceeded to the city of Charchemish, which rested between the Hittite sphere of influence and the Mitanni provinces. Jacob, remained with the caravan.

Through a series of trades and discussions, the caravan-master eventually encountered the recently elected ensis of the city. When, hearing of the caravan's travels through Elba and the intrusions of the Hurrians, the ensis demanded to meet the caravan-master.

As the merchants mingled their way through the crowded and colorful narrow streets, their eyes feasted on all wards that the other merchants brought from the distant lands to this marketplace. Eventually, and reluctantly, the merchants worked their way to the ensis's house. There, they entered through the hardened baked blocks that formed the doorway. The caravan-master and Jacob immediately met a large assembly who were debating the news of the Hurrians.

Prior to the caravan's arrival, several spies learned that the Hurrians' aggressiveness was the result of the Hittite advances into their territory. Displaced by the Hittites, the Hurrian refugees forced themselves into Ugarit and Elba. Soon, Charchemish would also be targeted by the Hittites.

The sudden displacement suggested Minoan influence and bribery.

"We have no navy to combat them!" One emphasized to the distaste of the other.

"We can pay for a navy's construction," the other countered.

"Where will we gain the skilled men to crew a navy?"

"Sailors can be purchased as well as lumber."

"The Philistines will not sell us any lumber."

"We can purchase it from the eastern countries. We will permit the sailors who work for us to travel on our roads to India and farther east to Asia."

"Those roads are the lifeblood of our wealth. If we permit foreigners to travel on them, they'll tell the whole world about them. Surely, the problem of the Hittites will seem small compared to the onslaught of greed that'll overwhelm us."

"If we do not bring the lumber from the east, eventually the enemy will overcome us! If we do nothing—and let's assume for a moment that the Hittites do forget us—do you think the Egyptians will forget us? The king of their Great House wants everything; especially since the Minos permits him such permanent inroads into the northwest."

The Speaker of the House quelled the outcries of the democratic assembly. "We will vote on what to do," he stated.

Jacob, quietly witnessing, spoke to the caravan-master, "What if they vote favorably for the sanctions?"

"Then a war leader, a lugar, will be elected from among the strongest of men. Then another vote will be taken as to what to do."

"I had read of such government procedures, but I had never witnessed the process. For all the voices being heard, however, the true voice of God fails to be heard. Such decisions should be referred to Him."

"God does not enter into a democratic society. How, among our hundreds of various beliefs, can we ask one voice to express absolute policy?"

Before Jacob could answer the ensis finished counting the votes. Recording the desire of the assembly, he left the room.

A few moments later he reappeared with an entourage of warriors. "Select the general. He whom you chose, I bequeath my powers to."

Just as he was about to leave again, he finally noticed the caravan-master and his guest.

"Welcome back, friend! May your wealth continue to increase! May your health never diminish!"

"Thank you for your open gates," the man returned his greetings. "Always, please, permit my caravans to pass unharmed through your province." He opened his garment belt and pulled out a small leather pouch. "This, my friend, is a small token demonstrating my appreciation for my safe passage." Handing him the bag of silver weights, he waited for the man's acceptance. Pulling on another portion of his belt he produced another gift. "And this," he placed a rhyton in his hands that resembled a striped bull which rode over a craggy rise incised on a sauceboat. He presented to his friend a tankard and a pyxis as well.

"What exquisite miniatures!" the ensis exclaimed. "Now, what about your friend?"

Jacob offered him a bundle of three scrolls and politely bowed.

"What's this? A treasure map of tin ore and copper mines?"

"A thousand times better. Infinitely more substantial," the caravan-master proudly commented on Jacob's behalf. He took the package from Jacob's outstretched hands and enthusiastically placed it directly on the floor. The ensis stooped down to examine the documents. He ran his fingers over the cuneiform wedges and nodded familiarity with the seal. He touched the hieroglyphics and nodded. He barely understood them. He studied the Hebrew characters for a brief time then he pushed the scroll away from himself. He appreciated the simpler style. It flowed easier. After he compared the three scrolls, he caught similarities and differences. The true linear writing deeply impressed him. The characters, when combined, recreated any sound, any word, any thought, any idea that a person desired to comment on. "I've never seen such a simple method of communicating. I don't have to memorize hundreds of characters. How did you come by this method?"

"I invented it," Jacob stated. "It's based on sounds. It's my gift to you."

"Truly?"

"Use it for your business activities and for your histories."

"Why not for your own people?"

"I will teach my children the linear characters that Shem, my great forefather, provided for me to have. That shall be our communication device."

"Absolutely amazing! What gift may I present to you in exchange for such a bold undertaking?"

Without hesitation Jacob easily answered, "No money whatsoever! I only ask for my safe passage to and from your province. I may need to reside here for a short time, then again, I may need to reside here for a long time. Circumstances won't allow me to guess as to which. Either way, I desire the road to be safe for me."

"The roads will always be safe for you and for your family." He clapped his hands and a servant quickly bolted through the door's opening. Another two servants carried a table between them. The scribe, slapping a fresh cake of mud into the holding frame, prepared his copper quill.

"Write his passport."

When the scribe had done so, the governor pressed his cylinder seal into the mud, testifying to all the nations the plate's authenticity. "Travel Jacob. Travel with the greatest of comforts."

Jacob left the city and turned to look again at the strange pillars that the hundreds of construction workers erected throughout the countryside. He momentarily wondered about them, then noticed that their smooth shafts ended with a cone-shaped top. He was disgusted by the phallic symbols. The golden bulls that had human heads carved on their shoulders weren't any better. He wondered why people would carve such things.

As he drew farther away he failed to see the priests bowing before the phallic symbols. They disrobed and publicly, the priests masturbated until they ejaculated, coating the poles with their semen. The nude priestess, orgiastically performing before the growing crowds, took large quantities of seedpods to the moist poles. The nude women then threw the pods at the poles. The women repeated the flinging of the pods until a few adhered to the semen. Younger priestesses then rubbed these grains into the poles until they powdered. In this manner the priests and the priestesses baptized the seedpods for the farmers' planting. In return, the farmers' worshipped the priests and the priestesses, presenting to them barley and animal and metal gifts.

ဆဝလ္ဆဝလ္၊ဆဝလ္ဆဝလ္

The territorial governor took Jacob's gift to the back room of his house and presented the scrolls to the lugar. "These works are the most important I've ever seen. Their value is greater than our city. And it came to us as a gift from a stranger who only wants safe passage from us. Interesting, isn't it?"

The lugar briefly looked at the characters. He didn't find it interesting, but he commanded, "Take these *'gifts'* to the new city of Byblos. Use them as an exchange for us to bond firmly our friendship treaty with them. Their commerce will require this invention far more than our commerce requires it. Do this quickly before we find ourselves trapped in a city of flames with nothing to trade for our lives."

ᏁᏪᏩᏁᏪᏇᏁᏪᏇᏁᏪ

Through the passing weeks Jacob feasted his eyes on new sights and sounds and cultures. The things that he read and studied were outmoded. Everything was different, and the histories would need to be expanded. "The men who wrote before me only had to master a few lineages, the names of a few locations, and required little scientific knowledge. The men following me will require far more knowledge and far more names to write about than I will ever have to know. History progresses and leaves everything behind in its wake." His eyes then turned to the soft rolling, rich green landscape that carried the caravan closer to his uncle's estate. The weeks seemed to pass too fast. Everything excited him. The son of the east returned home.

A group of children, frolicking around the main water well of Haran, ignored the approaching caravan. Every day some kind of caravan arrived at their well. The variety no longer intrigued the children as much as it used to. They grew accustomed to seeing the backs of camels and donkeys ladened with bags of spices, and wagons loaded with precious metals, and camels transporting thick cloth bolts. Military and civilian wagons crossed Haran's roads constantly. The children now played by the blacksmith, watching him shape the wheels and the bending of wood to exquisitely shapes. The colorful banners and distinguishing robes of the nations, in the eyes of the children, faded to a common occurrence. To pass from this day to the next, the children often spent their time chasing each other. The black-haired, brown-eyed, deep copper-toned children continued merrily playing tag and shouting and laughing as the caravan-master wiped the sweat from his brow. The mothers of the children, wanting extra money, quickly ran to the well, drawing up buckets of water for the travelers. A great cacophony of sounds filled the town square. Mothers shouting at children, children shouting at pets, the merchants shouting their wares, the caravan-master issuing orders to his men.

ℰℭℰℭℰℭℰℭℰℭℰℭ

By the near wayside of Haran's city gates a collection of cattle waited within a secluded pen. While the fat cows nibbled on the browning grass, teams of buyers lined the fences, waiting for the auction to begin. A second and larger collection of goats stood together by the greener wayside. A third and even larger collection of sheep flocked in the best grazing land. The three groups of livestock congregated by the engineered watering cutaway.

More important than the animals' thirst and crying was the food and watering and lodging needs of the excessively chaotic gatherings of men and women and children and priests and merchants and servants. Their presence brought silver and gold and precious stones. Their commodities purchased military weapons and paid the soldiers' salaries.

After the arriving guests quenched their thirst, the administrator pulled up the water gates for the herds, flooding the dry watercourse. The cows and goats and sheep, hearing the rushing sound and smelling the moist air, crowded the waterway.

Jacob, enchanted by the play of the goats, the jousting and bustling against each other, laughed. As he watched, a mystical moment captured his attention. In the midst of the crowded pens a single black goat leaped the highest and quickest to the waterway.

"A black goat?" he softly spoke to his friend.

"Yes. They're very rare. Very expensive."

"They wouldn't be so expensive if they were bred to produce more of their kind."

"Only a fool tries to breed what nature segregates from the rest. Goats are not dogs."

"Dogs? My people do not breed dogs! They are abhorrent to us."

"Who guards the herds, then?"

"Great, compassionate men do," Jacob answered. "Our shepherds and herdsmen and goatsmen judiciously carry out their responsibilities."

"These long months I've watched you carry out your responsibilities. You have been a true friend to me and to my men. May your God always travel with you, Jacob."

Jacob faced his dear friend and extended his arms to him. They embraced each other fondly and kissed each other's neck.

"Whenever our paths cross, my tent doors will always be open to you."

"When our paths cross, the door of my house will be prepared to serve you," Jacob responded.

"My friend," the caravan-master implored, "are you sure you want to stay in Haran? There's Ur to the east, then Babylon! We can travel into India and then into China! Come with me. There's really nothing for you in Haran."

"My father's law is here for me. He said: 'Go to Haran and procure a wife for yourself from your mother's house.' He did not authorize me to travel to Babylon, much less one foot beyond this province."

"What strange, unyielding obedience you have to your father. I became a caravan- walker to escape my parents. Later I became a caravan-assistant to escape my masters. Now I direct my own caravan. Let this caravan becomes yours as well as mine!"

"That is a generous offer. If I choose to walk with you, who knows what path I would neglect? Who is to say which road best suits one's travels?"

"Can you tell me why you refuse my generous gift?"

"A situation occurred with my grandfather and his nephew. A choice was given and a choice was executed. The nephew chose to seek the richest valley, the greenest walkway, the wealthiest citizens to reside beside. My grandfather chose the dryer climate, the less inviting landscape. Lot's problems became legendary! My grandfather rescued him once from disaster, then three angels rescued him from a greater disaster. That action portrayed a great symbolic battle! The first rescue was a freeing from evil bondage. The second rescue was total freedom from the captivation of evil."

The caravan-master smiled at his friend. "Must you always read heavenly actions into everything? Why not accept what happened as something that happened by the very nature of our folly?"

Jacob laughed. "My folly, then, waits for me here. Travel well, my friend."

The caravan-master ran his hand over his cloak. He wanted to add another statement, another pleasant gesture. There was nothing else to say. No other face to present. Stepping away, he renewed his journey.

Jacob stood still, remaining where he stood until his friend's caravan mingled completely with the horizon. When he could see it no more, he turned away.

ঽৡৠঽৡৠঽৡৠঽৡৠ

"Three?" Jacob questioned himself. "What does the number three have to do with me?" He hunched down and drew figures in the dirt. "They represent my emotional state of being," he answered himself. "Where, more than a century ago, did my grandfather bury his father? How odd? It appears that my new life must begin where my grandfather began his new life's ambition. Haran, Haran! A city named by Eber, dedicated to his favorite child. Who today remembers this? Everyone? No one?" Becoming sadder, Jacob continued to stare at the horizon. His fingertips played in the dirt. "Where do I go from here? North? East? To the road beside me or to the road behind me?"

Jacob sighed.

Unable to answer his own question, he rose to oversee the terrain. Without any more thoughts, he started walking on the road in front of him. Hours later he encountered several herdsmen gathered nearby. Being thirsty, he approached them. Oddly all the herdsmen slept while the cattle roamed loosely about. The men were wakened by the stranger's unwelcomed approach. Thinking he wanted to beg food and water from them, they turned aside. Each man covered his face with his blanket.

As he came closer, a snarling mastiff confronted Jacob. Several other large brown dogs eyed the transient. The dogs growled but held off, waiting for a signal from their masters to attack the approaching outsider. The larger mastiff, however, growing impatient and becoming alarmed at the man's unhesitating approach, lowered his head and prepared to lunge up. With his upper lips vibrating, the drooling dog showed his sharp teeth.

"Calm yourself, vomit-eater," Jacob commanded. The mastiff dropped his threatening stance. Instead the dog went to him and licked his hand, rubbing his fur against Jacob's leg.

"Bite me or love me, but make up your mind," Jacob grinned. "I suppose you want me to pet you," he added. When Jacob patted him on the back, the dog sat down.

"Look what that stranger is doing to our dog!" an astounded herdsman said to his companion.

They got up and hurried to the stranger. As soon as they reached the dog, the biggest man grabbed the dog by the neck and pulled him away from Jacob.

"This is a dangerous animal, stranger!"

"I'll say!" Jacob replied. "His tongue is big enough to drown a man in."

"Why didn't the dog attack him?" the companion whispered. "He's never friendly to strangers. Only family can get close to him."

The owner shrugged.

"Tell me, friends," Jacob spoke again, "where are you two from?"

Amazed at his audacity, they nevertheless answered. "From Laban's House."

"The son of Nahor?"

"We serve the House, yes."

Jacob raised his eyebrows and looked around. The land was thick with grass. Hundreds of cultured trees lined the land's borders. Jacob shook his head and recalled the story of how his father gained a bride from the House of Nahor. How Abraham's servant challenged Yahweh and demanded, 'Bring me directly to her.' No sooner than spoken, it came to be.

Jacob peered into the formation of piling clouds and challenged, "God, bring my wife directly to me."

No sooner had he thought his words, than a shepherdess came over the last ridge, leading a large flock of sheep.

"This is the fourth group of animals I've encountered today," he mused. "Three groups at Haran, another here. Three plus one equals four. Is there something significant about the number four for me? Yes," he hesitated, then resumed thinking, "the number four symbolizes the perfect completion of Yahweh's promise to me."

"Man," the herdsman shook Jacob's arm, dispelling his thoughts. "That girl, in fact, is Laban's daughter."

"Really?" Jacob's trance broke. He saw the girl's right shoulder before he saw her eyes. He focused on her delicate breasts. Her sensitive nipples bulged, stretching out her robe. But then her extraordinary face captivated him. Aroused by all of this, he breathed deeper breaths. He asked, "Her name is?"

"Rachel."

Unable to take his eyes from her, he watched her carefully walk toward a gigantic round stone that was blocking the mouth of a grotto. He turned to the herdsmen. No one bothered to move toward the blockage.

"Now, who is going to roll away the stone for the sheeps' watering?" he thought to himself. He sat down on the grass. The dog sat beside him. Seeing this, the two men relaxed.

The woman reached the stone and looked about. None offered to assist her. Jacob surmised the situation. The workers, repeating everything that the strongest member of the master's household, challenged her to succeed on her own merits. Jacob soon became ashamed of the men and determined to separate himself from them. As soon as he stood up the men's eyes followed him. He barely smiled at them. He nodded toward her and smiled warmly, trying to impress her.

Then impulsively, he dashed off and raced to the girl's side. Several mastiffs, excited by the running man, followed. The two men ran after the dogs. Others, noticing the odd event, also ran to investigate.

When he stood directly in front of the men, Jacob swelled his chest. He placed his hands on his hips and stared at the group. Not used to such a commanding stare, the men looked away. Jacob turned to view the sky's clouds. The sun had passed its zenith. The land's location was rotating toward midafternoon. "Why are you men resting from your chores?" he demanded to know.

Surprised by the stranger's challenge, they were unable to answer. Taking control of the situation, Jacob again raised his voice, asserting his newfound authority—an ability he had never before expressed. "There is plenty of sunlight left! It's much too early to be sleeping on your blankets."

Several men looked at their companions. One automatically began rolling up his blanket.

Rachel, standing among her sheep, was impressed with the stranger.

The men, confused by her weakness, looked to her for their instructions. She did not oppose the stranger.

"Gather the livestock for watering!" Jacob commanded them. "Then take them to the pastures."

The strongest man among them wanted to resist him at first, but when he saw the others cooperating with the stranger, he hesitated. After a long moment, he finally grew courageous enough to challenge him. "We are unable to take them to the pastures at this moment. It is our method to rest so we may be able to accumulate our strength to roll the stone away from the grotto. Afterwards, we water and pasture them at our leisure."

"Your leisure is not the sheeps' leisure. They are not here to be mistreated! Yahweh provided them to you so you would care for them. You, accepting them on your pasturage, accept the responsibility for their continuous welfare. These gentle animals trust you. Care for them."

"As you can see," the strong man retorted, "that large block prevents us from watering them. It has wedged tightly in its groove and cannot be moved by our numbers. We need twice as many men here."

Jacob examined the stone. Its flattened edge was fixed inside a deep groove that pinched its base against the rock. Jacob looked at Rachel and set his lips. He refused to be defeated in his determination to assert and maintain control over these men.

After studying the problem, Jacob motioned to the strongest man and called him forward. "Bring me your oak staff."

The man walked forward, but he held on to his staff. Instead, he bent ever so slightly forward and balanced his weight against his back leg. Quickly grasping the oak staff, Jacob pulled it out of the strongman's hands. Stunned by the bold move, the man gave in to Jacob's tug.

Jacob went to the large stone and reexamined it. It was smoother than he expected. No gripping holes, no push-pull rods. Yet, the front of the entrapping groove slightly dipped, giving a possible entry for exertion forward. After he analyzed the dip, he took a mid-sized stone and placed it directly behind the larger stone. Over the mid-sized rock he rammed the oak staff and wedged the point underneath the block. Without hesitation, Jacob jumped with his full weight on the staff and forced it as hard as he could downwards. It worked. The stone that had blocked the cave rolled past the grotto's entrance.

"Are there any other excuses? No? Then water the livestock and return them to the pastures. Hurry on with it."

The power of his voice and the cleverness of his intellect overwhelmed the grumbling servants. Believing he was a prince or a great master of one sort or another, they relented, obeying him.

"Who are you," Rachel asked. Her eyes were soft and her hair flowed with the wind. Jacob, holding out his hand, compelled her to place hers in his.

"I am Jacob, your father's nephew through his sister Riveka."

On saying that, his veneer of strength collapsed. He bowed. His voice betrayed his emotions as he embraced Rachel in his arms and held her tightly.

"A man such as this," she thought to herself, "so clever yet so tender."

She drew back and kissed him on the neck.

"Run ahead," he said. "Tell your father I am here."

"Seeing him for the first time," Rachel confessed a week later to her sister, "he appeared different from the other men whom I've met. He, like others before him, readily commanded. Yet his commands presented a greater authority than I have been accustomed to hearing. This man," she reflected "has an inexplicable, yet wonderful ability to assess and to perform."

From that time onward, she loved him dearly.

Chapter Twenty-Six

▼

Laban

Laban stopped counting the fleece hides that were separated into various quality-control piles in front of him. Tired, he rubbed his eyes then cleaned the brown wax from his ear and flicked a it onto the ground. "There's Rachel, running again. One day she's going to fall and skin herself badly," Laban commented to Leah, Rachel's elder sister.

Leah was holding a recently born lamb in her hands and playing her fingers through its curly white fleece. Occasionally she rubbed the lanolin through her own hair so that it would simulate the lamb's softness. When Laban saw how intensely she was stroking her fingers through the lamb's wool, he commented, "Don't rub on it too much. It's a delicate animal. Not a plaything."

"Daddy," she innocently replied. Her small voice betrayed her grown-up body. Her mind wandered for a moment. Unable to focus and assimilate what her father said, she stared at the vigorously running figure. As she watched the awkward wavering of the runner, she believed she was supposed to say something, anything. "I never fall when I run."

Laban brushed his daughter's hair away from her eyes and fondly replied, "That's wonderful, darling. But, nevertheless, let's allow Rachel to run whenever she wants to. You, however, keep walking. That way you'll never skin your knees."

"Father! Father!" Rachel shouted as she approached the center of the front gate. Then, catching sight of her skinny sister playing with the newest baby lamb, Rachel ordered, "Leah, be careful with that thing. Don't drop it."

Leah gently placed it on the ground and freed it.

"She was being careful with it," Laban admonished Rachel. "Stop being so critical of your sister. She needs to learn about these things."

"Father, you know how dim witted Leah is."

Realizing that Rachel's excitement was overwhelming her, Laban stopped everything he was doing. The 150-year-old man waited for his spoiled, younger daughter to speak.

"Your nephew from the south just arrived. Riveka's boy is here!"

"Which one?" he asked, startled by the news.

"I don't know," she answered, shrugging her shoulders.

Her manner delighted him. "Silly girl!"

He peered over her shoulder but failed to see anyone behind her. "Well, where is he?"

As soon as he spoke those words Jacob appeared over the rise and gracefully descended the steep incline toward the mansion.

Leah, as she observed the man, drew away from her father. The man appeared so tall on the mountain's rise! His brindled medium-length gray hair fell over his temples. His face had a quiet iridescent quality. "Maybe sweat," she thought to herself. Yet the sparkle of his white temple hairs intermingled with the jet black hairs, capturing her attention. Her heart felt strange. An air of breath escaped from her lungs. She stared directly at the man as he maneuvered down the trail. Even when she finally came to realize that he was much smaller than he appeared, she never lost from her mind the image of a giant man standing before her. When Leah stood beside her father, Jacob's head barely reached Laban's nose.

"Prepare a feast for us!" Laban commanded his servants.

Jacob, noticing the skinny girl standing beside Laban, spoke first to her, even before he had spoken to her father. "Hello. I saw you playing with the newborn lamb. I like little girls who know how to handle their pets."

She sighed and shyly withdrew from Jacob to hide behind her father. When she peeped around his back, she smiled at Jacob. Her face turned red. The stranger's voice was firm, commanding. More so than her father's. Yet the quality of his voice compelled people to come forward to him so they might hear more of his words. Somehow his voice had the power to transcend the normal voice of man. His face seemed as if he could understand everything.

She pulled on her father's garment and motioned with her index finger. Laban bent over to listen to her whispers. "I want him for my new daddy," she innocently stated.

"You mean, 'I want to marry him'?" he whispered back.

"Yes, Daddy. That's what I mean."

Jacob, intrigued by the scene, gently grinned. Leah's eyes caught Jacob's warm smile. Her faced turned deeper red.

"Come," Laban changed the subject, "let's talk inside my house."

Rachel then placed her hand on Leah's back and shoved her away. "Go and finish your chores."

"But I want to listen."

"Why? You don't understand anything that anyone ever says to you. By the time you do understand the spoken sentence, everyone's on another paragraph. So, what difference does it make?"

"I understand. You just speak too fast."

By this time the land's location rotated away from the sun, accepting the evening's crimson colors. At the supper table Laban learned the complete story of Jacob's eventful journey. He shook his head and pondered on how he could use this intelligent man on his estate.

ඩ‍ඏඩ‍ඏ‍ඏඩ‍ඏ

The first month that Jacob lived with Laban, he determined to prove himself indispensable to the household. Before the sun shone its rays on the landscape, Jacob rose to tend the fields. Before Laban's six sons shepherded the flocks to the watering wells, Jacob cleaned the troughs and buried the sheeps' excrement. As he traveled from outpost to outpost, he directed the workers' tasks and responsibilities even before Laban's sons could hand out the needed orders of the day.

Within that first month the tenants began to expect Jacob, instead of Laban's sons, to rouse them from their sleep. They looked forward to Jacob's placing before them the day's activities. The men began feeling a purpose in their chores. The daily tasks became meaningful. They began to understand the necessity of the day's operation and how important the day was for the fulfilling of tomorrow's work. The tenants appreciated Jacob's clear commands. With Jacob there were no contradictions nor changes of their mind halfway through the work, unlike the way it was with Laban's sons. "Logical reasoning always wins over irrational processes," Jacob explained to Leah, who nodded her head mutely.

The men obeyed Jacob, performing perfectly what he told them to do.

ඩ‍ඏඩ‍ඏ‍ඏඩ‍ඏ

Each new morning of the second month Leah personally took it upon herself to prepare Jacob's breakfast. Yet, later, during those same mornings, it was mostly Rachel who rode beside him. Attentively she listened to his adventurous tales.

Leah, occasionally riding behind the two of them, also eagerly listened to Jacob's stories. Somehow, the words that he spoke became imbedded in her consciousness.

One day it happened that Laban and his sons rode beside them as well. Laughing at every detail, the six sons prodded for more adventurous tales. "A true leader like you must resent having to work in the field." Laban's eldest son finally spoke what he had wanted to say all along.

"I've always enjoyed working in the fields," Jacob coldly responded. "I don't just sit and read throughout the day. I work."

Laban, seeing the jealousy developing among his sons against Jacob, prompted, "Neither I, nor my sons, read much. I heard how your great-great-grandfather read and wrote everything he could. Of course we know about Shem, who was called Melchizedek, and the great library, but that was a distant time and a distant place.

"Unlike your father's father, we choose to remain in Haran. We are a realistic family, not given to fantasies of grandeur.

"We work the land and we love the land. It serves us and it passes our time with meaningful hours."

"My work," Jacob intruded, "bonds me with Yahweh."

Laban tightened his lips. "My father told me of your grandfather's quest. He had this unremovable vision that only he, among all men, was blessed to present to the world the ultimate solution for genuine peace and nonending prosperity. When Terah died, he told my father only he and his children could carry the ultimate promise to the world. That was quite a vain statement from an old man who had, as of then, no children."

"But he came to have many children."

"Yes. Poor Sarai. What would she have thought if she could see her husband having children by Keturah?"

"Grandmother would have accepted it. Did she not accept Yishmael?"

"I don't believe she did," Laban's oldest son answered. "And I don't believe your mother accepts Esau's wives."

"You are probably right on both statements," Jacob conceded.

Laban again changed the subject. "At least you have incorporated into yourself the belief of one God: Yahweh. We, on the other hand, though we know His name and accept His existence, call on as many gods as we can.

We appease the population and benefit from it. We are not as rigid in our thinking as you are. We compromise and we prosper. When," Laban burned his eyes into Jacob's, "will you prosper?"

"I prosper every day. Do I not eat? Am I not clothed? Is my health poor?"

"Good statements," Laban's next son spoke. "Yet, cousin, you have worked harder than any of us during these past forty days, but you never once asked any wages from Father. It is obvious you are an intelligent man, even more so than any of us, so what is it that you want to gain from us?"

"Yes," a third son asked, "I know that what you say you'll do, you'll perfectly perform. Yet, I also wonder: What is it that you want from us?"

Jacob stopped moving forward. "Uncle," he directed his voice to Laban, ignoring his cousins, "as I had stated to you when I first saw you: I am here for a bride. Decades ago my father, Yitzhak, pledged me to remain in the land of the pagans. However when he faced the fact that not a single 'pure' Babylonian remained in our camp—because, as you well know, Abraham finally convinced the royal bloodlines to intermarry—he temporarily freed me from that pledge. That temporary pass allows me to seek a wife from your household. Once doing so, I must return home."

"It would be a shame to lose you. Already my pockets are heavier with weights of silver and my house is richer with possessions on account of your good trading sense.

"But, understand this: Decades ago when Eliezer, Abraham's servant and blood-relative, traveled to this very house, asking for a wife for Yitzhak, it was granted to him. Eliezer came, though, with ten camels filled with treasures and valuable commerce. Unlike your father we did not squander away the wealth. We nourished it and, like a tree's branches, it grew to shelter us underneath a protective cove.

"Jacob," Laban challenged as he focused his eyes on his nephew's, "where are your ten camels, much less one? Where on your person rests a single token to present me with? When you approached my house, what did you approach me with? A smile, yes. Good manners, absolutely! Yes, you do possess an intellect beyond anything I have ever experienced. But you have no money. No possessions. Not even a nose ring."

"Father did not 'squander' Grandfather's wealth. He 'nourished' it so we might survive the great famine. In the Torrent Valley of Gerar, the wealth returned to him. On my anointment, it passed from him to me."

"Anointment?"

I am the Mashiach of my people," Jacob countered.

"What people! Esau would have killed you if you hadn't run away from him! Abraham's vision is a fantasy gone berserk! Release that nonsense from you and settle to reality."

"My reality is Yahweh's dictate."

"Again! Esau controls your escape and he controls your return. Yahweh, it is said, called Terah away from Ur; yet, here you are, trying to run back to Ur!"

"I will not travel beyond Haran. Whatever may be, this is as far east as I will travel. Besides, I came here not to escape from Esau but to visit you. My wealth is intact."

"Only as long as Yitzhak lives," the eldest son tormented him.

"It," Laban interrupted his son's growing hostility, "may be as you said: you are a 'wealthy man'. Nevertheless, it is also just as my son spoke: 'Your wealth remains with your father, who yet lives'."

"Things will correct themselves."

Laban stretched his hands out. "I like you, Jacob. I love my sons. I love my daughters more. Tell me, intellect, how can I negotiate a marriage contract with you when even my poorest servant is a thousand times wealthier than you?"

"My grandfather's wealth, was it not large enough for his son as well as his grandson?"

"It was large enough for ten generations to come. But, and this is the point, it was pledged for only one son's wife. Not ten, nor even two."

"Then let that remain the case," Jacob answered back, controlling the explosion that wanted to erupt from his lips. "However, tell me, have any of your men or friends or sons possessed my intellect?"

"No."

"Have any of them my work ethics?"

"No."

"Have any of them my abilities?"

"No."

"What have they for you?"

"They have their labor, however filled with shortcomings it may be."

"That, then, is how I shall pay you for a bride. I will labor for her."

"A debtor stays with his obligation for seven years. It is your grandfather's very own law."

"I shall obligate myself to Grandfather's law. For seven years I will labor for you for a wife from your direct loins."

"I have two daughters. Both ride behind you. Leah is the eldest. Rachel, the younger. Which do you obligate yourself to?"

"Rachel?"

"The youngest?"

"She is my choice."

Laban, thinking, answered after a few moments, "I would rather see her married to you than to a stranger outside our race. Yet, I must return to the subject of my eldest daughter. Leah is slow-witted. She can, though, comprehend if someone takes the necessary time to explain the thing in question to her.

"Jacob, being more than a friend, help her to learn the way of things. It would please me greatly."

"The joy of your heart shall become the joy of my heart. I will teach Leah to read and to count and to watch over the flocks. I remind you, however, I desire a nuptial contract of obligation for Rachel. Is that agreeable?"

ɞCȝɞCȝCȜɞCȝɞCȝ

That Friday, the legal bond was transcribed by the special magistrate of the land. The scribe, bearing witness to the documents, presented Jacob's contract for him to examine. Jacob accepted the document and carefully studied the deeply etched characters.

"Sign the document," Laban restated. "Your signature testifies your pledge to me."

He nodded and signed the contract. Quickly, he concealed the agreement inside a flat, clay receptacle. A secondary servant, taking the tablet from Jacob, carefully carried the receptacle to the waiting scribe. Receiving it, he poured a thin resin of wet mud over the container, sealing it against the ravages of time. Afterward, Jacob imprinted his cylinder seal over the wet clay envelope. In this manner the two men publicly testified the conclusion of the agreement. Jacob now placed the agreement inside the courier's official pouch. Before the new sunrise passed, the courier placed the shallow box in the sacred covenant room of the government building.

Jacob, after all this, sighed out a long breath. He had just committed himself to seven years of enslavement: the number seven symbolizing total completeness, total perfection.

Through this manner Jacob became surrounded by numerical symbols, and gained the pledge of a bribe.

Chapter Twenty-Seven

▼

Jacob's work

As Jacob began his first seven-year cycle of obligation to Laban, his uncle, the farmers of the surrounding city-states concerned themselves with the gathering of the grains and their threshing. After harvesting the massive grape arbors, the people placed the grapes inside primitive stone grinders called querns. Completing the weekly-long work, the brew-masters stored the wine for trade with the southern capitals.

While the winemakers were finishing their assignments, the clay molders fashioned hundreds of faiences. Skillfully, artistically, they brushed varicolored opaque glazes over the clay objects. Small children placed the faiences inside a hollowed stone furnace. The firing hardened the crafts inside the ovens. After cooling, the merchants collected them for trade with the southern kingdoms that eagerly purchased the faiences for their temples.

"The bull's reproduction is as popular as the reproductions of the lions and warriors," Laban explained the images to Jacob. "I have images of Ashtoreth and Asherah and Anath in my house. They signify inheritance rights."

"And that one?" Jacob pointed to the other carvings.

"That one is Baal. His popularity grows every day."

"Why?"

"He is the god of male fertility. His semen fertilizes our soil."

"Who brought Baal to Haran?"

"The Armenians. They keep increasing their landholdings throughout our region. Their influence stretches even to the remote lands of Anatolia."

"Armenians? I've never heard of them."

"They drifted in from India and intermarried with the blond haired and blue eyed race. Their children travel to the extreme western lands. The Minos calls that land Europe."

After that Jacob explored the surrounding region to learn as much as he could about its people. Often Jacob and Laban whipped their camels to the outermost boundary stone.

"What's beyond this point?"

"The Kudurran! Their capital, Hattusas, is not far from my grazing lands."

"What's so special about them?"

"They specialize in weaponry. Their new war invention, the horse-drawn war-chariots easily overwhelm our donkey-drawn chariots. The dust of their troops arrives constantly into the surrounding cities. Their soldiers eat the vegetables set aside by the farmers on the corners of their land after the harvest. We call it gleaning."

"Horses? Why in the world do they prefer horses to donkeys?"

Laban, touching Jacob's shoulder, reminded him, "Jacob, Abraham rode horses, did he not?"

"He loved them."

"Like the Kudurran, it was in his character to love the very thing that everyone else rejected. It now seems that what he first saw in the horses everyone now sees in them also. They are faster and easier to control.

Nahor, my father, preferred the donkey. It made a wonderful pack animal, but it is not a good war animal. To Nahor, the purest animal on the face of the earth was the white donkey. Intelligent, strong, dependable. The horse, to Nahor, appeared stupid, untrainable, unable to survive in the deserts and incapable of completing the long hauls of the caravans' journey."

"Things and views change."

"I know," Laban answered.

"Look at our own history. Once, a time long ago, my father, Yitzhak, held thousands of animals. Now he has many fewer. Why," Jacob used this tactic to impress his uncle and win him over to his side, "you have twenty sheep for every cow my father has. Five goats for every sheep he has. That is wonderful husbandry!"

"Thank you, Jacob," Laban loved hearing Jacob's compliment. Jacob leaned over, asking, as a small youth would ask: "How did you gain so many animals?"

Laban laughed. "Do you not know?"

"No," he pretended.

"When the king of Ur chased Terah out, Eber made it a point to take with him all the varmints—the sheep—with him. All the farmers discarded them to him. Gradually, he traded them off. The going rate was twenty sheep per cow, sixty per bull, five per goat. What had once been a scourge, after the weavers learned how to spin and work their hair, quickly became a commodity. Eber forgot to look into that one!" Laban laughed again.

"He became interested in history," Jacob defended.

"You knew him?"

"I was nineteen when he died. I was playing with Deborah, our mother's faithful nurse, when an escort approached my father's tent, placing in his care the entirety of man's history. I read it all."

"So that's how you learned your accounting skills so well. Eber taught you."

Jacob nodded. Unable to prevent himself from asking, Laban blurted out, "Are you truly the Mashiach?"

"Father anointed me with the sacred oil."

Laban silently nodded. "So Terah's dream of becoming a king infected Abraham's household! Yet I am curious, have you never supposed that the anointment really went to my father? Look at it this way: my grandfather, Abraham's brother was as wealthy as he. Why a city rose in which he governed the people! My father was also a wealthy man—of course—your grandfather's ten camels helped solidify his wealth—yet think on this—your grandfather presented us with wealth as a humble token of our superiority to you family!

"Even this God that you worship submits to mine. I am wealthy. I am important. I have many grand, healthy sons who live in peace and in harmony with me. They do not disobey nor quarrel with me nor among themselves, whereas that's all your family seems capable of doing!

"So, if there is such a thing as an 'anointed one' and that 'one' is to come from Terah's loins—then surely I must be that man! No?"

Jacob was insulted. He turned his face away. Laban talked on. "What insanity to carry on such an invalid thought! Jacob, let it loose from your mind. Let the oil evaporate from your consciousness. Work the seven years. Marry Rachel as we contracted. Then, place it in your heart to dwell here."

"I vowed to return to my land."

"What land? The Canaanites, the Jebusites, the Horites, and now the Philistines live there. The Philistines are establishing cities in Lebanon, the Egyptians build roads through it, the Elamites practice their warring techniques there, the Hurrians surround it and make plans to control it. Who are you to dare dream such an incredulous dream?"

"I am the one who has been designated as the man to carry the genes of the ultimate Mashiach. Through my children's children will the power of reckoning come to the earth," he firmly insisted.

"I've been watching you ever since you've been with me. You are carefully plotting your return. You are inventing for yourself a new self. I watched you reinvent yourself. A personality transformation. Intentional. Deliberate. Yet, you do not publicly speak to raise armies nor weapons nor money for your cause. In this land, because you are a member of the House of Haran, you are entitled to do just that very thing. You do not run for election, which you are also entitled to do. So, without an army or political office, how do you propose to wrestle control of Canaan for yourself?"

"Yahweh has already committed Himself to that plan. Other than that I remain neutral of all political things."

"Ah, yes, Yahweh. El Khalil. But He is also Nahor's God, and I am his direct descendant. Please, never forget that point of absolute, sharply stated fact."

Jacob defended himself. Somehow, he never anticipated Laban thinking of himself as the possible carrier of genes to fulfil the promise of the savior to the world. "I did not choose myself for the anointment."

"Jacob," Laban grew stern, "never lie to me in my home. You cunningly schemed and manipulated to get Yitzhak's inheritor's rights for yourself. I wonder if I shall regret forging an obligatory contract with you? Let's hope not."

ഇരുടെ ഇരുടെ ഇരുടെ ഇരുടെ

Within several years the Hurrians from the highlands of Armenia began infiltrating the political system of Mitanni as the Hyksos had done in Egypt. The Armenian Hurrians' banners and gods slowly replaced the former Egyptian gods. Whenever a member of the *'Old Older'* objected, the Hurrians dispatched an armed escort to the house, presenting him with an irresistible bribe.

To appease the public, the Hurrian rulers permitted the ever-increasing traveling circuses to celebrate additional performances in their cities. Public arenas were built, accommodating the performances. The circus-masters, to gain privileged dates in these arenas, permitted the Hurrian political machine to place spies within their caravans, while they continued to circumnavigate the land.

To prevent a privileged social class of priests and worshippers from developing within the controlled cities, the Hurrians ordered all the temples to be opened to all travelers. To control the interests of the people, the Hurrian ruling class allowed daily banquets to take place throughout the region. Tables of dates and plates of geese and ducks welcomed the citizens as did the willing embraces of the prostituting priestess. As predicted by the Hurrian hierarchy, the society gradually lost its ability to freely elect its representatives. Eventually, the Upper House dissolved. The elite society degenerated into a feudal society of maryannu and khupshu (That is, the military elite and the barely free Semitic landowners).

ᎷᏣᎷᏣᎡᏎᎷᏣᎷᏣ

While the Hurrians solidified their power base in Mitanni, Hammurabi, the son of Sin-muballit, an Amorite, became the political choice of the Elamites of the city of Larsa, to govern the Babylonian territory. His procession traveled to the great ruins of the mysterious ziggurat that four hundred years earlier had been the epoch point of man's multi-languages.

"Who caused such a magnificent building to exist?" he asked his host.

"We only remember him as Marduk. It was erected during the time of the great flood."

"The legend of Gilgamesh? Utnaphishtim was quite the hero! Marduk must have been a great god if he challenged such a god as the god of the flood!"

"The antiquity of his name is so great, many, yes—many do worship him as a god."

"Reconstruct this temple," he excitedly demanded. "I have at last found a god to worship as my own! Dedicate this site to him. Marduk's name will be remembered. Such genius had a purpose. It is for us to discover it."

"Such an event will rouse the anger of the Elamites."

"Am I of Elam?"

"No, great ruler."

"I purpose to control this land. Whispers come to my ears, testifying of my great abilities. Rebuild this temple. Open again the impacted canals. Allow the caravans to pass through unhindered. Then, when we are confident of the camel-master's trust, buy all the swords and axes from them that we can. In a few years I plan to take the city of Mari for myself. Marduk needs it."

ฆผฆอฉลฆผฆ

Within a few, highly active and energized months, Hammurabi's war machines rose against the Elamites. First fell the city of Larsa! Then the city of Isin fell. The chained population grieved at the flames that engulfed their cities. Throughout the Mitannian provinces the hatred of the people increased against the Babylonians. Rumors of vicious conquests and merciless slaughtering circulated. Hurrian spies infiltrated the northern provinces.

Whenever Laban learned of their presence in his vicinity, he changed his national affiliation. To the Hurrian soldiers who were conducting a census, he documented, "I am Aramaean."

"And the others of your household?"

"What else could they be? Document all of us Aramaeans. And," Laban secretly handed him a pouch of lapis lazuli stones, "allow this to comfort your handwriting. I know it is an arduous task."

The captain flicked his hand and nodded. "So it shall be documented. However, I want you to know this," the captain smiled a selfish, greedy smile as if he had overpowered his most hateful enemy! As if he couldn't wait to spit in someone's face before plunging his sword into his stomach. "Your neighbors have already testified to your loyalty. I even understand you are descended from the founder of the city of Haran."

"I indeed am," Laban boasted, missing the cruelty of the captain's intent.

"So, then, no bribe was necessary. We know you're Aramaean. We just wanted to count the members of your household."

"The jewelry wasn't a bribe. It was prepaid taxes."

"I'll so place it in my care," the captain winked his eye.

"Laban, the Aramaean?" Jacob reminded him of the conversation moments after the military group left his vast estate and mansion.

"It is politically correct. I would be a fool to boast that my fore-parents are Babylonians. Isn't this the same ploy you would have enacted?"

"It was well construed. You once remarked to me: 'I am observing you,' well, I also am silently observing you."

"And what do you see?" Laban demanded to know.

"A man standing before me."

"Always you answer with the most prudent answers. One day I will out-guile you. On that day, the most you'll be able to do is to accept my terms. I look forward to that time."

ಬಂಡಚಬಂಡಚಬಂಡಚ

The first six years passed swiftly. The following six months slowed. The last six months seemed an eternity. The hot humid nights barely ended when the cold months came, bringing the frigid winds.

With the descending cold, the lions became braver, attacking the sheep and goats, killing a few every once in a while. When he discovered the bloodied remains, Jacob burned the corpse, replacing the lost animal with another newborn, assuring Laban an increase in the count, regardless of circumstances and disasters.

Chapter Twenty-Eight

▼

Marriage

In the year 1774 B.C.E., when Jacob was eighty-four years old, Laban ordered that a great feast commence, celebrating the marital contract between Jacob and his twenty year old daughter as well as the simultaneous completion of his newest mansion. The timbrel and lyre and flute players harmonized their musical notes with the dancing guests. Through the long night Laban freely distributed his finest wines to everyone.

Leah, mentally unfocused, dazed by the great emotion of the occasion, fixed her eyes on the ground to avoid having anyone talk with her. She wandered through the celebrants' clasped arms, disrupting their merry-making. No one dared shove her aside. Finally, after a hundred voices shouted in her ears, she tried to listen to everyone's words, she became more confused to the incomprehensible sentences. In her dazed state she got in everyone's way.

Rachel became frustrated and angry.

"But I was dancing with Father's guests!" Leah protested.

"Sister!" Rachel gritted her teeth. "Father's guests do not want you dancing with them. You're embarrassing all of us." She grabbed her by the forearm and escorted her to the servants' inner chambers, but looking back at the small hardened mud house nestled among the palm trees, Rachel felt guilty for having isolated her in that dank and hot place. "Zilpah, would it bother you to remain with Leah?"

"No, she behaves with me."

"Then come with me!"

The twelve-year-old servant ran after the fast-paced woman into the disarrayed quarters. Zilpah looked at Leah and at her tangled hair. She reached for an ivory comb and bowed in front of Rachel. "I will make her pretty." Rachel looked at her sister then at the thin, straggly servant. She stormed out of the house and collided with her father. "Keep Leah away from the party! She's ruining everything!"

"How so, Rachel?"

"She's your precious child. Go ask her."

Laban entered the servant's quarters where he discovered Zilpah combing the tangles out of Leah's hair. "How did you get it in such a mess, darling?"

"The wind keeps blowing through my hair whenever I spin around. I tried to work it back with my fingers, but they got caught in it."

"Come, let's go back home."

Inside the recently constructed grand estate, Laban stared at Leah's reflection in the polished bronze mirror. Catching his gaze, she blurted out, "Daddy, why does Rachel get to marry Jacob? Why don't I get to?"

Surprised, Laban hugged his daughter to himself. "Why do you want to marry Jacob? He's an old man. You're only twenty-three."

"You're an old man."

"Yes, I'm very old."

"You're older than Jacob."

"Yes, that I am," he smiled. A tear fell from his eye as he stared into his daughter's pained face.

"But you always knew I wanted to marry Jacob. You knew it from the first day I saw him. I believe you promised him to me. Isn't that why he's been teaching me, so I could learn to be his wife?"

"Has he taught you well?"

"I can write everyone's name and I can spell them just as well. I can count all your livestock."

"Jacob has taught you all that?"

"He has. So why shouldn't I be his wife? After all, I am older than Rachel."

"You never seemed upset before about your first-place role."

"That's because I didn't count on it beforehand. Jacob told me how important the firstborn is. He said that's why he feels no guilt about being the Mashiach instead of Esau."

"So, the conniver feels no guilt." Laban, releasing his affectionate grip on her, walked toward the thick, heavy, exquisitely carved oak doors. Bulls adorned his entryway as they did so many other elegant houses throughout the provinces. Beyond his entryway, on the paved road leading to his new grand mansion lay his Inn by the Wayside. Carved pagan images lined the hedges. Like the Hurrians, he placed his trust in multi-gods. Once he and Jacob had argued about them. Jacob wanted to destroy the pagan images exactly as his grandfather had destroyed the pagan representations in the city of Ur. Laban judiciously reminded Jacob about his family's origin. "Not all your ancestors aligned themselves with Yahweh." Proving it with recorded facts, Jacob silenced his arguments. "Truthfully," Laban insisted on winning the argument, "two to three centuries ago, before Abraham left the family for the promised land to seek his throne, Terah worshiped Sin, the moon-goddess. Terah crossed the Euphrates with Eber, and helped to establish this great commerce city. But Terah ever renounced his beliefs."

"Your father, Bethuel, was a witness of Yahweh."

"Yes, that is true. But the years in Haran slowly wore away many of his beliefs. Somehow, new thoughts replaced old conservatism."

When he saw the merrymakers frolicking throughout every bit of his courtyard and surrounding his vast imported fountain and eating in his spacious house, he turned to gaze at Leah again. "Her thin bones and narrow shoulders worry me. Her eyes droop. No one has ever offered me a gift for her. As much as I desire to sign a marital contract for her, no one ever approaches. No one wants her in their marriage bed." Laban paced the smooth and polished floor. Geometric patterns greeted his feet.

"Zilpah," Laban directed. "Place the strongest drink with Jacob. Never allow his cup to be empty."

Zilpah ran to the center of the courtyard, where the servants were distributing the meats and fruits and vegetables, and took a large cup of ale from them, placing it in Jacob's hand.

"Now, Leah, do this, and Jacob will be your husband. I will take you to his tent. Lie beside him. Whatever he wants to do with you, permit it. Say not one single word, no matter how much you want to. When he is naked, be naked also. When he places himself over you, remain silent. Make no resistance. When you feel a pain inside you, leave the pain alone. It is the right kind of pain to be in. If you listen and do exactly what I tell you to do, Jacob will be your husband."

Lead nodded and smiled. Laban watched her glowing face and returned her smile. "You have never been prettier."

He left to tour the house. There, he looked for his youngest daughter. Finally, he found Rachel conversing among her closest Aramaean friends. Rudely, he interrupted them. "Rachel, may I speak with you?"

"I hope you've straightened Leah out at last."

"That's what I want to talk to you about."

"Please, not another lecture on responsibility and caring. This is my wedding night. Let her have her own wedding night where she can do whatever she wants to do."

"Rachel, tell me," Laban began calculating his plot, "how much do you love Leah?"

Surprised by the question, she lifted her eyebrows. "You know I don't want to be mean to her. I love her as much as a sister can love a sister."

"As much as Jacob?"

"Jacob is wisdom personified. He has a commanding essence such as I've never felt before. Leah, is, well, you understand."

"Leah is slow. Yet, regardless, Jacob has been kind and patient with her. She can write, she can read, she can count. The more she stays with him, the more secure I am in her well-being."

"But she can't stay with us forever. She has you to care for her."

"For how much longer?"

Rachel grew silent.

"That is my problem. No one wants her. Soon, whether today or ten years from now, or even twenty or thirty years from now, I'll be dead—and she may be murdered by those who can't tolerate such people as her around them."

"Murdered?"

"You've heard of it a thousand times. We kill our weak cattle and our lame goats and sheep. People have done it to their own children. Who can protect Leah?"

"I can protect her."

"How?"

"I'll provide for her."

"How?"

"She'll stay with me."

"How?"

"Why, in my home. Wherever I go, Leah will go."

"How can I believe that to be true. Is it not our custom that a family must separate from a family? Who would want an old maid traveling with them? Also, consider your children. Would they be kind to a weak-minded old aunt?"

"No one would." She stepped aside and thought about what to do for her sister. Minutes passed. The sounds of the celebration completely erased from her ears and eyes. She saw nothing other than the problems of Leah. "Father, I have the answer."

"What is it, my dearest child?"

"We can force Jacob to pledge to her care. A formal contract."

"Jacob is the most cunning man I have ever met. He knows the legalities of the law, and when he tires of your sister, he'll place her on the beggar's corner. We need something more binding. Something that cannot be legally broken without threat of a vicious lawsuit."

"Only a marriage contract is that binding."

Laban smiled. His eyes gleamed. He had succeeded in manipulating her as he had intended. "Why, Rachel! How extraordinary! Of course you are right! A marriage contract between Leah and Jacob!"

Shocked, she shouted, "What are you saying? I did not mean to imply such a thing!"

"Why, I thought it was a brilliant idea. A loving and caring thought."

Rachel's face lowered, ashamed.

"It's my wedding night," her sullen voice teared out. She became nearly impossible to hear. "Jacob won't seal such an agreement once he has me."

"Again, you are correct in your assessment." Continuing his plot, Laban exclaimed, "But wait! Now I have an idea. After the celebrants quiet, permit yourself to come back here. I will take Leah to the marriage tent. After the night is through, the contract between them will be legal—and inviolable."

"Daddy! Didn't you hear what I said? This is my marriage night!"

"Yes, I'm sorry. I got carried away, thinking of Leah. Thinking of her lying helpless in the dung heap. Thinking of the boys who'll beat, rape and curse her."

"Stop it!"

"I'm sorry. I'll leave you now." Turning away, he headed for the courtyard.

"Wait. Do you really believe we can get away with this?"

"Our law will bind it. And Jacob is intent on forming a new personality, and what better ingredient to incorporate inside himself than honor."

"But what about me?"

"My dearest child, do this for me. Do this for your sister, Leah, and I promise you will also be married to Jacob."

"When?"

"After Jacob has proven to me he'll accept your sister."

"One week. Father, promise me! One week!"

"For this sacrifice, I so promise."

ഇൻഽൻൽഇൻഽഇൻഽ

Laban, finding Jacob completely drunk, escorted him to the marriage tent. He ordered his servants to extinguish all the lights in the courtyard. Not even a small candle or oil lamp flickered inside the tent's walls. The only light came from a bright torch that hung on the mid-wall of the courtyard. Gracefully its warm glow flickered alongside the carving of a false god. The flowing flame caused the trees by the stone walls to appear as fingering obstacles. The wall receded and waved, which was exactly as the way Jacob's head felt. He tripped over his own foot. Laban laughed as his two strongest sons carried Jacob into the tent.

Moments later Jacob heard the sounds of another person entering the tent.

"Walk toward my voice," he called.

The person, stumbling into the edge of the fluffed blankets, tripped, falling into his arms. Feeling the lithe body, he instantly became aroused. Quickly he stripped off her clothes. His nervous hands first felt her shoulders then her firm breasts. They were larger, harder than he recalled. Gently he pushed her flat over the blankets.

"Spread your legs wider," he told her, surprised at her ignorance of the act. "Didn't anyone prepare you for this?" But before she could reply, he managed to insert his penis into her. Thrusting it slowly inside, he heard her moan. Absorbed by his own desires, he felt the interior muscles of her walls rubbing against his shaft. Excited, he instantly climaxed. A powerful, addicting ejaculation burst from his penis. He never felt anything so wonderful, so awesome. She just lay still. Her arms rested by her sides. Soon afterward, both fell into a deep sleep.

As Jacob slept, Laban held Rachel gently in his arms, comforting her tears as his family rested outside the tent, vigilantly watching the entrance.

"You understand, don't you, darling child, why I am doing this?"

"My sister needs a husband. No one will take her."

"You love your sister, don't you?" Laban requestioned.

"Yes," she repeated.

"Then, what I did, is it not the by the demands of our customs?"

"Customs should not outweigh God's law. Man needs to stop falsifying God's truth to moralize their arrogant behaviors."

"It is so."

"Yes, it is. I pray, may this deceit not cause me to be hated by Jacob."

"My dear child, this is not deceit. This is taking care of your sister by the law's provision. Jacob could never hate you."

"The morning will answer that question," Rachel quietly commented, hiding her tears in his arms.

ℰℭ℘ℂℛℭℰℭ℘ℂℛℰℭ℘ℂℛ

Jacob woke from his sleep. He gently gazed over the lithe figure. "Strange," he thought to himself, "how is it that when someone is naked, they appear so much smaller?" He stared at her thin legs. "Funny, I never realized before how thin and frail she is." His eyes played over her narrow back. He bent over her and gently kissed her shoulder blades. She turned around and when she did so, he saw that the naked woman beside him was Leah: Rachel's sister! "What are you doing in this tent?" His trembling voice wavered as he demanded an answer.

"I am your wife," she replied.

In disbelief he snapped the blanket off her and looked between her legs. His eyes saw the dried blood on the linen cloth. A small coating also dried on his testicles.

He threw his purple and gold bridegroom's tunic on his shoulders and ripped the curtain door down. Before him Laban's family waited. Zilpah rushed inside the tent. Within seconds she emerged with the bloodied sheet. She presented it to Laban and he raised it overhead for the family to testify to the bonding.

"The marriage is consummated!"

Joyous cries filled the air. Word rapidly spread throughout the courtyard. Rachel, holding the soiled blanket in her hands, refused to look at Jacob. He walked to her and gently touched her cheek, which was covered with tears.

"I did not know," he replied, ashamed of his inability to discern one sister from the other.

"Father increased your beverage. He victimized you. He plotted the deceit."

"You also are guilty, but I love you too much to hate you for what you did."

Jacob then turned to Laban and demanded to know: "Why did you deceive me? I worked these past seven years for Rachel—not for Leah."

"Jacob, Jacob," he shook his head. "How could you reside in this land for these many years and not yet know our custom? When has any father placed the younger daughter in the bridal tent while the eldest remained uncommitted?"

"I believe, if the truth be known, you had committed her to me seven years ago. Everyone knew it except me. Your guile has been successful. But, how are you to know for a certain fact that I will be a kind and gentle husband to a woman who has been placed in my tent by intentional deceit?"

"What are you implying? Surely you could never harm Leah. She is mentally slow, and such a one needs your wisdom and intelligence to guide her. Wait! Let me be more frank. A man with your capabilities can surely guide my eldest into the world of learning and understanding. You are a patient man. A gentle man." He became afraid that his plot could backfire on him. After a few more moments of thinking about it, he determined to cement the contract. "Care for Leah, and you shall also have Rachel."

Jacob, peering into Laban's eyes, believed him. Still he tested him, "When?"

"Assure me that Leah will be impregnated by you. When the evidence is apparent, I will release Rachel to you."

"If you force me to wait nine months, I will take this case to the courts."

"I do not mean for you to wait nine months. I mean for you to wait only seven days more. Every night and every morning enjoy the marriage bed. We will wait outside the tent witnessing the intercourse. At week's end, Rachel will be placed inside your tent."

"I agree."

"But," Laban injected, becoming absorbed by his self-confidence. He knew he had bested Jacob. Now, taking advantage of the power of Jacob's committed love, he dared to demand an amendment to his marital consent. Laban spoke on, "Understand this; you now have two of my daughters by the rights of our former agreement" Laban's words became slower, more carefully spoken. Jacob absorbed each word in his consciousness. He didn't trust Laban. Jacob kept listening for a thought, a word, a hint, that would eventually allow him to beat Laban at his own deceit. Laban, understanding Jacob's concentration continued mouthing each word exactly right so no misunderstanding could occur. He was devising a concrete, indisputable agreement with Jacob, legally restraining him from leaving his household.

"I require from you an additional seven years of service."

"Seven more?" Jacob replied, not even raising his voice. Surprised by his own calm, Jacob kept staring at Rachel, thinking about nothing else than possessing her.

"And why not? The territories are infested with intrigue and brutalities. War and rumors of war harbor everywhere. My new house is at peace. We are family, and you fully know how much Esau resents you. So does it not make sense to stay here with me another seven years?"

He thought on his words. "Another seven years may soothe Esau's anger. Father will not forego his pledge to me, no matter what." Jacob took hold of Rachel's hand and nodded.

"Then go back inside your marriage tent. Your wife is waiting for you," he pointed straight out, "in there."

When the seven days passed, Laban fulfilled his promise. Along with Rachel, Bilhah, her personal attendant, also entered into Jacob's household, as did Zilpah.

೮೮೮೮ಉ೮೮೮ಉ೮೮

In his first night with Rachel he expected a more intense ejaculation. A greater throbbing of his penis. A greater flushing of his senses. Instead the climax was soft. Disappointing. His semen barely dribbled out. She, unlike Leah, became ecstatic! Her body quivered at his touch. She trembled when he entered inside her. Hugging him tightly against her breasts, she heaved her body against his, demanding more thrusting, more embraces. Her body squirmed uncontrollably. Rachel's voiced filled the tent, without regard to the neighbors. They, hearing, laughed. The more they laughed, the more she filled the air with her ecstasy! Her cries, though, hurt Jacob's ears. Yet he had the most beautiful woman in the province. Her presence delighted him. He fully and legally possessed her. To have such an incredibly beautiful woman in his bedchamber! He was the envy of the world.

Jacob was happy.

During the passing weeks, Jacob learned to take his time with Rachel, allowing his erection to stay firm as long as he could with her. He trained his body to last for her embraces. He gently held her in his arms. During the daylight he affectionately teased her inside his arms, displaying his love for her to everyone. In the night of sharing, Jacob quickly thrust his hips back and forth inside Leah. He instantly ejaculated. His orgasm was always more intense with Leah than with Rachel. After he dismounted off Leah, he abandoned her bed to sleep alongside Rachel. During the day he walked past Leah, barely acknowledging her presence.

"Jacob," Leah tried to impress her husband, "I made this wool coat for you to keep you warm during the night."

He stared at it for a few seconds. He nodded and took it into his hands. The threading was uneven, the lines poorly cut. The hair shagged. Unappreciative, he dropped it on the floor. Silently he brushed by her disappointed figure. Leah was devastated by his public rejection of her gift. She fell beside the long, laborious work, crying. Zilpah stroked her hair away from her eyes.

"My husband doesn't love me," Leah's voice cracked through her tears.

"At least he doesn't beat you."

"He does far worse! His eyes never see me! His mind forgets I am here beside him. Yet when he sleeps with me, I know that deep inside him he has great comfort for me. If only I knew how to take those moments of comfort and place them permanently over him."

"Talk with your father about it."

"He's delighted to be rid of me. If I offend Jacob, a writ of divorce could be written against me. I will never, never allow myself to dissatisfy Jacob. Whatever he wants from me, he shall have. My joy is being with him."

"I will help you all that I can," Zilpah promised her.

ᏇᏥᏇᏥᏇᏥᏇᏥ

Nine months later Leah gave birth to Reuben. While her stomach had increased in size, Rachel's remained flat. When Leah's period dried, Rachel's continued flowing. The household gathered around Leah's tent, waiting for the infant's birth cries. When the piercing cries greeted their ears, the household celebrated greatly. Leah, calling Jacob beside her, held his firstborn out to him.

"Jacob, did I do it right for you?"

"Yes, Leah. You brought to me a strong, vibrant son. A pure Babylonian!"

"Jacob, do you love me now?"

Startled at the simplicity of her question, he looked at her. Not knowing what else to say, he answered, "I have never been mean to you. I have even recited my books to you."

"You recite them to yourself, reinforcing your memorization of what you had read long ago," Zilpah angrily stated.

"Do not concern yourself, child, with this family matter."

"I am a part of this family."

"Young virgin," Jacob viciously retorted, "keep your mouth closed as tightly as your legs are closed."

୨୦୯୫୨୦୯୫୨୦୯୫୨୦୯୫

A year later, when Jacob was eighty-five years old and Rachel was twenty-four years old, Leah bore Simeon.

The following year Levi was born.

Leah surrounded herself with her three sons and gleamed! She publicly boasted about them. Whenever another person came by, she stood them in front of her, testifying to Jacob's miraculous potency! "These three prove to the world that Jacob loves me! How else, without the quality of true love, could I bear these sons for Jacob?"

Jacob, when he heard her boast, stopped to stare at his three sons. She was right. They were incredibly handsome, strong, vigorous. Their play surrounded the house with laughter and with happiness.

When Laban's sons saw the vigorous activities of Jacob's sons, they complained. Laban smiled. It was true! Jacob's sons were the envy of the world!

Jacob raised his finger to scold Leah for her boasting, but he was stopped by the sight of his three sons. He touched all three briefly on the head. "How is this possible? Such an intelligent comment from one so simple?" His eyes met Leah's. Hers never brightened. They never glowed. But her breasts remained firm. Her stomach robust. Her legs powerful. "Once, wasn't she weak and thin? When was that?"

He touched her cheek. She clasped his hand in hers. She wanted his hand to remain forever in hers. Embarrassed, Jacob moved his hand away. He turned his back and went to Rachel's bed.

"Rachel. Rachel. Barren Rachel." Soft tears formed in his eyes.

ßØCЗßØCЯßØCЗßØCЗ

One day it happened that the family members went for a picnic. Jacob and Rachel, leaving Leah behind with the children, strolled to the top of the hill. Once there, they leaned against a large oak tree. During the sunset, Leah wandered nearby, yet stood a distance away. She knew Rachel didn't want her with them. But the sun's colors deepened in the sky. A rich and deep silhouette outlined the distant mountains against a wondrous horizon. Leah forced herself to walk up to them. She sat by Jacob's left side and trembled. Jacob and Rachel looked at her. She smiled shyly. Awkwardly she placed her head on his shoulder. Ignoring her, he hugged Rachel tighter.

"She's always mimicking me."

"What greater compliment can she pay to you," Jacob defended Leah.

Leah's passions increased. She stared at the blackening sky. She remarked, "Some women think my existence is denigrating to themselves. Some should have compassion for me."

Jacob was surprised and turned to stare at her. "What words you've spoken! Do you realize what you've said?"

"I spoke them, did I not?"

"What influence has this sunset on you?"

"Jacob," Rachel became jealous, "pay attention to me!"

"I will, but you weren't speaking. Leah was."

That did it. She snapped at Leah. "Leah, you have three sons to be breast-feeding. Put one on each tit, and shut up!"

Leah couldn't take it. She left the two alone. Rachel continued: "Since when have you ever listened to Leah's words?"

"She's learning to discern. Sometimes she says the most wonderful things. Profound, insightful."

"She says nothing that you haven't taught her. She only repeats those same things. She's assimilating you into herself. I know you love saying those words to her so she can replay them to you whenever you want. A speaking mirror is all she is. A cold reflection."

"Sometimes I hear original words. She is maturing."

"You're rubbing off on her."

He nodded. He thought on the matter. "It's good that I married her." He became proud. "I see I am able to teach, and that my teaching has effect."

"Jacob!" Rachel broke free from his embrace. The sun had set. The indistinguishable clouds blurred into one another. "Are you falling in love with my sister? Are you now so wrapped up with her you've forgotten me?"

"You are, and always will be, my favorite."

"You only say that to be in my bed tonight. But I see how you draw closer to her children day by day. I think, Jacob, you no longer love me because I am barren."

"My mother was barren until she was much older than you and my grandmother was barren until she was real old. You'll produce children for me when the time comes for you to produce them."

Rachel stood up and looked down at Jacob's darkened figure. "Our custom and our law says that if a child is born to you through a woman that I give you, that child also belongs to me."

"I know the law. Grandmother did the same with Hagar. Those arrangements usually don't end up so well."

"I didn't ask you for a lecture or moral statements. In fact, Jacob, you are violating my morality by refusing to place with me a legal heir through my designated bearer." She raised her voice, "Is that not so?"

"It is the law. It is the custom."

"Tonight you will therefore sleep with Bilhah. Unlike Hagar her bloodline is not impure. She is Babylonian."

"Aramaean, you should say."

She laughed and fell beside him on her knees. He pressed his head close to her breasts as she commented, "I so say. Now, give me a son."

ຉ໙ຉໟຉໟຉໟ

When Jacob was eighty-eight years old he fathered through Rachel's handmaiden, Bilhah, Dan. She was fourteen when she gave birth to her firstborn. In the morning of her birth pains the fourteen-year-old servant girl sat on top of Rachel's spread legs, giving birth to Dan. Rachel screamed as she screamed, wiping off her perspiration as gently as she could.

"At last I am vindicated," Rachel whispered to Jacob. "God has heard my anguish pleas and has truly answered them."

As the week passed, Dan's newborn cries filled the household. Jacob, pacing the floor with his son laughed alongside Rachel: both content with their newborn child.

ຉ໙ຉໟຉໟຉໟ

"Each child I brought forth to glorify Jacob," Leah jealously stated to Zilpah. "Each son I conceived, I did so for Jacob's love and affection. For such dedication, I have been wronged. I do not desire to bring a child into this world hoping it will bind my husband permanently to me—to force him somehow to fall desperately in love with me. No, the next child I bring forth I will dedicate to Yahweh. Only He can love me forever. Only He can touch the deep fibers of my heart."

In that same year, while Jacob was still eighty-eight years old, Leah conceived Yehuda. Leah dedicated Yehuda to Yahweh.

ഇരുഇരുഇരുഇരു

When Bilhah was fifteen-years-old she became pregnant, bearing Naphtali.

ഇരുഇരുഇരുഇരു

Then Leah became barren.

"As Bilhah has proven her love to Rachel, prove your love to me."

"I am still a young child!" Zilpah protested.

"You are a year older than Bilhah. Her bearing went well. Her pain passed. She is beautiful again."

"I don't know what to do. I am afraid."

"My father told me not to be afraid of my first night with Jacob. I promise you, it is not such a bad thing."

When the night fully enclosed the house with its veil of black, Leah walked into Jacob's bedchamber, bringing Zilpah with her.

"She is for you, husband."

"Am I to lie with this child as well?"

"The same as you did for Rachel, you must do for me."

"Will you stay and watch as Rachel watched?"

She shook her head no, casting down her eyes to the floor.

"If you do not watch me penetrate her, I will not perform your request."

"You have never been mean to me. Why are you now?"

Her simple words stung him. Tears moistened his eyes as he looked at Leah. He saw her bent stance and her cowering shoulders and he knew that he had been mistreating her by ignoring her. "When I do wave her to my side, it is only to tell her to find something to do. To busy herself away from me and Rachel. When she insists on staying by my side, I walk away from her. Often, I tell her not to follow so closely behind when Rachel and I stroll through the dim twilight of evening through the blossoming meadows." His guilt intensified.

"I isolate her," Jacob confessed. "Rachel and I always delegate the task of baby-sitting to her. While she carries out the boring task of watching the children, Rachel and I enjoy the cool rise of day. We race, without forethought, through the valley to the hilltop, dancing in the frost of the dew."

Jacob reviewed his guilt, then gently nodded to Leah. He held out his hand to her and was ashamed of himself for wanting to avoid her request. "Leah," his voice became sensible, gentle, "you do not have to watch. I will impregnate her for you."

Smiling, tears ran down her cheeks. "Jacob, thank you. Thank you." When she withdrew from his room, her smile mixed with her tears. And her love continued for him.

ॐ૭ॐ૭ॐ૭ॐ૭

When Jacob was eighty-nine years old, in the year 1770 B.C.E., Zilpah, Leah's handmaiden, gave birth to Gad. On his exit from her womb, Leah wiped clean the newborn, laughing. "What good fortune!" she exclaimed over and over again throughout the house, showing him off to everyone.

ॐ૭ॐ૭ॐ૭ॐ૭

In the month of Sivan (about the middle of May), when Reuben was a little past five years old, he went out to play by himself behind the encampment. While he was playing near the rise of an isolated slope, he happened to come near a cluster of purple flowers. Intrigued by the beautiful, oblong dark green leaves that grew in front of him, he went to the patch.

He sniffed the sweet aroma and explored the richly colored yellowish-red mandrakes that were about the size of a plum. Their taproots fanned out beneath the under-brushing of the ground. Unknown to Reuben the women of the land believed that the perennial herb possessed aphrodisiac powers and coveted the mandrakes. The traveling merchants, encouraging this mythology, purchased the herbs to process as a narcotic and to use as an antispasmodic.

He bit into one and his eyes grew wide at the delicious taste. "This will make Mommy happy!" he cried out. Running with an arm full, he shouted for his mother to come and see his newfound candy!

Rachel, tired of his screaming, along with the constant noise from the other undisciplined children, broke loose a stick from the nearby tree to spank him with. "That damnable brat," Rachel hissed between her teeth. Leah, in exact contrast, was proud of the energy of his exuberant displays.

Reuben began to slow down when he saw Rachel waiting. He saw the stick swinging behind her tunic. That stopped him completely. Leah soon arrived at the scene and approached Rachel's right side. She failed to see the punishing stick.

"What are those pretty things?" she asked her son.

"I don't know," he replied. "That's why I brought them to you. They're delicious!"

When Rachel caught a glimpse of the purple flowers, she dropped the stick and kicked it deftly to the far side. "They're mandrakes," she answered for Leah. She rubbed her hands dry on her tunic and walked to the two. She knelt beside Leah and gently rubbed Reuben's forearm. "Where did you find them?"

"I don't remember. Somewhere."

"How many were there?"

"This many," he nodded with his chin to the pile in his hands.
"You picked all of them?"
"Yes."
"What are you going to do with them?"
"Make Mommy happy."
She laughed, then faced Leah. She placed her hand on her arm and motioned for her to rise to her feet. "Leah, I have a special purpose for them. May I have them?"
"You always want everything I have!" Her face flushed red. "You took my husband's night embraces from me. He always sleeps with you and with the two young girls. But he doesn't sleep with me."
"Do you want him to?"
"Yes, I do. I miss it when he doesn't have sex with me."
"Well, why should he? All you do is lie still. You never hug him or get excited. You just lie there like a wool blanket."
"I still like what he does to me. And why shouldn't I get to lie down with him? I never say no to him. He's the one who says no to me."
"Give me Reuben's mandrakes and I promise you he'll have sex with you tonight."
"Reuben, hand them to me."
He obeyed his mother, and she patted him on the back. When Leah saw that her son had gone a short distance away where he couldn't see what she was doing, she gave the mandrakes to Rachel.
"Your unruly child was fortunate today!" Rachel tauted Leah.
Leah walked away, glancing for a moment at the discarded stick on the ground. Quickly forgetting it was there, she went into her private room.

 ෨ஊ෨Ⴂ෨ஊ෨ஊ

As the earth rotated on its axis away from the sun, another part of the earth lit up. A weary Jacob returned from his night-watch over the cattle and goats. The night was difficult, bothersome! His mind kept reviewing the vision of black sheep, black goats, and spotted and speckled flocks. Worried, he examined the livestock and wondered why he kept seeing them in his dreams. Frustrated at his inability to understand the vision, he shook off the dream and buried it deep inside his subconscious.

⁊Ↄ⁊Ↄ⁊Ↄ⁊Ↄ

ℒeah, carrying a pitcher of water, met him on the road.

"Leah, how nice of you to meet me. Is this water for me?"

Proud of herself, smiling radiantly, she nodded. "Rachel said you're to have sex with me tonight. I paid for you with Reuben's mandrakes."

"You paid for me? Mandrakes? My, my! I haven't tasted mandrakes in quite a while. Did you save any for yourself?"

"No. They're all Rachel's."

He placed his hand on her cheek and returned her smile. "Well, I can guarantee you she didn't save any for me either. All right, let's go into your room."

As Jacob thrust his erection inside her vagina, she prayed for conception. God, hearing, answered her prayers. When Jacob ejaculated, his breathing increased, his penis throbbed hard. In that terrific moment he vividly remembered how among the four women, only Leah could cause him to achieve such an intense orgasm.

He looked at her. Her body still remained youthful, in spite of the number of sons she gave him. Rachel's stomach now bulged where it once had been flat. The two teenagers breasts sagged, whereas Leah's body remained firm. He laughed and pressed her closer to himself.

That night Jacob slept soundly alongside his first wife, Leah.

⁊Ↄ⁊Ↄ⁊Ↄ⁊Ↄ

𝔚hen Jacob was eighty-nine years old, he fathered Issachar.

Then, through Zilpah, he fathered Asher.

When Jacob was ninety years old, he again renewed his sexual relationship with Leah. Zebulun was born nine months later.

When Leah finally learned now how to respond to her husband's passion, she embraced him tightly to her and hugged him proudly every time he climaxed. This new arousal in her encouraged Jacob to come back night after night into her bedroom.

It occurred that Leah's seventh child was a girl. Dinah was born when Jacob was ninety-one years old. He held her in his arms and tenderly kissed her forehead. "Leah, you gave me a daughter. She vindicates you."

₭₮₭₮₭₮₭₮

In Jacob's fourteenth year of service to Laban, Rachel fervently prayed to Yahweh.

"Dearest Lord, please forgive me for my behavior against my sister." Yahweh listened to her prayer and opened her womb the same night that Jacob had sexual intercourse with her. His semen traveled deep inside her cavity, fertilizing her. The warrior cells fought the opposing cells, killing them until the correct sperm cell forged a clear path to break through the membrane. The correct cells instantly joined together. Nine months later the adjoining cells matured, producing his eleventh son. The male child was Rachel's first.

While Jacob was still ninety-one years old he fathered Joseph.

₭₮₭₮₭₮₭₮

Soon afterwards, when Rachel regained her full strength, Jacob appealed to Laban, seeking a discharge from his household.

"I have served you long enough. My contract has been fulfilled. I must now leave you to return to my own father and mother."

Laban panicked and looked at his men. A new warehouse rose high over their heads. In front of his laborers, Laban's magnificent new courtyard opened into the vast landscape. Great quantities of burlap sacks bulged with the harvest grains. The heavy sacks covered the courtyard, ascending to the very top of the side walls. Barley grains, rye grains, ram skins and wool threads covered the sum of his palace.

"Jacob," Laban begun after a few silent moments, "long ago I accepted you as the person you revealed yourself to be to me. Even today I have no problem accepting you as the revealed and anointed Mashiach. Certainly everything you have done for me has reinforced my belief in you.

"I am wealthy. I am respected. The Hurrians leave my house alone. They tax me lightly. The caravans buy my grain, my wool, and my food-stuffs. I have never suffered a plague nor suffered a shortness of water.

"And now Jacob," Laban became terse, "I have a grave problem. I and my sons have grown accustomed to the life-style that you have freely given to us. I do not want this fortune to leave me." Laban grabbed Jacob by the arm. He stared intensely into his eyes and coarsely whispered, "Jacob, tell me, so I may know: How does a mere mortal hold on to a god?"

Jacob shook off his grip and returned his stare. "You cannot control what is not yours to control. As for your wealth—I know you say that I made it possible for you to gain such materialism in order to appease me, but truly, I know you think you did it on your own merits. You have never accepted me as the Mashiach. You inwardly believe you are he and that the oil never truly poured over my hair. As for my God, I know you think He is inferior to your gods! You often—by word and action—remind me of those beliefs."

"It may be as you say, or it may be as I say. But this much is certain: I never witnessed the oil poured over your head, nor even your father's nor even Abraham's. Regardless of these things, though, I know you will con-tinue subjecting yourself to me."

"What makes you so confident that I will again serve you for a third seven-year contract?"

"The power of love guarantees me of more than another seven-year contract. It guarantees me a life-long bondage. So what else do I need?" He held his hands out and both of Laban's daughters went to him.

Automatically the grandchildren followed their mothers. "Look, see how much your family loves me! See how much they love this house! What a burden it would be for them and for yourself—and, yes, even to me—if one day you and they should leave here! But I will not haggle with you, today. So tell me, Jacob, what wage should I pay you to stay?"

Jacob hesitated to answer. He lifted himself away from the Hearing Chair that stood in the center of the large reception hall. He walked behind the Chair of Judgment and stared deep into Laban's eyes. The two men faced each other; staring each other down.

Silence.

Even the children remained quiet.

At last, when Bilhah walked to the edge of the courtyard to quiet Reuben from his confounded squirming, the standoff gave way.

"Laban," Jacob replied, "you know full well that I have served you with total obedience. For your kindness and by the law of our contractual agreement I presented to you all my talents. Your cattle have increased. Your goats are fat. Your rams are the envy of the world. Your sheep's wool is the thickest and softest in the land. I taught your women to weave the broad cloth as my father had taught me from his mother's hands. Yahweh has blessed you considerably since I've been staying with your house."

Another period of silence followed. Jacob at last added, "So, answer me this: When is my own house to prosper?"

Laban, not knowing how to answer this large question repeated his smaller one, "What should I pay you to satisfy you?"

Jacob walked again around the chair. The children began acting up. One began crying. Then another and another. They became unmanageable. "Take them to the fields," Jacob commanded.

"No, leave them here," Laban countered Jacob's command. "They're part of my household. They must witness this."

"The children need to be playing outside."

"Let them play in this courtyard. I won't mind."

"What if they break your pitchers or faience!"

"They've broken so many already. Another one or two won't matter."

"Let them play," Jacob raised his voice, making the request his own command. "Laban, it appears you insist on maintaining the upper hand. I acknowledge this is your house. I publicly declare: I agreed to serve under your name and titles. I freely state: whatever I had performed, I did it for your improvement. It had to be such because a contracted man must fully serve his contractor.

"Therefore, let this new pledge take place between us. As before, pay me nothing for my services to your house. Yet," he raised his arms, emphasizing his words, "you must in return do this for me.

"First, I will return to my shepherding duties and herdsman's task. I will continue to face the bitter cold and humidity and heat of summer. I will fight the lions and the thieves! I will continue to account for you every lost livestock with a replacement digit. Your accounting will never diminish!

"Second, for this, allow me to travel through your flock. Today, I will commit myself to removing from them every spotted and every speckled and every dark-colored sheep for my own camp.

"Third, the same will be committed to with every speckled and dark-colored and spotted goat.

"That will be my wages.

"Furthermore, let us not allow any misunderstandings to prevail over us!

"Therefore, let us both clarify our new contract. Let us not allow a single word of confusion to fall between us. I state this because I desire that my honesty remain untarnished before you and your sons and your household and your servants. I have always proven my honesty to you and to your sons and to your house.

"Therefore, let this be known: should it happen that any non-spotted or non-speckled sheep or goat appear in my campground, they came to be there by another's theft!

"I testify and swear," Jacob placed his hand over his head and raised his other hand toward the heavens, "all white sheep and goats are legally and rightfully yours! I have nothing to do with them!"

Jacob kept his right hand raised to the heavens waiting for Laban to acknowledge his gesture.

Laban thought about it and placed his chin on his open hand. He leaned forward and smiled, almost grinning. Laban looked at the children, thinking, "They always roughhouse with each other. They're spoiled. They're careless with my things. My own sons, in contrast, respect everything in my house. They never ran through the house. Never shouted. Never touched what I or my servants placed on the table. Jacob never disciplines his children!"

Laban looked at his two daughters, and though about their inability to control the eleven children. "How dangerous these spoiled children are! Yet, if one could harness and channel their energy, who could ever conquer them? Yet, how does one keep eleven different houses united?"

Out loud, Laban replied, "I agree. Let the contract be drawn up."

After placing his seal over the moist clay, Jacob shouted at the top of his voice, as if he had been reading Laban's thoughts, "Reuben, Simeon, Levi, Dan, Yehuda, Naphtali! STOP PLAYING! We have work to do!"

"But Jacob," Laban countered, "they're only five and six years old. What work can you possibly require from those babies?"

"All are circumcised men. So let them act as men, regardless of their youth! Children, mothers, separate what is to be mine from what is his!"

₨ಳ₨ದಜದಳ₨ಳ

From that mid-morning to the very time of darkness the family worked in the fields, removing from Laban's flocks the black and multicolored goats and sheep.

That night Jacob and Laban met with the magistrate of the courts. Under the soft glow of the candles, the two finalized a legal contract of inheritance. With this decree Jacob's children became the responsible owners of the flocks. This ownership the children exercised until Jacob returned to the House of Yitzhak. Once across the Canaanite borders the ownership of the flocks reverted to Jacob. That way if any harm came to Jacob, the family's property would stay with the eldest son, thwarting Laban's claims.

The council member placed the legal work in the temple of the city.

ཀ

Before daybreak, Jacob's household gathered together. In the stirring morning breeze, Jacob's two wives and two concubines stood behind the boys. Over their shoulders the sun began its rise. The rays painted the earth with its myriad of colors, but Jacob saw only his sons and not the beauty of the colorful, awakening earth. In front of his young women, his three-and four-and five-and six-year-old sons waited.

Jacob just stood there, contemplating them. The boys looked at the old person, wondering why he was staring at them so hard. Leah, caught in her husband's stare, tried smiling. Rachel stiffened her back, while the two servants looked away.

Jacob walked to Rachel and grasped her hand in his. Together, the two began their long trek away from Laban's vast mansion. The rest, uncertain, followed.

Through the quickly diminishing day the family traveled toward the city of Carchemish. The next two days passed swiftly also! Within seventy-two hours the entourage traveled thirty-six miles away from Laban's house. Feeling secure, Jacob camped.

"Rachel, stay here with the boys," he directed. "Teach them what I have taught you. Never fear the nights nor the strangers. Always remember this: Yahweh's angels travel with us. They surround us. Every other week I will return to stay with you for a week."

"This doesn't make sense to me. Let's take all of these sheep and goats back to Father. You needn't be so stubborn!"

"And remain under subjugation to his house? Am I to receive his inheritance or his blessings? I am the master of my own house! Do you want me to remain your father's lifelong servant and then your brothers' servant until I die?"

"I, husband," Leah bravely spoke up, "want you to be your own master. You shall never be subjugated to anyone, other than Yahweh."

"Leah," Jacob admiringly stated, "six sons are yours! Let it be as you say!"

Rachel envied Leah for her proper answer, but silently agreed.

"How long will we remain here?" Rachel asked.

"Until each of you learn to speak Hebrew and after my herds have grown sufficiently large for us to return to my home."

"Why are we going to learn to speak Hebrew?"

"Because no one speaks Akkadian where we're going."

So during the next few years. while Jacob worked at Laban's estate, his household spoke Hebrew. Leah, amazingly, had few major difficulties learning the language. The children quickly absorbed the new sounds. When Leah regressed, Reuben lovingly corrected her, reinforcing the new language in her mind. After a while, Jacob completely forbade the Akkadian language in the camp.

After the first two weeks in the new camp, Jacob decided to return to Laban's camp. First he went to his herd and from among them selected a single goat. With it, Jacob walked back by himself to Laban's house.

As the distance between Jacob and his family increased, Yahweh's angels materialized around the camp to guard it against any vicious intrusion.

And for the next few years, all was well.

ഇൽ ഇൽ ഇൽ ഇൽ

When Jacob reached Laban's estate, he paid a supervisory visit to the shepherds, checking on their care of the flocks and herds. Then, going his separate way, he traveled to the hill country where he patiently waited for a horse's appearance. Only recently had horses begun becoming popular in Haran. Decades of tradition had established a preference for donkeys.

After hiding for a long time, permitting his clothes and hair and body to take on the smells of the surrounding country, and hiding downwind, Jacob saw a horse wandering into the pasture.

Jacob acted. Nature blocked the three sides of the small, steep valley. Contentedly grazing, the horse failed to notice the long branches that the person dragged across the field, entrapping him.

Over the next few days Jacob patiently talked to the animal and gradually gained its trust. He hand fed the horse and began petting it, confidently touching its nose and neck. At week's end Jacob mounted the horse, determining to be its master. After he subdued it, he trained it to obey his foot movements. Soon, it responded to him as Abraham's horse had responded to him.

Jacob returned again to his camp. He explored the sparse forest and found within its midst a grove of almond trees. The lovely shiny pink serrated blossoms radiated in pairs from the branches. As he studied them, his mind raced to the depths of his intellect where he again recalled the strange dream of so long ago. The meaning of that dream became clearer to him. From its secret depths he culled it interpretation and acted on it. He broke off dozens of the branches and carried them to the drinking troughs where he laid them on the ground.

Not too far from his camp the stately plane trees grew sixty feet high. The wide-spreading branches cast protective, provocative shadows on the earth. After chopping off dozens of thick branches, Jacob cleaned off the dark-green vinelike leaves. He then transported the collection of branches to the water troughs.

After he obeyed his vision, he traveled to the distant and dry hillsides of the country. Out of the caked earth, dozens of the flexible twigs of the storax tree grew. Its fragrant white petals filled him with delight. Obsessed with the various collections of branches, Jacob protected them underneath his body while he fell asleep. Rachel, puzzled by his actions, became afraid to disturb him from his sleep. "Perhaps, when he wakes, his senses will return to him."

Sixteen hours later Leah approached him. "He has never slept so long. It is time for him to wake up," she said to Reuben.

"Is it smart to wake Daddy?"

"You wake him," she smiled at her son. He nodded and shook his father's shoulder.

Groggy, he moaned. "Didn't I just go to bed?"

"You slept a long time," Leah said.

He gazed at her eyes. Lately, they seemed brighter, more intelligent. He looked at his son. He smiled then stretched.

"Daddy, what are these sticks for?"

Jacob's smile increased.

He grabbed the nearest branch and started stripping the leaves clean from the twigs.

"Both of you, sit beside me and help me."

"If you think I can handle it," Leah said.

"Of course you can."

She smiled and set to helping him as much as she could. Throughout the afternoon and late evening the three of them laughed as they worked.

The next morning they woke beside a large pile. Days later he mixed the various leaves together. After he crushed them into a finer mixture, he carried it to the water troughs where he dumped handfuls into the clear drinking water.

He returned to the nude branches and proceeded to cut from them long strips of bark. When he had finished his work, he summoned his wives and concubines, "I want my flock to view these branches as they drank at the trough," he directed them. "I want their eyes looking only at these," he held the branches high in the air.

The two wives obeyed Jacob's strange commands while his two concubines went to the pens. The children laughed at their mothers' efforts as they corral the collection of goats and made them face the swirled peeled branches.

When the women noted the shavings they were afraid to step on them. "What curse lay within the fragrance?" one thought. "What Egyptian traveled nearby when they were asleep? What mystic spoke to Jacob? Has his tremendous intellect finally affected his common sense? Is he totally insane?"

Jacob walked up to the laughing children and sat with them. He also laughed at the women who were working hard on his project.

"Daddy," Reuben asked, "why are they playing this game?"

"It's a game I invented to fool the people who happen by. They will think I created magic and fail to realize that I am practicing breeding methodology."

"Breeding meth-od-a-what?"

"I'll explain it later," Jacob embraced his son. "Right now, I've got to help them play this game to its conclusion."

By the first hour past the sun's height, the eyes of every sheep and goat directly faced the troughs where the spotted twigs and branches rested: wholly white against brown. Satisfied with his family's tremendously hard effort, Jacob himself led each goat to the water trough. There, he forced their eyes to see first the peeled and spotted twigs and branches. A few seconds later, he let them drink the leafed mixture from the trough.

After each drank a few swallows of the brew, Jacob brought another animal to the trough. He then selected the most robust spotted and streaked goats. These, he fed the leaf mixture that he had not diluted with water.

An observer, standing at the far wayside, wondered about the strange commotion. He stood by, idly watching an old person forcing ugly goats to drink a foul smelling brew. But he gazed in amazement when the released rams instantly sought a mate to breed with. "Somehow," the observer thought, "the rams become incensed with sexual desires on tasting the water." The observer watched the animals mate by the rods and staffs of the almond and plane and storax trees.

Jacob continued with his task and followed the course of the dream that God entrusted to him. As he performed the details of his dream, he realized that whenever a multicolored animal mated with another multicolored animal, their offspring would carry the same traits as the parents. By breeding within the same family with the same characteristics, the children would portrait their parents. If their offspring displayed the parents' markings, so would the offspring. As soon as he discerned what was going to happen, he eagerly pushed himself through the night to make sure all his animals were bred in similar fashion. Thus it happened that Jacob developed his own special class of goats.

ဆဣဆဩဆဣဆဩ

Months later it occurred that a passing merchant stopped his journeying caravan at Jacob's camp.

Jacob and the merchant immediately recognized each other and joyously hugged. The stouter merchant kissed his old friend on the neck. "All of these children are yours?"

"Yes!"

"These four women also?"

"The two in the middle are my wives. The other two are my concubines."

"Are you sure you didn't travel to China behind me?"

The two spent the evening laughing. Fascinated by the beautiful and unusual colorings of Jacob's herd, the merchant, before departing for the western seacoast, insisted that magic caused the effect. "Everyone practices it in India."

"Yahweh hates magicians," Jacob said. "They serve Satan, not truth."

"Then how did you manage to breed such unusually beautiful animals?"

Jacob laughed. "My knowledge, dear old friend, did not come not from magic. Rather, it came from a vision given to me by God.

"God? Oh, you mean the God that you used to talk to me about."

"Yahweh's truth," Jacob reminded him. "is always truth. His truth can always be culled from acute observations and sincere listening."

"What do I listen for?"

"A whisper in the night."

The merchant listened, but failed to grasp what Jacob meant. "Never mind," he finally said. "Nevertheless, friend, no matter how the feat came to be, I insist on buying as many colorful goats and sheep as you'll sell me."

Before continuing with his journey, the merchant reached a mutual and satisfactory agreement. The merchant happily paid for the animals with gold.

"For your second escape," his friend beamed.

The two men warmly hugged, then forever parted.

స౧౩స౧౧౩౧౧౩స౧౩

Jacob devised a separate tactic for the sheep. Following the impulse of his vision, he took the multicolored animals during their heat time, placing them face to face with the discolored flocks that had been in Laban's camp. Jacob again surprised the observing shepherds.

The strongest livestock bred with the strongest. The multicolored ones stayed with the multicolored ones. The weakest solid-colored offspring he placed with Laban.

Within months his flocks increased so much that he recruited from Laban's work forces other skilled Aramaean shepherds. He deceived them also with the trickery of the sticks and the brew, hiding from them the truth of the principle of genetics.

Some, believing that the peeled storax and almond and plane trees held a special chemical within their branches, tried to do the same with their solid white and solid black animals. They failed.

By the third year his camp had become so large he was able to trade the solid black skins and excess livestock for camels and asses. In the middle of his third year he hired dozens of men and women servants.

Soon, the remarkable coloration of the animals became the fashionable desire of the society residing around the province. The wealthy and ruling classes insisted on buying the uniquely beautiful animals for themselves.

The herders, wanting to profit from these desires, kept trying to breed their own stocks of multicolored goats but, the solid colored animals refused to breed multicolored offspring. Within months the asking price for the mysteriously beautiful animals skyrocketed, making Jacob the wealthiest breeder in the province.

Chapter Twenty-Nine

▼

Hammurabi's War

Hammurabi gazed beyond the luxurious walls of his palace and longed to leave the confines of his city. He was bored. Anxiously bored. High-strung, energetic, unable to contain himself, he vigorously walked the ramparts of his recently refurbished palace. It rose from Nimrod's original foundation stones. The walls anchored in firmly with Chedorlaomer ambitions. He patterned himself after the last two rulers and had established for himself the greatest throne in the world.

Large baked blocks of hardened and painted clay frescoes surrounded his palace. The thickened walls fortified the reconstructed city of Babylon. The great walls rose sixty feet high. The members of an entering caravan, passing through the three armed guard towers and two heavy gates, were awed when they encountered the patterned, heavily flowered city streets. Massive fountains stood at major intersections. The high fountains were shaped with small openings at the top that permitted the water to run against the visitors' faces. As the travelers stared in an amazed trance at the architecture of the city and its fountains, the languid afternoons cease-lessly drifted by.

A young girl, touching the hardened brightly painted clay blocks, shook her head in grief. "Such beauty. Such beauty," her father heard her whispering to herself.

Over the smooth plastered troweling highly skilled and respected arti-sans painted magnificent frescoes that boasted of Hammurabi's accom-plishments to the world. Beneath their wobbling ladders, team leaders briskly shouted orders, rushing the artisans to complete the remaining tasks.

Hammurabi, always eager to boast, invited the world to feast with him at the city's rebirth! "In this great celebration I want the conquered ruler of the city of Larsa to publicly bow before my throne. I want him to acknowledge me as the world's supreme authority!" Hammurabi laughed and sat in the middle of the gold-leafed council room. "Only I, of all the men in the world, am strong enough to humiliate the Larsa Dynasty! On my own merits and skills and genius, I thoroughly vanquished the ruling son of Rim-Sin I! All praises and glories come to me!"

A trembling servant, who happened to pass Hammurabi, flinched. Hammurabi, disliking the cowardly flinch, stopped to stare at him. "Why are you afraid of me?"

"All lower ranking men must be afraid of higher ranking men," the ser-vant's voice trembled out.

"Why?"

"It's the way of things."

"I came from the same background as you did. I never tremble in fear against anything or anyone. It may be that that is what separates us."

"No, Great Ruler. What separates us is the inequality of the law."

The royally clothed man touched his lips as he studied the dingy ser-vant. "Laws?" he whispered.

ಬುಲ್ಬುಗ್ಬುಗ್ಬುಲ್ಬುಗ್

In 1768 B.C.E. Ishme-Dagan I ruled the city of Ashur. On the civilized eastern front the Kassites began their embryonic rise while on the uninhabited western frontiers, the Hurrians infiltrated Anatolia from the Kirghiz steppe. All descended from Yefet. Eventually these tribes immigrated to Germany, Persia, Russia, India; from the Altai Mountains the people migrated into the Tarim Basin and into China. After several centuries of unrest, remnants of the tribes returned to the Caspian Sea. Repopulating, restrengthening, their children's children migrated back into Europe, India, and China.

ᛥᏣᏣᛥᏣᏣᛥᏣᏣᛥᏣᏣ

The Western powers were afraid of Hammurabi's military expansionistic intrigues. They agreed to attend a private meeting with Zimri-Lim of Mari. The Minos of Crete who was visibly concerned about Hammurabi's imperialism, arrived arm in arm with the Egyptian ambassador to the conference of united nations. In the highly ornate room, other kings from various city-states waited for them. Respectfully, the assembly of kings bowed to the strongest and richest sovereign as he entered. The Minos, accepting the bows, applauded them in return.

The servants, dazzled by the Minos's immeasurable powers, stole awestruck glimpses of every movement he made, while they worked to serve the guests of the attending nations luscious fruits and exotic wines. They placed large solid gold bowls of fruit and exquisite beer containers on the tables. The delegates feasted and boasted loudly among themselves of their capacity to stand against Hammurabi.

ᛥᏣᏣᛥᏣᏣᛥᏣᏣᛥᏣᏣ

Simultaneous with the secret meeting, Hammurabi paced on top of the rampart of his great ziggurat, conducting his own meeting.

"How shall we commemorate Rim-Sin's defeat?" his chief administrator asked.

Hammurabi stared at the great valley that stretched before him and answered, taking the administrator's hoped for procession in an unexpected direction. "This grand structure collapsed once before. Surely it may do so again. Only a few today remember the original name of the man who inspired this ziggurat. Marduk may be the god of today, but even that may change according to man's whim. Already the god of the sun, Shamash, is a powerful god. Our caravans carry his thoughts even to Egypt! Like those man-made gods and fanciful inventions of the priest, I want a powerful reminder of myself to penetrate the people's consciousness. I want something eternal to be made of myself so my name will never vanish from the face of the earth."

"Is not your war against the world enough to make men remember and tremble before you? Grand-Sovereign, what kingdom does not whisper your name!"

"Such is true," another general spoke up, wanting to assert his position in the power hierarchy. "You've already beaten the Elamites and the war is going favorably against the Hurrians."

"When the war is over and I've conquered the world, what then? I'll just die. How long will my carved image last before the sand's onslaught and time's chisel?"

The chief scribe came forward. "The public library's have your history recorded in Akkadian and Sumerian. All the great knowledge of the intellectuals rests there."

"The math and science books?"

"And the astrology and astronomy works."

"All are dedicated to me?"

"All."

Hammurabi paced the open deck of the world's tallest temple and looked about him. His vast kingdom stretched from the foot of his man-made brick and mortar mountain to the plains of the southeastern sea to the dividing mountains beyond India.

"Babylon has been rebuilt twice before me. My third rebuilding shall be the last rebuilding. Unlike Babylon's other two predecessors, I will be eternally remembered! During their conquests they both forgot to leave something behind to be remembered by. That shall not be my mistake!"

He walked to the chief-librarian and took the accounting tablets out of his hands. After inspecting them, he turned to the man. "It's a shame no one knows how to write the sounds of music. That part is missing from my library."

"How can anyone write musical sounds?" the scribe remarked, then wondered if it wouldn't have been better for him to keep his thoughts to himself.

"See!" the ruler shouted out, smashing the tablets against the floor. The shattering clay flew everywhere. "Sounds vanish! Images collapse! I am caught in the framework of time! I cannot transcend it. My stomach aches when I realize my mortality. I want to be remembered!" he nearly cried.

"Everyone knows your name," the priest reaffirmed.

Hammurabi glanced out from his balcony and turned his attention to the distant tenant farmers. They appeared like members of an organized beehive. Each human being properly cultivating the land as must be done. Each knew their responsibility to the ruler. The irrigation workers, the herdsmen, the scribes, the soldiers, the diplomats, the artisans! Everybody! Hammurabi swiveled toward the scribe and pointed at the beehive of men and asked: "Who is their lord and master?"

"You are lord and master of all."

"Are they loyal to me?"

"If not," the great general injected, "my sword will make them so."

"Yes, loyal by the power of the sword," he commented more to himself than to them. "Let us do this for them, for I know for a certain fact that it is they who carry from generation to generation the veneration of a man-god. The generals and the chief priests and the great scribes only formulate for today whatever they desire in order to attain ambition's rewards for themselves."

"We are loyal," they all bowed.

"I have collected and placed in my library a collection of laws that, when obeyed, can stimulate and govern society. Men should not be so free from the law that they can haphazardly do to one another whatever they want to do. There must be a preventive measure and a system to oversee the laws of that government. Thus, let us incorporate Ur-Nammu's codes among our own codes. Their effect may be the necessary matter to bind us together. United in such a manner, we may be able to press our attack even faster and better against the Hurrians. Thus, let this happen: place on the high points of the major commerce roads the laws that I will share with you. Carve these laws on diorite steles. From this effort I will gain an immortal name."

"Are we to be subjugated under those laws as the workers are?" the priest inquired.

After a slight pause, Hammurabi answered, "I have never known a priest who has ever subjugated himself to man's laws."

The priest, grinning widely, folded his arms.

"But you shall be the first," Hammurabi concluded his conversation.

꧁꧂꧁꧂꧁꧂꧁꧂

Simultaneous with the Amorites' third reconstruction of the city of Babylon (the first being by Nimrod, the second by Chedorlaomer), the Hittites engineered their new city of Hattusas. During this same time-line the Minoans discovered the break of water between the African and European continents. Rowing past the precipice, the Minoans turned their ships southward. A few brave ships, staying on course, discovered the Azores. Returning to Crete, the captain of the expedition reported the event to the Minos.

As the rich caravans continued rushing throughout the Eastern Empires, traveling beyond the Yellow River of China and into deep eastern India and extreme western Thailand, the Hurrians determined to end Hammurabi's heinous presence and challenge.

৪০৩৪০৪২৪০৪৪০৪

While the new Philistine city of Byblos in Phoenicia rose from the imaginations of the fertile mind to constructed reality, the Canaanites, taking advantage of the Philistine presence, traded with them their vegetables and grains. The Philistine sailors continued intermarrying with the Canaanites and within short generations their offspring became the great sailors of the Mediterranean Sea.

৪০৩৪০৪২৪০৪৪০৪

Exactly at this same time the Canaanites, utilizing and propagandizing the region's war-panic against the eastern tyrants, enriched themselves at the bargaining tables and bazaars. Jantin-hamu, the Philistine mayor of Byblos, sensing an opportunity to expand his powers and solidify his position, renegotiated and finalized another trade agreement with the Minos of Crete.

The scribes inscribed the new stipulation on detailed tablets. The Minos ambassador sealed it with his official stamp. The mayor, presenting it to his friends, swore renewed loyalty to the Minos. He created the impossible contract. Officially, the Canaanite and the Philistine offspring would become the exclusive carriers of the purple dye from the murex shells to the outer ports of the world.

In turn, the wood purveyors of Phoenicia promised to cease trading their cedar planks with the Egyptian king. When the Egyptian representative protested, the Minos's representative stared him down. "To win this war, all lumber must become exclusively available to the Minos! Or do you prefer that the Minos forget Egypt?"

"In this international war against Hammurabi of Babylon, take all the cedar trees you need," he acquiesced.

Three hundred years later the forests of the land had vanished.

Chapter Thirty

▼

The Minos

The Philistines dispatched their skilled metallurgists to Arabia and there they conducted preliminary testing for copper veins in the south junction of Seir. The Kenites (who descended directly from Abraham and Keturah), permitted the investigation, but followed behind them closely to assure proper procedures. They traveled together, exploring the various encampments. After the Philistines learned everything that they could, they drew detailed maps of the lands. The following month they bargained for the exclusive copper mining rights in the land and river opening to the Red Sea.

The roads that wound from the interior of Arabia to the vast western sea, Esau protected. Four hundred soldiers bravely served his banner, bringing with them their wives and children. A total of 2,500 people lived under Esau's protective care.

Near the forked tip of water that led to the Red Sea rested the Gulf of Aquaba. At the apex of that waterway the Kenites established civilization's largest copper smelting operation. Abraham's skilled descendants forged the thick copper swords and battle axes and multilayered metal uniforms.

While the children of Abraham forged these new weapons of war, a Minoan ocean traveler reached the southwestern island of India. In Sri Lanka the captain of the ship personally concluded a trading agreement with the inhabitants to buy all the tin bar-weights that the Malaysian miners brought out from the bowels of the eastern earth. When the ships returned to the port city in the Gulf of Aqaba, the Kenites mixed the tin with the copper, fashioning swords and other weapons of war from hardened bronze.

ᏇᏣᏇᏌᏡᏓᏣᏇᏌᏣ

In Crete, the Minos applauded the naval commander's great discovery and victorious expeditions. He examined the soft wavy-haired and dynamically black-skinned men of Sri Lanka and was awed by them. "You are our remote relatives. Your Aryan roots are undeniable! Travel with my men in their ships. We will transport you to the far western lands and to distant horizons of the world."

The Sri Lankans signed the agreements.

The Minos turned his attention to Mesopotamia and closed the door to his conference room. "Send bribes to the city of Mari. Let King Zimri-Lim close his eyes and thoughts to our mercenaries."

"I beg for you to forgive my intrusion," another explorer asked permission to express his views, "but are we not freemen to speak what we believe?"

"Yes. It is by such empowerment that we rule the world."

"Permit me, then, to suggest this: Allow the Mesopotamian nations to fight the war among themselves. Allow us to concentrate on peacefully exploring the lands in front of Africa. Who knows what we may discover when we submit to the ocean's great breadth?"

"Why continue west?" the Minos challenged.

"Already our European provinces are the envy of the world. How much more so the lands west of Europe? Let the east remain with the east."

"If we do not align ourselves with the Orientals, the Mesopotamians will force their way to Anatolia, then on to Greece, then on to us. Like dry grass the Kingdoms will crumble. Then we must stand alone. That is not economical."

"As always, the Minos understands our economic situation the best."

"And so I must. This great Utopia of ours shall endure," he added.

The two naval commanders took pride in the wisdom of the Minos: the seventh generation to serve in the elected position. "It is true," the recently decorated commander stated to his admiral. "No poverty exists anywhere on our island. We have no walled cities. No standing army. No policemen. Only the marines carry long weapons."

"Our wealthy island may be the envy of the world," the admiral commented, "but our luxuriant lifestyle spoils us. Our constituents, loving the luxuries that our trading vessels present to them, indulge in whatever pleasures they desire."

"Yes, and why shouldn't they? What other land has the attractive allure to compel so many strange and beautiful women of the world to come to our island?" he smiled. "The delicate, white-skinned aristocrats marry as many of them as we can import."

The admiral smirked. "These foreign women breed far too well. Our population increases much too rapidly. The parents need to expand their households on the mainland before we crowd ourselves out of our paradise."

The lesser ranking man laughed. "Who will leave here? Every person of this specific generation has large accumulations of gold and silver and jewels and land and shipping grants. Each lives as he desires."

"With what result? Boring and uninteresting lives. Luxurious existence means only that. Look about you! The idle rich invent new games and sports. These new pastimes dominate their lives."

"Admiral," the handsome young commander smiled, "Don't you enjoy watching the acrobats play with the bulls?"

"It's unnecessarily dangerous!"

"As long as we all abide by the codes of the Prince of the Lilies, everyone prospers, and isn't that what really matters to us?"

ಬಿದ್ಯಿಬಿದ್ಯಿಬಿದ್ಯಿಬಿದ್ಯಿ

The Prince of the Lilies looked at the large battle-axes of the Bull that represented his empire throughout the world. Centuries later a modified version of this battle-ax would become the universal symbol of pagan Christianity: the cross!

Executing his plans in Mesopotamia, the Minos sent a delegation to Zimri-Lim. The long caravan emptied in his palace baskets of spices, carved gold rings and wrist bangles, bead and reel necklaces, ornamental glass oxen and bull impressions.

Hammurabi, sensing that his erstwhile ally secretly sought an alliance with the western powers, conducted an earlier than expected war campaign against the west, catching the Marians off guard. Unexpectedly, the new morning's breath moved across long, unbroken lines of disciplined warriors. With the trumpet's sounding, they charged. Their horse-drawn war chariots trampled the unprepared army, vanquishing the inept defenders.

In the victorious aftermath, silence filled the frozen battlefield. That dreaded quiet was replaced with the cries of thousands of vultures flying into the battlefield to consume the remains of the tens of thousands of corpses. The breeze stopped blowing. Open eyes stared into an abyss of total nothingness.

ಬಿದ್ಯಿಬಿದ್ಯಿಬಿದ್ಯಿಬಿದ್ಯಿ

When the news of the rapid conquest reached the Hurrians, the husbands and fathers and sons frantically purchased as many brass weapons as they could from the Minos's merchantmen.

An emergency meeting was called.

The Philistine representative paced the floor in front of the Minos.

"We don't have enough ships or men to defend our shores, much less transport our warriors from the coasts of Africa back to our lands. We implore you, great Prince of the Lilies to send your navy to help us bring our warriors back home so we may defend ourselves."

"If we permit our navy to help you transport your warriors back to your land, what will you concede to us?"

The representative stopped pacing. He simply stated, "We concede our port-cities to our Minoan cousins."

The Minos smiled. He pointed his finger to the clay tablet. The representative rolled his cylinder of authorization over the wet clay. After a long pause he officially declared with stilted language, "In return for your generosity," the Minos said, "I promise your people complete political autonomy for the interior lands after the crisis abates."

The two men nodded and sealed the contracts.

Of all the harbors on the western shore, the ports of Gaza, Tyre, and Sidon held the deepest and the widest waterways. The Minoan-Phoenician Alliance, fearing an attack by Hammurabi, constructed new defensive forts along the coastal lands of Lebanon.

With the near-completion of the deep fortifications on the seacoast, however, the reestablished colony in the city of Sidon wanted extra survival assurances. Demanding a meeting with the Minos, the ambassadors hammered out a new trade contract whereby the Sidonians granted the Minos their deep-water harbor as an eternal port city for the Minos's caravans and fleet in return for his promise of trade-route grants into Mesopotamia and in India.

While the political and commercial debates took place in the council chambers, the loyal harbormasters and engineers continued building and fortifying the cities. Meantime, in the nearby northern provinces, the defeated, uncertain, and frightened refugees of the eastern provinces crowed into the city of Ugarit. The merchantmen, realizing the enormous profits of the panic, debated with the king the issue of keeping the gate perpetually opened for the escapees. When the decision was made to open it, Ugarit became the largest metropolis in the world: 45,000 people coming and going every week of the month.

Soon afterwards the Minos's ambassadors coerced a trade agreement from the small fort of Troy and from the Etruscans who were beginning to filter into Italy from India.

About the Author

Walter Schenck is an avid Bible student who has written ten books.

He also holds numerous certification in the computer field.

CCNA 2.0, A+, MCP, MCSE, ENP, AutoCAD, MCT

Other Books by Walter Schenck

First Voices
is a novel based on The Book of Genesis

The no-nonsense, straight-to-the-gut,
CCNA Study Guide
*is a Cisco course exam reference to help students
prepare for the CCNA 2.0 test*

The Birdcatcher, Part One:
The Formation
*is a moving, violent tale that takes place in Vietnam
during the Tet Offensive of 1972*

The Birdcatcher, Part Two:
The Reformation
*is the dramatic and powerful conclusion of Part One
depicting graphic and intense helicopter battle campaigns
and vibrant characterizations!*

The Handbook of Jesus' Parables
*has 37 black and white illustrations to accompany
the sayings of Jesus and John the Baptizer*

Jesus of the Four Gospels
*Is a complete integration of the Gospels
on the life of Jesus*

The Final Comparative of the
Synoptic Gospels: Part One
*this work represents the most complete harmony ever written
on the four gospels with Old Testament references and
historic commentary. Nothing is better!*

Printed in the United Kingdom
by Lightning Source UK Ltd.
99867UKS00002B/17